I0716957

Deal with a Djinn

··

S.N. Moor

Copyright © 2023 by S.N. Moor

All rights reserved.

No portion of this book may be reproduced in any form without written permission from the publisher or author, except as permitted by U.S. copyright law.

This means placing my book on a pirate site. If you do, I wish you death by 1,000 papercuts and curse you and your cum maker, be it dick or vagina. May you never orgasm for the rest of your life.

Contents

Hey Dad

WELL SON OF A b***h! I did it again. I wrote another freaking book you can't read. When I tell you that I'll write one you can read, I really mean it... even though it may not seem like it. I have a couple of ideas I'm noodling on, but until then, here is your one page. To summarize this NSFD (not safe for dad) book into a SFD (safe for dad) book...Everlee meets her male friend companion guys (definitely nothing crazy there) for the first time again. Crazy! This is a paranormal twist on the first book.

True fae were the first fae that ever existed, but they were killed off several hundred years ago. Evil power play. Fast forward to present. Everlee is a squib. A fae born without supernatural powers... or so she thinks! Dunt, dunt, dunnnnnn! When at a se club on Halloween, a troll tries to steal her away to make her his bride and when she fights against him... BOOM! Magic. But not just any magic. No that would be too easy peasy lemon squeezy. She had the true fae light ball, something that hasn't been seen in hundreds of years. So obviously she has to go on the run and into hiding until she can figure out who she is. But as we all know... easier said than done. Lots of other stuff happens in between that would simply bore you out of your mind, which is why it's NSFD. All you need to know is that it all ends with a happily ever after!

*To all you kinky fuckers who love to dress up on Halloween
so you can be fucked by a monster*

Introduction

<u>Deal with a Djinn</u> is the fifth book in the series, however, it can be read as a standalone. Like some of our favorite shows do, Deal with a Djinn breaks from the series and our favorite characters are transported to another realm- a paranormal world, where they meet again for the first time. It's a paranormal retake on Cupid's Contract. If you've read the series, then you will likely see Easter eggs that have been planted throughout in this book. Hope you enjoy!

It's recommended you read Cupid's Contract, Bunnies and Bowties, Rainbows and Unicorns, and Stars and Stripes first. If you haven't read those yet, stop here, because there are spoilers below (the title links will take you to the books).

In **<u>Cupid's Contract</u>**, Everlee meets her four delicious men who give her the time of her life and the confidence she lost after dickface, Rich, destroys her. The only problem is the men make her agree to only sleep with them two times before they part ways. By the end of the arrangement, Everlee gets attached but doesn't know how the men feel, so she honors the agreement against her own desires and leaves. She's scared of getting hurt again.

<u>Bunnies and Bowties</u>, picks up two months later. She's been absolutely miserable, and unbeknownst to her, so have the men. Lizzy, being the amazing BFF she is, gets her back out on the scene, but she runs into her men and things are as hot as ever. She wants to talk with them about a future, but she's already committed to visiting her family for Easter. We get to meet her eccentric brother, Beckett, and her mother and father. Her mother is hellbent on a marriage and grandkids for Everlee and uses every opportunity to remind her, going as far as setting her up on a date with a lawyer. Everlee does her part but is missing her men desperately. The church her family attends is hosting a birthday party for one of their members and during the celebration Everlee comes face to face with her men (while on her date). They were all in foster care together a few towns over from Everlee growing up. Small world. As you can imagine, fireworks ensue, and Beckett picks up on all the sexual tension between them all and calls out she's in a poly relationship. Our favorite fivesome is formed and it is HOT! HOT! HOT!

<u>Rainbows and Unicorns</u> picks up soon after Bunnies ends. This one centers around Memorial Day and Pride Month. Sammie, a woman from the men's past enters the picture with a proposition for them that is hard to refuse. Because of personal reasons, Sammie has to go back to Texas, but offers to sell Allure back to the guys. Allure was their first successful business, a sex club, that gave them the funds to open Vixen and Bo's. Scared of how Everlee will react, they are hesitant to tell her, but when they do, she shocks them when she's excited about it. Sammie sets up a night where our fave five can visit Allure and experience Eden and Infernus (hello fave wood scene), two other areas of the club she added. While at Allure, Knox and Everlee participate in a Shibari demonstration that is... ahem... hot AF and we learn that Knox's nickname in the SEALs was Knots. In the end, they all decide to buy the business, Everlee included, so she's now an official owner of a sex club with the boys. Things continue to progress with the relationship and by the end of the book everyone says they love one another with hints of something more developing between Emmett and Jax. Lizzy is still in wedding planning mode so who knows what she'll decide about her wedding, and we also finally get to meet Betty's husband.

Stars and Stripes gives us our summertime vacation feels! Our fave five head away for a week of fun in the sun, with Beckett, Will, Lizzy and Tony, but when Beckett stupidly invites his and Everlee's mom, things get tense. She never travels alone, so why would she now? Several days later, the knock on the door shocks them all. Dearest Donna took a page out of Ev's book and travelled on her own... to the beach house... the forbidden love nest with Ev and her men. Things are awkward and their bedroom activities are put on hold, but when Everlee's life is in danger and all the men jump in to save her, the cat is out of the bag. Everlee and her mom talk, and Ev admits she's in a poly relationship. With the weight of the world off Everlee's shoulders, she can finish out the week relaxing and Donna can really meet the men. Also, in Stars and Stripes, we see Emmett and Jax's relationship start to heat up as Jax begins to explore the feelings he's been pushing down. Everlee's love and unconditional support give him the courage to explore. What does this mean for the future?

EVERLEE - HALLOWEEN AT A SEX CLUB

IT'S BEEN THREE MONTHS since I've had a semi-decent fuck and that was with a Dullahan who was so ashamed of sleeping with me he took his head off and faced it in a corner. It's like the entire bag on the head situation, only worse. Do you know how weird it is to fuck a guy with no head? I mean, the upside is that he's not trying to suck your face off or slobbering all over you, but still. It was awkward as fuck when I was climaxing and tried to wrap my hands around his neck, only to have them slip off, causing me to punch myself in the face. Talk about an orgasm to remember.

And it's not that I'm ugly, because I'm not. I'm not the prettiest thing that walked the earth, but I'm a solid eight, maybe eight point five, depending on the phase of the moon.

No. My appearance is not what makes me undesirable. It's the fact I'm a Squib.

A fae born without superpowers.

A nobody. Someone seen as barely more tolerable than a mundane, or a human.

In my case it's almost worse because Helsgard, the high court over the fae, thought I was going to be super powerful... the firstborn of an interspecies coupling. I wasn't the first, but I'm rare. For the most part, fae species don't mingle. Too much history and wars for most to see past.

Blood never forgets.

But historically, when there's an interspecies union, their offspring, especially the firstborn, is more powerful than others of the species they become. My mom is a succubus and my dad is a werewolf. I could have become one of those, or something else entirely. Or, even more rare, a true fae. Each fae holds a recessive gene for the true fae, the sprite little fairies that once existed long ago.

Some believe they still exist and have gone into hiding. Others say they've all been killed off. True fae were very powerful and were natural healers, but some didn't like that.

All that to say, I'm none of that.

When I turned nineteen, we waited like all families do for my powers to reveal themselves, but nothing. Year after year, we waited. Sometimes it can take longer... at least that's what everyone who was in denial would tell me. But when my brother, Beckett, burst into a flame and was re-born into a phoenix at midnight of his nineteenth birthday, it all but solidified the fact I'm a squib. My parents still held out hope, but I knew. I just didn't have the heart to tell them. I felt nothing. Although, there was one time I had a glimmer of hope, but I think it was just a really powerful orgasm.

My best friend Lizzy, a witch, felt bad for me and my pussy and gave me a 'sorry you're not super, but you're still super to me' gift. Her words, not mine. She has an unhealthy obsession with my pussy health, because she thinks I may have inherited some special powers from my succubus mother, but it works out well for me. She gets to try out new magic spells, and I get enchanted dildos. The one that caused me to think I was not a complete waste of space was the tentacle shaped dildo she gave me on my twenty-second birthday.

Good year.

Not really. More like good night. Well, if I'm being honest, good forty-three seconds. This tentacle looking dildo was dark and sparkly, and when I used it, it would come alive. At least that's what it felt like. Once I put it in, it would move back and forth and side to side and would expand inside of me. Almost like a knotting. Although no one has ever knotted me. Someone would have to enjoy sex with me to want to knot me.

Anyway. GLORIOUS. The first time I used it, I came so hard I thought I saw stars and felt a flush sweep across my body. That was the moment I thought I was becoming a fae. Which, to my disappointment, obviously I did not. Which completely ruined my orgasm.

Nothing like thinking you're about to find out you can rejoin society to bring you off an orgasm high. That was several years ago. Have I masturbated with a magical dildo since then? Yes. Does part of me think that maybe if I have a powerful enough orgasm, it will jump start the fae magic that's obviously tucked away and hidden inside of me? Also, yes. Have I tried to recreate the orgasm by edging myself repeatedly to the point I've used all the magic in the dildos? Also, yes. Do I know that is batshit crazy? Ding! Ding! Ding! Yes. Fortunately, there aren't too many people in my circle I can scare away and the only one I care about, Lizzy... well, I can't scare her away. I've tried. But she doesn't care about my super status, or lack thereof.

Which brings me to tonight.

It's Halloween. The human holiday where they all dress up in silly costumes and parade around looking for candy. This holiday truly baffles me, but that's why we don't really deal too much with mundanes. The ones who know about the fae are usually contracted to houses to render a variety of services. Cleaning, sex, blood donations, and some more that are too dark for me to even think about.

Now you may say to yourself.... Self, why doesn't she just fuck a human? She looks like a human and has no powers like a human. Both valid points, but no. That is the best way to destroy any remaining possibility I have of being accepted by the fae community.

No. Tonight is this Halloween holiday and a full super blood moon. The latter being the most important, even though others would argue. They would say Halloween is the one night a year that fae can walk around in their true form. Most fae can easily blend in with humans, but others need to be careful because of their non-human features.

There are fae businesses set up all around town, and most have an underground system you can use to travel. There are some who try to target a certain clientele and operate on the fringes of the underground fae system. This means you can only reach them from above ground. Those are the places the underground fae, or under fae, go when they can. A lot of animosity between those two groups.

But again, I care more about the latter. With the super blood moon out tonight, everyone is going to be... more. More aggressive, more horny, more powerful. This is what I care about. I need a good fuck. A fuck to last me until the next full moon. So I plan to go to Allure, a local sex club that has all variety of fae- light, dark and if I get desperate enough, then under fae who don't choose to go to those other clubs. I've never fucked a troll before, but I've heard they have enormous, possibly ribbed cocks... so...

My phone rings with an incoming video chat.

Lizzy.

Preparing for the tornado on the other side of the screen, I take two deep breaths, then swipe to answer.

"Hey hooker! What are you doing?" she chirps, full of spunk. She braided her hair with hints of purple and pink weaved throughout that glow against her light brown skin. The green in her hair matches the green in her eyes, making them pop. She's beautiful, but doesn't act like it. Model tall, with those legs you'd die to have. Tonight, she's wearing a revealing black v-neck top with various colorful necklaces, one of which is her favorite - the seeing eye. It's kind of weird, but it's her thing. She's also wearing a black witch's hat she got from one of the mundane's stores. She loves Halloween, especially with the full moons because her coven is tasked with walking around and keeping the peace between fae, which means she can use her magic in the open if needed. It's typically frowned upon, and you get pulled in front of the fae council if you do anything that could expose us. But tonight is the exception.

"Oh. Nothing much," I mumble, trying to sound as cool and calm as possible.

"Batttshit! I know you're lying. You're going out tonight, aren't you?" She's carrying the phone around the room as she continues to get dressed for the night.

"No."

"Your pussy's happy meter is at like negative two! I know you're looking to get your pussy pummeled, your peach waxed, looking for a date with the thunder sword."

I cut her off. "For the love of... well, whatever you love a lot, can you please stop? Thunder sword? Really? Who even says that?"

"It's better than the other ones I could've used like one-eyed-"

"Stop." I cringe and laugh at the same time.

"Fine. So what are you doing? Really?"

"Nothing much. I may go out. See what trouble I can get into. You know how much I love *the* Halloween."

"You hate Halloween. You're just horny. Are you not using my gifts?"

"I have." A lot.

"Oh my goddess! Have you used up all their magic?"

My brows furrow. "What? No? Why would you think that?"

"You have, you little freak toad! Damn, are you sure you aren't a succubus in hiding? You do need a good fuck, then. Find an alabaster and see if they can suck some of your sexual chi out of you, because I'm not sure my spells can keep up with you." She adds again for good measure, like she's proud of me. "You little horn toad."

"I'm not a succubus, and you know that." I frown. For a long time, I was sensitive about my predicament because I, like everyone else, thought I was going to be something. Until I wasn't. When most people look at me with pity in their eyes, or disgust (because I get that too), it bothers me. But when Lizzy does it, I don't know if it's something about her personality or her delivery, but it doesn't make me want to punch her in the face. We are practically sisters from different misters and have been getting in trouble together since we were in our single digits.

She shrugs her shoulders and lets out a hmph, completely dismissing what she said. "So, do you want to come out with us tonight?"

"With your coven? To watch them use magic? To have the young witches look at me with pity and have the elders poke at me, begging to do just one more spell, because they're this close to releasing my trapped fae power?" My fingers show an infinitesimally small space.

"They wouldn't do that."

"HA!" I tilt my head to the side and just stare at her incredulously.

She huffs, "Fine. They would, but you can ignore them and just hang with me."

"Liz," I pout.

"I know," she huffs. "Fine. Tell me what club you're going to and I will try to swing by and see you later."

"Liz."

"Damn it, Everlee!" Her face falls, and she stops moving around the room and stares at me.

Her sudden seriousness catches me off guard. "What?"

"I worry about you, ok?"

The words she left unspoken are, *because you are a squib going out on one of the most dangerous nights of the year.*

"Liz. I'll be fine and if not, I'll call you."

She stares at me through the phone with restrained irritation. I'm used to it though.

The look.

It's the same look I get from my parents and my brother every time I see them. Most squib don't move out on their own because it's too dangerous. But fuck that. I went to a mundane school for self-defense and learned the basics. Well, they call it a black belt, but they've never been toe to toe with a vampire, werewolf, or any other super.

The elders in Lizzy's coven call for her in the background and she stares at me.

"Go. I'll be fine," I urge.

"Fuck Everlee." Her lips pinch into a thin line.

Trying my best to convince her, I plaster on the biggest and brightest smile I can.

She growls at me, then hangs up.

My phone dings a second later.

Lizzy: *I love you and please, for the sake of all dick, don't do anything stupid.*

Everlee: *I love you too.*

Everlee: *And no promises.*

I stare at myself in the mirror and try to figure out what to wear. *You could wear nothing...* the devil on my shoulder chimes. I shake my head, clearing it. No. I need to leave something to the imagination.

That's it!

With a pep in my step, I walk over to my closet and grab my little black skirt and sheer black crop top.

Yes. This will do nicely.

EVERLEE - WHERE'S MY DDD BUDDY?

....

Two hours later, I'm standing in front of Allure. From the outside, you wouldn't know it's a sex club because it looks like a large rundown brick building with vines running up the walls. But that's how most of the fae businesses are. They don't stop mundanes from walking in, but they also don't flash signs encouraging it either.

The set of aged-oak double doors with large black knockers stands between me and my night. The wood bears the symbol of the seven-pointed faery star, which some fae burned onto it, symbolizing earth, air, fire, water, above, below, and within. A protection spell for the fae who enter.

The bass from the music inside is pulsing through the doors, tempting me like a siren song - even though all fae, including sirens, are forbidden from using their magic in Allure. However, there are two other exclusive parts of the club which allow the use of magic for pleasure. Pleasure being a very general term. Eden is mostly for light fae, while

Infernus was created for the dark fae. Either can transcend, but rarely do.

Light fae are gentle by nature, using their powers to help others and even occasionally mundanes. Dark fae, however, are quite the opposite. They use their powers to help them get ahead in life, oftentimes, using mundanes and other fae to get them there faster. Lines have been drawn as to what is acceptable and not acceptable behavior, so rarely do you get any that would voluntarily go to the other side.

They aren't required to choose a side, but it naturally happens over time. Some fae decide to go out on their own in the woods, or build a small cottage by a brook, living their life in solitude away from other fae. I thought about doing this at one point, but I'd be miserable.

When I hear several others walking up behind me, I grab the handles and push the doors open. The thick, dark air hits me in the face as the music amplifies to a deafening sound, but seconds later, my hearing adjusts and I can feel it moving within me. Pulsing, dancing.

The woman behind the desk looks at me, then nods towards the door, allowing me to enter. Because I'm a squib, I don't have to listen to the same lecture about not using my powers and how Allure is a neutral territory for all fae. Her words about Eden and Infernus fade away as I step further into the room.

The room is dark and there are lights shooting around as the beat of the music continues to pulse through my body, making it tingle and hum. The excitement and power from the blood moon is pumping through the air, charging it, causing the hair on my arm to stand- seeking connection. As my eyes continue to adjust, I can make out figures moving around on the edges of the room. A large Minotaur-like figure pulls two women behind him and leads them into one of the rentable rooms. I've never fucked a Minotaur or had any desire to. I'd be scared their horns would poke me, but I guess they could make great handles to hold him to my pussy as his tongue. Thick... wide...

Oh fuck.

My stomach clenches and my pussy pulses at the thought of being eaten out by a Minotaur. Maybe I should expand my horizons, because the images running through my head right now. It's like I can almost feel his tongue swiping up my center, brushing over my clit.

My knees buckle slightly and a whimper escapes between my lips.

His tongue is huge. Like as big, or bigger, than most cocks. It slips inside of me and the pressure... my eyes roll into the back of my head. *What in the hell is happening to me?* My plan was to come here and orgasm tonight, but in the middle of the damn floor?

A puff of air escapes between my lips as my stomach clenches, pulling me over. My hands brace on my knees like I'm about to hike a football or something as my orgasm is about to crest. Then it stops. Fucking washes away like the freaking tide back out to sea.

Completely stunned, I stand there, bent over, catching my breath and letting my pulse slow down. "What the fuck was that?" I mumble to myself.

"Everything ok?" A hand slides up my back to around my neck, pulling me up.

"Yes. Fine," I say, stumbling over my words as my eyes settle on the woman beside me. She's slender with long dark hair to her waist, wearing a shiny black leather outfit.

"Are you sure?" Her voice is light and airy, but there's a hard edge hidden beneath.

My hands nervously pat down my skirt, and I stand up straight. Well, more straight. Ok. In my mind, it feels like I'm standing up straighter even though I don't think I moved very much. "Yes. I'm fine."

A tingly feeling prickles on my neck, like someone behind me is staring at me. Curiosity prances inside of me like a cat walking on a fine line, but I don't know if I should turn around. Something about the woman in front of me has me in a trance. Not really, because using magic would be against the rules, but something. Obviously, someone in here is using their powers, perhaps a Mesmer, exercising their mind control over me to nearly make me orgasm in the middle of the floor. But why?

Her eyes dart up to the second level, and before I can stop myself, I'm turning as well. Standing there is a man. A God, with electric blue eyes that are piercing through the darkness. His hands grip the rail as he stares at me. No. At us. At her.

It's dark in here, but with the bouncing neon lights flittering across the second floor, I can tell he's dressed in all black. Black slacks, black jacket and a black button-up shirt. He has dark hair, a chiseled jaw with the hint of a five o'clock shadow. And he's tall. And damn. Muscular.

His eyes lock onto mine and for a moment, I forget how to breathe. We stare at one another, neither of us breaking our eye contact, until another man in a dark suit walks up to him and looks at us. He whispers something, then with a huff, blue eyes turns to leave.

Is he a Mesmer? Though I've never met a Mesmer who can make you feel things. Yes. They can usually control your movements and make you do whatever they want, but that. That was something else.

When I turn to ask the woman who that man is, she's gone. Disappeared without a trace.

Do they know each other?

Who are they? Granted, I don't come here a ton, but I've never seen either of them before.

Get it together Everlee!

This is the first time in a while I've been to a bar without my wing woman Lizzy. I almost don't know what to do without her here. She's my DDD buddy. Drinking, dancing, and dick buddy. She's made it her mission to make sure I'm sexually satisfied. Although, I think part of it is her projecting onto me. As one of the high-ranking members of her coven, they frown on her having a relationship. She's at the stage of her training (there's always training, apparently) where focus is priority. Most elders in her coven are single women who have never married or experienced any meaningful relationship. I think seeing that worries her because she doesn't want to be a spinster. She's always dreamed of having a family with children. Unfortunately (some would say the opposite) for her, she's powerful. Not exactly right now, but according to her coven, she will be. The Oracle has seen her future and said it's so. Which means she will go through more years of training, then in a tight little window they will bring men in to impregnate her. She can only have one child because more than that can diminish her power. Unless it's twins, then they become the Gemini pairing, which is a whole other ball game.

When Lizzy tried to push the Oracle on other parts of her future, the Oracle refused to answer. Lizzy, of course, read into that and was coming up with all sorts of theories as to why. It didn't matter that the Oracle never gave any other information. Nope. Lizzy saw a look on the Oracle's face and *just knows in her bones it's bad.*

Sometimes I can't help but wonder if she's still friends with me because part of her wishes she was also a squib. There's a lot of pressure on her and her life isn't really her own. I guess in that way I'm lucky. For the most part, people leave me alone.

Unless they want to fuck with my head like that fae just did.

I glance around to see if there's anyone out of place, but everyone seems to be off doing their own thing.

Wishing Lizzy was here with me, I pull out my phone and dial her quickly then hang up.

No!

You're a big girl. Pull up your panties and jump on that dick train. I quickly stuff my phone back in my pocket, then make my way over to the bar and pull up a seat.

The bartender, a beautiful harpy with whitish golden skin that sparkles, walks over to me. She has long dark hair and purple feathered wings with flecks of gold sprinkled throughout. Her bright emerald green eyes look me over for a second, then settle on me, but her head twitches from side to side. "What can I get for you, darling?" Her voice is airy, with a steel edge weaved throughout.

"Goysuxin, please." My cheeks flush under her gaze as she continues to watch me, her nose slightly tilting into the air like she's smelling me.

Oh Goddess! What if she can smell the arousal that has puddled in my panties?

Fucking Mesmer or whatever in the hell that was that got into my head!

A few moments later, she's bringing over the glowing bluish white drink. It's one of my favorites. A delightful and potent fae concoction with hints of raspberry, orange, a sprig of thyme and a liquor that glows and dances like a blue flame that tastes like vanilla and honey. I'm not sure how it's made, but my gosh. Delightful.

The drink, cold like ice on the lips, but hot as a blue flame when you swallow it down, sends goosebumps across my body.

"Want another?" she chirps.

"Yes, please."

Her golden speckled brows peak. "Everything alright? Most large fae can't handle much more than two back-to-back."

"All is great. And I'm not most fae." I wink with a smirk.

She smiles back, then hands me the drink. "Name's Harlow... if you need anything else." The look in her eyes causes my pulse to quicken.

"Harlow the Harpy. Nice ring." My cheeks are starting to hurt from smiling. Why am I smiling so much? "Thanks." Our eyes stay locked for another second until a troll sits down, grunting for a drink.

I drink this one a little slower, savoring all the intricacies of each flavor and hoping Harlow will come back by for a chat.

But she doesn't. The bar gets quite busy as she floats from one guest to the other. She's almost mesmerizing to watch. What is going on with me? I feel like someone or something has planted themselves inside of my head tonight. I mean. I knew I was horny, but damn! And the man from earlier on the balcony.

The soft chime of a gong filters down one of the halls calling interested patrons to the observation room for a demonstration. Perhaps I can get called on stage. I've tried most every time I've been here, but still haven't been picked. Who knows? Maybe the blood moon is the magic I need tonight.

EVERLEE - HOCUS POCUS YOUR ASS BETTER FOCUS

Colored ropes are hanging across a silver bar on the main stage. A Shibari demonstration. How exciting! The room is quickly filling, so I push my way to the front as best I can. Something about being tied up in ropes causes a flush to sweep across my skin. Images of me suspended from ropes, with hands firmly gripped on my hips and swinging me onto a cock, causes me to scream out and clutch my chest as my pussy pulses.

Just as quickly as the images appeared, they fade away.

My gaze quickly flits around the room and again, those blue eyes are focused on me from the back corner. My eyes narrow to thin slits as my head falls to the side, watching him. Why is he doing this to me? I've never seen this man before, which is a tragedy because he's gorgeous.

"Is everything ok?" a woman's voice asks, as her hand gently touches my shoulder.

Embarrassed by my outburst, I turn around and start to concoct some lie when my eyes fall on the woman from before who came up to me right after my near orgasm. "Oh. Hi. Hello. This is awkward. I'm not usually this awkward. I don't know what's going on with me tonight."

She laughs. "The super blood moon is very powerful tonight. Perhaps you're simply responding to that."

Something between a snort and a chuckle escapes sounding like I swallowed a toad. Which before you ask yourself... yes. I have swallowed a toad before. Blame Lizzy's coven and one of their surefire ways to unlock my fae. "Shit. Motherass. I'm sorry. I don't know what's come over me."

"Well, enjoy the show tonight." She tosses out her arm at the same time the lights dim. I hurriedly take my seat in the second row in the corner. Not the best view, but for showing up after the gong, it's not too bad.

The lights slowly turn back on and standing center of the stage is the woman I was talking to. What the fuck? That's-

The room erupts with gasps and applause.

"Good evening, fae folk. I'm Madame Dubois, your teacher for tonight." Her eyes lock on mine with the hint of a smile playing on her lips.

Madame freaking Dubois. Is here. At Allure. She travels the world with her shows and demonstrations and reviewers always rave about how wonderful they are. How was this kept quiet? Her shows are famous within the fae world. More importantly, how did I not recognize her? I mean, I've never seen her in person before, so I guess that would totally explain it, but still. Someone that famous, someone you want to be like- badass domme- you would think your mind would just instinctively know that's who you're talking to.

Twice now.

Two times she's touched me and talked to me.

Fuck yea! I nearly thrust my fist in the air, but regain control of myself.

First time tonight, it seems, my subconscious chimes.

"Tonight, we have a special treat for you. Shibari. How many of you have seen a Shibari demonstration or practice it?"

Less than half the crowd raises their hands.

"Ooh, not many. Not many. Well, this will be most exciting for all of us then." She claps her hands softly, then clasps them and rests her chin on them. "No demonstration would be complete without my helper." She fans her arm to the side of the stage where a delicious man, wearing only a pair of black boxers, bounces in. He has golden hair and a bright smile spread across his face. On his right side are several rune tattoos, meaning protection, loyalty, honor and a fourth I've never seen. His opposite shoulder has a tattoo that creeps down his arm and back, but it's just a series of lines and symbols, perhaps specific to his fae tribe? His soft green eyes flitter around the room and land on the back corner.

Realization hits me. He's the man from earlier. On the balcony, with tall, dark, and blue eyes. Before I can turn around to see if he's looking at blue eyes, the crowd goes wild, standing and waving their hands.

Madame Dubois must have asked for a volunteer. A delicate hand snakes its way through the first row and points at me. "You," her delicate voice chimes.

"Me?" I choke out, full of surprise.

"Yes. Let's give our volunteer a round of applause."

A few clap, but most look at me like I have five heads.

"Oh. We can do better than that, can't we?"

Suddenly, the entire room smiles and begins clapping. Like she has the room under her mind control.

Standing here on stage between this glorious piece of man candy and this domme, I feel so small. They are both taller than me, and I'm not short by any means at my five-foot-eight, but he has to be like six four? Six five? And Madame Dubois, with her spiky black six-inch heels on, has to be six feet at least.

"Are you ready?" she asks me.

I nod, scared I may croak if I speak.

"No, darling. Words. Use your beautiful words." Her fingers gently lift my chin up.

"Yes...ma'am," I mumble out, scared that I may melt into a pile of goo on the stage.

She looks at me, pleasantly surprised. "Would you two like to introduce yourself to your partner?"

Sticking my hand out, I turn to look at the man. "Everlee."

A smile curls on his lips. "Knox." He takes my hand and lifts it to his lips, gently brushing a kiss across my knuckles, making my nipples hard.

Pretty sure I just whimpered out loud. Fuck. Get it together, Everlee.

"I'd recommend you wear a few less clothes for this demonstration if you're comfortable with that?"

I nod my head, waiting for her to tell us to begin, and then realize she's talking about me. Obviously, Knox can't wear less. I mean, he can, but then... my mind wanders and before I know it, I'm staring at his boxers.

Oh my. Big dick. Big dick energy.

Well, I'm fairly certain after tonight, I'll no longer be able to show my face in here. My cheeks blush red for the what? Millionth time tonight.

I shake my head to clear it and nod again, "Right. Yes. I don't mind." No, I don't. I came prepared for this.

Well, not being in front of a room of strangers, disrobing into my bra and panties about to be tied up in rope by a hot as sin man. But this is a sex club, so it's not the craziest outfit. Half the audience is topless and I wouldn't be surprised if they are bottomless too. Is that what you would call it? Why is the word not coming to me right now? Bottomless sounds so weird. Like bottomless salads, soups, food things. It sounds normal. Fuck, Everlee! What is your deal tonight? It's like the whole nervous thinking thing where your brain just flits from one random thought to the next instead of focusing. But I'm not nervous... am I?

No. Why would I be nervous?

My gaze moves around the room noticing everyone looking at me, waiting, others glowering. But not blue eyes in the back corner. He's still standing there, arms crossed in front of his chest, shoulder leaning against the wall, watching me.

Who is he? Why does he keep watching me? At first, I thought he was looking at Madame Dubois, but now... now his eyes are definitely locked on me. Why have I never seen him?

His eyes narrow, as his focus on me deepens. If he was a Mesmer, couldn't he just control my body and have me remove my clothes? Does he own part of this club?

Fuck it.

If he wants to watch me, let him. Keeping eye contact with him, I pull my shirt over my head and drop it to the ground. My pulse quickens when I see him push off the wall and stand upright. Trying to push him a little further, I slip my fingers into the elastic band of my skirt and slip it over my hips. It puddles on the ground around my feet, So I step out of it.

He takes a step forward, almost possessive like, then stops.

Interesting.

Using my foot, I nudge my skirt and shirt together and push them out of the way, then move back to my place between Knox and Madame Dubois. I'm so glad I decided on this outfit for tonight. The bra makes my breasts look a cup size larger and my panties sit low on my hips and are very cheeky. Almost a thong, but not quite.

"Beautiful," Madame Dubois approves, looking at me for a moment before turning back to the crowd. Knox mumbles something, but it's incoherent.

He's the epitome of confidence, standing with his hands clasped behind his back, feet spread apart, tongue swiping over the bottom of his lip.

"Let's begin," Madame Dubois says. "Have you ever practiced Shibari before?"

"No."

"I've played in the ropes a time or two," Knox answers with a smile and only a hint of cockiness, smirking at blue eyes.

Oh God. What if blue eyes was looking at him? My inner demon is laughing hysterically at me for thinking he was looking at me. I could have sworn he was, though. Maybe he has a lazy eye or something and I just completely missed it.

Madame Dubois's voice brings me back. "Excellent, however for tonight's demonstration, I would ask you let me lead."

"Of course," Knox says, nearly bouncing with contained excitement.

He strikes me as the type that is always happy and full of energy. Even standing still, his muscles are flexing so much his pecs are nearly dancing on his chest. He clears his throat, catching my attention, so I look up at him. He nods to Madame Dubois, who is talking to us, and I've completely missed what she's said.

Damn it!

"Ready?" she asks, walking over and handing Knox the rope.

He runs the rope through his hands and something about it gliding through his fingers is so erotic.

"Step behind her," Madame Dubois commands, and Knox moves without question. Just the thought of him standing there causes a shiver to move up my spine. He's close. So close, I can feel his body heat, but I don't dare turn around. "Tonight, we're going to work on the diamond harness. An intricate, but beautiful design."

Knox lets out a moan.

"Knox, what I want you to do is start from her back and wrap it around her chest, crossing it over. Keep it high because we're going to come back around the other side and cross it back up. We want the cross to be just above the sternum."

Knox's hand grabs on my shoulder, causing me to jump. He leans forward, his chest brushing against my back, and whispers, "Do I have permission to touch you?"

I nod, since the words are caught in my throat.

"Baby girl, I'm going to need words."

Fuck me sideways Gandalfus. Did he just call me baby girl? I want to look down to make sure I'm not seeping arousal down my leg, but I feel confident I'd feel that? Right?

A few men in the crowd sit more erect, their heads tilting in the air.

Ah, shitballs. Must be werewolves or some sort of other shifter. They can smell my arousal. My pheromones must be shooting out of me like a firehose.

Damn it. Can Knox smell what he just did to me? I can't even look at him to find out.

"Yes. Yes. You can touch me," I pant out, then cringe almost immediately. I didn't mean to sound like I was hungry for his dick. I was simply trying to move the demonstration along since I realized I was having a whole internal monologue while Mr. Hot Crotch was still waiting on an answer from me.

His fingers trail up my back and my butt arches out like a cat in heat. Fuck me.

Focus, Everlee. What would Lizzy do?

She'd say something stupid like hocus pocus, your ass better focus! Wave her arms around, do some sort of jiggly dance, then end it with a pow pow, or something else equally dramatic and silly.

Knox curves the rope over my shoulder and steps forward, pressing his chest completely against my back and I try to ignore his bulge rubbing against my ass. I don't think he's doing it on purpose because his concentration seems to be fully on the ropes. He uses his hand to guide the rope across the top of my chest to the right under my armpit before he brings it back.

The rope feels different than I expected. A little rougher on my skin, but not prickly like some ropes feel. Though I'm not a master ropes woman by any means.

"Excellent. We don't want to cross between her breasts yet. Now, can you create a quick release?"

While Knox works on the quick release, Madame Dubois walks everyone through what that is and why it's important. Once Knox is done, he steps back and Madame Dubois walks around to the back and asks, "May I touch you to examine his work?"

"Yes. You may check the ropes," I say, turning my head to the side as her fingers trail along my back, checking his knot and the tightness of the ropes. The tail of the rope is currently brushing gently along my ass from side to side, tickling me. Who knew? My ass is ticklish.

"Very nice work. Perhaps you can travel with me for demonstrations," she says to Knox.

He laughs awkwardly, but doesn't say anything else.

Madame Dubois moves around to the front of the stage. "Ok. Now we have the quick release completed, we need to create some cross tension, so let's loop this around and back up, creating a cross at the top. But here we want to use the Munter's Hitch," she says, pointing to the front of my chest.

She walks the crowd through creating the knot while Knox wraps the rope under my right armpit and brings it around to my chest, walking with it so he's standing in front of me again. This time a little closer as he creates the Munter Hitch where Madame Dubois pointed earlier.

"Are you ok?" he whispers.

"Me?" I stutter, looking up at him.

"Who else would I be talking to?" He chuckles.

"Right," I mumble, sucking my bottom lip into my mouth.

"Oh, don't do that, baby girl." He swipes his thumb over my bottom lip, pulling it from my teeth and watches me, waiting for a reaction.

My lips part, stunned, as I take in this beautiful man who is bewitching in his own right. It's like I can feel myself being sucked into a vortex surrounding him and I want to say don't touch my lips. Don't call me baby girl. But it's all I can do not to combust on the stage right now. Who is this man? What kind of fae is he?

His hands continue to work the rope while his eyes stay locked on mine, working skillfully as he moves around to my back, creating the necessary loops and cross tension needed. He's like a shark circling its prey. *Hi, it's me. Yes, I'm the prey, it's me*, I sing in my head as Madame Dubois continues to give instructions. Following her words, he moves back around to the front, bringing the rope just under my armpit, his fingers gently brushing my skin.

A very sensitive spot for me. Potentially an erogenous zone. My nipples perk right up, nearly stabbing him through my bra. Stabbing may be a bit of an over exaggeration, but that's what it feels like. If I wasn't in front of an entire room of people, I'd try to push those fuckers back in. I know it doesn't work like that, but damn. It's like two little light sabers, weeeerrr weeeerrrr pew pew pew.

Knox's eyes are on my face, like he finds me the most interesting thing in the world, with a hint of a smile on his lips. Holy shitballs. What if he can hear my thoughts? Fuck! I look around the crowd to see if anyone else can. No one is dying of laughter, so chances are I'm safe. A few people look a little pre-occupido with their hands or mouths and aren't paying me much attention.

Damn it. Hocus pocus your ass better focus!

Knox has created a knot just above my breast and is now running the rope between them. He reaches around me like he's giving me a hug and my dumbass hugs him back until I realize he's just wrapping the rope around my back.

"Thanks," he whispers, dragging the rope up between my breasts with a hint of a smile on his lips.

"I'm sorry. I'm not usually this weird. Well, I don't think. It's just a very... odd night for me. I'm all in my head."

"Such a pretty head to be in." Before I can say thank you, he continues, "How is the pressure?" He gives the rope a gentle tug on my backside, cinching the rope tighter.

"Good." I swallow, as I watch his eyes drop to my heaving breasts, where he works to create another Munter Hitch between them. Lost in his thoughts, he sucks his lip into his mouth and I watch as his tongue and teeth work into it. A lip that I find myself wanting to touch. To feel. Anyway I can. Each time his hands graze my body, it leaves a wake of goosebumps across my skin, causing my nipples to press against the thin fabric of my bra.

Determined to concentrate on anything but him, I look into the audience and watch them while Knox continues to work the rope, pulling, knotting, and wrapping it around my body, checking in with me every so often. The further he works down my torso, the more I'm getting turned on, especially when I find blue eyes watching me from the corner still. Does he like ropes too?

I'm jerked back to the stage when Knox gives a final pull on the ropes, then moves to stand beside me and everyone's clapping. Feeling like I was just splashed in the face with a bucket of cold water, I look down and see a beautiful diamond pattern across my torso. It's a weird feeling. Somewhere between pain and pleasure, leaning more towards pleasure.

"Beautiful job, you two."

"Thank you, Madame Dubois," Knox answers as his eyes rake over my body. They seem almost feral, even though his breathing is slow and controlled. Very much the opposite of mine. I'm panting like a dog in heat.

Madame Dubois asks me to turn around so the group can see how *beautifully* Knox finished the knot. I feel slightly exposed with my ass on near display, but my eyes find Knox and his look is both electrifying and calming at the same time.

Out of the corner of my eye, Madame Dubois waves her hand in the air and a bar lowers from the ceiling.

My gaze flickers from the bar, to Knox, to his crotch where I most definitely just saw his cock twitch, back to his face. His lips part as he readjusts his stance. Blue eyes takes another step forward, eyes locked on me. It's almost a possessive stare, which I don't understand since I've never met him. But the things it's doing to me... Typically, I'd be pissed, but for some reason, it's turning me on.

"The thing about some harnesses is they're great for dominating and control." She looks at me. "Do you like to be dominated?"

Flabbergasted, I choke on the air surrounding me. "Well, I. Um... I don't know."

A wicked smile pulls at Knox's lips, causing a wave to pulse through my body, making my stomach clench.

"Let's find out."

"Mmhmm," I mumble out and know I should use words, but shit. Thoughts of Knox dominating me here, in bed, everywhere, flick through my mind like a movie. "Shit. Yes. There was a period between those two words. Like shit, I forgot to use words and yes, we will find out. It wasn't like shit yea!" I finish thrusting my fist in the air with tears prickling at the corner of my eyes. I'm not a crier usually, but the number of times I continue to embarrass myself here is truly astounding. Praise the high court that Lizzy isn't here. She'd be having a fucking field day with this and I would never hear the end of it.

"Knox, let's test Everlee."

KNOX - ROPE PLAY

Dominate Everlee? Fuck me.

My eyes move directly to the back of the room where Callum is standing. He's been watching us the entire time and even though he isn't sharing his thoughts, I know what he's thinking. He wants her. And wants to murder me.

Not really, but he is jealous as fuck. Jealous, I got to touch her first. Talk to her first.

He hates that Madame Dubois came to me for tonight's demo and not him. However, to be fair, he typically hates demos and anything attached to them. But when he saw her on the stage, I could nearly feel him shake.

I don't know why he's reacting to her like this. He hasn't even said one word to her, or even touched her. *Not like I have.* Thoughts of my fingers between her perfect fucking breasts play on repeat in my mind. She's so responsive to my touch. Fuck. To my look. Imagine how responsive she'd been with my cock between her legs or Callum's. He'd definitely want to put his dick in her first while the rest of us watch. Claiming her.

I swear... it's the oddest thing.

I need to talk to Emmett and Jax about this at our house tonight. Maybe they'll know what's going on. The way he is with her, the way he responds to her looks. When we were in the office talking earlier, his eyes flashed a bright blue silver and he rushed to the railing on the main floor like someone called his name. He's acting like she's his mate, but I don't think that's the case. Not in his -

"Knox. Grab her from the front and pull her towards you."

Damn it. I definitely don't look in the back corner. I can't deal with him right now.

My hands latch onto the rope and I pull her hard, with authority, and she easily moves across the floor, her chest pressing to mine. I'm not usually the dom in our relationships, that's Callum's territory, but I'm not going to lie. This feels nice. I can't help but laugh on the inside, because I know his dick is probably harder than Thaleon's crystal right now.

"Spin her around."

With the same speed and authority, I spin her around, then a primal instinct takes over and I pull her in close, pressing my cheek beside hers, inhaling her scent. I can't help but smile when she lets out a needy whimper.

Movement catches my attention from the back of the room and before my brain can catch up to my eyes, I see Callum gnawing on his bottom lip, eyes flickering between blue and silver. For both our sakes and for everyone in the room, I push her away from me just a bit.

"Very sexy. The chemistry on this stage is electric."

"Thanks Madame Dubois," I sigh. As if living in this prison wasn't bad enough, she's making it nearly unbearable with her comments and directions.

Does she know?

Surely she hasn't missed Callum in the back. On a good day, he's nearly impossible to miss with his height, his look, and sheer presence. But tonight? Tonight, he is all dominance, authority, and pure sex. Is she doing this on purpose? I know they've had their words in the past. Is she doing this to fuck with him? Using me like a pawn?

"Knox, let's walk her over to the bar. Have you worked with suspensions before?"

"A few times," I say, hooking my finger in the rope near Everlee's ass and dragging her over to the bar. Did I purposefully choose that location to grab, so my fingers could brush against her ass? Yes. Yes, I did. Her reactions are becoming addictive, and I occasionally have a reckless streak in me that enjoys pushing Callum.

She smiles, "Excellent." She looks at Everlee. "We're going to try some face down suspension with this harness. It can be one of the more restrictive suspensions in terms of asphyxiation, so communication is key here. Do we have your permission?"

She stands up straight, "Yes, ma'am."

"Don't think because you're the bottom, that you're not in control. You have the most power. You say the word and you come down immediately. If you are having a hard time breathing, or feel too much pain, you need to tell us. Don't try to tough it out."

"Ok."

Her shoulders are rising a little faster as her breath picks up. She's nervous. Wanting to ease her nerves, I grab her shoulder and rub my thumb up and down her neck. Her head bobbles for a moment, before her shoulders relax. I step forward, closing what little distance is left, and whisper, lips barely touching her ear, "If you don't want to do this, then just say the word. We can stop."

She turns into me and looks up, her lips inches from mine. Her eyes are bouncing between my eyes and my lips as her breath slows. She shakes her head and regains her thoughts. "I want to do this."

"Good. Me too." I wink and shift her to the bar.

Madame Dubois hands me another rope and I run it through my fingers like a long-lost friend. Rope at one point in my life was my enemy, but I learned about it. How to use it. How to manipulate it. Now... now I have a new enemy. An enemy, who in my weakest moment, took from me what I valued most-

"Knox?" Madame Dubois asks, looking at my hands with her brow furrowed.

The rope was cutting into my skin because I was pulling it so hard.

"Yes. Cuffs," I answer without thinking. Calming my sudden onset of rage, I drop to my knees in front of Everlee and take a deep breath. The sweet scent of her arousal dances around me. So sweet, it's causing me to drool. Is this what Callum has been reacting to all night? I need to focus because I don't even know this woman and here I am, getting lost in her. I work the rope high on her thigh, to give her better control when she's suspended. If the rope is too far down her leg, it will cause her back to bend too much. Careful not to swipe against her pussy, I knot the rope a few inches from her center.

Madame Dubois keeps talking, and I follow along. I need this demonstration to be over. I need to talk to Everlee, figure out who she is. After ten minutes, I've successfully hoisted Everlee into the air. With her body fully suspended, she lets out a small cry of pain as her body adjusts to the ropes.

"How are you doing?" I ask her, trying to focus on her well-being instead of the carnal need ripping its way through me. The need to sexually ravage her and sink my cock deep inside of her.

"Good," she grunts out.

"How's your breathing?" I can tell it's shallow, but steady.

"Good," she says, wiggling in the ropes.

"Pain?"

"Not too bad."

She's strong. A fighter. She doesn't want to admit any kind of weakness, which in this case is stupid. It's not weakness. She's new to this. She's never had a rope tied around her. Never felt it cinching tighter and tighter with each movement. Her skin is turning pink where the ropes are cutting in.

After another minute of Madame Dubois giving her speech, I lower Everlee. When she stands, her legs wobble and give out, causing her to fall into my arms and I hold her. She curls into me like she's never experienced this kind of embrace before, and the thought of that pisses me off.

Fuck. Now *I'm* becoming possessive.

There's an electricity between us. A heat. At first, I think it's in my head, but she feels it too. I can see it on her face.

Lights flicker in the room and pull her out of whatever trance she's in.

"Sorry," she mumbles quickly before pushing off me. "Can you help me out of these ropes?" She thumbs over her shoulder.

She's antsy, nearly bouncing in the spot she stands.

"Knox," she presses.

"Yes. Yes. Sorry," I mutter, still trying to understand why the sudden change. She went from cool and collected to one rung short of freaking out.

Tugging at the quick release, I make quick work of the ropes, untying them at the same time she's wiggling and pulling them down.

Madam Dubois stares at Everlee and then looks to the crowd, asking for a round of applause. That does little to calm her down. If anything, it makes her more antsy.

She pushes the rest of the ropes to the ground and steps out of them, bends to grab her clothes, and darts out of the room. Callum's eyes are boring holes through me like I did something, but I didn't. I simply caught her to prevent her from falling.

Madame Dubois continues to talk about safety, pulling the crowd back in, and I'm stuck between running off stage or staying put.

When I don't move, I pump my eyebrows at Callum and he turns out of the room.

EVERLEE - BETTY'S BITCHIN' RIDES

WHAT THE FUCK WAS that?

The heat. The lights flickering. My body. It felt like lightning, preparing to unleash.

My chest continues to heave rapidly as I stand in my bra and panties in the dark hallway, bent over with my hands on my knees. Footsteps are moving down the hall with a heavy thud, so I push off the wall and move deeper into the club. I can't be around anyone. See anyone.

Did I make the lights flicker?

Impossible.

I have no powers.

A growl sounds behind me, from where I was just standing. Not Knox, but who?

They are angry. Frustrated. I can understand them.

What is going on with me?

"Hey," a deep voice groans.

My hands continue to rove over my body, the ripples and indentions giving my mind something to focus on.

"I said hey," the voice groans as a set of large moist hands grab my shoulder and yank me around.

"What?" I snap back and then look up. Like way up.

A fucking troll. He has to be every bit of nine feet tall and six times wider than me.

"Mine. You're mine."

Trolls aren't known for their intelligence or ways with words.

"The fuck I am."

"Pretty."

"Thanks, but I'm not looking for anything tonight."

His finger and thumb wrap around my wrist like it's a twig in his large grasp.

"Let go of me," I cry out, trying to pry his fingers off of me.

He's walking through Allure, brushing past tables, and people like they're nothing. Did I really consider sleeping with a troll earlier tonight? What the fuck was I thinking? Definitely a hard pass. I don't care if I never have sex again. I can't sleep with a troll. He smells like fish and sewage. I'm surprised they allowed him to come in.

"Let go of me!" I yell, trying to set my heels into the ground to stop us, but he's probably five hundred times stronger than I am.

"Let her go!" a voice yells beside me and I recognize it immediately.

Lizzy.

"Lizzy! You're here," I say, reaching out for her to give her a one-armed hug, but the troll is still moving. He's heading towards the large door that says Infernus.

"No shit Sherlock! What in the hell are you doing here? Where are your clothes and what happened to your body?" Her hand latches onto mine and we both pull.

My wrist plucks out of the troll's slimy hands and we both fall on our butts.

"I wanted to come out tonight and have some fun. My clothes are here," I say, shaking them. "And Madame Dubois picked me as the volunteer for the Shibari demonstration."

"Shi-whatty?"

"Decorative rope bondage."

"You kinky fucker!" she says, shoving me to the side. "Next thing I know, you'll be wanting me to call you a good ghoul."

"Ha. I see what you did there."

"You. Come here!" The troll commands.

Lizzy and I both scramble to our feet.

"I don't think so, buddy. She's my bitch. I claim her."

"Aww boo." I smile at her, tilting my head to the side.

"I didn't have time to get a ring or anything," she continues, playfully.

"Lies. You lie. She's mine. She's Wilpus's."

"No. I'm not!"

"Will puss what?" Lizzy goads.

"Wilpus. Me. She's mine."

He grabs at my hand, but I quickly snatch it away and grab Lizzy's hand as we move through the crowd, trying not to draw attention to ourselves.

"What's going on?" I pant, looking over my shoulder.

"A fucking troll wants to make you his bitch stick. His glory hole, his-"

"Stop. Stop with all your names. Why are you here?"

"You called me, then hung up. I thought you were in trouble, so I ran a locator spell on you. It looks like I wasn't wrong."

"I have the situation under control. And a locator spell? Don't you need something from me to do that?"

"I'm sure you don't," she says, flapping her arms in the air. "And hair. I keep a jar of your hair in my bedside drawer for cases like this."

"Mine." The troll swipes at the air in front of me again, trying to grab my arm.

"You realize how fucked up that sounds? You don't really have a jar full of-" I stop speaking, realizing she's probably not kidding. "Lizzy!" I bark.

"Stop. Let's not pretend you wouldn't do the same!"

"Keep a jar of your hair? No. I wouldn't do that!"

"Well, easy for you to say," she stares at me indignantly.

I growl out in frustration as the troll tries to grab at me again. "Can you do something?"

"You said you have it handled," Lizzy says clasping her fingers and placing her hands behind her head.

"Liz!"

"What? You came here looking for a good time."

"Liz!"

"Fine. Go back to your bridge, troll!"

"No."

The troll snags my arm in his hand and Lizzy and I fight to get free, and that's when I feel it again. The charge.

The lights flicker.

Fuck.

Something's happening.

My eyes dart to Lizzy as I try to grab her attention, but she's too focused.

A ball of light shoots out of my hand, hovering for a second, then disappearing. It was small, but it lit the entire room and everyone freezes.

"What the fffff–" Lizzy starts, staring at me, then jumps. "Fuck." Her word was less of a question and more of a statement.

Several people gather around us, intrigued, and even the troll is stunned.

"You want more of that?" Lizzy shouts, stepping forward, conjuring up a light ball in her hand and holding it there for a second.

What the fuck was that? A ball of light just shot out of my hand. A small bead that was as bright as the sun. Me. My hand.

Lizzy's ball of light fizzles, but it was nowhere as bright as mine, but she's trying. She's lying to protect me.

Protect me?

Why?

I stare at both of my hands.

No.

I can't be.

No.

"Let's go. Now. Ride's outside."

"Liz."

She turns to me, all jokes aside. "Shut the fuck up and listen to me for once! Don't say a word. Let's go now."

Fuck. She's thinking the same thing I am.

She flicks her wrists, pushing the doors open as we approach them. The first set, then the second.

"You can't use magic inside!" a woman yells from the front desk.

"Eat glass, Karen!"

Lizzy waves her hand in the air and the doors shut back. "Jump on," she insists.

"When did you get a motorcycle?" I ask, hesitantly climbing on, reaching for the handlebars.

"It's not mine."

"It's mine!" A voice barks at me. "And hands off the bars."

I look around, trying to find the voice as the bike roars to life.

"Liz. Who is this chick? She looks like she's a few ladles short of a cauldron."

"That doesn't even make sense."

"Hold on," the voice chimes as the bike peels off down the road.

"To what? You said not to grab the handles!"

The bike veers a hard left.

"Coo coo caa-choo this one L bean."

"L bean? Where are you?"

"Hoo hoo. Down here."

A little bobble head figure suction cupped to the body of the bike is looking at me. "There she is. Welcome to Betty's Bitchin' Rides. I'm Betty, your driver du jour."

"You're a talking bobble head."

"The fuck I am. I'm incognito."

"As a bobble head."

The bike screeches to a halt, throwing us both forward. "L bean, put a zip on those lips."

"Ev."

"Fine. Not a bobble head." *Even though you are literally bobbing on a spring from side to side.*

"I can hear your thoughts *Ev*," Betty says pulling her tiny little bobble head face.

"What?"

"Kidding, of course. That's fucked up. Now hold on." She pulls forward again.

"We need to hide, Betty."

"Of course you do. I could tell by the way you came storming out of there. What did you do?"

I look at my hands, scared to say the words.

Lizzy answers, "A troll was trying to drag Ev back to his lair, and I used magic to stop him."

"Seems innocent enough."

I wish that were the case.

"Not in a place that is neutral territory and prohibits magic."

Betty sighs, "Fine. I have a place. But no one can know where it is."

"I won't say anything."

"I know." Her little bobble head hand twitches and blackness sweeps in like a raptor for its meal.

CALLUM - BLUE BALLS, LIGHT BALLS

MY BLOOD BOILS LIKE hot lava inside of me. It has been for some time now. Watching Knox on stage with her. With his hands on her. Watching what it does to her. Smelling her arousal. I'm typically not a jealous man when it comes to Knox and our women, but something about her... I wanted to be the one who was turning her on. Wanted to be the one causing her to whimper and flush.

She ran out of the demonstration room before I could get a chance to talk to her. To figure out who she is and where she's from.

But she ran!

Where did she go?

The echoes of my footsteps bounce around in the hall like sounds bounce around in an empty cave, pinging off the walls, hitting me from all sides. Mocking me.

Taking in a deep breath, I let her scent fill my lungs. It's pocketed here, against the wall. She was standing here for a minute. What was she doing? Catching her breath?

Calming her rapidly beating pulse? She was standing here until she heard me coming. Rage erupts inside of me, and the wall and my knuckles feel my wrath.

"Where is she?" Knox asks, running up to me.

He's put his slacks and black button up back on, but it's still not tucked in.

Unprofessional.

"Tuck your shirt in. You're on the floor."

"Cal. Half the club just saw me in my boxers." He stops speaking, holding his hands up in defense when he sees my eyes set on him. "Fine. I'll tuck it in." He slips his pants down and works on his shirt. "Where is she?" he asks again, pulling his pants back up.

"Gone! She's gone!"

"Who is she?" Knox presses, looking into the crowd.

Why the fuck can't he leave me alone? I need to find her, not answer a hundred fucking questions about where she is. If I knew, I'd be with her right now. Not standing with him in the middle of a dark hallway.

"I don't fucking know Knox. That's why I'm trying to find her, so I can talk to her," I snap. I don't mean to, but this woman. I growl out in irritation. "There's something different about her." When she walked into the club tonight, my skin felt this tingle sweep across it. I *felt* her presence.

"I can tell."

"You can? What can you tell? When you were touching her, did you feel something?" The words rush out of my mouth as I step towards him, pressing him against the wall with my chest. I had to know. Know what he felt. Know any and everything about her.

Knox holds his hands up. "Fuck, Callum. I simply meant that you're losing your shit over her. Over a chick you've never seen before. You're possessive. I haven't seen this side of you since-"

"Don't you fucking say it." I've never laid hands on Knox, and would never want to, but he knows the rules. We don't talk about the past. We can't fucking change it, just endure the present.

This prison.

We've known each other for nearly two hundred years, which is only a fraction of my one thousand and fifty-four years. He's my brother.

Not by blood, but by choice.

I choose to be by his side, mostly because he's never left mine. Even when I wanted him to, he wouldn't. An annoying little shit that just wormed his way in and embedded himself into the depths of my skin. Like fungus on a tree.

A piercing bright light explodes through the club, illuminating the dark confines of our hell before it vanishes again.

"Fuck!"

"What was that?" Knox asks confused, taking a step forward, but not leaving my side.

My lips flatten into a hard line. "Her."

"Her? Everlee? The girl I–"

"Yes. Her. We need to find her. Now."

"Why? What was that? I've never seen a light so bright."

"I know."

"What?"

Irritated, I bat the air and tear across the floor towards the middle. Her scent is faint, but hints of it still dance on the air. I wasn't sure before, but now I am. It's been so long since–

"Callum," Knox huffs, grabbing my arm. "Is this a good idea? Going after her. Could she hurt us? She clearly has no qualms detonating a light bomb in the middle of a club full of fae."

Yanking my arm out of his grip, I continue to push forward through the crowd. Some are confused, others don't care, but a few... a few know. Or think they know.

"She's not safe, Knox."

"Are you sure it's her that's not safe?"

Frustration boiling over, I stop and turn to look at him. "Listen, if you don't want to come, then don't. But I'm telling you. She's going to need our help."

"Why?"

"I don't have time to explain right now. We just need to get to her."

Pushing through the rest of the crowd I see her, standing toe to toe with a troll that is several times her size with a woman beside her, hand clasped to her wrist.

My heart pulses. Is it too late?

Discretion is of the utmost importance right now. If the others don't know what's going on, then I don't need to charge in, tipping my hand.

Everlee looks from the troll to the woman, baffled, but not scared. She knows the woman. Perhaps the woman is a friend?

Tilting my head up in the air, I inhale slowly, focusing on her friend. Moments later, the stench of herbs and dead animals attacks my nose.

A witch.

She's friends with a witch?

A ball of blue and white light dances in the witch's palm and she aggressively steps forward, closing the distance between her and the troll. "You want more of that?" she taunts.

Her witch friend has a potent smell. She's more powerful than most of the other witches here. Does she know about Everlee? Is that why she's friends with her? To use her?

The tips of my nails bite into the palms of my hands, and seconds later a warm ooze is trickling down my hand.

Fuck.

I'm bleeding.

The room shifts again. The few vampires that frequent our club smell me.

"What the fuck Callum? Get yourself under control. I'm not trying to fight off half the damn club because of you."

The warm iron taste coats my tongue as I swipe it across the cut on my palm. Seconds later, it's sealed. The few heads staring at me, salivating over me, turn away. They'd have no chance against me. I don't care how fast they are or think they are. I'm faster. They are feeble minded and think their speed and strength are no match for anyone. I have years of experience they can't touch, even without my-

"Callum," Knox murmurs, capturing my attention. He nods to the crowd where the witchy woman is pulling Everlee.

When I start to go after her, I feel the whoosh of air around me.

A vampire.

Reacting without waiting, I turn and my hand clamps around the throat of the would-be attacker.

My eyes focus at the same time the bone in my arm cracks.

Shit. Emmett. I release my grip from his throat, and Jax releases his from my arm.

"What's going on?" Jax barks.

Trying to get the feeling back in my arm, I give it a hard shake and feel the small cracks heal.

They're gone. Everlee and her friend just ducked through the main doors that just splintered open. Yea. The woman with Everlee is powerful. I just don't know if that's good or bad.

"Callum!" Jax barks again.

"What?"

"What in the hell is going on?"

"Jax. Don't," Knox warns.

"Let's go to the office."

"Where were you two?" Knox coos playfully.

"Shut the fuck up," Jax retorts.

"You've got something there," Knox points at Emmett's lip.

Emmett quickly runs his tongue over his lip. "No, I don't."

"Made you look."

Jax shoves Knox on the shoulder and before Knox can retaliate, I walk through the middle of them and head towards the office.

"We need to find her," I call over my shoulder to no one in particular and ignore the questions from Emmett and Jax, who are trying to catch up.

EVERLEE - THE MORNING AFTER

THE HEAT FROM THE morning sun warms my face, pulling me from my sleep. When I try to roll over, I feel an arm draped over my side and begin to silently freak out.

What happened last night?

Scared to move and find out what happened, I freeze and try to put the pieces of last night back together. I went to a sex club looking for sex... had two goysuxin, which probably wasn't the best idea because they're pretty potent. My eyes travel down to the hand hanging across my bare stomach.

Fuck.

It looks petite. A female's hand.

Did I go home with the bartender?

Working my way through my memories, I remember I was on stage with Knox being tied up in rope, blue eyes, and the troll, Lizzy and then... oh shit. Remembering the light orb that shot out of my hands, I pull them up to look at them. Lizzy dragged me out of the club and we got onto a motorcycle with a bobble head for a driver.

Am I in bed with Lizzy?

Fairly confident I wouldn't find a stranger, Lizzy's contorted face meets mine when I roll over. Unable to hold it in any longer, she bursts out laughing. I push against her, creating a space between us. "What the fuck, Liz?"

"Oh, stop." She bats her hand and rolls out of bed fully clothed. "I just saw a perfect opportunity to fuck with you. I know waking up in a strange bed is a fear of yours."

"So you thought it would be ok to make me think I went home with a stranger?" I throw the sheets off and notice I'm in my underwear and a crop top that isn't mine. "Where are my clothes?"

"Yes. Again, I saw an opportunity and love watching that little scrunch in your brow when you're panicked. I thought the hand on the stomach was a wonderful touch."

"You're such a bitch." I swat at her, laughing.

"A bitch who is currently washing your clothes. Careful or I will dry them on super hot and shrink them."

"Is that how you shrink clothes?"

"I don't know. I just wash them all together on normal, then dry them on normal and see what happens. It's a crap shoot."

"You know, if you read the directions, that would help."

"Directions schmections."

I scrunch my nose at her and she cackles. "Come on. Breakfast is downstairs."

"Where are we?" I ask, looking around. It's a large room with tattered industrial wooden floors that have knots throughout. There is a large open window on the far side of the room with a hazy film on most of the picture sized frames, and a hole in one. There's only one bed with a tattered blanket on the end, and a mismatched dresser along the opposite wall with a dead plant in a pot on the corner.

"A safe house. It hasn't been used for a while."

"A safe house?"

"Yea, until we figure out what to do with you. About you. Just you, in general."

"What was that? Last night."

"Thanks for qualifying with last night. When you simply asked '*what was that*', I had no idea you were talking about the giant light ball you made with your hands, putting our lives at risk."

"You're being sarcastic?"

"Yes. Yes, Everlee, I'm being sarcastic. I don't *know* what that was. I have an idea, but I need to talk with the elders to see, but if it's what I think, then I don't want you to talk with anyone."

A knot lodges itself in my throat. "You think I'm a–"

She flicks her hand, and my hand flies to my mouth, covering it.

"Don't."

My eyes nearly bulge out of my head. She just used magic on me. Something she swore she'd never do again after she thought it would be funny to enchant my bed to keep me in it when we were little. She got the spell just a bit off and the sheets were attacking me, trying to pin me down.

I moan and stomp my foot so she'll let my hand go because it feels like she's superglued it to my face. She walks over and gets close to me.

"Don't talk."

My eyes pulse wide, the obvious sign for *ok I won't talk and get my fucking hand off my mouth.*

She flicks her finger and my hand falls. "Was that really necessary?"

"Hungry?" she asks, completely dismissing my question.

"Yes. I guess I am," I huff.

When she starts to walk out of the room, she looks over her shoulder at me with those eyes that tell me she's not kidding.

The stairs down to the main floor creak under our weight. It's obvious this was an abandoned building of some sort and hard to tell what was really safe about this safe house. The walls look like they're made of paper and the floors look like they're one wrong step away from another hole in it.

"There she is!" A voice yells from the kitchen, causing me to jump into the wall. "Calm down, deary. Didn't mean to startle, didn't mean to startle." The woman is moving the hot pan off the stove and putting it on the counter. "I just finished up these eggs. Come sit down and get something in your belly."

The woman standing in the kitchen is a normal human sized version of the bobble head affixed to the bike from my memory. She has short, light pink hair that looks like one of those LED fiber optic lamp things with the thin little strands that you just want to run your hand across and pet. Only I'm pretty sure if I tried to pet her head, she'd knock me out. Which I couldn't blame her, but her hair. I just want to touch it.

"Are you ok?" she asks looking at me.

"Ev?" Lizzy asks, nudging me and breaking me from my trance.

"Yea. Sorry." Not sorry. "I'm still just wearing off the drinks from last night."

"Wild night last night." She watches me cautiously walk into the kitchen. "Name's Betty. Don't know if you got that from the Betty's Bitchin' rides, or if you remember that. You seemed a little loopy last night, then for good measure, I gave you the whammo blammo punch and knocked you out."

Either I'm still drunk, which I didn't think I was before, or she's just a lot to process.

"So what happened last night? Liz Whiz here was in a hurry to get to you, then a few minutes later yuns are boltin' out of the doors with an 'eat shit and die fuckers' look on your face. Well, Liz Whiz, not you. You looked like you were a bit in la la land."

Is she talking fast or am I listening slowly? "I-"

Liz interrupts, "Like I said last night. Some ginormous troll was trying to bring her back to his lair. He had her by the wrist and was dragging her across the floor. I showed up, used a little magic, and then we bolted. One, because

I'm pretty sure I pissed off the troll, and two, because you aren't allowed to use magic. A point, the lady at the front desk, harped on several times before she let me in the club. What about this?" She runs her hand up and down her body several times, "Says I won't follow the rules and use magic."

"Did you use magic?" Betty asks.

"Yes, but that's beside the point."

The grumble from my stomach echoes around the tiny little apartment space. Judging by the blanket thrown over the back of the couch, I'd venture to say Betty slept down here. I take a bite of eggs to help soothe the ick feeling that's churning in my stomach. I'm pretty sure it's because I'm hungry, but it could also be nerves. Lizzy is in overprotective mode, so there's something else going on. Something she won't let me say.

"How was last night?" I ask, shoveling a forkful of eggs into my mouth.

"It was fine. Not much drama," Lizzy slumps her shoulders.

"You're mad because you didn't get to use magic on anyone?"

"Yes."

"Sorry." I pump my eyebrows, picking up another forkful of eggs and putting them on a biscuit. "These are great," I say, stuffing a bite into my mouth. I didn't realize how hungry I really was. "How did you two meet?" I ask, pointing my finger between them.

"I used to be in the coven Lizzy belongs to."

"Used to be?"

"They excommunicated me. Banished," she says, flipping her hand in the air dramatically.

"What happened?"

Betty slams both hands on the counter in front of me and a can of three spatulas on the end of the counter clangs loudly together, startling me.

"Now you've done it," Lizzy says, looking between Betty and me, scooping some eggs up to put on her biscuit.

Confused, I look back at Betty.

"I's targeted."

"Targeted?"

"I may have done a few things I wasn't proud of, but," she points her finger rapidly in the air. "I was proud of what I did, which got me kicked out. Even though it's complete batshit. I's in school. Witch school. Training. Whatever they want to call it nowadays. Any whoozle, they had all those frogs in those jars just sitting there on the shelf croaking. Over and over and over and over again. I couldn't take it anymore. It's really too much for one person to handle. Like medieval torture and I even saw it in BethAnn's eyes and Morley's too. They didn't like the frogs locked up."

"So, what did you do?"

"Well, I may have cast a spell that let them out. But in my defense, how was I supposed to know they'd go straight for the dean's room? She'd just gotten in a nice variety of flowers in her bedroom, which apparently attracts frogs better than shit attracts flies and that's saying something. I say the dean shouldn't have been napping in the middle of the day, but she's yet to answer for that!" She slaps the table.

"It was several hundred frogs," Lizzy adds.

Betty just groans. "Well, they shouldn't have been locked up. We could have retrieved them as needed from the ponds around the compound. Plus, who puts that many flowers in one room?" she retorts, defensively.

"Is this your house?" I ask trying to change the subject. I'd hope this isn't her house, because it looks like a solid wind could come through and knock it out. There are walls that are nothing but two-by-four posts standing up. You can walk between them.

"One of them. This is my July house. I've got one for each month."

"You have twelve houses?"

"You gotta stay busy. Be prepared and always moving."

"Why?"

"Well, after they banished me for the frog incident... well, I's mad. It was a silly mistake and I's only trying to free the poor things and–"

"What was that?" Lizzy asks, standing from her chair and running over to the exterior wall, looking outside.

"Probably some underfae working their way back home after last night," she answers without concern. "One of the underground entrances is at the end of the alley."

Pushing away from the table, I join Lizzy by the window. "I don't see anyone."

A second later, a bright purple light flashes against the wall at the end of the alley. "Is that it? The entrance to the underground?"

"Yea. But don't get any ideas. While the underfae are not aligned to either court, they tend to be more dark fae and a pretty little thing like you... they'd have a field day with," Betty adds, walking over to look out of the window. "Oh yeah. That's Tompkin. Mean son of a bitch with cards."

"Cards?" I stare at the oversized troll trudging down the street, ignoring the screeching cats running for cover. He gets to the wall and holds his hand against it and a purple light flashes before he walks in.

"Is it magic?"

Betty laughs. "Yes sweetie. Most portals aren't like that. They did me a solid a few years back, so I gave them that portal opening. A little quid pro quo. Makes it easier on some of the older, larger fae who don't enjoy climbing down sewer grates or jumping off bridges into water."

My eyes stay glued to the wall as the purple light fades and the clay red bricks return with hints of graffiti letters sprayed on it. I've never seen an underfae entrance, magic or otherwise, but often wondered how they move around. Obviously, I didn't wonder hard enough to go search them out, but it crossed my mind. Especially at first, when I didn't turn and some of the fae community turned their backs on me.

An outcast.

Like the underfae.

But I was nervous. Underfae are underfae because their appearance can't pass as human. I could pass. I was just a squib. Who could be more human looking than me? Well, who knows after last night? Humans don't shoot blue balls out of their hands. So there's that.

Clanking dishes from the kitchen grabs my attention and pulls me out of my thoughts. "Hey girls," Betty starts. "I need to run out. Grab a few supplies if you two plan on staying here for a while."

"I don't think we are." I look at Lizzy.

"We may be."

"Liz. I'm not going to hole up in a stranger's house."

She grabs my arm and pulls me close and whispers, "I don't think it's safe for you out there."

"Why?"

"The blue ball."

"Fluke."

"You don't believe that and don't even try to make me believe you believe it."

"How many times can you say believe in one sentence?"

"How ever many times I want. I don't think it's a good idea to go out until we know what we're dealing with."

"You're really nervous."

"Well, I'm not *not* nervous."

"I can't just stop showing up for work."

"What? The books can't dust themselves?"

"Rude."

"It was kind of a serious question."

"That is my book shop. Mine. There's no one else to run it if I'm not there."

"Are there really that many people that come into it?"

"What the hell Liz? Yes. It's not some cool fancy fae job for Helsgard, but I abandoned that hope when they all but turned their backs on me. No. I went out and worked my ass off to open my dream book shop. It's old and quaint. I just finished the romance themed room."

"Whips and chains and handcuffs?"

"Not that kind of romance."

She frowns.

"That's downstairs."

"Shut the front door."

"Well, technically back door. Its primary access is at the back door."

"Shut up. You don't have a sex room."

"I mean, not really a sex room. It's just a themed room with some toys and such. Partners can reserve the room for couple reads, or if someone wants to just be in the environment of their books..."

"Why didn't you tell me?"

"I started to, but then you fell asleep."

"I wouldn't do that. I love books."

"You don't love books. You would literally practice your spells on them, catching most of them on fire."

"The teacher said to focus on something you ha- Oh. I see what you did there."

"You two are cute," Betty jumps in.

"What?"

"You two. Your banter. You're like sisters."

"Sisters from different misters," Lizzy says, punching my arm.

"Ow." I rub it, holding my hand up to her like I'm going to shoot a light ball at her. "Too soon," she mumbles.

"Ok, well, I'm going to head out. I'll be back later. Make yourself comfy. There's not much, but what's mine is yours." She waves her arms around at the nearly empty apartment. "You are welcome to come and leave as you please. Spells on the apartment, so it's well protected, but you step outside of the door and no protection."

"This is great. Thank you so much. Again. Really."

"Anything for my Lizzy Lou."

"Lizzy Lou?" I ask, nudging her arm.

"Long story. Not worth the retell."

"We literally have nothing but time on our hands since you have me holed up here."

CALLUM - VISIT FROM THE DJINN

"TEN HOURS!" I SLAM my fist on the kitchen counter. The hard stone does little to echo the anger that's boiling inside of me. "It's been ten hours and we have nothing. No trace of her. How is that possible?"

"Who is she?" Emmett asks, pulling the bag of O positive out of the boiling water on the stove. Even though he changed clothes, it looks like the same outfit from last night. Dark slacks and a white button-down shirt. It's what he wears every day. Something about being born in the late eighteen-hundreds, then being turned into a vampire at the turn of the century, has not allowed him to move on. He still speaks of those days like they were yesterday.

He was a promising chef, studying under the world-renowned Chef Jean Pierre Pantoffier in the beautiful Paris. But as he tells it, one night after closing up the restaurant, a pair of men and a mistaken identity later, he was dying in an alleyway without a prayer in the world. Then this woman appears from around the corner and sees him, descends on him like some dark angel. She recognized him and called him by name, her voice light and melodic, hurriedly ripped into her wrist with her teeth, then fed him her blood. Before she could say anything else, footsteps were running towards them and she was gone in a flash, never to be seen from again. Darkness swooped around him and the next thing he remembers was waking up in a hospital with an insatiable hunger. He looked at his stomach where he felt the knife enter and didn't see so much as a scrape. He checked his arms and legs. Nothing. The only thing that remained was his hunger. He bolted, and that night was the first night he killed someone. Racked with guilt and confusion, he tried to hide himself away until the hunger became too much for him to handle and he attacked again. What he knows now is that he could pace himself, only taking what he needs and letting the human go on their way. Even though he knows better now, he doesn't allow himself the indulgence of a fresh feed. Instead, he warms up days old or weeks old blood in bags on our stove.

"I've already told you. I don't know. Well, I know her name is Everlee, and that she has a friend who is a witch. Potentially a powerful witch, but they're both young. I wouldn't put them a day over seventy and that's being generous. They smelled younger, like fresh out of the womb young, but if that were the case, there'd be no way they'd be able to evade us for this long."

"Maybe you're losing your touch," Jax mumbles, using a chicken bone to pick between his teeth.

"Watch it," I growl.

He's smug, watching me. Waiting to see what I'll do. How I'll react.

"Why do you want to find her so badly?" Emmett asks, pouring his blood bag into a coffee cup that Knox made him last Christmas that says 'Bloody good Chef' with a pair of vampire teeth under the oo in bloody.

"Because," I start, then stop. I trust these boys with my life, but this. If I'm wrong, I don't want to get their hopes up. I don't want to tell them there's a chance we can get our lives back and get out from under the Djinn's hand. "I just need to find her."

Jax studies me for a moment, then stands from his chair. "What aren't you telling us, Callum?"

I stare at him in shock. Why can't he let this go? "Nothing. I'll just find her on my own if it's that big of a deal."

"I don't think that's what he's saying," Emmett defends. "I think he, we, us, just want to know why this girl is so important to you."

My hands clench at my side. I can't tell them. I need to protect them. Their hopes. We were all thrown together years ago when we found each other after the Djinn had tricked us. We had each gone to her on our own, searching for answers, searching for help. Being the powerful dark fae she is, she used our words against us. Giving us what we wished for, but in turn taking from us the very thing that made us... us. And now we're under her thumb until we can get back what she stole.

The shrill ring of the doorbell tears through all our stares. There's typically only one person who comes here this early in the morning. I'd been expecting her today, just not so soon.

"Are you going to get that?" Knox asks.

"Do we have a choice?" I don't want to. I want to ignore it and ignore her. Pretend I never heard her name whispered on the winds. Knowing that I can't, I set my coffee cup on the counter and make my way to the front door.

"Hello," I try not to bark out my greeting as I open the door, but I hate her. I hate everything about her. Her look, her sound, and most importantly, the power she has over us.

"Callum, dearest," she chimes in a fake singsong voice. "Aren't you going to invite me in?" Samara is standing on the front porch with her long, stick straight, black hair hanging down to her waist, wearing a deep purple dress that touches the ground.

Grinding my teeth together, I force out a smile. "Samara. Please come in on this beautiful morning. The guys are in the kitchen. Follow me."

"Formalities, darling. Call me Sam, or Sammie. We've known each other long enough." She cackles behind me as we move through the hall to the kitchen. I refuse to call her anything but Samara. To use a nickname or a shortened name would imply we are close and friendly and we are anything but.

"What can I, we, do for you today?" I ask as soon as I get in the kitchen, my eyes meeting each of the guys.

"It appears there was a fae using their magic in my club last night."

Fuck.

I close my eyes slowly, trying to figure a way out of this, then grab my cup and turn to face her. "The witch. I know. Her information has been recorded and I'll banish her from the club."

Samara laughs as her fingers lightly swipe along the edge of the counter, her sound grating on my very last nerve. "No. Not the witch. The other one. The one Knox was with. What was her name?"

My eyes meet Knox's and I subtly shake my head from side to side.

"Hey Samar- Sammie." He chuckles softly. He's always been more fearful of her, but he's also the one of us that has a gentle soul and likes to avoid conflict.

"Knoxxy." She steps in front of him and runs her fingers from his temple, along his jaw, to his chin. "Beautiful. Your eyes twinkle like the sun on the ocean."

A gentle dig to remind him who she is and what she's capable of.

She steps back from Knox and claps her hands like she's breaking a spell he's cast and looks at everyone. "It's so wonderful to see the four of you together. Such good friends. Your own little makeshift family. To think it's all because of me."

Rage simmers within me and it's all I can do to stop it from boiling over. Because of her? Her! She took everything from us. Everything. She left us as mere shells of the fae we used to be.

Jax steps towards me and runs his hand up my back and squeezes my shoulder. Hard. Causing me to release the muscles in my arm. "We couldn't be more grateful to you, Samara. You gave us something we didn't even know we needed."

"So wonderful. It's amazing, really. The four of you. The way you've all bonded. Anyway, back to what I was saying. The girl Knox was with."

"I don't remember her name," Knox lies.

"Knoxxy. I don't believe you, darling." She runs her finger down his chest.

"Sammie, you know I wouldn't lie to you." His eyes meet mine and I can tell he's uncomfortable. "It was something that started with an E. Like Emily, Emory."

"Everlee?" she asks with all hints of amusement drained from her voice.

Knox's eyes widen as he stares at me, shrugging his shoulders. "Yes. That sounds familiar."

"Yes. Perfect. Well, I need you to find her."

"Why?" I spit out, garnering glances from the guys.

"Why?" Her head snaps back in shock. "Do you forget who you speak to Callum? What I have the power to do? To give? To take away?"

"Only if we wish it to be done."

An evil smile stretches across her lips. "Yes. If you wish it."

"Tell me, Callum." She sets her sights on me and walks over, standing toe to toe with me. "What do you wish for?" Her eyes glow and pulse a soft purple color as she watches me. I notice the guys take a step away from her and watch cautiously.

Keeping my lips sealed, I shake my head from side to side. I will not wish for anything else from her. Not until I figure out how to reverse what she did to us before. She's very conniving and uses and twists words that make the wishers wish blowback on them in the worst way possible.

Emmett asked her to help him control his bloodlust because he wanted to feed on people without killing them. She gave him his wish by removing all pleasure and taste from feeding. When he consumes blood, he feels nothing. There's no urge, no hunger, nothing. He uses bags of blood because they are premeasured and he eats when we do because he has to. For him, food was everything. He was an aspiring chef before he was turned, and even after that, he loved the taste of blood. For him, he could taste hints of what they consumed. The spice. The flavor. It reminded him of what he once was. But it's all-consuming and dangerous. He didn't want to be a monster, but he couldn't control his hunger.

Until Samara.

The glow in her eyes dims, and she steps away. "Very well." She looks around the room. "I want that girl. Perhaps see what she wishes for most and add her to my little collection of misfits."

Without thinking, I step forward and growl.

She throws her head back laughing. "Callum. So protective. How is it you're so protective of a woman you just met?"

Fuck.

"I care nothing about the girl. I have a problem with you."

Knox jumps in. "A problem with you not telling us where we can find her," he says lightly, trying to make it a joke.

With no amusement and eyes focused hard on me, she snaps, "Knox, you idiot boy. If I knew where she was, then I wouldn't be reaching out to all of my minions, sending them after her."

"How many people are looking for her?" I ask, tone more controlled.

"That's for me to know and, well, you'll never find out. I'm thinking about gifting a wish reversal to the one who brings her to me."

"A wish reversal?" Emmett and Jax repeat softly.

"Yes. Does that sound appealing enough?" She turns to Emmett. "Would you like your taste of blood back? Jax, would you want to feel your wolf again? To know he is still alive inside of you, eager to stretch his legs and go out for a run? Knox, would you want your skin back so you can shift and swim in the ocean with the rest of your family? Callum-"

"I get your point."

"I hope so. Unfortunately, for you four, though, I'm only granting one wish reversal, so you'd have to fight over it. Which I'd love to see. Perhaps shirtless in a pit with oils at my house." She looks to the ceiling, picturing it. "Yes, that could work out very nicely for me. Hopefully, none of the others win." She pats the counter a few times. "Well, I must be going. More people to visit." She turns and walks towards the front door. "Ta-ta."

The front door closes with a thud and Knox starts to speak, but I hold my finger up, stopping him. "Samara is no longer welcome in our home," I say out loud. While I don't think she's still in the house, disinviting will push her out painfully, even if she's shifted into a fly on the wall.

We wait a minute, then I give Knox the nod.

"What is going on? Who is she? What aren't you telling us?"

"I don't know why Samara wants her. I doubt it's anything good. And there's nothing I'm hiding since I don't know who she is."

"Damn it, Callum!" Knox pounds his hand on the counter. "Stop lying to us!"

"I don't know anything Knox. I'm not fucking lying to you."

"But," Jax adds.

I stare at him, then sigh. They won't let this go. "But."

All the guys step forward.

"She may be a true fae."

They all take a step back and look for support against the counter or the wall, whatever is closest.

"I don't know. I really don't. It's been hundreds of years since I've seen or even been around one. But the way my body responded to her last night. The way my skin prickled and then the light. Her friend that left with her is a witch. A powerful witch. Well, she's untrained, so she's not there yet, but she has potential. Anyway, she saw it too and tried to protect Everlee by casting her own blue ball of light. It wasn't the same and anyone that has seen a fae light before would know. Fortunately, I don't think many in the club have, but I'm sure there were a few."

"A true fae? What does this mean for us?"

"I don't know yet, but she may be able to destroy Samara and free us all."

"Which is why Samara wants her?"

"That's what I'm thinking."

"We have to find her," Knox says, clapping his hands.

"Slow down Romeo," Emmett reminds.

"We have to be careful about this."

"Not too careful. Samara wants Everlee, and she'll stop at nothing to get her. Even using the underfae to do it. She'd have a field day granting wishes for them. She could turn everyone against Everlee. We have to hurry. We don't know how far behind we are."

EVERLEE - THE UNSAFE SAFE HOUSE

I'VE MOVED AROUND FROM the couch to the kitchen, to the wall, to the bed, back to the couch and now I am standing in the kitchen staring in a mostly empty refrigerator. There are three eggs, a splash of orange juice in a container without a lid and a jar of pickles. It's almost lunchtime and I'm starving, but I'm not allowed to leave.

"Lizzy." I stomp my foot. "I'm so hungry."

"She said not to go anywhere and that she'd be back soon."

Exasperated, I throw my hands up in the air, "Soon is relative. Is soon a few minutes, hours, or days."

"I forgot how hangry you get."

"Stop. It's a reasonable hour to eat lunch. Can't you conjure up something for us?"

"No can do mon frere. Magic doesn't work inside the charms she put in place."

"What can I do? Liz, this is ridiculous."

She looks at her phone. "I'm trying to protect you."

"You've been doing that all morning."

"What?"

"Checking your phone."

"So. I need to see what time it is."

"Lies. Who are you waiting for?"

She sighs. "Fine. I reached out to a few elders and I'm waiting on them to call me back."

"Do they know how to use a phone?"

"They may be old, but they've learned to adapt to the modern wonders."

"So that's a no?"

"I'm still teaching them, but they know enough."

"Why don't we go to them?"

"Why don't you learn how to listen?"

"You think I'm a true fae," I spit out, tired of beating around the bush.

She gasps louder than I've ever heard her gasp before.

"Stop being dramatic. I don't think I am."

"You don't want to think you are, so you are going to tell yourself that you aren't until you have undeniable evidence to the contrary. It's your defense mechanism, which is why I have made the calls, so you don't have to beat yourself up."

"Well, who's the bestest friend of all?"

"Me. Obviously. I give way more to this friendship than you do. I mean, until last night, you were no better than a muggle."

"Ouch."

"Truth hurts," she says, pinching my arm.

Another purple light pops on the street.

"Do you think they do this all day, every day?"

"What? Walking through the portal?"

"Yea. Do you think she sits here and counts the number of purple flashes?"

"No. That sounds horrendous."

Bored out of my mind, I flop on the couch, sprawled out like a starfish. "Can you call Betty to see where she is?"

"Oh my goddesssss. Fine. I will call her." She walks out of the room, which is probably more from habit than anything else, because the walls are paper thin, where they exist. She's talking to her about lunch and groceries, so I walk over to the window and play spot the underfae.

SMACK!

I scream and jump back, clutching my chest, blinking rapidly, trying to steady my breathing.

"What? What!" Lizzy yells, storming into the living room. "What happened?"

"A bird. I was standing at the window watching the underfae portal, and a bird flew straight at me into the window."

"Flew at you? Like it was aiming for you?"

"Well, no. I wouldn't say it was aiming for me. It just happened to hit the window I was standing in front of."

"Where is this bird?"

"You don't believe me?"

"I believe you. I just want to see the bird."

We look out of the second-story window. There on the sidewalk, laying with its wings spread out on the cement, is a little bird. "There."

She stares at it for a minute too long, then sighs and sits back on the couch. "Betty got delayed. She's having some food dropped off for us. She said she gave instructions to leave it at the door."

"Fan-tilly-tas-tic! When?"

"Always with the when and gimme gimme. Patience, dear child. It's a virtue."

"You're hilarious." Between the two of us, she is the most impatient person I've ever met. She waits until the last possible second to use the bathroom, because she hates sitting on the toilet for too long. She's nearly shitting her pants before she allows herself to go. I've told her it's a bad idea to do that, because one time she's going to get burned, but she doesn't listen.

We settle on the couch and stare at the wall, and I can feel the air changing around us. "So... you think I could be true fae."

She looks at me, all humor dropped from her face. "Possibly. Probably. It doesn't make sense, though. Everyone thought you were going to be a strong fae. Then nothing. What if it was something, but we just didn't know what to expect since it's been hundreds of years since anyone has seen or been around a true fae?"

"I've had no powers. Not an inkling of anything, well..."

"Well?" She sits up and grabs my hands.

"There was this one time."

"When? Why didn't you tell me?"

"Because you're going to laugh at me."

"I always laugh at you and that's never stopped you from telling me all the dumb shit you do."

I snarl my lip at her, causing her to laugh.

"Tell me. What's up buttercup?"

"So one time. When you gave me a magical dildo..."

She sucks her lips in and her eyes go wide, but she doesn't speak, even though I can tell she's about to burst like a volcano.

"I had a really powerful orgasm and thought I felt something. Like a pulse of heat, or something."

"And your bitch ass tried to recreate it, which is why you've burned through my magic dildos? You know. This makes so much sense now. It's why I thought you were a succubus. I mean, I put a lot of magic into those dildos and for you to go through them that fast. I was really concerned."

"I've tried everything to recreate the pulse of whatever it was I felt after that one orgasm, but I haven't been able to."

"Man. Such a hard life."

"Shut up."

There's a knock on the door.

"Oh thank Goddess, our food is here," I groan out and start walking over to the door.

Lizzy grabs my arm and yanks me back. "What are you doing?"

"I'm getting our food."

"What if that's someone who was sent to kill you?"

"Liz. You're being dramatic."

"Am I? I don't think you're taking this seriously enough."

"Because I don't believe it."

"I can't with you."

"Plus, Betty gave directions for them to drop at the door. They probably just did a curtesy knock."

Lizzy peeks out of the door and opens it a second later, quickly grabbing the food and dragging it inside.

"Oh, my... that smells divine. Where is that from?"

"I don't know?" She looks around the bag, but there is no name on it and pulls out the sandwiches, but there is nothing written on the paper either. "No name."

"No name restaurant. Doesn't sound sus at all. Are you sure we should eat it? It may not be safe."

"You're right." Before I can stop her, she opens both sandwiches and takes a bite out of each. "Nope. They're both fine. But I'm keeping this one."

"You took a bite out of my sandwich."

"To be fair, it wasn't your sandwich when I took a bite out of it. It only became your sandwich after I did. And really, you should thank me."

"Thank you? For eating part of my sandwich?"

She clutches her chest. "I risked my life for you. Who knows if they were poisoned?"

"Whatever would I do without you?"

"I ask that question most days."

"Shut up!" I laugh.

We sit in silence as we both shovel our food into our mouth. For someone who was giving me a hard time about complaining about being hungry, she demolished her sandwich.

"Oh. Excuse me." She stands quickly and I know that look in her eye as she squeezes her butt cheeks together while she runs across the room to the bathroom. Fortunately, it's the only room that has four walls and a door.

She lets out a blood-curdling scream and my heart drops.

"What? Lizzy?" I race over to the door. "Lizzy? Are you ok?"

"I'm fine," she calls through the door. "The toilet seat shifted, and I thought I was falling off the toilet. Most terrifying thing ever. One moment, you're feeling safe and confident, the next you're reaching out for anything to prevent your ass from falling in toilet water. Terrifying."

"I'm done with you."

"Doubtful."

Still on edge, I walk back over to the window and look for the little bird, but it's gone. Did something eat it? A cat shrieks from the garbage can, startling me and doing nothing for my nerves. The garbage can lid is still rocking back and forth from where the cat just jumped on it, presumably to get away from the dog lurking around. It's a massive dog.

"So, what do you want to do for the next couple of hours?"

"Hours? You mean days? Do you have a long- term plan, or is it to keep me locked up in here forever?"

"I have a plan. However, the length of time of said plan is uncertain. I don't want to leave you locked up, but I want to protect you Ev. You're my bitch and if anyone tried to hurt you. I'd...kill them. Have you called your parents yet? Your brother?"

"And tell them what? That I may have been drunk at a sex club and after being tied up in rope on stage, I may have created a light ball in my hand when a troll was trying to drag me to his underground lair to make me his wife."

"That's right! I forgot about the rope!"

"Will you focus?"

"Yes, of course I will. After you tell me about the rope, you little kinky fucker. No wonder why the troll wanted you."

"It was interesting. At first I was nervous, but Knox... he was great."

Her brows peak, "Knox... was great?"

"He was my partner."

"Go on."

"There isn't much to tell." A warm wave passes through my body and my stomach tightens at the memory of his hands brushing against my skin.

"Lies! Dirty little lies! I can smell your arousal just thinking about him."

"No you can't!"

"You're right. I'm not a shifter, thank God. Can you imagine what you had to be doing to them last night? How wet were you? I bet you were soaked."

"Lizzy!" I yell, slapping her arm.

"What? I know you were." She smirks. A moment later, her phone rings and she looks at the caller ID and pulls her face. "This can't be good."

"Who is it?"

She holds her finger up and answers the phone. "Elder Angorica. How are you?" she asks with a smile. "Yes, I know I left my group last-" She stops talking, and the smile drops from her face. "Right now?" She shakes her head, as her lips hardened into a flat line. "No. I haven't seen her." Her eyes close.

She's talking about me. Rather, they're asking questions about me and she's having to lie to her coven. For me. This isn't good.

"A what? No. I don't think that's the case."

She starts pacing around the room. Not a good sign. She's quiet for almost two minutes as the voice continues to talk on the other end. I can hear them, but can't make out what they're saying. I just know they're talking very fast and don't seem to be thrilled.

"Ok," she sighs. "Have them pick me up on the corner of Folly's Bridge and third." She cuts her eyes at me. "I know. I was out last night and just stayed with a friend. No, not Everlee. I don't know where she is." She rolls her eyes.

I can tell she hates having to lie to her coven, but something's going on. Why is she having to go in? And if she reached out to the Elders, and this Elder is calling her, then who did she reach out to?

She hangs up the phone a moment later and hauls it above her head, ready to chuck it against the wall.

"Woah. Don't do that!" I run in front of her and grab her arm.

"Ev," her tone is soft and there's a pain in her voice.

"What's going on?"

"This is getting away from us too quickly."

"What is?"

"The coven suspects you are a true fae. They're calling an emergency meeting to address the possibility."

"And what if I am?"

"Well, it didn't work out for all the other ones that were killed."

I laugh out loud, then stop. "Sorry. But come on. Do you really think they'd kill me?"

"I don't know. If I had to guess, they would lock you away and do all sorts of tests on you. Study you like a lab rat. Try to drain your power. Weaponize it."

"Sounds very dark fae, plus, I don't have any power."

"That you know of. Last night, you weren't even trying when you created that light ball and it was a hundred times brighter than mine. Imagine what other powers you have and how powerful you could be if you trained."

"I think you're getting ahead of yourself."

"And I don't think you're taking this seriously enough. They're looking for you. The covens and I'm sure others, too. For all I know, everyone is looking for you. Each with their own agenda, which I'd bet money on, won't be good for you."

"So you have to go?"

"I don't want to, but yes. I have to help in the search for you." She rolls her eyes. "Which makes it even more important that you don't leave this place."

"You can't be serious."

"Damn it, Ev! For once in your life, just listen to me. Let me figure this out. Let me protect you." A tear wobbles on the bottom rim of her eye.

"Fine." I hold my hands up in retreat. "But I can't stay her forever. This place looks like it would barely survive a powerful gust of wind."

"I know, I know." She pats the air. "Just let me think."

"Do you trust Betty?"

"Yes. She hates the covens, so she won't join them. More likely to tell them to snort coke off a cock."

"I get that with the covens, but they aren't the only fae in town. You have all the other pockets. You don't think she'll align with them?"

"Look. I'm going to be honest. I don't know. I'd like to think she wouldn't, but you're the first true fae we've seen in several hundred years. The bounty on your head is high and makes people do baffling shit. I mean, once they get up to a million quid, you shouldn't trust me."

"A million? That's all I'm worth to you? I'd bet you could at least get five," I tease.

"Three and you have a deal," she laughs, but only for a second as the gravity of my situation sets in.

"When are you leaving? And I guess you won't be back?"

"I've going to leave in a minute, so I can make the meet point. I want to be there before Tony shows up so he can't see from which direction I'm coming. And no, I don't think I'll be back, at least for your safety."

"You should always travel with your broom, in cases of emergency."

"Hilarious."

"I'm fae-bulous."

"Idiot." She laughs.

"Maybe try to plant seeds I'm not a monster, and probably not even a true fae."

"You know I will. I wouldn't recommend calling your parents or Beckett. Most likely, they'll be tracking those calls."

"Liz." A knot forms in my throat and prevents any more words from spilling out.

She walks across the room and wraps me in her arms. "Ev. I'm scared."

Mustering up all the courage I can, I push her away and stare at her. "We'll get through this. I don't know how yet, but we will." She nods a little, eyes still worried. "Tell me... who's Tony? I've never heard of him."

She rolls her eyes and wipes the tears off her face with the back of her hand. "He's some high-ranking warlock from the Seelie Court at Helsgard."

"From Helsgard?"

"He just got into town a few days ago."

"Why? Why leave the Seelie Court and come here to Elloree Falls?"

She tilts her head to the side.

"What?"

"It will be time for my quickening soon."

"They brought in a stud to mate with you?"

She pulls her face. "It's bad, but that makes it sound so much worse. I imagine they want us to get to know one another." She flops on the couch and puts her head in her hands. "Ev. I don't want to have sex with him."

"You love sex. What if he's hot?"

"I do and apparently, he is. The girls have been talking about him since he arrived, but I've kept myself busy."

"So, what's the problem?"

"It's all very transactional. You know me. Before I met with the oracle, I thought I was going to do my time at the coven, get trained, then move off and start a family. With a man I love and have lots and lots of children. Now, because of what the oracle saw, I'm going to be impregnated by a man of their choosing, and we will produce one child who will be raised by the coven. I mean, sure. I'll be there, but it won't be the same."

"We could go on the run together and live on the Cliffs of Morgai and meet random men and hook up with them and raise children on our own."

"That sounds equally parts nice and fucked up."

"Maybe." I shrug.

She takes in a deep breath. "I have to go, but I don't want to leave."

"I hate to see you go, but I love to watch you walk away."

She shakes her head with a hint of a smile. "Only you would make jokes when your life is on the line and the entire fae community is out searching for you with pitchforks and wooden stakes."

"As long as it's not iron."

"Funny, not funny."

"I love you."

She gives me another hug, holding me to her so tight, it's hard to breathe. "I love you."

She turns and walks towards the door. "Don't open this door for anyone."

"Yes, ma'am." Overwhelmed by a thousand thoughts and emotions, I close the door and press my back against it.

Fuck!

What am I going to do?

EVERLEE - FACE TO FACE WITH DICKFACE

IT'S BEEN TWO HOURS.

Two hours with no one here. Betty is still MIA and Lizzy is gone. I have looked in every room in this little apartment, made the bed, folded the blankets on the couch- three times, and stared out of the window. There are more cats that have claimed the trashcans as their playground, while others are using the curb as their lounger. Every time I look out of the window there are more- close to twenty now- and a little kitten that prances around with its tail in the air like it's hot shit. He or she is orange with white stripes with a black and white face. It's the most interesting color combination I've ever seen.

What am I supposed to do? If Lizzy is right and most of the faedom is looking for me, then my days are numbered. I can't stay in this apartment. There is literally nothing to do and nothing to eat. I will die of boredom before any fae kills me.

I need to come up with a plan, though. Where to go, contacts, backup plans.

Excitement prickles my skin as I hurry into the kitchen to find some paper and a pen. I quickly flip through all the drawers and find a pencil, but no paper.

"DAMMMN ITTT!" I yell out in frustration, sinking to the ground. A wolf spider the size of my palm climbs out of a hole and scares the ever-loving- shit out of me. "Where the fuck have you been hiding?"

The spider stops and stares at me, and I stare at it.

"Are you hungry?" I look around the apartment. "I have nothing for you to eat. Shit! I'm talking to animals. Sorry, spiders. Oh!" I remembered the paper wrapper our sandwiches came in. Standing quickly, I run to the trash and fortunately, it's still on top. On top of what? Air? I scoff. Because there is nothing in this place.

I get Lizzy wasn't prepared to hide me away, but damn. And seriously, where in the hell is Betty?

Shit! I don't even have her number to call her for food. I'm going to starve to death.

No.

I refuse to die of boredom or hunger. I'm a fighter and I will fight. I'm really regretting not paying attention more in fae history class now. Learning about the true fae seemed like a waste of time. I'm wondering if this is karma. She is a fickle friend.

I grab the pencil and the wrapper from the sandwich and start planning and plotting. Where I can go, people I can see.

My list is pretty much non-existent. I have my parents, my brother and Helsgard. I wonder how long before they ca-

My phone rings.

No freaking way.

Nearly breaking my neck with speed, I run into the bedroom and grab my phone, and press the answer button.

"Everlee? Everlee? Are you ok?"

"Yes. Yes, I'm-"

"Stop. Don't tell me where you are."

Because the phones are being monitored.

"I was only going to say I'm fine. I guess you've heard the rumors?"

"It's true?"

"I don't know."

"You don't know if you killed a man?"

"Wait, what?"

"Last night, you revealed you're a true fae, created a light ball, and killed a man."

"Not quite. I don't know I'm a true fae. No one died, but a light ball did form in my hands."

"So you didn't shoot it at anyone?"

"Shoot it? No."

"They're saying you killed someone. The courts of Helsgard are looking for you."

"Convenient." I mark them off the list. "I don't know what to do."

"I know baby," I can hear the break in her voice. "Your father and I are going to figure out something for you. Until then, just stay where you are."

I look around and groan.

"Where ever you are is better than a laboratory or the dungeons of Helsgard. I have to go. I'll be in touch soon. I love you." She hangs up before I can respond.

For good measure, I mark my parents off my list. I stare at the one name, despair seeping its way in, and start pounding my fist repeatedly on the floor, screaming out.

"Ow!" Pain radiates up my wrist. A small piece of the wooden floor breaks off and is sticking out of my hand. "Son of a bitch, that hurts." I grab the little wooden shard with my fingers and pull it out slowly, then toss it to the ground.

Cans clank, and a cat shrills outside, grabbing my attention. Grabbing my chest as if that can slow my racing heart, I run over to look out of the window and see a bulldog running around, snapping at the cats, who are trying to get out of his way. I bang on the window, and the dog looks up at me for a second, then goes after the cats.

"Leave them alone!" I yell through the window. "Oh, no!" The bulldog has its sights set on the little kitten, whose tail is tucked between its hunched legs. "Stop! Stop!"

The bulldog's teeth are pulled back over his gums as he inches forward, step by step.

"No!" I bang on the glass, but this time he doesn't look up.

He lunges at the kitten, who jumps backwards, barely escaping.

"Screw it."

I run across the apartment and throw the door open. I run down the little hall, then down the short flight of stairs, and bust the exterior door open. "Go away!" I yell, chasing after the dog. His head lifts and sees me running at him like a lunatic, then darts away.

I slow to a stop and watch the little kitten walk out from between the trashcans meowing at me, like it's talking.

"I can't understand you, little guy. Or girl. But if you're saying thank you, then you're welcome. I couldn't let that mean dog get a hold of you."

Everything goes quiet around me. Even the wind stops blowing. When talking to the kitten, I hadn't noticed the other cats were slowly making their way closer to me. Oh shit.

"You aren't a kitten, are you?" My heartbeat is nearly pounding a hole through my chest.

The kitten shifts before my eyes and standing in front of me is a woman with shoulder-length blonde hair. She's just a touch shorter than me, and completely naked.

My hand fumbles behind me, searching for anything to grab on to.

"Where're you going?"

"I... I." How does this work? If I run back inside the apart-ment, do I still have the protections I did before? Will they be able to break down the door to get in? How did I not see this was a trap? I'd been watching them all day, and they have not acted suspiciously at all.

Seconds later, several other cats shift into a variety of men and women, standing behind the woman in front of me. Are they waiting on her?

A moment later, a scrawny-looking man with dark hair and a heart tattoo on his shoulder steps around the corner of the building. He was the large dog? Oh yeah. Definitely compensating.

"We did it Rich! We did it! We got her!" The woman with short blonde hair yells, running into his arms.

"Calm down Wendy. We still have to take her in."

"She ain't going anywhere." She flaps her hand out like I'm nothing.

I need to figure a way out of this. If not, Lizzy is going to find me and kill me. *Stay in the apartment.* What's so damn hard about that? I groan in frustration.

Think Everlee.

Think.

You can outwit these two jokers.

And the ten others in their little group.

"Let's go fae," Rich commands, stepping forward.

"I'd rather not."

He laughs and does a sort of bow, looking at his friends, "She'd rather not gents. Let's go. Sorry Wendy. Maybe when *she'd rather* we can try again."

"What? We're leaving?" she asks, exasperated.

"You heard the lady," Rich says.

"But? What? We've been here all day because your damn friend saw her through the window. He broke his nose for you."

The bird.

Rich grabs Wendy in his arms and tilts her back into a disgustingly long, wet kiss, then pops her back up. "I'm just kidding babe!" He unhooks his arm from her waist and walks over to me and grabs me by the throat and pushes me backwards. "Would you rather now?" His breath smells like dirt and rotten bananas.

"You're a dick." I thrust my knee right between his legs.

He drops my jaw and I push him away while he's bent over, sucking wind. I tear off down the street and duck between two houses, back pressed against the wall. This entire area of town seems to be abandoned, which worked out well for me when I was trying to hide, but now, not so much. I need to find someone, anyone.

"Here, little freak fae," Dick calls. I'm changing his name to Dick, because that's what he is.

I look down the small alley between the houses and see cats skittering under the decking and jump. Fuck. I don't know if they're real or shifters!

"Come out, come out. Wherever you are?" Wendy laughs.

Back still pressed against the side of the house, I inch further from the main street. There's a break in some boards under one house and I debate crawling and hiding, but then realize I'd be at a disadvantage. If they can shift into cats, they can move through here easily.

DAMN IT!

My phone's in the apartment. I close my eyes and take a deep breath.

True fae are fast and powerful. That's what I remember. All I remember. Fuck!

It's like that one time in class they were like 'hey learn this, it will come in handy one day' and then you spend your whole life pissed you had to learn something you will never use, and then that one day comes around when you're stuck between two abandoned houses being chased by a bunch of idiot shifter cats and dogs, who you're fairly certain don't know their ass from a hole in the ground, and you wish you hadn't forgotten it... I take a deep breath from my internal word vomit.

"I found her!" One guy shouts, jumping up and down.

Being the smart ass I am, I jump up and down too, "Where? Let's go get her!"

He stops jumping and looks at me, confused.

I wave him on, "Let's go!" I say, walking the opposite way as he stands there, confused.

"Not so fast," Dick says, stepping from around another corner. What is it with him and corners?

Ta-da bitches! Only I'd slide out with jazz hands or something.

He grabs my hair and pushes me through the alleyway to the main street, where everyone else is waiting. "Let's go before she tries anything else."

"Where are you taking me?"

"Shut up!" He pulls my hair, yanking my neck around. "You'll find out."

"Do you know who I am? Why they want me?"

"No, and no."

"Don't you think that's important information to have?"

This is totally going to backfire on me. Stop mouth. Stop moving. Stop producing words.

"Did you hear what happened last night?"

Seriously! Shut the fuck up!

"No," Wendy answers, a hint of worry in her voice.

Good, use it.

No! Don't use it.

Why am I arguing with myself?

"At the club?"

"Oh yeah!" One guy shouts, and everyone stops.

"What?" Dick asks.

"They think a true fae was at the club."

"True fae?" Several people repeat in unison, looking around.

"Yea. Apparently, she produced the true fae light ball and killed a man."

"I didn-"

You're going to admit to a group of people who want to hurt you and take you to someone else who likely wants to hurt you that you didn't kill a man?

"I did."

"You? True fae?" Dickface laughs.

Now would be a really good fucking time to create a light ball.

"Yea. Why do you think everyone is looking for me? Why do you think I was hiding out in a run-down building?"

I can tell they are all putting things together, but I have nothing else to really drive home the point.

"I don't believe it. True faes don't exist."

"That's what everyone believed until I created a light ball in my hands and killed a man."

"Do it again," Dickface challenges.

"No. I'm not some circus clown you can get to perform for you."

"Do it, or I'll do the fae community a favor and kill you here. Tell Samara that you were resisting and accidents happen."

"So, let me get this right... I need to prove to you I'm a true fae, or you'll kill me for being a true fae. Seems like a damned if you do, damned if you don't situation if you ask me."

"I don't care what kind of situation you think it is. Do it, now!"

"Who should I direct it at? Who do you want to kill?"

Rich chokes on his words and looks at his crew, who are all looking around nervously.

"In order to show you, I have to direct the ball *at* someone."

"No you don't. You can just create a ball."

"I can't. You won't know if I'm a witch creating a light ball or a true fae. Only the true faes can kill."

Who the fuck knows? I don't and I'm certain they haven't read a book in probably like ever.

"That's a lie," another woman chimes, at the same time she's taking a step back.

Her actions contradict her words. She doesn't believe what she's saying, so I double down, pulling my hands up to my chest and stepping towards her.

She shifts into a cat and bolts.

One down. Am I too hopeful to think I can mind-fuck them all enough to run? Likely.

Dickface steps towards his group. "If anyone else leaves, you're out of the club."

"The cool cats club?" I laugh out loud, so fucking proud of myself. Hell, if I'm going to die today, I'm sure as shit going to do it my way.

Dick smacks me hard across the face, bringing blood to my lip.

"Ass wipe," I say, clutching my cheek and swiping the blood away.

My hair whooshes around me and I can feel them surround me.

Vampires.

"What do we have here?" The one in the front asks, tilting his head to the side to look at me. He's wearing black pants and a black shirt, which is a stark contrast to his pale white face.

"Back off, she's ours."

He leans from side to side. "Doesn't look like your pack has marked her, so I'd say she's fair game."

"She. Me. I'm not fair game."

"The bounty on your head says otherwise."

"Out of curiosity, how much is it up to now?"

"Two mill."

"Quid? Fuck me. Only one and a half more before my best friend turns on me."

"What?"

"Can I run upstairs and grab my phone, before we leave to wherever it is you're taking me?"

"No."

"Worth a shot."

A gust of air blows my hair back and his cool fingers trace along my jaw to my bottom lip where his thumb pulls it down. Remnants of my blood show on his finger, "Mouthy little thing, aren't you?"

"So I've been told a time or two." I grab his hand and wipe my blood from his finger before he can put it in his mouth. Something about him tasting any part of me makes me feel sick.

"I was going to enjoy that."

"I know," I smirk back.

"I like you. You have spunk. Perhaps Samara will let me keep you as a little pet."

"My breath is bated," I retort back.

The vampire grabs me, his grasp feeling like a boulder is crushing my arm. "Let's go."

"She's not going anywhere with you."

Looking at my options, I'd much rather the shifters. They are slow and dumb and with them, I have more time to outwit or escape. Vampires. Not so much. They are cunning and quick.

Dickface shifts into his dog and the rest of his pack shifts.

"What? What are you going to do? Meow me to death? We fight werewolves, who are like twenty times the size of you."

It's true. Looking at them, it doesn't seem like it's going to be a fair match.

"Let's go." The vampire jerks my arm. Suddenly, cats are leaping onto the vampire. They're everywhere. Do they have the ability to communicate with the other cats in the area? Because wow. There are like a hundred. Maybe not quite, but there are a lot and they are jumping and scratching at the vampire holding me.

"Get off of me!" He growls.

He releases my arm, and I take off running. Screams and shrieks and slams of trashcans echo behind me, but I don't turn around. One foot in front of the other. The apartment building gets further in my rearview, and I don't know the area well enough to figure out how to get back. That's the only safe place for me right now and I'm running away from it.

My legs are burning, and my lungs are begging for air. I'm not a runner. Never have been. I have this innate ability to cross my legs and plant myself face down. It's like my legs are two best friends who haven't seen each other in a long time and when they run, they just want to hug each other because they're so excited.

Pushing myself, I wait until I get to the corner of the street. I look up and realize it's where Lizzy was earlier today. It seems like so much has happened in that short amount of time. This entire area of town is run down. There are no cars, no people and all the buildings are empty. How does this happen?

Echoes of the fight still linger behind me and I don't know who's winning. Admittedly, the shifters are holding their own more than I thought they would, but it won't last. As their numbers continue to dwindle, the vampires will be left the victor, so that's what I have to plan for while I have the time.

I need silver. Doing a quick scan of the area tells me I'm probably going to be out of luck. Moving down the street, one abandoned building at a time, I peek in each window. Shoe shop... seamstress... book store. Oh, I want to go in there and look around. There are old dusty books on the shelf. Who knows what treasures could await? *But no silver*, my subconscious reminds. Reluctantly, I keep walking and come across a restaurant. The door is cracked open, so I slip in without trying to move the door at all. A lot of times, these restaurants have bells hanging above the door and I didn't want it to ding, alerting anyone to where I am.

The restaurant is dark, with small slivers of light shining through the dirty windows in the front. They have a thick layer of dust and dirt covering them, obscuring the inside. There's a rancid smell in the air like old meat, or likely dead animals who have met their match in here, or perhaps have been dragged in here. My heart beats a little faster as I stare into the dark voids in the back of the restaurant. Suddenly, the hair on my arm is prickling and my feet are glued in their spot.

Danger is close by, but how close?

Outside close? Or inside, a few feet away close?

My stomach is tied in knots as I try to get my feet to move forward. Backward. Anywhere.

"Hello? Is anyone or anything in here?" I whisper and pause, listening for any sound. "If there is, I'm not going to hurt you. I come in peace. I'm just looking for silver to defeat a bunch of vampires outside who want to... well, I don't know what they want to do to me, but it's not good."

Something shifts in the back.

Oh fuck. I'm going to die.

There's something here.

"Fuck, fuck, fuck, fuck, fuck," I whisper, looking around.

This is the last damn time I'm saving a cat from a dog. I feel like shit just keeps snowballing.

There's nothing in here but a few round tables with scattered wooden chairs. Some on top of the tables, others on the floor, or against the wall. Maybe I could grab a chair and break a leg off. It's not as effective as silver, but a wooden stake to the heart would stop him, and in the chest would slow him down.

Him. I laugh. Because there's only one. Not.

Maybe I should get several wooden legs and carry them around.

Like you have time to break and whittle points onto the ends.

Ugh! Life was so much simpler when everyone didn't want me dead and just ignored me!

A bucket from the back clangs to the ground and I jump, clutching my chest.

Give me a freaking break!

Staring at my hands, I try to create a fae light ball. But nothing. My fingers are stretched out and my hands are shaking. It looks like I'm trying to hug air and losing. You got this. I change my stance a little. Holy spirit activate!

Holy spirit activate! Flaming blue balls!!! My face is strained so hard, a tear is trickling down my cheek.

Useless.

I'm useless.

Why am I going to have some power that just pops up out of nowhere, calling out my potential powers to just vanish? It's like the Gods are mocking me.

"Look, if you can understand me, I really don't want to fight. I just want to be left alone. From everyone. I've spent most of my adult life as a nobody. A squib. While I didn't like it, I got used to it. The one that everyone ignored. Last night, I may have created a light ball with my hands, and everyone thinks I'm a true fae. I don't know if I am. I don't feel any different. But now everyone seems to want to kill me and I would really appreciate it, if like just one person didn't. I'm tired and I'm hungry and I'm scared."

Silence.

When weapons don't work. Try pity.

"Oh Everlee?" A wicked voice calls from outside.

The vampire. He's back.

"Hopefully, you didn't think those shifters were going to help you..."

Slowly, I creep to the wall by the back counter.

Is that what it means to be between a rock and a hard spot? I'm literally in the middle of a vampire and something that uses the dark as its lair to hide its dead... I don't even know what it eats. Humans? Cats? Something else.

I try to create a ball of light with my hands again, but nothing.

"I smell your fear pulsing off of you."

Can they do that? I know they can smell blood, obviously. But fear?

"I want to taste you. Taste *all* of you."

Cringe.

His shadow moves in front of the window.

"Everlee?" He stops in front of the window, his hands cupping his eyes as he moves closer to look in.

My heart is racing. This is it. Stop running because it's futile. You're alone and need to conserve your energy for whatever happens next.

A hand clamps around my mouth and drags me over the counter into the dark.

I'm dead.

KNOX - FINDING COCKBUSTER

"IT'S BEEN HOURS. HOW do we know someone hasn't already captured her and we aren't out here wasting our time?" Jax groans behind Callum and me.

"Because. She's a fighter. I feel it," Callum says, glancing at me.

"You don't even know her," he mumbles, barely audible.

"Anything?" Callum asks to the group, ignoring Jax.

"N–" Emmett starts, then stops. "Other vampires."

"Where?" Callum asks, taking a step back towards Emmett and Jax.

He throws his head up in the air, smelling it. "To the left." He lifts his ear into the air. "They are talking about Everlee." He listens for another moment, "But haven't found her. Incoming."

Before he can finish saying the word, a gust of wind smacks us in the face.

"Jordan," Emmett says, seeing the vampire in front of us.

He's tall, not as tall as us, above average, but scrawny. He's also young. Only sixty years old, even though he looks like he's in his early twenties. His hair is dark and slicked back and looks like an absolute dickwad.

"So let me know if you've heard this joke before. A werewolf, a selkie, a vampire, and-" he looks at Callum. "What are you again?"

"None of your fucking business."

"Harsh," Jordan chuckles, patting him on the back. "Well, I can't finish my joke unless I know what kind of fae you are. You seem to be a mystery." He stares at Callum and waits for him to speak, but when he doesn't, he continues, "Fine. I will make one up. Are you a Mesmer?"

Callum blinks slowly, but gives nothing away. He's over a thousand years old and has had plenty of time to perfect his 'eat shit and die' face.

Jordan shrugs. "Well, now I don't feel like telling my joke. You've ruined it," he whines.

"Nooo," Jax mocks. "I was almost looking forward to it."

"You werewolves. Always the same. Tell yours I said hi." Jordan leaps back in a flash as Jax charges him and Emmett grabs his arm.

"He's not worth it, Jax. You don't want to get called to the courts at Helsgard."

Jax shakes his arm free of Emmett's grip and pats his shirt down.

"Good boy," Jordan presses.

"Keep coming, asshole. I may not be able to talk to my wolf, but I can guarantee you he's there and my bite can still release the poison to slowly and painfully kill you."

"Down boy."

"Jordan," Emmett warns.

"Betraying your own kind, Emmett, I would have expected better. I suppose lay in a bed with wolves and wake up with fleas or however the saying goes."

I'm usually a fairly peaceful guy, but right now, this guy is making me want to punch him.

"Why are you still here?" Callum asks, trying to bring the conversation back to him.

"I came over to see what brings you boys out here," he says, wrapping his arm around Callum. Emmett and Jax both take a possessive step forward, but Callum waves his hand, so they retreat a few steps, but are still tense.

While we're all different species of fae and aren't related by blood, we have formed a bond that's as strong as blood, if not stronger, and Callum is our unnamed alpha.

Calmly, Callum answers, "I imagine the same thing you're doing. Searching for that girl." Callum tries to downplay his interest in the girl, but we know. She isn't *some* girl to him. She's hope.

"That girl." Jordan drags. "Do you know why Samara wants her?"

"Not a clue." He pauses, then adds, "Well, she used magic last night in the club, but aside from that, I don't know."

"Hmm, I was there. Was it that light ball?"

"Yea. I think she concocted it to scare someone away," I add, and Callum looks at me, so I add, "Her friend did it, too."

"Yea, I saw that. Wild."

"I wonder if Samara will get mad if I have a little taste beforehand? What do you think, Emmett? Care to join?" Before Emmett can answer, Jordan is unhooking his arm from around Callum and walking away. "It's been real. Good luck."

"What did Samara take from him? His humanity?" I ask.

"I heard that!" Jordan yells over his shoulder.

"Fucking prick," I add for good measure, and Jordan laughs again. "We really need a witch in the group that can cast barrier spells and privacy spells."

"And spells to make your dick bigger," Jax chimes with a smirk.

"My dick is plenty big. I call it the pocket rocket."

"Because?" he presses laughing.

"Listen. I didn't hear you complaining when I was fucking the last girl while she was moaning around your cock."

"Boys. Can we focus? We need to find Everlee."

"Yes. Everlee," Jax retorts.

"Let's go this way so we can put as much space between us and Jordan as we can."

"Wait." Emmett holds up his finger. "Shit."

"What?" we all ask in unison.

"They have a scent." His nose goes in the air.

"Fuck," I say, watching the veins around his eyes pulse.

"Can you smell that?"

"No, we all say in unison."

"Emmett?" Jax asks.

Emmett's fangs drop.

"Emmett!" Callum commands, using his alpha voice.

He snaps out of whatever trance he's in. His fangs retract, and his eyes settle on Callum. "It's her and my Goddess. Her blood."

"She's bleeding?" I ask, worried.

He smells the air again and frowns. "It's gone. It was just right there, but now it's gone."

The pain in his voice matches the pain on his face. I'm not sure, but that may have been the first time he's smelled blood and craved it since Samara took his bloodlust and general desire to feed from him. If that's the case, then maybe Everlee is a true fae and can help us. But if that's the case, then I'm sure all the other vampires in the area smelled the power on her blood like Emmett did, which means she's in more trouble than Samara simply wanting her.

"We should go." I grab Callum's arm, and he nods, thinking the same thing.

"Are you good, E?" Jax asks.

"Yea." He pauses, then continues, "Just stop me if I go after her. I don't want to hurt her."

"E." Jax's face looks torn.

"It's ok." Emmett smiles and pats him on the shoulder like two friends who are discussing something trivial.

"You're going to be fine, Emmett. You can do this and we will be there," Callum encourages.

"It just smelled..."

"Better than anything you've ever smelled? Penetrating the depths of every cell within you?" Callum asks, sounding like he's speaking from experience.

"Yes," he sighs in appreciation of the understanding.

"Let's go." I dart off down the street and the others follow.

Shifters are fast. Not as fast as vampires, but we won't be far behind and Emmett is staying with us. A few minutes later, we come to a street full of run-down buildings with storefronts that look like they haven't seen a patron in years. Doors are partially open, with leaves scattered into the doorways. Old wooden benches line the streets with chipped paint and missing slats, and the overall smell in the area is of death. Effective for keeping mundanes away.

"Do you know where she is?" I ask over my shoulder.

"She's close," Callum says, looking at the hair on his arm.

"Someone's coming." Jax nods his head in front of us, so we duck to the side of the building that has 'ockbuster' in faded paint on the side of the wall.

"Was this a sex store named Cockbuster?" I ask, trying to calm my excitement. "Do you still think they have toys in there?"

"Who needs sex toys when you have the pocket rocket?" Jax jokes.

"Keep it up and my pocket rocket will shoot up in you when you least expect it."

"You'll only do it one time. I promise you that."

"Not if I make you like it."

"Guys," Callum says.

Jax peeks around the side of the building and watches Jordan. He's taunting Everlee from outside of that building. Did he find her? "I smell your fear pulsing off of you," he says. "I want to taste you. Taste *all* of you."

Curious to know what's happening, I peek over Jax's shoulder and see Jordan has stopped in front of a window, cupping his hands and looking inside.

"Everlee?"

Pushing off Jax, I turn to look at the others. "I think he found her. Wait. Where's Emmett?"

Callum looks around and then his eyes fall on mine. "Shit."

EVERLEE - IN THE ARMS OF A VAMPIRE

"EVERLEE?" THE VAMPIRE FROM outside says again as I stare into the red, pulsing eyes of the man who pulled me over the counter.

He holds a single finger over his lips, telling me to be quiet. Who is this man? Judging by the pulsing red eyes and pain on his face, I'd venture to say he's also a vampire. A vampire who's fighting with himself. To what? Not kill me?

His face is twisted in pain and he keeps staring at my neck like it's a steak on a silver platter.

"Everlee. I know you're in here. Your scent is all over this place. You smell like a dream. A delectable, tasty morsel of heaven. I'm supposed to bring you back to Samara, but honestly," he laughs out a puff of air. "I don't know if I'll be able to control myself."

A chair crashes to the ground, making me jump, but I don't make a sound. The man beside me is staring at me like he also wants to taste, but something about his eyes... There's a pain there. Both a physical and emotional pain battling for control. Will he attack me or won't he? I don't think either of us knows the answer to that question.

"You have someone else with you?" the vampire says.

My eyes dart to the man beside me. His fangs are slowly descending and he's licking his lips.

Fuck me.

There's no use fighting against him. His arms are wrapped tightly around me from when he pulled me over the counter. Fighting him would be the equivalent of trying to push a boulder up a hill. It's not going to happen.

He leans in and inhales my scent, his nose nudging my hair away from my neck, causing goosebumps to erupt over my skin.

"She's mine!" the vampire commands.

In a flash, the vampire holding me stands us up. His arm is wrapped around my chest, nearly crushing my ribcage.

Struggling to breathe, I reach up and grab his large forearm and try to pull it down, but it doesn't move.

"Emmett," the vampire says, looking slightly amused. "You're squeezing her to death," the vampire in front of us says. "Fine by me. We can still taste her after she's dead."

Emmett eases his grip, but still has his arm wrapped around me.

"Jordan," Emmett retorts unamused. His voice is burly, sexy, and he's huge. Both tall and muscular, like a lumberjack, but... not. *This* is a vampire. Everything about him ensnares the senses, making you swoon and fall for him. Bedazzling you with everything he has to lure you in. The vampire in front of me, Jordan, does not. He just looks sleezy and repulsive.

Jordan throws his head back, laughing. "Did you follow me here? I found her first." He takes a step forward.

"But I have her," Emmett returns, not moving.

"She's also listening to both of you talk like she's not right here and she doesn't appreciate it," I add. I've never been one for damsel in distress vibe. Although I guess to be fair, this would be my first time. Problem is, I'm not the damsel type. I'm the snarky, loud one that fights until the last second.

"Where's the rest of your crew? Trying to catch up?"

"We're right here," a voice booms behind us.

I try to turn around, but I'm locked fairly tightly in Emmett's arms.

"E, you good?" Another voice asks, taut with tension.

"Yea," he says, inhaling my scent again.

It makes me nervous when he does that, because judging by the massive boner that is pressing into my backside, I know my smell is driving him wild. Is he torturing himself?

"I think you can leave now, Jordan. She's not going with you."

A second later, several other vampires run and stand behind Jordan. "See. I think she is."

"I don't think I am," I chime.

Jordan's eyes fall on me with only a hint of amusement. I can't help but imagine he's thinking about all the horrific things he's going to do to me.

There are six vampires in front of us, and I've only heard two voices behind us. And I don't think they are vampires. Odds seem to have reverted back to Douche McDouche in front of me, although I'm fairly certain Emmett could take on several of them on his own.

"Isn't she cute?" Jordan asks.

"Fuck off asshat."

"With a mouth too. I love the ones with spark. More fight, harder to break."

"I don't know. She seems like she may be a little too much for you to handle," Emmett says, his fingers brushing my arm affectionately.

"I love a challenge."

"A challenge is what you're going to have if you and your little posse want to go up against us," another man from behind Emmett chimes, stepping into view.

Fuck. He's hot. He's equally as tall as Emmett, his muscles are pressing against the seams of his suit jacket and the confidence he's exuding. It's enough to melt your panties.

"Jax. You're a werewolf without a wolf. You don't scare me."

"He's inside and he'd love to play with you."

"Did he tell you that?"

Judging by the tone of his voice, I can tell he's trying to taunt Jax, to get under his skin.

"Enough," the voice from earlier booms again. He steps up and stands on the other side of Emmett. When he glances at me, I recognize the blue eyes almost immediately. The man from the club last night.

A second later, another body is moving up on the other side between Emmett and Jax. He glances at me and gives me a wink.

Knox.

My muscles relax, but only for a second. What are they doing here? Why did they come find me? Do they work for Samara too? I guess they do, since they work at her club.

Shit.

But the wink. Knox winked at me. Would you wink at someone you were going to trade over? Perhaps if it was all part of your plan to deceive and manipulate.

We don't know each other. Sure, we shared several... intimate moments on the stage last night and he made me feel things I wasn't sure I could feel, but... no! No, we don't know each other and if push came to shove, he'd turn me over faster than a burning pancake.

"You think you four misfits can take on us six?"

"You're young. And if I had to guess, you turned all the guys behind you, which means they're even younger. We are not. We have time on our side. Skill. Power. All things you think you possess, but do not. Not to mention we have her."

He's looking at me. I know he is because there's no other her in this room. I am it. I am the her. Usually, I'd be fine tooting my horn, but right now, no. Right now, I have no horn to toot. I am a hornless her. Am I going to advertise I seem to have misplaced the temporary power I had last night? No. But they also don't need to rely on me, or count me in. In fact, count me out, coach. Not it. Time out. New number, who dis? Yea. I'm not the one they need to be looking at.

Jordan continues to look at us, his eyes scanning back and forth, calculating in his little pea-sized brain if he thinks they can take us. His shoulders slump and I see his resolve fading. He's giving up.

"Come on, guys," Jordan turns and bats his hand.

"Really?" one guy behind him scoffs.

Jordan unleashes, spinning and grabbing the guy by the throat and shoving him against the front door. "Yes, really. She's probably not even a true fae, anyway. If she was, she'd be using her powers on us and not running like a pathetic coward and hiding behind a bunch of misfits." He glances over his shoulder as he says the last words.

Emmett's grip lessens on me, like he's expecting someone to lunge and react. By the looks of it, my money would be on Jax. He's seems the most on edge and seems to really hate this guy. Knox seems happy and jovial and along for the fight because he's loyal. Blue eyes seems to have a cool and level head and is the possible leader of this group, and Emmett. He's still hard to read. Clearly a man torn. It's obvious from the way his fingers grip into my arm then seconds later he's rubbing it affectionately, or the way his eyes look like he wants to devour me while at the same time he seems like he's fighting against himself to do just that.

Waiting another beat to see if he's pushed the guys enough, he speeds out of the door and seconds later, his guys follow.

I'm now standing in the empty restaurant with at least a vampire and a werewolf and two others. Emmett still has his arm wrapped around me, his cool fingers gently digging into my skin. I can almost feel the battle that's raging on within him. The two opposing forces, one wanting to whisk me away and likely kill me and the other who doesn't want that.

"Well, that went better than expected," Knox says, bouncing up and down, clapping his hands. "Although I would have liked to put Jordan in his place. I really hate that guy." He stops talking when his eyes fall on me, still in Emmett's arms. "Callum?"

"Emmett? You can let her go now."

He doesn't speak, and his grasp doesn't loosen. If anything, it tightens. I try not to react because I don't want to spark him into whisking me away, because I have a feeling if he did, they wouldn't be able to stop him, or at the very least catch up to him before he drains me of my blood.

"Emmett," Callum warns with a soft, but stern, voice.

Emmett snaps his head to look at Callum and they stare at each other in silence.

"Let her go now. She's safe," Callum says, calmly.

"Callum," Emmett sighs painfully.

"You did good. You protected her. Now let us."

Emmett's grip on me tightens, and he steps backward. Instinctively, I grab on his forearm and hold.

Knox steps forward, but Callum shoots his hand out to stop him.

"Emmett, let me have her."

"Her blood Cal. I've never smelled anything so sweet before. It's like a drug calling out to me. I hear it. I feel it." His grip tightens with a bruising strength.

"It's a trick. It tastes like shit," I add.

Emmett chuckles. "You're lying to me because you don't want me to rip your throat apart."

"Well, that took a dark twist."

Callum and Jax both stare at me with confused looks on their faces and Knox is just staring at me in shock. I have nothing to lose. The only thing I can use is my mouth, and that thing has gotten me into more trouble than I can count, but perhaps just once it can get me out of trouble.

If he is battling with himself, then he needs to be reminded of his humanity and not of the monster he thinks he is.

"Look. You seem like a good guy. Nice. You helped me. Saved my life." I rub his arm affectionately. "Thank you. Without your help, those monsters would have killed me. But you didn't. You saved me."

"I don't want to kill you."

"I know. That's what makes you better than Jordan and his group."

"You don't know me."

"I don't. But I'd like to. You seem like a really nice guy who wants to make the right decision. The thing holding you back is that my blood smells good to you. But I'm telling you. If you like the taste of cat piss, then you'll love it."

"Cat piss?" He scoffs, his hand relaxing a little more.

"Yes. Wretched."

"How do you know?"

Drive home the fact he's better than Jordan. "That monster, Jordan, smacked me hard across the face and caused me to bleed."

His grip tightens, but my gut tells me it's because Jordan hurt me instead of blood.

"I smelled it then."

"You did? And you smelled cat piss?"

"No. It was the most heavenly scent I've ever smelled."

"Emmett," Callum warns, and a prickle goes down my spine.

I can't see his face, but the entire room tenses.

"Emmett!" Jax snaps, stepping forward aggressively. "Let her go now or I'll make you."

Callum and Knox both look at Jax. Apparently, he'd had enough of the soft approach and decided to use dominance.

In a second, Emmett releases me, pushing me towards Jax, who grabs me in his arms. A gust of wind tousles my hair as Emmett runs away.

"Thank you," I say, looking up doey-eyed at Jax. He's a beautiful man with a hard expression.

"I didn't do it for you," he snaps and pushes me away to run after Emmett.

Stunned, I look between Knox and Callum.

"We need to get you out of here before anyone else finds you," Callum says.

"I need to grab my phone."

"Leave it. They'll track you."

"But..."

"Do you have your speed yet?" Callum asks.

"No, I don't think so."

He turns around and lowers to his knee. "Climb on."

"Your back?"

"No. My head. Yes, my back."

Standing there, looking at Callum's back, the angel and devil appear on my shoulder.

Everlee... don't do it. Don't go with these men you know nothing about. Just because they're hot as sin- The devil chimes in with a thank you - doesn't mean you should go with them. They have no allegiance to you. You're nothing more than a pawn in their game.

Conversely, they did just save you, so they clearly want something from you, so they'll keep protecting you until they have what they want. It just buys you more time.

Time. That seems to be what I need most right now. Time for Lizzy to work her magic and for me to find mine.

"Don't kill me," I say, climbing on his back.

"A little late for that now, don't you think?" In a flash, he's standing and running through the door, and my arms and legs tighten around him. Knox is right beside us, smiling at me. They are moving so fast the world around us looks like a blur. I'm taken back to my childhood when my father would give me rides around the neighborhood, but we never moved this fast. No, this speed could almost take your breath away. And to think the vampires move faster than this.

I hope I don't regret this decision, even though I'm fairly certain he was trying to be nice and make me think it was mine to make. I'm fairly certain if I said no, I'd still be going with them. Just unconsciously.

EVERLEE – JOGGER FROGGERS

It's dark by the time we get to their house. We've been walking for the last thirty minutes, mostly in circles through the city, to confuse anyone who may try to follow us.

Their house is a three-story brick building nestled between two other homes that look just like theirs, with large oak trees casting shadows on the walls.

"Come on, let's go inside and get something to eat."

Knox bounces up the stairs gleefully, already grabbing at his shoes with Callum behind him. When I try to step through the door, it feels like I've walked into a wall.

"Um?"

Callum turns around and smiles. "Everlee, please come in."

"I thought that was just for vampires."

Knox smiles. "We hired a witch to cast a spell to block anyone from entering without our invitation.

"Apologies for the theatrics, but I want to show you, rather than tell you, there were protections on the house."

Nodding, not sure what to say, I step through the doorway and pause. Their house is not at all what I expected. Open floor plan, with wooden floors, high ceilings, exposed beams and grays and blues that tie together nicely.

"Come on!" Knox waves, skipping down the hall.

There's an innocence about him that is all-consuming and brings a level of comfort and calmness to the environment around him.

"You'll have to excuse Knox. He's always like this."

"Not all the time," I mumble under my breath, but forgot they have super hearing.

Callum turns to look at me, confused.

A heat races across my body. "Last night." Goddess, was it only last night? It doesn't seem right. "He wasn't like this last night on stage."

Callum's eye pulse as the memory of last night replays in his mind. "Right," he mumbles out, clears his throat and turns. "Let's get some food."

"Yep." I swallow the knot in my throat. His eyes in those last seconds... did things to me. Made me... want things.

Fuck, I'm horny!

Their kitchen is no less impressive than the rest of their house. The kitchen has stainless steel appliances, white granite countertops with gray webbing, and ocean blue cabinets with brushed golden hardware. The ceiling has exposed beams that run the length between rooms. An oversized island takes up most of the space in the middle with seating for six.

"Wow. Your house is beautiful."

"Pull up a stool," Knox calls over his shoulder, rifling through the refrigerator. "I'm sure we have something in here we can reheat."

Callum walks upstairs and calls over his shoulder, "I'm going to shower and change."

I watch him for a second, then turn back to Knox, who's still digging and mumbling to himself. "At this point, I don't know if I care what it is. I'm starving." As if on cue, my stomach gives a loud gurgle.

He looks at me wide-eyed with a boyish grin. "Yes, I suppose you are." He pulls out a few slices of turkey, a half-eaten slice of pizza, and a bowl of grapes. "Well, this is depressing."

"I'll take some grapes."

"You mean you don't want the half-eaten piece of pizza?" Jax says, walking through the door. "Seriously Knox? What the fuck?"

"You know I don't cook. I'm hardly allowed in the kitchen!"

"Where's Callum?"

"In the shower."

"Really?" Jax asks, confused.

"Yea. I thought it was weird too, but whatever." Knox turns back to the fridge to see if he can find anything else.

"He carried me home. Well, most of the way."

Jax looks at me but doesn't speak. Look was probably being too friendly. Glare is probably a better description.

"How's Emmett?" I ask quietly.

Jax's head snaps in my direction as his glare has turned into a scowl. "What do you care?"

"I do. He saved my life. Jordan was definitely going to find me before he did. So I wanted to say thank you."

"Save your thank yous."

"Jax," Knox softly reprimands.

"What Knox? What? She's been in our lives for hours, not including whatever the fuck you were doing with her last night on stage, and she's already caused a riff. This is our family and she... she's going to destroy it!"

I push away from the counter, quickly, hunger getting the better of me. "Fuck you! I never wanted to be here. I never wanted you to come after me, or anyone else. I didn't ask for any of this."

Jax rushes me, grabbing my wrists and pinning them above my head, while his hips press me to the wall. "You didn't ask for this?" His face inches ever closer, lips parted ever so slightly. "Then you should have fucking kept your light ball to yourself. Fucking true fae."

We stare at each other for a moment, breathing one another in. Goddess, he's beautiful in a shadowy and callous kind of way. My pussy clenches as moisture pools in my panties. I know I should fear him right now, but... he's turning me on.

Fuck Everlee, get control of yourself.

Jax huffs and drops my hands before walking away. "I'm going upstairs. Take Emmett a blood bag in an hour. He'll be in his room for the foreseeable future until *she's* gone."

The way he says she makes me flinch.

"What's his deal?" I ask when he's out of sight. I don't care if he can hear me or not.

"He's always like that. Kind of a grump. Him and Emmett are close, which is kind of funny since they're supposed to be sworn enemies."

"I'm sorry. I didn't mean too..."

Callum comes bouncing down the stairs wearing a pair of black joggers low on his hips, tugging a white t-shirt over his head. His hair is slicked back and his abs are on display for a second before the shirt drops and I nearly moan out in my seat. I saw hints of tattoos on his chest and on his hips, working their way down, and I want to see more. See them up close. Know what they look like and mean. I swallow hard when I follow the trail down to his...

My head falls to the counter.

His package. His dick. It's bouncing around freely in his pants like a flag that says, salute me. That thing is... I whimper this time. A loud, audible, fucking whimper. Oh my goddess. "Fuck me."

"Everything ok?" Callum asks, with humor playing on his voice.

"Fucking, no Callum. Your cock obviously," Knox says, throwing his hands in the air. "Here I am trying to prepare her a nice dinner and you come down in *those* pants with your gigantic cock swinging all over the place. You know those joggers do nothing to hide your man candy. Why do you think women love fall so much? Hint. It's not because of the sports. Sweater weather and pumpkin spice, my ass. Jogger Froggers. That's what they love. Watching cocks bounce around freely like a frog inside of those joggers." He flicks his hand from side to side, simulating a cock bouncing around. "And no boxers Callum. Seriously!"

"I..." There was too much to process. Jogger froggers? No boxers?

"See!" Knox continues, "Robbed her of her breath."

"Do I need to change?" he asks, holding back a chuckle.

My eyes go back and forth between the two of them, completely in shock. "I... no. No. NO!" Why am I yelling? "I mean, if you want to, but no. I don't want- need. I don't need you to change."

Callum laughs, "Ok then. Do you mind?" he asks, pulling up the stool beside me.

I nod, unable to speak.

"What are you cooking for us, Knox?"

"Callum, you know I don't cook."

"I can," I offer.

Knox laughs out loud, then stops. "You were serious. Yea. I can't let you do that. Emmett would kill me."

"Kill you?"

"This is his kitchen. He always cooks for us."

"But he's a..."

"Vampire. Yes. He was an aspiring chef before he was turned. He still loves to cook, even though it tastes like cardboard to him now."

"That's horrible."

"Yea, and what's worse is that Sam-"

"Knox," Callum interrupts, stopping him. "How about you just order us some food and have them drop it at the door? I don't think Everlee wants turkey slices and grapes for dinner." He looks over at me and smiles.

"Well, she's starving, so she can snack on the grapes until the food gets here," Knox huffs, walking out of the room. "Maybe you can feed them to her!" He shouts, and it's hard to tell if he's joking or serious.

Awkward silence hangs around us as we sit in the kitchen. I pop a few more grapes in my mouth, then look at him. "So?"

His brow quirks up a little as his brilliant blue eyes flash at me. "So?" He waits a minute, then says, "I can show you to your room if you want to take a shower while we wait for the food."

"Room? How long do you plan on keeping me here?"

"You are free to go whenever you want."

"So I could just get up right now and leave?"

"You could. But I wouldn't recommend it. You do have the entire fae species in the area, it seems, looking for you."

"But not you?"

"Obviously we aren't looking for you since we found you."

"But why? Why did you find me? Why did you bring me here?"

He inhales a deep and thoughtful breath.

"I think you can help us."

"So you're using me."

"Not in the way you may think."

"Enlighten me."

"I can't do that right now. I need to do more research."

"Research?"

"Yes."

"About true fae?"

"I know about true fae. I'm over a thousand years old."

My eyes nearly pop out of my head.

"Needless to say, I know true fae. I've had many close friends that were true fae. I've also lost many friends."

"I'm sorry." My lips pinch into a flat line.

"It's why I wanted to find you. I genuinely want to protect you."

"If you can use me?"

"Call it what you want, but don't pretend like you aren't getting anything out of this deal. You don't end up as some lab rat with Samara running all sorts of tests on you," he snaps out.

"You're right. I'm sorry."

"Seems tense," Knox says, walking back in.

"I'm going to take a shower," I huff, pushing away from the counter. When I get to the stairs, I realize I don't know where I'm going and turn back around to find Callum looking at me with an amused grin on his face. "I don't know where I'm going."

"I was wondering how long it was going to take before you realized that."

Ugh. I stomp my foot. I imagine he's not used to being told no, or stood up too. He's had over a thousand years to perfect his charm.

He slides off the seat and walks towards me and his fucking cock is coming along for the ride to. Like a freaking mundane child in a bouncy house, ping ponging all over the place.

"My eyes are up here," he jokes.

"Shut up. Wear some boxers then. I can't help my eyes follow things that move."

"I'll take it under consideration." He places his hand on the lower part of my back and gently pushes me up the stairs. His hands feel like they're spreading molten lava across my skin, but it a good way. A great way. The hairs on my arms stand on end and a tingle shoots up my spine to my nipples and a pant parts my lips. I suck my bottom lip into my mouth to prevent my moaning or saying anything stupid.

"Down the hall, second door on the left." We pass several other closed doors and I can't help but wonder whose bedrooms they are.

"My bedroom is across the hall from yours. Knox's is further down on the right and we just passed Emmett's and Jax's."

"Oh. They're together?"

He looks at me, surprised, then answers slowly. "No. Jax's is the room beside yours and Emmett's is across the hall." I feel like there's something else that he's not saying.

The door creaks softly as I press it open and pause. There's an enormous fireplace on the right side of the room with a chaise lounger in front of it, and on the left is a four-poster king sized bed with a dark red velvet comforter.

Callum presses both hands on the doorframe and leans in, his muscles flexing tightly under the cuffs of his shirt. He smiles at my reaction before he speaks. "The bathroom is behind that door in the corner."

"Yep. Ok."

"I'll bring some clothes up here for you before you get out."

"Clothes?"

"Yes, unless you don't want to wear them."

"I... uh."

He adds. "The clothes I bring you. I can also just wash what you're wearing."

"Oh." Oh my Goddess. "Right. Duh. Umm. You can bring some clothes up."

"Ok. Well, if you need anything, let me know."

"Thanks."

"You're welcome."

"No. I mean... thanks for saving me earlier and bringing me back here."

"Oh. You're welcome for that too." He pats the doorframe and backs into the hall, dragging the door closed with him.

His feet pad down the hall further and further away until it's just silence.

Exhausted, I fall face first onto the bed. It's so soft. The velvet feels like clouds against my skin and hugs me perfectly. "You're a dangerous bed." Reluctantly, I walk to the chaise and fall into it with one leg up and the other still on the floor with my arm slung over the back. "Fetch me some tea!" I say with an accent to nobody.

My stomach growls, reminding me I need to eat, but first, I need to shower. When I get to the bathroom, it has a modern, but rustic feel. The shower is a gigantic glass stall the size of the bedroom at my place and the sink has a wooden base with a large white bowl resting on top of it. I slip out of my clothes and turn the shower on. Showers always make me feel like a new person. No matter how tired or crappy I feel, it's like they wash everything away.

After my shower, I'm going to figure out more about me and my powers and how I can help them. The stronger I get, then the sooner I can get out of here.

CALLUM - DON'T GET OFF IN THE SHOWER IN A HOUSE OF SUPERS

THE MORE STEPS I take down the hall, the more I want to turn around and run back into her room. I want to press her up against the wall in the shower and run my fingers over her wet skin, through her hair. I've been around hundreds of true fae before, but they never caused me to react like this.

Needing someone to talk some sense into me, I push the door open for Emmett's room. I know Jax will be in there with him. And who better to set me straight than Jax, who's already pissed she's here.

Emmett's room is like the rest of ours. Large with gray walls, wooden accents, king sized bed in the middle with a balcony on the wall opposite of the door. The only difference between our rooms is the large piece of artwork we each had commissioned to hang over our beds. Well, all of us except Jax. Emmett has a large painting of the Eiffel Tower, Knox has a picture of ocean waves crashing on the banks of a lighthouse, and I have a picture of the Cliffs of Morgai. Since Jax decided not to get a painting commissioned, Knox took it upon himself to decorate Jax's space with enormous posters of himself posing in a leopard print thong in Jax's room. Jax rips the posters down and within days, another one with a different pose is in its place. It's shocking Jax hasn't killed him yet, but that's their relationship. Below the bickering and jabbing most see on the surface, there's a deep bond that has formed over the years. They would go into battle for each other in a second, without question.

"What's going on?" Emmett looks up, his eyes a mixture of the man I know, mixed with torment.

"Is our savior resting in her new bedroom?" Jax snides.

"Jax." Emmett puts his hand on his knee.

"What?" he snaps. "I wasn't ok with her staying here before and now that you have to hole yourself up in your room like a prisoner because of her..."

"It's not her fault."

"If she wasn't here, would you be in your room? Torturing yourself?"

He cocks his head to the side, staring at Jax.

"I'll take that as a no, which further supports the fact that it's her fault."

"She can help us. Right Callum?"

"I think so. I mean, the fact Emmett is having this reaction to her should say as much."

"So she fixed you? You want to feed again?"

Emmett shakes his head. "No. After I ran off after we found her, I ran across several humans and couldn't smell any of them. I even went to a bar and kissed a woman, but nothing. I was kissing her throat, breathing in her scent, and nothing. Couldn't even get my fangs to descend and simply being in the same house as Everlee has my fangs out and my cock hard as fuck."

"What's going on in here? Why did I not get the invite?" Knox chimes, bouncing in.

"Obviously, because we're trying to exclude you," Jax chides.

"Oh, you silly goose!" Knox bats the air and prances across the room to sit on the arm of Jax's chair.

"What the fuck are you doing?" Jax looks up at him.

"Sitting."

"Get the fuck out of here!" Jax pushes him off the chair, but Knox has the reflexes of a cat and bounces to standing.

"You could have simply asked," Knox says, snarling his nose.

"I would have thought you're old and wise enough to read the expression on my face."

"You have resting fuck off face, so it's hard to know if you're happy, sad, want me to go or want me to stay."

"Always go."

"Got it," Knox winks hard.

"There's no winking."

"Ok." Knox winks hard again.

"Fuck me," Jax sighs.

"I thought you'd never ask." Knox clasps his hands together and rests them under his chin, batting his eyelashes.

Jax stares at him incredulously.

"What was that?" Knox asks, completely ignoring his banter with Jax.

"What was what?" Jax asks.

"That's Everlee. She's masturbating in the shower. I've been listening to it for several minutes now, hence the even harder erection," Emmett sighs.

Silence fills the room as we all listen to her moans dance around us.

"Her orgasms even sound heavenly," Knox says in awe.

"Someone should go in there and stop her," Emmett grunts, his eyes rolling into the back of his head.

"Not it!" Knox touches the end of his nose.

"No," Jax says simply.

Inhaling a deep breath, I push to stand up from the chair.

"No," Knox furrows his brow and whines. "Just a little longer. Let her at least have her moment. It's your fault with your cock swinging all around earlier. She was practically drooling over it. I mean, look at it now!" Knox motions to my cock, which is hard and pressing against the seam of my joggers. "That thing is massive!"

"Please stop her." Jax nods towards Emmett, whose tongue is rubbing over his fangs.

"Got an idea!" Knox yells, then dashes out of the room.

"This should be good," Jax quips.

Another moan, this one louder. She's getting close to her release.

Knox races back into the room, pouring the warm blood bag into a mug and thrusting it in front of Emmett's face. "Here. See if you can taste it."

Emmett snatches the mug out of his hand and drinks. A moan echoes through the room and he tilts the glass up, guzzling it down at the same time his hand rips his pants off and he fists his cock. "Oh my. Oh my!" He tosses the mug across the room and Knox races to catch it before it crashes into the wall.

Emmett pumps his cock to Everlee's moans and a moment later, her orgasm hits and a pulse vibrates throughout the house. Emmett releases, Jax's eyes glow gold, and a tingle moves up my spine. In a second, it's gone and we're all staring at one another.

"Fuck," Knox says, looking down. "I just exploded in my pants."

"Stop her!" Jax commands with restrained anger.

Bolting down the hall, I burst into the bathroom and find her crumpled on the floor of the shower with a water jet pelting her in the back of the head.

She looks up at me, startled, but also satiated. "Cover up!" I grab a towel and throw it at her as I race into the shower and cut it off.

"What are you doing?" She asks, staring up at me.

"What are you doing?" I fire back, panting. My shirt is clinging to me and she's sitting there on the floor with the towel sitting on her lap, and her breasts on full display. Fuck me, she's beautiful.

Her teeth scrape over her bottom lip as her eyes move down my body to my hard cock.

No. No, no, no. I cannot fuck her.

"You... put a towel on."

"What? I put a towel on?" she asks, confused.

"No. Put a towel on." I motion to the one sitting on her lap and then to her breasts. She needs to cover them up, because if not, I may lose all control and take her right now. I've wanted to sink my cock into her since I first laid eyes on her. Fuck that. Since I felt her presence.

"Oh. Goddess. Right. Fuck." She quickly pulls her towel up.

"You..." I start, but can't seem to formulate thoughts. Images of her perky little breasts bouncing while she rides my cock play on repeat in my head.

"What's so hard?" She grunts. "To say. What's so hard to say?"

"You were... masturbating."

Her entire body flushes pink.

"I..."

"You're in a house of supers."

"So you heard..."

"Yes."

"Which is why you..."

"Yes."

"Oh, fuck." Her head falls into her hands.

What do I do? Do I try to console her? That's not going to fucking work. If I so much as touch a hair on her body, I'm going to fuck her. Self-control has never been a problem for me, but with her... My wet hair is dripping into my face, so I run my fingers through it, pushing it back.

"Fuck," she mumbles out.

When I look down, I find her eyes staring appreciatively at my body. I've worked hard for it and have taken great effort and time with how I mark it up. I have fifty-three tattoos, some small, some larger, but each is important, telling the story of me and my history. Battles I've fought in and friends I've lost. While I'm not immortal, I feel like it sometimes. My body is my greatest artwork, a key to who I am, so that I may never forget.

"You're beautiful," she whispers.

Space. Space and distance. I turn to leave, but my manners will not let me leave her on the floor. Offering her my hand, she slips hers in mine and I lift her. Her touch causes a wave of ecstasy to spread across my skin. She wobbles and I catch her, causing her breasts to brush across my chest.

She moans and I'm frozen. Our eyes lock on one another, breathing each other in. My hand brushes the wet hair from her face before my fingertips slide down the curve of her jaw and rest under her chin. I lift just the slightest, giving me better access to those perfectly pouty lips.

Her hand slides up my chest before inching down slowly. Further and further, her eyes never breaking from mine. Her hand presses against my stomach and slips beneath the hem of my joggers.

I know I should move. I know I should stop her, but I'm frozen in place. I'm curious to know what it will feel like with her hand wrapped around it. Her mouth.

My cock twitches.

She slips her hand down further and glides it along my shaft and an appreciative moan escapes my chest.

Her hand wraps around the length and slides up.

Fuck me.

She lets out a whisper of a breath as her teeth bite into her bottom lip and her grip tightens.

I've never wanted to take someone's lips with mine so badly before.

I swear to Helsgard you better not be fucking her, Jax mindlinks.

Damn him. "Stop," I groan out.

She looks up at me, hand pausing on my cock.

"We can't. I can't."

"What?" She's confused. Fuck, I'm confused.

The doorbell rings.

"Dinner's here."

Greedily, I plant my lips on her head. This can't happen again, so I will take what I can get while I can.

She pulls her hand out of my pants and picks up the towel that fell and wraps it around her.

"I'm sorry." Damn it. What was I thinking?

EVERLEE – ANCESTRAL MEMORIES

WHAT IN THE HELL was that? What was I doing and why am I mad he stopped me? The way he's been looking at me. At the club, on the stage, here. And then nothing?

So embarrassing.

The other's voices are echoing through the hall as they clamor down the stairs.

What am I doing here?

Get your head in the game, Everlee.

When I walk into the room, there are no clothes on the bed. Or in the drawers. Did he forget?

Probably because you were masturbating, you fairy fucker.

Oh my goddess. They heard me. Well, this is going to make for an awkward fucking dinner.

There's a soft knock on my door. With the towel still wrapped around me, I crack it open to find a small pile of clothes in a bag. Opening the door wider, I look both ways down the hall, but don't see anyone. There's some weight to the bag when I bring it into the room. I dump it out on the bed and rifle through all my options. Shockingly, I don't hate it. There are several plain colored tops and some plain colored bottoms. A few pairs of shorts, a few pairs of jeans and some joggers.

I shouldn't do it... but I do.

If you can't beat them, join them. Although in this case, I won't draw the same attention a man does in joggers. I could always grab a banana and shove it down my pants and that would probably get their attention. Perhaps. I grab a t-shirt and slip it on without a bra. One, because there isn't one in the bag. Two, because I don't want to put mine back on since it wreaks of nervous sweat. And three, because I simply don't want to.

I'm bouncing downstairs and a few minutes later and Knox, Callum, and Jax are laying out the food on the counter.

Callum looks me up and down and a smile tugs at his lips. It's the same outfit he's wearing. Black joggers and a white t-shirt. Only mine is tighter fitting and hugging my breasts.

Knox shoves his fist into his mouth and clamps down on his knuckles, while Jax rolls his eyes.

"Cute," Callum says.

"This ol' thing?"

"I'm going to go back upstairs and eat," Jax groans. He grabs a plate of food and brushes by my arm.

"I can go to my room to eat. This is your house; Emmett shouldn't be tucked away in his room."

Jax pauses on the stairs and looks at Callum.

"Tonight, you can eat down here. You're our guest and Emmett wants you to feel welcome," he says pointedly at Jax, who scoffs and continues to walk up the stairs.

"Ignore him," Knox says, walking over to grab my hand and guide me to a chair. "Did you have a good shower?"

"For fuck's sake, Knox," Callum growls.

"What?" he asks innocently. "Oh, the masturbating. I wasn't talking about that. Well, fuck. Thanks a lot Callum. I was just trying to be nice and now you've made me make it awkward."

"I think you did that all on your own."

Wanting to put Knox at ease, I rest my other hand on his arm. "It was lovely. Both the shower and the orgasm."

"I think I'm in love," he bows as he backs away. "What would you like to eat?"

"You don't have to get my food. I can do that."

"I insist. You've had an eventful twenty-four hours."

His words remind me I'm not just staying at a guy's house I just met. I'm on the run, hiding.

"I'll take some lasagna and bread, please."

"That's it?"

"She's not a shifter, Knox. She won't consume as much food."

"Right. I knew that."

"Sorry. He's just a little excited."

I laugh, "He's fine. It's sweet."

Knox is the kind of person who just makes you feel calm and happy. Like the days by the water. No matter your troubles, there's nothing that water can't seem to fix. He has the same qualities, it seems. Although he doesn't seem to make Jax happy. Quite the opposite. He seems to take pleasure in making Jax mad, although I get the impression it doesn't take much, which could be why he does it. It seems... fun.

Callum is more of a mystery. He brings a calmness to the house and direction. He steers them and they follow, although judging by Jax's reaction with me, it seems like they don't always agree.

Callum thinks I can help them, and until he figures out how, he's going to keep me safe. The only thing is, I need to figure out who I am and what my powers are before he figures out how to use me to get what he wants. Once I have my strength and power, I won't need them anymore and can leave.

Dinner was delicious, and it was nice to have someone to talk to while I gorged myself on enough pasta to last me for a year. Knox is hilarious and didn't stop talking the entire time he was eating. So much so that while I was cleaning up the dishes, he took his first bite. Callum insisted I didn't need to clean, but I needed to contribute somehow to show my gratitude for them watching over me.

After dinner, Callum showed me the library, which is absolutely massive. It's two stories on the back of the house with floor to ceiling shelves full of books. Callum said he likes to read and I guess being as old as he is means he would have collected a ton of books. There's no telling how many first editions he has in the room. I'll have to do some exploring tomorrow.

He walked straight to a section where the books looked ancient, with leather backings and buckles to hold the pages together. He pulled one out and handed it to me. The writing on the front had been worn away, but he said it's full of history about the true fae.

Back in my room, I grab a blanket off the bed and perch myself on the chaise in front of the fireplace. Even though the book looks like it will disintegrate into a pile of ash with one strong flick of the wrist, Callum assured me it's in solid condition.

Even still, I gently flip the cover open. The title page is written in some sort of ancient lettering that I can't make out with words written below that I try and fail to sound out, so I flip the page. The top of the page has the number one written in a fancy font, but the letters underneath it are in the same odd lettering.

Why would he give me a book that I can't read?

Should I be able to read it?

Is this the true fae language?

I stare at the pages, tracing every line with my eyes, hoping that something magic will happen and they will rearrange themselves into something I can read. Page after page, I do the same thing, and still nothing happens.

It's a beautiful font. Curls and lines, dashes and dots. I just wish I could understand it. This book has all the answers to who I am. I just know it.

After a while my eyes start to burn, so I close the book and sit it on the chaise and pad over to the bed. When I crawl in, it feels like I'm rolling on a cloud. It's soft. Majestic. If that's even a thing.

I roll over to my side, curling into a ball and bring the covers under my chin, and watch the flames of the fire dance. It's so beautiful. The way it moves and juts into the air. The way the colors meld between yellows, reds, and oranges.

Darkness slowly creeps in and before I know it, I'm spiraling down into the sweet abyss of nothingness.

RUN!

"Run little one. You must get away. They are coming for us."

"Mama. I can't. I can't leave you."

"You can and you must. You're the one. You're the one that will save us all. All of our power, our bloodline. It's all in you now. You are the future of the fae. You little one."

"Mama. No," The warm tears feel like fire against my cold cheek.

"Take her! Get her to Morgai!" Mother commands, and a pair of hands wrap around my stomach and whisk me off the floor. My little hands and feet stretch out, kicking and clawing to get back to her. To get back to them. They are stained red with the blood trickling down my arms.

A crash echoes down the hall as flames engulf the house moments later. The cries of the fae echo through the land as sharp claws hold me in their clutches, and I ascend higher and higher into the sky. The wind grows colder the higher we go.

More harsh.

More angry.

The houses in the little village are nothing more than orange specks on the horizon. Like orange dots scattered across the dark green grass. An arrow flies through the sky, zinging by as we bank hard and to the right.

Wings sound like thunder as they flap harder and harder, pushing us higher and higher.

So cold.

Freezing.

My little body has stopped shaking and darkness creeps in.

A hot fire dances in an orb around me, warming me up. My eyes open, but they're tired.

"Hold on, little one," the man's voice says. Gentle, yet commanding.

The sounds of the waves crashing below are the only noise I hear as the large wings of the dragon glide over the landscape. There's nothing out here but grass and water, except for a few small houses with smoke billowing out of the top.

"Tired."

"I know. Just a little further and then you can rest. Rest for a long time."

"Mama?"

The man doesn't answer, but his talons grip around me. Not in anger or to punish, but to support. I feel what he feels, his pain. His sadness.

"You will see her again soon, little one. We just need to get you to Morgai."

"Morgai, the ancess- ancess..."

The man laughs, "Yes. The ancestral burial ground of the true fae. You will be protected there. They won't be able to hurt you."

Moonlight shimmers on top of the waves below like snow on a mountain. Ahead is a large body of land jutting out of the ocean, trying to touch the sky.

"Morgai."

"Morgai. Hold on little one."

His wings flap harder and faster. Wind whips by, but the flame of warmth stays intact.

Darkness pulses at the edges of what's real and what's make believe.

"Hold on. We're almost there." The man's words do little to hold back the darkness.

My eyes close. "So... tired."

We're descending.

Fast.

Falling to the ground.

Falling.

Faster.

Wind whips by harsh like anger.

Everlee!

Everlee!

"Everlee! Wake up!"

My body is shaking.

"Damn it, Everlee," the man growls.

No. Not the man, Callum.

Callum.

Slowly opening my eyes, Callum is standing beside my bed panting.

"Move over," he commands, and I listen. "You weren't ready." His words are quiet, like he's scolding himself rather than anyone else.

He scoops me into his arms as my body molds perfectly into his. His knees curl into mine, and his arms wrap around my side and under my head like a pillow.

Strength.

Safety.

"What happened?" I ask, drowsy.

"Go to sleep. We'll talk tomorrow."

A breath pushes its way out of my lungs and with it, the part of me battling to stay awake.

JAX – ALL BARK AND NO BITE

A SCREAM PIERCES THE night like claws tearing through flesh.

Everlee.

I bolt upright in bed, listening.

Her soft whimpers and groans feel like needles poking my skin.

She's having a nightmare.

Damn it! I knew he wouldn't be able to wait. She wasn't ready yet, but no. He had to know. He had to put his conscious at rest.

Selfish.

I knew him bringing her here wasn't a good idea, but he didn't want to listen to me. All she's going to do is bring chaos and trouble. Two things I don't want or need in my life.

Another scream.

She's terrified. I throw the covers off and race across the room and down the hall. By the time I get to her door, Callum is sliding into her bed, wrapping his arms around her. Anger feels like molten lava coursing through my skin.

Not jealousy.

I don't care about her. Not like that.

I just want her gone.

Out of this house and out of our lives.

But the more Callum gets attached, the more she intertwines herself into our family...

My family.

By the time I get downstairs the next morning, Callum, Emmett and Knox are sitting at the counter enjoying their drinks of choice.

"Good morning, gents." I smile, running my hand down the handrail.

"Who died?" Knox asks, turning in his seat to look at me.

"No one. Why would you ask that?"

"You're smiling. So clearly, something horrible has happened."

"Shut the fuck up!"There's my little cupcake," Knox says, holding his mug of maple apple cider tea up, cheersing me.

"Everyone have a good night?" I ask, walking over to the coffeemaker to pour myself a cup. One of the best advancements mundanes have made.

Callum cuts his eyes at me because he knows I'm speaking directly to him.

"I told you it was too soon and to wait." I take a breath and sip my coffee. "How is she?"

"She's fine. She just had a nightmare."

"A nightmare? Is that what you're pretending it was? Is that what you told her?"

"Told me what?" she asks, walking down the stairs throwing her hair into a messy bun on top of her head. She's wearing those fucking joggers again, with the tops rolled over several times, so they sit low on her hips, causing a gap between the tops of her pants and the bottom of her shirt.

Emmett tenses and starts to move.

"Stop," she commands, holding her hand out and we all freeze. She doesn't move and waits to see if anyone is going to say anything. When no one speaks, she continues, "You aren't going to run away every time I walk into the room."

She's got a set of balls on her, that's for sure.

"Everlee," Callum starts, then stops when she holds her hand up to him.

Knox and I exchange a shocked glance. This woman. She has no power, yet, and is in a house with a bunch of strangers and commanding a thousand-year-old dragon. If I wasn't so pissed she was here, I may actually allow myself to like her. But that's not going to happen.

"This is your house. I'm a guest."

"I could kill you. I want to," Emmett grits out, his eyes pulsing with lust.

"No, you don't."

The fuck?

"You don't want to kill me. You are good. I said it before and I still say it now, Emmett. You lose control and that's what you don't want to happen. Perhaps if you're around me, then I can help you. Desensitize you, if you will."

"I don't think I could ever become desensitized to you," his words are soft.

She smiles. "You stay down there and I will stay down here."

"Ev." Callum glances at her.

Ev. Fucking Ev. Pet names? I knew he felt a connection to her when he told me about her at the club. He's obsessed. He's been beating himself up for the last several hundred years because he held himself responsible for the true fae getting wiped from existence.

Was it him that hunted them?

No.

Was it him that fought for them? With them?

Yes.

He hasn't told me much about the night he had to save little Aleida, only that he thought he failed and that guilt has stayed with him for all of these years.

And then Everlee walks into the club. Our club.

She's the first true fae born in several hundred years.

Hiding. Waiting.

I don't pretend to know as much about the true fae as Callum does. He's scoured the earth one hundred times around to find any and all documents related to the true fae. What their life cycles are like, their powers, their ability to reincarnate, everything. When they were hunted and killed, the hunters tried to wipe their entire existence from the world by setting everything on fire. So Callum set them on fire.

For years, he traveled around to the towns that killed off the true fae and killed them all. A lot of it was his own guilt for not saving Aleida and feeling like he let his friends down. His family.

He doesn't talk about it much, but he was abandoned when he was younger. He was told hunters killed his mother because they thought she was protecting gold and treasure in her cave. It was *her* treasure. Him.

Sofrai and Feyra, the two fae that found him, said they believe that in his mother's final act, she used her tail to slide him over into a crack in the cave wall. He was dying because it had been days since he ate, so Feyra and Sofrai made quick work and carried him back to their village where they used their combined resources and magic to bring him back to good health. He grew and became their guardian. Protected them. Until he couldn't. When he lost them, he lost his family. He lost everything.

His home.

That's what he's trying to get back. It's what he was trying to get back when Samara took his wings. I've been able to figure out what everyone asked for to get their most prized possession taken from them but him. I can't figure out how she could have used his words against him to take his wings.

But he doesn't need his wings to be alpha. He just commands it.

Except with Everlee. She doesn't seem to give a shit, which I find amusing.

"It'll be fine," Everlee says, taking a seat behind me at the bar.

"Do whatever you want, but I'm not playing go between if he decides he wants a taste."

"Jax," Emmett warns.

"What? It's not my fucking fault if she wants to do this."

"She's doing this for me."

And to try to score points with me. I know her game and it won't work. I want her out of here. When I look at her, my blood boils. "I'll tell you what. While I'm out today, I'll go buy some cookies and give her one, since she's being so... thoughtful."

"You're an ass, you know that," she fires.

"So I've heard," I call over my shoulder without turning to look at her.

"It's fine though. I've dealt with worse."

"Doubt it."

"Harder they are, bigger the crack."

Knox laughs, no doubt thinking of something childish.

"I'm out." Needing to get away from her, I push back from the counter. "I need to run some errands. Care to go with E?"

"Yea."

I ignore the quiet sigh from Everlee. She doesn't need to try to break Emmett's hunger for her. She won't be here long enough to see it happen.

"Let's go." I wave over my shoulder.

"Are you going to be here later, Ev?" Emmett asks.

She hesitates a moment, looking at me before answering. "I think so."

"Yes. She will be. She hasn't come into her powers yet."

"Always taking in the strays, Cal."

"He took you in," she snaps back.

"Oh, shit!" Knox says, eyes wide, jumping up and down.

Before I can stop myself, I'm standing in front of her again, chest pressed to hers with my hand wrapped around her throat and her eyes glued to mine.

"You don't scare me."

"I should."

"Try harder," she grinds out. "You seem to be all bark and no bite."

"I bite, *Ev*. But you'll never feel it."

Her eyes dilate and her lips part.

Damn it. She likes that. It turns her on. Of course she would be into that.

Irritated, I drop her from my grip and she falls to the ground and grabs her throat. She snaps her teeth before she sits back down.

Fucking hell. "Let's go." I kick the chair under the bar and walk towards the back door.

Emmett is there a second later, licking the remaining blood from his bag off his lips. "You want to fuck her."

"No. I don't."

"You do," he says, smiling.

"She gets under my skin."

"You want to fuck her," he says, climbing into the passenger seat.

"You can shut your fucking mouth or you can stay here and sulk in your room all day while she prances her blood around in front of you."

"Admit it and I'll stop."

"What the fuck, E? Why are you pressing this?"

"Because I haven't seen you like this with anyone in a long time."

"I don't want to fuck her."

He blows out a cool breath. "You can't get enough of her. The way you just were with her."

"That. You think because of that, I want to fuck her?"

"If you don't think that, then you're lying to yourself. I'm surprised your cock isn't still hard."

"Still?"

"Oh brother, I saw it twitch in your pants when you had her by the throat. She liked you being rough, and you liked that she liked it."

"Shut the fuck up."

He zips his lips with an imaginary zipper, then locks it with a key and tosses it out the window.

"Really?" I smirk.

He winks and after a beat asks, "Where are we going today?"

"I don't fucking know. Away from that house and her."

EVERLEE - LIBRARIES ARE KINKY AF

WHAT AM I DOING? Playing chicken with a vampire and going toe to toe with a werewolf. And last night? What was that? A nightmare? It didn't feel like a nightmare. It felt more like a memory, like an ancestral memory. The bone crushing sadness I felt when that man, no, that dragon shifter, was pulling me away from... my mom? Only that wasn't my mom. It was another woman. And the Cliffs of Morgai. I've only ever heard of it, almost like it's a mythological place that doesn't really exist, but I saw it. Well, I think I saw it.

Overwhelmed, I fall into the freshly made bed and stare at the ceiling. I need to figure out more about the true fae, and the book Callum let me borrow last night was no help. I couldn't read anything.

Did Callum think I could? Is that why he gave it to me? Is the book what caused those dreams... no, memories? Last night?

Giving myself a few more minutes to put as many pieces together as I can, I roll out of bed, and grab the book off the chaise, and head back to the library. The goal for today is to learn all that I can about the true fae and try to figure out if Morgai is an actual place and where it's at.

A few minutes later, I'm walking into the library and find Callum sitting at the oversized desk in the middle with a book laid on the desk. The library looks more impressive in the daylight. Larger somehow, if that were possible. The large arched floor to ceiling window on the wall opposite the door, behind Callum's desk, is inviting. There's a bench that lines the wall in front of it- a perfect reading nook to relax in and waste the day away.

He looks up at me and smiles, "Back so soon?"

"I couldn't read this book. It's in some other language."

He shrugs.

"You knew that?"

"Yes. It was a test of sorts."

"A test? Is this all some sort of game to you?"

"A game? Not at all."

"Then what? Why give me a book I can't read?"

"You can read it. Rather, you'll be able to soon."

"Soon?"

"Yes. You've only recently discovered you're a true fae. As your powers continue to come in, I imagine the ancestral knowledge of the true fae will also return."

"What are you talking about?"

He slowly closes the book he's reading, like he's formulating his thoughts carefully, then stands from the desk and walks over to the wall with the ladder. "Come here."

He climbs a few rungs on the ladder and stretches out for a book. I can't help but look up and notice his physique, the ripples on his chest and the delicious hook over his hips, guiding my eyes straight to his pants. Jogger Frogger, I chuckle, thinking back to Knox's name for it. He wasn't wrong. Sweater weather and pumpkin spice are nice, but men in joggers... Especially Callum. He's huge. I felt it, if only for a second, but goddess, I want more. No amount of masturbating will get him or it, out of my mind.

Callum clears his throat, pulling me back.

My lip falls from my teeth and I look up at him like a kid who's been caught with their hand in the cookie jar.

He climbs down the ladder and hands me the book, "Here." Our fingers brush as we both stand there, hands on the book, looking at one another. The spark I feel with his fingertips brings back memories of last night. Were we going to talk about it or pretend like he didn't come into my room and hold me in his arms until I fell asleep?

When I woke up this morning on my own, I thought it was a dream. That it was all a dream, but I smelled him- his scent, on the pillows.

"Here," he says again, like he too is having a hard time with words. He gently pulls the book from my fingers and walks over to his desk and opens it. He scoots his chair out of the way and stands, palms pressed, to the desk and looks over it. "Are you going to come?"

I'm about to. Fuck. Focus Everlee. Something about this man just... causes my senses to go all haywire. I can't think when I'm around him.

His brows perk up, looking for an answer.

"Oh, right! Yes."

His eyes track me as I move across the room to stand beside him.

"You ok?"

"Yep, all good."

He smiles, then flips through the book. This book is a deep blue with golden foiling on the front cover. It looks old, but not nearly as old as the one he gave me last night.

"Last night," he starts and stops and I think he's going to talk about climbing into my bed, but he doesn't. Not exactly. "What did you see? In your memories?"

"You mean nightmares?"

"No. Memories. I imagine you saw something pretty horrific that felt like a nightmare, but was likely an ancestral dream."

"Ancestral dream?"

"Yes."

He's serious.

"I... I don't understand. How can I have a memory of something that existed way before I was born?" I really wish I would have paid attention more in school.

He smiles, moving his hand over mine. When our eyes lock, he slowly slides his hand off and balls it into a fist before he speaks. "Every species of fae came from the true fae. They've been around since the creation of the great universe. As fae powers developed, each had strengths and weaknesses that altered their appearance and powers over time. However, the purest and strongest stayed true fae. With unique powers and different fae, there was a battle for control. Some chose to use dark magic to advance their agenda, while others chose light. That's how the light and dark fae came to be, and when that happened, Helsgard created the Seelie and Unseelie Courts to watch over their people."

"This I remember. It's taught from the time you start school until you graduate. But it still doesn't explain the dreams."

"Overtime, members of the Courts motioned to have seats at Helsgard to ensure both Courts were being represented equally. As the Courts moved into Helsgard, the true fae wanted to step out of the politics of the Courts, so they found their own place they could call home."

"Cliff of Morgai."

"Yes."

"So they aren't a myth? It's an actual place?"

"Yes."

"They were in my dream... sorry, memory last night."

"Your ancestor, Aleida, was taken there and buried. She held the bloodline of the fae."

"A dragon took me there. Her. Took her there."

"Yes. On the night of the Great Fall."

"The Great Fall. The night true fae were wiped from existence. A series of coordinated attacks by hunters."

Callum's lips flatten into a fine line and he looks at me, eyes broken. "Yes. It was a sad night."

His pain. It's radiating off his body and washing over me in waves. My hand moves to cup his cheek, bringing our lips within an inch of each other. Breathing each other in.

I could just tilt my head a little and feel his lips pressed to mine. Taste him. Savor him.

"Everlee," he whispers. His words are equal part soft and sweet, hesitant and pained. "We can't." He pulls away.

"Sorry. I... I don't know what happened."

He smiles without speaking. "This book will talk about the Great Fall and the ancestral memories of the true fae."

He's dismissing me. Putting space between us.

"Ok. Do you mind if I stay in here? The reading light is better and if I have any questions..."

His hand brushes my cheek, but he pulls it away and again, he balls it into a fist like he's mad for letting himself want... me. "Of course. What's mine is yours."

His cock?

As if reading my mind, he adds, "Well, most of every-thing."

I blush because I feel like he caught me, but there's no way he knew what I was thinking. Right? Oh Goddess. Can he hear my thoughts?

Callum?

My eyes thin to narrow slits as I study him for any sort of reaction. Nothing. Not even a twitch of his head.

Wanting to give him the space he clearly wants and that I need, I grab the book and walk over to the bench by the window. I crack it open. Chapter 1.

I don't know how much time has passed, but it's been several hours. Even though there's considerable space be-tween us, I still *feel* him. *Hear* him. His breaths, the way it picks up or slows down based on what he's reading or perhaps what he's thinking. The way his fingers tap on the desk when he's lost in thought. When he moves around the room, grabbing books or putting others back, the hairs on my arms follow him like a magnet. My stomach feels like there are a thousand butterflies in it, dancing and swarming.

His eyes catch mine staring at him, but I don't hide it. It's no use. We've been playing this game all afternoon. Stolen glances. Brushes of the hand when I have to ask him a question. It's almost torture staying in this room with him, wanting to touch him. Taste him. But leaving would be worse.

I'm halfway through the book and there's so much about the true fae I didn't know, but if he wasn't here, I'd probably be done. I'm a fast reader and not stupid, and the number of silly questions I've asked just to be near him or create that bridge to him is almost embarrassing. But I have learned a lot.

The ancestral dreams connected all the fae together, their lifeline and story. Being true fae, they were the only ones that could do it, as long as they were buried at Morgai. It's believed that Morgai was the first place the fae came to be and holds all the magic of the fae. When Aleida was buried on Morgai, she joined the ancestral realm and waited. Waited for the right time. While I'm not Aleida, I have her blood and memories pulsing throughout me. I have her strength, her passion, and her magic.

The sun is setting and turning the sky an orange, pinkish color, casting long shadows on the ground. Knox has flittered in and out of the room several times, but hasn't been here for some time after he got called in to speak with Samara. Jax and Emmett still haven't come back yet, which isn't a bad thing, but I can't help but wonder where they are.

"Are you done?"

Startled, I turn from the window and see Callum turned around in the chair with his legs casually sitting open. Inviting. The smart thing would be for me to stop staring at him. To leave. But I'm not always smart.

It feels like someone else is in control of my body as my body lifts off the seat and slowly walks across the floor to stand so close to him our legs touch. Heat radiates up from the spot they touch to my aching pussy. Aching for a glance, a touch, a feel. He has bewitched me, need and lust overriding logic.

"Everlee," he pants, eyes looking up at me, wanting.

"Callum," I whisper back, not moving. My heart feels like it's pounding a hole through my chest and breaking my ribs at the same time.

"This isn't a good idea." The tips of his fingers run up the back of my leg, just behind the knee, causing it to buckle.

"Horrible." My right-hand rubs along the side of his cheek, pressing into his hairline.

"But I can't stop thinking about you."

"Samesies." Stupid. Why did I say that?

A smile tugs on his lips. "Fuck it." His other hand grabs my other leg and pulls me towards him and my hand reflexively grabs the other side of his cheek, holding him in place. Our lips are less than an inch apart, pausing to give the other person the chance to back out before this line is crossed. I give him two seconds, that's all, before I close the distance and press my lips against his. His hands rove over my ass and up to my lower back, pressing me to him before he hooks them around my hips and pushes me down on his lap.

A moan escapes when I feel his hard cock pressing at my entrance through our pants.

His tongue pushes its way in past my lips and I let him. Goddess, do I let him. Kissing him makes my head feel like it's in the clouds and I'm spinning. My hands wrap around the back of his head, holding him to me as I grind my hips on him, desperate to feel his cock inside of me. It's been months and my pussy is desperate.

He pushes me away. "Everlee. We need to stop."

"Yep," I dive back in, pressing my lips to his and continue to rock on him. My clit is so sensitive right now, I'm about to come from the friction alone. "You feel so good."

"You've not felt anything yet." His hands grab my hips and lift me off his lap and twist to sit me on the desk. His arm sweeps across the desk, knocking its contents onto the ground.

"The books." Why the fuck am I worried about the books right now?

He chuckles, "They're fine." Then loops his fingers into the hem of my pants and pulls them down in one quick motion, exposing my glistening wet pussy to him. He looks at it in appreciation. "Goddamn it's beautiful."

He leans forward and plants soft kisses on the inside of my knee and I moan out, slapping my hands on the desk behind me for support and arch my back.

He growls as he slides out of the chair onto his knees and pushes the chair away. "Mine."

His words elicit another moan as my stomach tightens. This man. His looks. His words. They're going to make me come before he even touches me and my goddess, he's going to touch me. He wants my pussy as much as I want him to want it.

His lips trail kisses further up the inside of my leg and I'm a writhing, wriggling mess, anticipation tightening my core to the point it hurts.

"Callum," I cry out as his lips hover just above my pussy, as his warm breath dances across it like smoke over a flame. My fingers latch into his hair and I hold him, waiting. I want to take him right now, press his face to my pussy and make him fucking eat like he's never eaten before, but I wait. I need to know he wants it, because I've never felt that before.

"Everlee," he whispers, his voice broken.

Our eyes meet for a second before he leans in, so agonizingly slow tears nearly form on the rims of my eyes. His tongue swipes up and the sound he makes causes a shiver to run down my entire body. At the same time, our bodies in perfect synchronicity grab at each other to pull us closer. His hands wrap around my ass and pull me to the edge of the desk, while my hands grab and hold him to my pussy.

"Oh my Goddess!" I cry out, staring at the ceiling.

"Shirt!" he commands.

Obeying, I quickly release his hair and yank my shirt off, tossing it to the ground. His tongue leaves my pussy for just a second so he can admire my body. He saw it before in the shower, but not like this. Not fully wanting. Not his to do with what he wants.

He goes back down and pulses his tongue in, then slides it out, running it over my clit, before slipping a finger in.

"Callum!" My legs lift to his shoulders and my ankles clasp together, locking in place.

"Callum," a voice booms from the door, and we both freeze.

No! I was so close.

We both look at Jax standing there, hand on the frame, watching us. His eyes are glued on me, scouring every inch of my body. His eyes pulse a golden color, possessive. Feral.

Not breaking eye contact with Jax, I tell Callum, "Don't stop."

"You want him to watch?"

"Yes." It was a lie. I didn't want him to watch. I wanted him to join. I wanted to feel his hands and his lips on me while Callum made me come around his tongue. Just the thought of Jax's mouth on my breasts causes my pussy to pulse and a moan to escape.

Callum hesitates for only a second before he starts again. My right hand runs through his hair at the root and locks in, holding him to my pussy while my other stays firmly planted on the desk so I can watch Jax watch Callum tongue fuck me.

Rubbing my tongue over my lips, I suck it into my mouth and slowly scrape my teeth over it. Jax watches as the bulge in his pants grows. The immense feeling of satisfaction I have right now, knowing this turns him on, sets my body on fire even more.

My orgasm is building faster and faster, and threatening to be more intense than any I've ever had before. "Callum," I call out, moaning as I rock onto his face as his tongue spears into me. Jax twitches his hands, unmoving as he watches, but I know his cock is aching. It's pressing at his waistband, begging for release- for freedom. Goddess, what I would give right now to feel it in my mouth. The thought of it sends another shiver down my spine. "Oh... Oh..."

Goddess, I want to fuck you.

I hear the words in my head, but I don't know who said them. Was it Callum? Jax? I heard the words, but I know neither of them spoke.

Jax's teeth scrape over his bottom lip as he stares at me through his hooded gaze. We break eye contact, as my head drops back and I let my orgasm claim me. I cry and moan out a string of words as every muscle in my body clenches. My pussy is pulsing and I don't want it to stop as tears trickle down my cheeks.

When my senses come back, I look at the door, but Jax is gone. Callum stands and grips the back of my neck and takes me in a hungry kiss, remnants of my sweetness still on his tongue. My hands ride under his shirt, feeling the ripples of his chest, before they move around to his back and run over two ridges. He lets out a growl, then jerks up straight, causing my hands to fall away from him.

He's panting heavily, eyes locked on mine. I feel like I've done something I shouldn't have, but I don't know what.

"We-"

The doorbell rings, and we both turn towards the open door to the office where Jax was, then look back at one another.

He holds his ear out, then his face falls. "Fuck."

"What?"

He looks at me, then wipes the back of his hands across his lips. "Samara is here."

CALLUM - DON'T LOSE THE UNDERWEAR

Fuck!

Stall! I command through the mindlink.

This is such the wrong fucking time for her to be here. What does she want? No doubt, she wants to get an update on where Everlee is. My eyes fall on her beautiful body, still sprawled on the desk- on *my* desk- with her pussy still glistening.

My goddess, she tasted divine. I could live on my knees in front of her.

"Where's Callum?" Samara asks from downstairs.

"He'll be here in just a moment. He's in the library," Jax says with an obvious strain in his voice.

My gaze falls on Everlee. I need to get her out of here. Fortunately for us, while Djinn can shapeshift, they don't have super speed, smell, or hearing that other shifters have. They can just grant wishes for unknowing victims.

When I bend over, my still half hard cock presses awkwardly against my stomach. I grab her pants and hand them to her. "Put these on and follow me."

She slides off the desk and slips them on. "My underwear. Where's my underwear?" She looks around on the floor.

"They were with your pants."

"*We can just go to the library and meet there,*" she suggests.

"*No, here is fine. He's on his way.*"

"*He wouldn't be trying to hide a true fae in there, would he?*"

She's welcome to come up here, I mindlink Jax.

"*No, he's not. Would you like to go look?*"

"*You want to share your house with me?*"

"*We aren't hiding anything.*"

"*I'd love a look.*"

"Let's go. We don't have time to find them. Samara's on her way up."

"Where the fuck am I going to go, Callum?" she whisper-yells at me.

My fingers slide over the bindings of the books until I find the right one. *The Cask of Amontillado.* I pull it out, revealing a small button inset on the shelf. When I press it, the click of the lock releases.

"A hidden room?" Everlee asks, eyes wide with excitement.

"Not your tomb."

Her brows furrow for a second before she looks at the book in my hand.

A cool gust of wind hits us in the face as the seal for the door is broken and the entire bookcase swings out.

"She's on her way. Hurry down the stairs. We will get you when it's safe."

She ducks behind the wall and looks at me, giving me a quick kiss on the lips, and my stomach tightens. When she pulls away, I watch her descend the dark stairway before voices down the hall spring me to life.

Quickly moving, I close the bookshelf door, move my seat back under my desk, and pick up as many things as I can off the floor. In the heat of the moment, clearing the contents of my desk seemed very much needed and romantic, but the aftermath... Papers litter the floor. Mostly, my research around true fae and their powers. It's been so long since I've been around them that I've forgotten so much.

Forgotten?

Made myself forget.

After I buried Aleida at the Cliffs of Morgai that one night, I waited. I waited for weeks, months, years and nothing. Thoughts of failure slowly seeped in and I blamed myself for the death of the entire species. I wasn't the one moving through the towns and torching their places, but I should have been more proactive. I should have been watching and following the patterns of the Hunters. Seen their growing numbers and anger. Stopped the dark fae who were twisting the minds of these feeble mundanes, putting fear and hate in their heart. No. I was too concerned with other things and I let my people down. My family. The ones who took me in and saved my life.

"Hello?" Samara says, poking her head in, looking around the room.

"Over here," I say, crouching on the floor by my desk.

"What happened in here?" she laughs, and again my body cringes in pain.

"Frustration."

Sexual frustration, maybe, Jax pokes through the mindlink.

"So you haven't found her yet?" Samara asks thoughtfully.

There's only one group of vampires that know we have her, and I don't know if they've said anything.

EVERLEE – MAKING A DEAL WITH A RIPPER

It's dark.

Too dark.

I can't see my hand in front of my face.

Did he forget I can't see in the dark? Is that something I'm supposed to get? I should know, but I haven't gotten to that part in the book yet.

Flashbacks of me on his desk and his mouth between my legs flip through my mind like a movie. His tongue. The way it moved with perfection. Butterflies swirl in my stomach.

Voices echo just behind the door.

Samara... she's laughing.

Using the hard stone wall as a guide, I follow the steps down one at a time and notice there's a slight spiral in the shape. Maybe it's a good thing I can't see shit, because the wall to my left seems to have fallen away, which could mean the center is open. My heart thumps harder and harder. Well, it would be awkward as fuck if I fell to my death while they were trying to hide me from the person who wants to kill me. Well, I assume that's what she wants to do... eventually. I imagine she would try to extract as much out of me as she can.... What, I don't know, but I sure as shit don't want to find out.

The images of me, tied to a device with my limbs chained and tubes draining my blood, play on repeat.

A moment later, the stairs end and I'm walking on flat stone. Reaching my hand out tentatively, I find the wall to my left has reappeared. I look up to see how far I've come, but still can't see shit. I would have thought my eyes would have adjusted by now, but there is literally not an ounce of light in here. For all I know, it was a short flight of stairs even though it seemed longer because it took me forever, testing each step before I took it.

Something I should be doing now. Fuck! I walk straight into a door, my face taking the brunt of it.

"Fuck!" I groan, then quickly put my hand over my mouth. Shit! What if she heard me? Heard the bookcase yell fuck?

Damn it!

A warmth tickles my nose and when I swipe it away, I realize it's blood. Quickly, running my fingers over my nose, I try to feel if it's broken, but it doesn't seem to be. Just bleeding.

What am I supposed to do now? Callum didn't give me instructions for when I get to the bottom of the stairs. My hands slide over the walls, feeling for any sort of button or lever. When I don't find one, I push on all the stones, thinking there's some hidden stone, but nothing shifts.

What the fuck, Callum?

I'm scared to bang on the door because I don't know what's on the other side, and I don't want the noise echoing back up to the library. Why would he let her come up there? Oh Goddess, what if she finds my underwear? How's he going to explain that one?

Nerves crackle through my skin like electricity. I feverishly run my hand over the door in front of me and find a handle.

Fucking Everlee. Why didn't you check that first?

I twist, cautiously, and push the door open and low light pours into the small space, as well as hushed voices I don't recognize. There are several females talking and a few men.

Where am I?

Did Callum know where he was sending me?

I step through the door and find myself in a storage room of some sort. There's a hint of light filtering in from underneath the door, but after coming from complete darkness, it seems like an abundance.

Fully stepping into the room, I look around and find shelves with a mixture of things. Mostly plastic bags, and tubes, some chains, locks, metal bars.

Where am I?

I push the door closed, which is on the back side of a shelf. Even though it appears to be weighted down with a lot of boxes, it glides along the floor easily and clicks locked with a thunk.

Trying to force my heartbeat to slow down, I take several slow and deep breaths with my hand on the handle. Building up the courage, I twist and push the door open.

What the fuck?

It's a large open room with lights on in only half of it, so the left side is too dark to see anything. Sitting in a chair in the corner is Emmett, talking to three women and a man who are also sitting in chairs along the back wall. They have tubes coming out of their arms hooked to blood bags, with trays and a drink beside each of them.

Emmett looks at me, then at the four individuals, before his eyes snap back to me. His eyes settle on my face. On the blood that is still trickling out.

Fuck.

His eyes pulse at the same time his body becomes ridged and his hands grip tightly onto the handles of the chair he's sitting in.

The four individuals don't notice the tension in the room, or the micro movements of Emmett trying to restrain his bloodlust.

"You need to go," Emmett says through gritted teeth, eye set on me. The girls stare at me casually with a smirk on their face.

"I don't think he's talking to me," I retort, suddenly feeling a little jealous. Jealous he can be around them without wanting to drain them. Jealous they get a relationship with him, even if they are just donors. What's wrong with me?

"But..." the one pretty blonde pouts. "E?"

E? That's not his name. That's a nickname. One that Jax uses. Another twinge of jealousy hits. Is this where Jax and Emmett have been today? With them? I have absolutely no right to be upset or jealous, but that doesn't change the fact I am. The way Jax was looking at me earlier with Callum. The way it made me feel.

I want him.

I want them.

He slowly turns his head to her. "Go," he says, barely moving his lips. Do they know he's a vampire? Do they know right now that he wants to feed on them? On me? That he could move with the swiftness of a jaguar and drain them in seconds?

"Emmett, what's wrong?" She sits up, alarmed and confused.

He rubs his hands over his face and covers his mouth like he's frustrated. "I will call you when I need you." They pull the needle out of their arm and place it on the tray beside them and take the band-aid laying there and put in on the inside of their elbow. Something that seems to be practiced. Something they've done hundreds of times.

Acting like drones, they stand up and walk in a line and stand in front of him. He grabs each of their faces and stares them in the eyes and repeats the same thing before they leave through a door behind him. "You may feel a little lightheaded from giving blood today, so be sure to drink plenty of fluids and rest. We had a good time talking about Greenlee Marie's new album, and it was just the five of us after Jax left. You did not see anyone else and you will not talk about coming here today *to anyone*."

He walks them out and keeps his hand on the handle, gripping it tightly. "I meant for you to leave too," he growls.

"I can't." I take a step back.

"You should."

"Samara is here. Callum sent me down here. I couldn't see and hit the door, hence the..."

"Blood." The word slides off his tongue like a sultry mistress.

He's still not looking at me and I know it's taking everything he has to control his bloodlust. If I thought I could run and get away from him, I would. If I thought running back through the storage room and trying to open the hidden door would save me, I would.

"I don't want to hurt you."

"I don't want you to, either."

He chuckles and slowly turns around. "You're brave."

"Maybe a little stupid, too."

His lips quirk up in a smile. "Back up some more."

Without waiting, I take several steps back, at the same time he presses himself into the corner.

"You aren't bad," I whisper.

"You don't know me."

"I know enough. You've saved me once already, and you don't want to act now."

"I can't control myself. I couldn't." He shakes his head. "Samara... I went to her and asked for her help. Asked her to take the bloodlust away. She took away everything. My desire for blood, the desire to feed. She took it all away. And then you... your blood." He takes a step forward, eyes narrowing to thin slits.

"Emmett."

"I just want to taste it. Just a small taste."

"You wouldn't be able to stop."

"I... I'll want to."

He takes another step forward.

"Emmett!" I bark, hoping to break through his fixation.

Silence.

Another step forward, so I take another step back.

His tongue runs over his teeth. "It's been so long since I've wanted to feed. Your blood. It's driving me wild."

"E!"

Silence.

"What if I draw some blood for you? Put it in a bag."

He pauses.

Fuck. What am I saying? It seems to have slowed him down.

"You can... you can taste my blood, but not feed on me. We can teach you control. I will teach you control."

His eyes look at me. "Teach me?

"Yes. Yes."

"It doesn't matter. You blood is the only blood I want. No one else's smells like yours. It all tastes the same. Like nothing. But yours... I can smell the sweetness on it. The floral notes, the earthy undertones. It will be..."

"Horrible," I spit out, like my words could convince him otherwise.

I take another step back and the next set of lights click on, illuminating the next part of the room. It takes a minute for my brain to catch up with what my eyes are seeing. A large cage with cuffs on the left. A transition cage? For Jax? Across from it is a large X with leather straps at each end of the X and just to its side is a wooden chair with a U shape type seat. Are these sex toys? What will I see if I keep going deeper into the room?

"Emmett..." I look between him and the cage. "I have an idea."

He pauses, the distance between us less than a breath apart if he were to lunge.

"Do you want to learn control?"

"Yes," he pants.

"I will give you my blood, but you have to get in there." I point at the cage.

The wheels in his head are turning as the anguish and pain on his face grows.

"You're a good man. You saved me. You don't want to kill me... and that's what you will do if you try to feed on me. You won't be able to stop and you will kill me. You're good. You saved me. You aren't a monster." I feel like a broken record, but I don't know what else to say or do. I'm giving him what he wants. What he's struggling against...

He shakes his head no, and the soft ground we've been standing on starts to crumble. Fuck, crumble? It washes away like a goddamn avalanche.

"I'm sorry," he mumbles, then rushes at me.

The last thing I remember is his hand clasping around my throat.

CALLUM - WISER THAN THE DJINN

▪ ▪

SAMARA WALKS INTO THE room slowly, looking around like she expects something to jump out at her. I finish stacking the papers up and shuffle them into a neat pile, then stand, sitting the papers on the edge of my desk.

She's staring at me like she's waiting for a response.

Right. Have we found her?

"We found her."

Jax and Knox both scrunch their foreheads, staring at me.

"But she got away."

Samara laughs condescendingly. "She got away. She's a nobody. How did she defeat a dragon, a selkie, a werewolf, and a vampire?"

Rage surges through me, so I clamp my hands on the edge of the desk.

"Care to take a seat," Knox offers.

She looks coolly over her shoulder at him, then continues walking around the library. "Speaking of... where's Emmett?"

"He's out," Jax says.

"Out?"

CRASH.

Echoes of screams and bars crashing together sound through the house. Faint, but there.

My eyes go wide as they fall on Jax and Knox, who also heard it. Fortunately, Samara doesn't seem to hear.

Where's Everlee? Jax commands through mindlink.

I sent her downstairs via the library wall.

Fuck! That's where Emmett is.

What the fuck is he doing down there?

What do you think? We couldn't very well setup his blood bank in the middle of the fucking kitchen with your precious Everlee here! Jax barks.

"Hello?" Samara asks. "Emmett's out?"

"Yes. He's getting supplies for dinner."

Hopefully not Everlee, Knox chimes.

Shut the fuck up, Knox. You aren't helping, Jax snipes.

Sorry just trying to bring light to the situation.

You won't be trying to bring light to it when you have to pry her lifeless body from Emmett's grip, or deal with the fall-out and guilt he's going to have afterward, Jax says.

"Would you like to stay?" Jax asks. "For dinner?"

Samara's finger glides over the spines of the books on the bookshelf and her finger pauses on the Cask of Amontillado. Is she playing with us?

"Not tonight, but I will take a rain check," she says and continues walking.

I let out the breath I was holding. It's a proven fact that if you hold your breath in a moment of suspense and angst, it actually slows the event down, allowing your mind to process.

Not. It just makes your lungs hurt, because they're crying out for oxygen.

"So you don't have her? You aren't hiding her here."

"Emmett. You need to stop." Everlee's voice filters through the air.

At least she's fighting, Knox encourages.

We need to get Samara gone, Jax urges.

"I'll be right back. I need to go check on something," Knox says, thumbing over his shoulder.

"What could be more important than filling me in on how you had her and then lost her?"

"You're right. It can wait." *I hope.*

"Please sit," I encourage. Her moving around the room is making me anxious.

And there. That's when I see it.

Them.

Everlee's panties.

They're off to the side of the room near the other bookcase. How in the fuck did they get over there? Did they grow wings and fly?

Everlee's panties. By the bookcase. Your ten o'clock.

Fucking hell, Jax groans.

You fucked her? Knox asks.

No.

Is that really the most important thing to be focused on right now? Jax scolds, then moves across the room towards the panties.

Samara moves to the bench by the window and flips over the book. "Reading about the true fae?"

"Yes," Knox answers. "I'm trying to learn about them so we can track her."

Samara tilts her head up, studying all of us. "So tell me again that she's not hiding here somewhere."

Taking a deep breath, I explain what happened at the restaurant with Jordan and his band of dreary men, then add... "And as we were leaving, she used that light ball on us. Knocked us out and when we came to, she was gone."

"Gone?"

I don't hear anything anymore, Jax says, worry thick in his voice.

"We tracked her all around town for hours, then came back here and figured we could learn as much about her as possible."

"I see."

"Have your other scouts found any trace of her?"

"No. It's like she just completely vanished, which makes me wonder if someone found her and is hiding her for their own selfish reasons."

"They'd have to be pretty stupid to do that."

"They would have to be *very* stupid."

She stares at us for a minute, then sets the book back down and continues walking around the rest of the room. By the time she gets to Jax, he has his foot planted firmly on Everlee's underwear and tucked out of view.

She stands by the door to the library. "Tell Emmett I hate I missed him."

"Are you sure you don't want to stay for dinner? I'm sure he's preparing something amazing."

She smiles, but it doesn't reach her eyes.

"I'd love to, but I need to check in on everyone else. I really must find this girl. I fear she may be a great danger to all of us. Unbridled power."

"Fortunately for us, she doesn't seem to know how to use it."

"Yes. How fortunate."

"Let me walk you out."

"Thank you. That would be lovely."

My fists clench into balls, then release as I move around the desk.

Go to Everlee now, I command. "Right this way."

"You have a lovely home. Shame, I've only been able to see parts of it."

"Would you care for a tour?" If she's testing me, she will not win. I may not be older than her, but I'm definitely wiser. She was trapped in some totem for hundreds of years and when she was found and freed, she unleased hell on all of those around her and hid her totem, so no one could ever find it and put her back in.

"Thank you for the offer. Perhaps next time I come over."

"Just let us know before you show up so we can have it in tip-top shape."

"No," she laughs, her grimy like fingers brushing against my arm. "Where's the fun in that? I want to see how you all really live. No filters."

How is she? How's Everlee?

Silence.

JAX - FEELING... THINGS

<hr>

As soon as the click of the front door opens, I run over to the bookshelf, toss the book on the floor, and press the button. I take the first three steps, then jump down the center of the spiral staircase and land with a hard thud on the floor. My heart is pounding out of my chest. I can hear soft gasps of air and know what I'm about to walk into, but just hope I'm not too late.

Goddamn it, Everlee!

Rage sears through me like hot lava.

Ignoring the crash of supplies as I push the door open, I run into the middle of the floor and see Emmett huddled inside the locked cage. Everlee is slumped on the outside, against the wall, weak with her wrist on the floor.

"What the fuck happened?" I growl out, racing over to her.

Her eyes are open, but she's weak. In that space between life and death.

"I said what the fuck happened?"

"She... she... wanted to help me." Emmett wipes her blood from his lips.

"You almost killed her!"

Everlee slowly puts her hand on mine. "He stopped. He did good."

"Fuck that."

Emmett flinches out of the corner of my eye, but I don't feel guilty. Maybe I would if she wasn't laying pale in my arms right now.

"Get over here!" I bark at Emmett. "Give her your blood. Heal her!" I nearly cry out.

Emmett looks up at me, startled, bites his wrist, then crawl-slides over the floor and sticks his wrist through the bars of the cage.

"I'm fine," she whispers.

"Shut up." I gaze down at her and brush the hair out of her eyes.

Fuck!

I'm worried about her and I don't want to be. This isn't how it's supposed to be. I'm not supposed to care about her. I hate that she's here. In this house. In this room. In my arms.

A growl rips through my chest that is low and gravelly. My wolf. I feel him. Inside of me, pacing around like a caged animal. My eyes fall back to Everlee in shock. Is it her? Is she doing this to us?

She lets out a meek little cough and rolls onto her side.

I snatch Emmett's bleeding wrist and hold it over her mouth. "Drink."

"No."

"Fucking drink, or I will make you."

Her eyes set on me full of fire, but it fades quickly. She's in there, fighting.

"Drink!" I growl again, shifting her in my arms so her head falls back.

She grabs his wrist and holds it to her lips. At first she resists, but like a shot of epinephrine, her eyes shoot open and her fingers clamp tightly around his wrist and she holds him to her, sucking. After a few minutes, her body flushes red, and she moans and wiggles in my lap.

"Everlee, that's enough."

She shakes her head and continues to suck.

"Everlee!"

Emmett's arm that is holding him up goes out. He won't stop her, even if it kills him. He feels guilty for doing this to her and feels this is what he deserves.

"Fuck! I can't deal with you two!" I rip Emmett's arm from her mouth and he scurries away from her and sits in the corner. She looks up at me with blood on her lips and fire in her eyes.

"Holy fuck. What is that?"

"Vampire blood."

"I feel..." she rubs her hands over her body. "Oh my Goddess, I feel... everything. Every hair that moves with the air and I hear... your heart..." She presses her hand to my chest, "It's beating so hard. Were you worried about me?"

"No," I spit out.

"And fuck... I'm horny. Holy shit," she says, rubbing her hands over her body and then between her legs.

"Should have told her of the side effects," Emmett mumbles through the bars.

"This is amazing." Her hand slides up her chest, exposing her breasts, and I feel my cock twitch in my pants.

"Pull your shirt down," I bark, yanking her hand away.

"That's not what you want? I feel your hard cock pressed at my ass right now. I want it inside of me. I want you to fuck me. I saw you earlier."

"It's not *hard* for you." *Yeah, that didn't sound very convincing.*

She looks at Emmett in the cage. "You want to fuck him?"

"It's not you."

She smiles knowingly. "I'd love to watch you two. Would you let me?"

Emmett shifts uneasily. I know he's as hard as I am right now.

"No. This feeling is temporary... it only lasts for a few minutes and when it wears off, you're going to crash."

"This isn't temporary." She runs her hand up my chest.

My wolf lets out a low growl of appreciation. He likes this. Likes her. Fuck! Maybe it was a good thing I haven't been able to feel him. I forgot what a selfish prick he can be.

That's rich, since you're trying to ignore me because you don't want to admit you want her, he snipes back.

Wolf?

Hello, friend.

Shut the fuck up.

The wolf presses his face to the ground with his ass up in the air. He's excited. He's missed me. Could I shift?

No. Don't do it. Not yet. Too weak.

You'll be fine.

Not me. You.

Another growl escapes, this one full of anger and frustration.

She's evil. Everlee. She's torturing me. Giving me a taste of what I want. What I most desire. Dangling it like it's a carrot in front of me, but always out of reach. I had given up on feeling or talking to my wolf ever again, but here he is. I've felt it several times now. Inklings, hints, but I was able to push it away until now. The feeling is too overwhelming.

"I... I... don't feel so good," she mumbles.

"I told you... you're going to crash." I stand, holding her in my arms. She's so light.

"Tell her I'm sorry," Emmett says, pressing his back and head against the wall.

"You stopped Emmett. We will keep trying." She smiles and reaches back.

"The fuck you will."

Her head rolls up and lies on my chest, her head nestled under my chin. "We'll be fine."

"You almost died."

"Careful. Some may think you care about me."

"I don't care about you," I snap. "I don't want the guilt to hurt Emmett."

"Always Emmett, huh?" Her hand slides up and curls around the back of my neck.

Damn this woman.

Callum and Knox meet me at the top of the first set of stairs in the kitchen. "What happened?"

Everlee moans, but is incoherent.

"She's fine. She's coming off Emmett's blood."

"Emmett?" Callum asks.

"He's fine. He's locked in my cage. I don't know the story, but she was trying to help him. She gave him her wrist, and he nearly drained her. But when I got down there, he had stopped. On his own, I presume. Just not soon enough. She was mumbling something about him doing good and them trying again."

"That's not going to happen," Knox says.

"No shit."

"Yes. Need to... help him," Everlee murmurs with her eyes still closed.

"Get her to bed. We'll talk about this tomorrow morning," Callum commands.

"Samara?"

"She's gone for now."

"Does she suspect anything?"

"Hard to say. I would be prepared for surprise visits, though."

"Ok. I'm going to get her in bed."

"Sounds good. She's going to be ok, though?" Callum asks, with a hint of worry in his voice.

"Yea, she'll be fine. She's a fighter and stubborn as shit."

"Sounds like someone else I know." Callum pumps his eyebrows at me.

"Shut it."

"Man, why does he just get shut it, but I get the whole shut the fuck up!"

"Because you're more annoying."

"I think it's because you like me better."

"Keep telling yourself that." I laugh and shake my head as I walk to her bedroom, then call back down. "Knox. Can you get Emmett?"

"Aye, Aye, Captain my captain." He whispers to Callum, "He asked me, not you... because he likes me better. He just won't let himself admit it."

I'm still smiling at his dumbass when I get her to her bedroom.

I sit her on the edge of the bed and pull her comforter down, then carry her over and slide her in.

"Take my clothes off," she mumbles, half asleep.

"What?"

"Don't like... clothes on me... when I... sleep."

Damn it.

Grabbing her legs, I spin her around and hook my fingers around her pants and drag them off. Her skin is smooth... and...

Focus, Jax.

You don't want to fuck her.

Tell that to your cock, my wolf chimes.

You're back.

I never left.

Focus, Jax.

I finish tugging her pants off and nearly fall over when I see her beautiful pussy right there in front of me. I forgot her panties are in my pocket from earlier. She must have forgotten too, because she casually looks down then up to me, a soft pink tinging her cheeks.

"I'll grab you another pair," I offer, hurrying to the dresser behind me. It takes me two drawers before I find the one with her underwear in it. Quickly, but gently, I slip them up her legs and over her perfect ass. When my fingers graze her hips, she lets out an appreciative moan, even though her eyes are still closed. This woman and her noises, I sigh. I pull her to sitting so I can take her shirt off, gently pulling it over her head. Her breasts are on full display and my cock twitches again. Ignoring the need to wrap my mouth around her pink nipples, I grab her clothes and walk them over to the chaise by the fireplace.

When I walk back over, she has turned her body, so she's lying on her side, with the covers still by her ankles. Grabbing the comforter, I tug it up over her body, my fingertips lightly grazing the side of her hips. She lets out a moan and shifts her body, then reaches her hand behind her and grabs my wrist. "Stay," she whimpers. Gone is the fire, and present is the need. The need to feel safe.

Damn it! I growl out again.

Before I know what I'm doing, I slide out of my shoes, remove my pants and shirt, and I'm climbing into bed with her. I wrap my arms around her and she scoots back into my body, molding into me.

Fuuuuccckk. This is not supposed to be happening.

"Thanks," she murmurs and then she's out.

My wolf is purring with desire inside, curled up and relaxing. I plant a soft kiss on the back of her head and close my eyes.

EVERLEE - VAMPIRE SEX DREAMS

His rough and calloused hand slides up my body, starting at my hips, moving over my stomach and up to my breasts. He rolls my nipple roughly between his thumb and forefinger before moving to the other. A pant escapes as my body tenses, eager to feel more as my ass grinds back into his hard length. My pussy clenches at the promise of what's coming.

Me.

Hopefully, with his cock so deep inside of me that my lungs will feel it.

Another moan escapes as his lips find their place on the most sensitive spot on my neck. He's rough. Teeth exposed and sucking hard enough to leave a mark for days, but I don't care. Let him mark me.

My hand glides behind me, tangling through his hair, holding him to me for a second longer before I turn into him, taking his lips with mine.

Jax.

His dark eyes study me, full of lust and fire.

He licks his lips before they crash to mine, taking me in an unapologetically rough kiss. His tongue pushes its way in and my body responds, bending and angling up into him. He grabs my leg and pulls it over his, so his cock is lined up at my entrance.

"Oh my..." I pant between kisses.

Straddling his lap, I look at his cock laying against his stomach, sitting between my pussy.

"You want it?" he asks.

"Very much."

"Good, because it wants you too." He thrusts his hips up, bucking off the bed and sending his cock through my slickness. "Ride it."

Rocking my hips back and forth, we watch as my arousal coats the outside of his cock. My hands glide and push up his ridged abs and over the tattoos stained on his skin.

"You feel so good," he moans as he grips my hips and holds me down while he continues to rock.

"I want you inside of me. I want to feel you stretch me." I rotate my hips up to the head of his cock and slide back down, letting my clit rub against him. My eyes flicker behind my lids as my orgasm builds.

"I want to taste you first." In a quick motion, he thrusts his hips into the air and flips us over so he's on top of me. "Fucking perfection," he groans as his lingering gaze rakes over my body. His hands cup both of my breasts while his cock continues to slide up my pussy.

He leans down and clamps his mouth around my breast and runs his tongue over my nipple before he sucks hard. Eager for more, my back arches off the bed and presses my breast further into his mouth. His finger leaves a wake of goosebumps as he slides it down my body, around my clit, then presses it inside of me. Rough, claiming.

White hot pleasure rips through me as I ride the building wave inside.

"You're so tight," he murmurs against my ear, adding another finger. He was stretching me, prepping me.

"Everlee..." his voice sounds different.

"Jax," I moan out, trying to hold on to this moment.

"Everlee."

I could feel it slipping away.

No. No. No.

"Everlee!" The harshness of my name pulls me the rest of the way out of my dream.

When I open my eyes, I'm laying on my back with one hand in my underwear and Jax propped up on one elbow watching me, eyes on fire, lips parted.

"What?" I shake my head and slide my wet fingers out of my underwear. "Oh... shit."

Jax's hard length presses at my hip, but he doesn't look like he's in the mood to fuck me. He looks pissed.

"I'm sorry. I..."

"Fucking Emmett," he growls, rolling out of bed.

"Emmett?" I flinch and sit up.

Jax walks over to the chaise and tugs his pants and shirt on at a speed I don't think I've ever seen before.

"I don't understand."

"His blood. It's inside of you. He's fucking with your dreams."

"He can do that?"

"Yes. You two are connected until his blood is out of your system."

Rage fills me as I throw off the covers and jump out of bed.

I don't know if it's because he gave me that fucked up dream, or because he did and I wasn't able to finish. My body is so primed right now and my panties are so wet it feels like I'm walking around with a fucking pool strapped to my ass.

"Where is he?" I bark.

Jax looks at me in shock.

"Stop and tell me where he is!" My body feels like an inferno- hot with equal parts rage and needing release.

Hell, I've needed a release for a while now, and this was the last straw. I don't like to be manipulated or toyed with.

"His room," he concedes, looking down.

Throwing the door open, I stomp down the hall until I'm at his door. Without knocking, I push the door open and feel gusts of wind as Knox and Callum stand behind Jax at the door.

EMMETT - TOE TO TOE WITH A TRUE FAE

WELL, THIS WON'T BE good. She's yelling from her room and only getting closer. The book I'm reading falls onto my stomach and I just wait for the hurricane that is Everlee to storm in. She's not like most girls I've met. And I have met my fair share. She's a little spitfire who routinely seems to get in over her head, but manages to find a way out. She doesn't let our age or power deter or impress in her, and probably my most favorite thing is she doesn't care about Callum's alpha status within the house. She does what she wants and screw anyone else.

My door bursts open seconds later, so I grab my book and reach over to put it on the nightstand.

"It's not my fault," I say before she can say anything.

"You can fuck with my head all you want, but sex dreams? That's fucking off limits unless I can finish."

I can't help but smile. She doesn't mind the sex dreams. "Technically, that's Jax's fault. He woke you up. The sexual tension between you two is..." My eyes get big. "So I was just helping it along."

"What the fuck, E?" Jax mumbles, but my attention is back to Everlee as she races across the room in a fury and climbs onto the bed, mounting me.

"Technically. You want to get technical?"

Typically, I'd be worried that I was going to lash out and want to attack her, but earlier... in the cage... she did something to me.

Sure, I wanted to taste her. And my goddess, when I did... she was a dream. Her blood is orgasmic. When I lunged after her, my fingers wrapped around her throat and I saw the lights going out in her eyes. I didn't want to hurt her, but the monster inside was trying to overpower me, overpower us.

For fear of killing her, I tossed her to the ground like a rag doll and watched her lay there lifeless. I was so mad at myself for giving into temptation, for not being strong enough to stop myself. Her body started glowing, and then she opened her eyes. She nearly floated to a standing position and looked at me, her eyes a brilliant, glowing blue. It was absolutely mesmerizing. Like she was transforming before my eyes.

She landed with a soft thud on the floor and a small ball formed in her hands. She pushed it out towards me and all I could do was watch it as it sailed through the air and hit me in the chest.

It burned.

It burned like a white-hot flame, sent straight from the sun.

The pain knocked me on my ass and sent me skittering backwards into Jax's transition cage.

She had a slight snicker on her face, and when she spoke, this voice that was deeper than hers came out, warning me. Warning all of us.

A moment later, Everlee collapsed on the floor and when she opened her eyes again, she was back and exhausted.

She glanced at me in the cage and was completely confused. I realized she didn't remember what happened.

She saw the large red spot on my chest just before I collapsed. The light ball seemed to have lingering effects, which is good to know for the future. By the time I was born, it was after the Great Fall, so I know nothing about the true fae. Hence, why I picked up a book in Callum's extensive library this evening.

"Well?" she presses, looking at me.

While I still want to suck her blood, the monster inside of me knows our place where Everlee is concerned. She's strong even if she doesn't know it. I can trust that even though the true fae within her lies dormant unless needed, it will come out to protect her. I don't need to be scared for both of us anymore.

"I'm sorry." I was just trying to do something nice for her, give her the release she needs and nudge Jax into taking what he wants. I see it on his face even now, even as she's mounted on me. He wants her, but he won't let himself.

"You're sorry. Fucking with people's dreams..."

"I was just trying to give you what you wanted."

"I don't want the dream of sex. I don't want the dream of a cock filling me. I want the actual goddam thing pressing inside of me. Stretching me."

Spitfire.

She slowly rocks on me, teasing me. "Isn't that what you would want? To feel a hot, tight pussy hugging your cock? Sliding up and down until you come so fucking hard you see stars?" She rips the sheet off the bed and her eyes nearly bulge out of her head as she looks at my now hard cock laying on my stomach with the glints of metal pierced through it. There's a ring at the tip and several barbells pierced on the underside of my shaft.

It shocks most people when they first see it, because of my everyday dress. I had a bit of a wild side when I first turned and did some really wild shit. This being one of them, but I kept it because the men and women I've used them on seem to really like it. It's been a while, but she looks irresistible mounted on top of me, breasts out and a pussy so wet I can feel it through the thin fabric of her panties. And to smell her... it's like she's in heat right now.

"Fuck me," she whispers, and I don't know if it's a request or an exultation.

A smile pulls at my lips. This woman. I'm obsessed. It hasn't been very long, but something about her. I think because I know now, she can and will hurt me without reservation. It's like the monster inside of me knows that and is not pushing with her anymore. "Not what you expected?"

A switch in me flips, and I want her so fucking bad. I wanted her before, so many fucking times, but now... she's on my lap and we're both in need. The monster inside of me growls out, wanting too. Not to feed. No, he got his fill earlier.

When she found me in the cage and hurt, the guilt on her face was immediate. She wanted to help me, so she offered me her arm through the cage. She thought it would protect her that way, but it didn't.

Not completely.

She went on about how she can help me keep my humanity while I feed. She doesn't understand what it's like when I taste blood and want it. It's all-consuming.

The light ball injury on my chest wasn't healing. It felt like it was still there, slowly cutting away at the tissue, muscle, and bone within. Imbedding itself deeper and deeper.

I still refused until she stupidly found a piece of jagged metal on the cage and sliced her wrist across it. I'd like to think if I wasn't dying, I could have held out longer, but within seconds, like a moth to a flame, I was across the cage with her wrist cradled to my mouth.

When her blood touched my tongue, my entire world lit up like the fourth of July. It was the first time in nearly seventy years I fed on someone and her blood was like all of my favorite foods I'd been missing.

After a few minutes, I knew I needed to stop, but I couldn't. Not couldn't. I didn't want to. I was terrified this feeling would go away, and I'd never experience it again.

She called my name in warning several times and when I didn't stop, her blood started changing again. The flavors were fading away and her blood was becoming boiling hot.

It was enough to stop me.

I stopped.

I'm not stupid enough to admit I had self-control, rather I valued self-preservation and was fairly certain if I kept on drinking from her, I'd kill myself via her blood. It was like she was changing it. Weaponizing it.

The fact she can kill me... makes me feel safe with her, as baffling as it sounds. I can bring my whole self to the fuck and not fear hurting her.

"Were you planning on coming in here with your half naked body to taunt me and tease me, only to walk away leaving me wanting, like you are right now?" My fingers delicately glide up her arm then back down, and I see how she responds and fuck it's addicting. Goosebumps erupt across her skin and her perfectly pink nipples grow even harder, if that's possible. "Did you even think this through?"

She looks at me wide-eyed, not speaking.

"You prance around this house and you're making us fucking feral. Your scent is a goddamn wet dream for all of us, even though some can't admit it." I glance over her shoulder at Jax. "I was just trying to help you get what you wanted." Needing to smell all of her, I lean forward and inhale her scent, in the sweet spot on her neck, just under her ear, and my dick gets even harder. "Do you feel that? How hard my dick is for you?" My stomach muscles are clenching something fierce as need consumes me. "Just the smell of you lights my entire body on fire and when I tasted you earlier, your blood. Fuck me, it was so good." My hands glide down her arm and grab her hand, bringing it to my mouth. "Are these the fingers you were fucking yourself with before Jax woke you?" I breathe in the scent on her fingers, then slide them into my mouth. "So fucking good. I bet your come tastes as good as your blood."

Her pupils are so blown, her eyes are nearly black, and her chest is rapidly falling and rising with want.

"Touch yourself," I command without using my glamor on her. Just a simple request, because that's all it will take. I won't force her into anything, but I can also be a selfish bastard and right now I want to feel my cock inside of her and I know she wants it too. She may not have wanted it when she stormed in here, but the room has shifted along with her intentions.

"E," Jax warns.

Her eyes pulse with a hint of excitement at the realization they are still in the room and watching. Or maybe it's the fact Jax is watching. She seems to like to get under his skin and he just gave her exactly what she wants.

"I'm not doing anything to her. She's the one who came in here and climbed on my lap trying to prove a point, but I think she's changing her mind on what exactly she wants to get out of this little show of power."

Her eyes narrow at me as she realizes that she's lost control. "Fuck you."

A throaty laugh vibrates inside of my chest. "I know you want to. I can hear your heart beating out of your chest. I can feel your arousal seeping through your underwear onto my cock. I can almost taste your want on the air. Do you want me to fuck you, little fae?"

Her eyes grow wide because her brain wants to say no, but every other part of her body is screaming, fuck yes.

"E, that's enough," Jax warns again.

Her eyes pulse. Jax should know her well enough by now to know that she enjoys pressing his buttons, and this is a big fucking red one that says, press me! Press me!

The wheels in her mind are spinning and I swear if Jax speaks out against it one more time, she will be on my dick faster than a balloon pops.

"This is your decision. I'm not controlling you at all. Well, not on purpose. My blood does make you a little more horny and well, you were already spooled up ready to snap, so I can only imagine how you're feeling now with my cock throbbing underneath you."

Her teeth grit as she stares at me. One thrust of my hips, one touch on her skin, and that would seal the deal. But this needs to be her decision, not mine. I'm a selfish bastard who's wanted to sink my cock into her since she stood in our kitchen.

Glancing over her shoulder, Jax looks pissed, but harder than I've ever seen him. And Knox and Callum both have their hands resting on the outside of their pants, trying not to jack themselves off.

The room is deathly silent as we all just stare at her... waiting.

It feels like an hour has passed and then she rotates her hips on my cock, eyes still narrowed on me, but I don't move.

Her hand presses to my chest as she thrusts her hips slowly, the piercings on my cock rubbing against her clit. She closes her eyes for a moment, basking in the feel.

When she opens them, she looks at me.

"Fuck me."

EVERLEE - WHEN SEX DREAMS TURN INTO THE REAL THING

HE'S STARING AT ME. Waiting for an answer. This is not what I had planned when I barged into his room, but something about the way he's looking at me right now, combined with the need to release, is all it takes. It's been six months since I've felt a cock inside of me and that one wasn't all that impressive. This one... my mouth is like a dam ready to choke me on my drool, because it is large, hard, and pierced. And his eyes... they are drinking me up with want.

Emmett and I shared something downstairs earlier. I don't know what you would call it, but it was an understanding. We battled for dominance, each of us pushing the other to the brink and then we fed each other our blood. We are connected, at least for now, and perhaps that's what's driving these feelings... this need. I don't care what it is. I may care in the light of day, but right now, I'm selfish.

"Fuck me," I answer.

The words are barely out of my mouth, before he has me flipped over on the bed and pulling my panties off. The guys are at the door watching, and it turns me on even more.

"Are you sure you want this, love?" He smells near my neck, causing a shiver to move up my spine, hardening my nipples even more as his chest brushes against them.

"Don't make me ask again," I grind out.

He chuckles as he moves down my body. "Yes ma'am."

"E," Jax groans by the door and my eyes catch his. His face has a mixture of expressions. One of concern, one of anger, and one of wanting.

Emmett waves him off as he works his way down my body. His mouth planting gentle kisses on the inside of my leg.

"I don't think this is a good idea," he warns, body tense.

"You need to shut up and join him, or lea-" My moans cut off the last word as Emmett's tongue presses inside of me. "Fucking fuck." My hands clamp to his head as my hips buck off the bed. I was close before and just the brush of his tongue across my clit with a gentle suck has me seeing stars and clenching around his tongue, but my eyes stay locked on Jax. Something about the way he watches me when I'm orgasming makes it even more intense.

"Your come tastes better than your blood," he groans against my skin, slipping a finger in, pushing my orgasm even further.

"Did she taste this good earlier, Callum?" Emmett asks, swiping his tongue up from base to top.

"She tastes like heaven," he murmurs from the door, his hand rubbing slowly over the fabric of his pants.

I hold my hand out to him, "Feed me your cock, while he fucks me."

Knox whimpers, knees buckling.

"You can join too."

"Thank you, Poseidon!" Knox rejoices, throwing his clasped hands in the air, causing me to laugh for a second before I'm back to moaning out Emmett's name.

Callum is climbing on the bed a second later, tossing his boxers on the ground and waiting for instruction.

I feel like I'm in some sex crazed dream right now, where orgies happen in mist-filled darkened rooms... only this isn't a dream.

Emmett scoops his hands under my back and lifts me, so we're sitting chest to chest. The way the men move around the bed, into positions, tells me this isn't the first time they've done this together. And I don't know if that excites me or terrifies me more. I've never had a threesome, much less a foursome. I mean, Lizzy used to say the goddess gave us three holes for a reason, but really? My skin prickles with nerves, but then I catch Jax shift from the door. Not moving closer, just more... alert? Could he feel my nerves? Was he worried about me? Why wasn't he over here? Earlier tonight, when he slipped into bed behind me, I thought we were progressing towards something. What, I don't know, but something. He seems to hate me and I can't figure it out, which is infuriating because at the same time he looks at me with hate, there is also something else in his eyes.

I'm pulled back to the present when Emmett falls back and shifts me on top of him, with my pussy perched at the tip of his cock. His hands dig into my side to stop me from sinking on him. "Do you want it bare? We're all clean. Weekly tests requirements from working at the sex club."

I smile. "I'm clean and yes. I want to feel your come explode inside of me."

Knox lets out another whimper, making me chuckle.

Emmett slides his hands down to my thighs and gives control over to me. The tip of his cock is teasing me, making me wetter as I drip down his shaft. "You fuck me, princess."

Licking my lips, I slide down slowly, his size stretching me out as my tight pussy vibrates over each piercing.

"We can go slower," he offers.

Trying to get leverage, I press the palm of my hand against his chest, and glide my pussy off his cock, then slide down again, this time moving a little faster. I sit upright on him and grind my hips into him, rocking my body back and forth, letting his size fill and stretch me. The pressure is immeasurable as he fills me completely.

"You feel so good," he says, and his fangs pop out.

Startled, I stare at him, waiting, but the guys don't seem to be phased. Well, Jax does. He's still watching from the door, and I can't help but wonder if he's punishing himself or if he really doesn't like me.

Emmett smiles shyly. "They pop out when I get excited."

"Me too," says Knox. He shrugs. "I'm a grower, not a shower. It's the seal in me, but watch out!"

"Watch out little fae, when he comes he'll bark like a seal too," Jax taunts from the door.

"Man! That was one time. And technically she asked for it, so..." he bats his hand.

Jax slowly blinks his eyes and sucks on his teeth.

"Are you going to join?" I ask, watching him.

"I'd rather not. Grower, over there, tried to peg me last time we had a group fuck."

"It was an accident and you know it!"

He shakes his head, but doesn't speak.

"So you're just going to watch us?"

"Does that bother you, little fae?"

I don't know how I got the nickname, but when he says it, it makes my spine tingle. "Not at all. I rather enjoy it."

"I know." His eyes darken.

Emmett rocks his hips, sending his cock swirling inside of me, while his cock rings hit areas I didn't know existed. My skin feels like electricity is moving through it, over it, under it... one spark and I'll combust.

Callum runs his hand up my spine and tangles it in my hair, before gripping tightly and pulling my head back. "Are you ready for your orgasms, little fae?"

"Yes."

"Yes, what?"

Daddy? Sir? Dragon? Fuck if I know.

"Sir?"

His eyes darken with appreciation as a wicked grin curls on his lips. "Good girl." He takes me in a kiss, pressing his tongue in as I grind my hips on Emmett.

A second later, I feel a warm mouth over my breast, sucking and playing with my nipple. "Heaven," Knox says, rolling my other nipple between his fingers.

With his mouth still on mine and hand still fisting my hair, Callum moves to standing. He releases my lips from his kiss and his hand from my hair. "Let me feed you my cock, little fae."

Eager to suck him in, I open my mouth, but he tilts my head back up and walks around the bed and stands over Emmett's head. "This will be a better angle for you. Plus, we can show Jax what he's missing."

Knox takes the place behind me that Callum just left and whispers in my ear. "Have you ever had your ass played with?"

Quickly glancing over my shoulder, I find Knox's eyes dancing with excitement. "Once, but it hurt."

"Oh, little fae. I'll make you orgasm from your ass."

I nod, nibbling on my lip because words seem too silly. What do you say? Sure? Ok? Yes, please? Betcha can't! Thank you. So many options that all sound equally idiotic.

His hand glides up my spine and pushes me over so my hands fall back to Emmett's chest. Callum uses his finger to tilt my chin up as he guides the tip of his cock in.

Jax shifts again, and I can't stop watching him watch me. It's as erotic as these men and their words and their cocks. His eyes are fucking me just as good as the others are.

The head of Callum's cock presses at my lips and I slowly suck him in, eyes still fixed on Jax. I can see his jaw grinding and clenching and part of me wonders if I push him just a little further, will he join? Where would he join?

Lizzy would give me shit for not magically growing a fourth hole to be fucked in. Belly button doesn't count even though I had a guy try once. I mean, really?

Callum's hands tighten in my hair as he pushes his cock in slowly, hitting the back of my throat. I shift and try to swallow, sending his cock to the roof of my mouth, as I lean into him, taking him a little further.

"Oh... little fae. Do you enjoy taking our cocks?" he asks, dragging his cock out.

Knox's finger plays around my ass as something wet and slippery slides over it. "You're so tight. Just relax. If you want me to stop, you just say the word, or think it." Without waiting, he presses his finger in. "Relax."

"I thought I was."

Emmett has stopped thrusting for the moment, but his finger continues to circle my clit and my eyes flutter.

Wet gel slides over my ass as Knox drags his finger out before he pushes back in again, this time a little quicker. Between Knox fingering my ass and Emmett toying with my clit, my muscles tighten as pants come quicker.

Callum is watching Knox, waiting, teeth scraping over his lip, while his hand slowly fists his cock.

"Give me your cock," I command softly, looking up at Callum.

He smiles, "Gladly, little fae." He presses in and I suck hard until he hits the back of my throat, causing me to gag. He drags out and pushes in again, holding my face while he begins to fuck it. "You suck cock like a queen, little fae."

Tears trickle down my face as he claims me, pressing in harder and faster, abandoning caution to the wind.

Hold up, Knox says in my mind, and it takes me a minute to realize what it was.

Callum pulls his cock out and leans down, kissing me hard, his tongue swirling in my mouth. Years of practice have made him an amazing kisser.

Knox's cock presses at my forbidden entrance, and anticipation causes my stomach to clench. He pushes in slowly and my body zings to life as a deep, guttural moan escapes. "Fuck me, that feels... amazing."

He presses in a little further and then slowly drags his cock out before he presses in again. The muscles tighten in a wave through my body, starting at my feet and working its way to my fingertips.

"Your ass takes cock so... good," he sighs in appreciation. He presses in a little faster and when he pulls out this time, I push back on him, swallowing his cock. His hands grab my hips as he and Emmett match pace, thrusting into me at the same time. Callum waits a moment, then lines his cock up to my lips. After a few uncoordinated thrusts, we're all moving as one, with Jax still watching and fucking me with his eyes. This is definitely not how I saw my night going, but I'm not mad.

Grunts, moans, and wet slaps of slick skin on skin become the soundtrack for the room. Tears fall down my cheeks as Callum presses in deep and slow, hitting the back of my throat repeatedly, a contrast to Emmett and Knox thrusting in quick unison.

My eyes catch Jax and watch him, his cock hard in his boxers, but his hand remains unwavering, gripping the frame of the door. I can't figure him out. Wanting to distance himself, but stay close. Saying he doesn't care, but lays with me in bed to comfort me.

Balancing on one hand, I grab Callum's cock at the base and squeeze, twisting, and his deep growl echoes around the room. His skin ripples, changing from flesh to scales, then back to flesh. He hesitates a second, noticing his shift, then thrusts faster.

"Don't you come before her," Jax barks from the door.

My eyes snap to him, then back up to Callum, who glances at him over his shoulder.

"Hurry," Callum orders.

Knox's hand slides around and circles my clit, causing sparks to fly across my body as it begins to pulse and tense and something else. There is a buzz that is vibrating through my body.

"She's getting close," Emmett chimes.

"Fuck, she feels amazing. Her ass is choking my cock and E... I can feel your cock rings."

Knox presses in further and I swear he just hit a button in my ass that causes me to see stars.

My body loses control and moves on its own, pressing back onto Emmett and Knox, riding their length, and seconds later, my body is convulsing. Callum thrusts his cock into my mouth, hitting the back of my throat and holds it there as he shoots down my throat. He tastes sweet like sugar and I can't get enough. Need consumes me, so I grab his cock and suck it hard, like I'm trying to get every ounce out.

His moans send me over the edge and my orgasm slams into me hard and fast. I push him out of my mouth as soon as he's finished and press my hands to Emmett's chest to hold me steady. He and Knox use their super speed and fuck me, pushing my orgasm further and further until I'm screaming out. It feels like a heat is dancing across my skin as Emmett's eyes grow wide.

"You're glowing."

"Well, I just had a pretty fucking big orgasm. Like in two spots at the same time."

"No. You're actually glowing. You aren't going to like... combust or create another light ball, are you?" Emmett's eyes look worried.

"I don't know. I don't know how to control them."

"This should be good," Jax chimes.

"Shut the fuck up," I bark at him, and his eyes flash with fire. He doesn't like when I come at him, but his response is addicting.

"It's the succubus blood in her. She's getting stronger, taking from us," Callum pants, breathlessly. "I felt it when I came. Her orgasms strengthens her."

Knox is chuckling before his moans cut him off and his orgasm tears into him. His cock is throbbing inside of me at the same time Emmett releases. His eyes pulse with fire as he hisses out his moans.

"Her ass sucked me in and tightened around me," Knox mumbles, pulling himself out. He walks across the room, stumbling for the first few steps like he just got off a ride. He grabs a cloth and cleans himself up, and I collapse onto Emmett before rolling off to lie beside him.

"Are you happy now?" Jax asks, standing above me, looking down.

"Very." I don't think I've ever had that many orgasms in a row and that intense. My body feels like it's still humming and buzzing and my arms seem to have a slight glow, which has dimmed a little.

"Let's go," Jax says, reaching down for me.

"Where?"

"Your room."

JAX - WOLF VS VAMPIRE

MY COCK FEELS LIKE it's going to explode inside of my pants, watching them with her. Had I known she was going to incite a group sex event when she stormed out of her room, then I would have stopped her. My subconscious laughs at me. There's no way I was stopping her without physically going to battle with her. She's a little spitfire, and she was angry earlier. And horny. Very horny.

She watched me the entire time she was on their cocks and sucking on Callum like she was trying to piss me off. I've got news for her. It didn't.

I don't care they fuck her, I just don't think they should. She's an unknown. An unknown who's being hunted by Samara, who's made our life a living hell and will continue to do so. Sure, Callum was close with the true fae before the Great Fall, but she's not the true fae who raised him. She can't control her powers and almost killed Emmett earlier tonight, and then tried to save him, in turn, almost killing herself.

Overall, it's just a bad idea and one of us has to be smart about this and not get involved. And it has to be me. Ever present shadow to make sure my family is protected, because they are who matters.

Not her.

When she climbs off Emmett and rolls over on the bed, I walk over and stand above her naked, spent body. I try not to look too long, because my cock doesn't need any help to stay hard. I'm going to have to relieve myself soon before irreparable damage to my cock is done.

"Let's go," I say, reaching down for her.

Her eyes shoot open and glare at me. "Where?"

"Your room."

Her brow furrows.

Frustrated, I snap, "I'm not going to fuck you, but you aren't staying here with him." I thumb over my shoulder and look at Emmett, who flinches.

He's a biter. When we've fucked girls in the past, he loves to bite while he's coming inside of them, or during. A couple of times tonight, I thought he was going to lose control and bite Everlee's wrist. I saw him looking at it, wanting it.

But he refrained.

I won't say it's because of anything she did. She can't give him her blood one time and think she's fixed him. He's not fixed. He has bloodlust and if they think she can fall asleep in his bed tonight and wake up in the morning, then they're both fucking idiots.

"Now," I command.

She glares at me again and slowly starts to roll away from me.

"I will fucking drag you out of here if you don't come."

"Already did. Four times," she remarks with a smirk, then looks at my bulging cock. "Looks like you need to, as well. Maybe if you did, you wouldn't be such a prick."

"I plan on fucking someone, just not you."

Her face falters for a second, flashing a mixture of pain and defiance.

"Let's go," I say again. "I'll give you to the count of five."

"You aren't going to count me down like a child."

"Then stop acting like one and let's go."

"You're an ass."

"So I've heard. Fortunate for me, I don't give a shit what you think."

What's your deal? Knox mindlinks.

I'm not having this conversation with you right now.

Maybe you should have joined. Her ass felt amazing.

So happy for you, I remark, deadpan.

Everlee is still laying on the bed, watching me, "Five... four... three... two... one."

She doesn't move and I feel the hair on my arms stand as a growl escapes my mouth.

My wolf.

He's stirring inside.

Her eyes widened in shock and she rolls over and glares at me.

"You're going to unleash your wolf on me? You're a fucking ass. I was just playing around."

Wolf? She saw him? "Well, stop fucking playing around. Does it look like I want to play?"

"Jax," Emmett says, sitting up and my eyes cut to the right, staring at him. "Take it easy."

Irritated, I throw my hands up in the air. "Fine. I don't even know why I'm trying so hard. You want to stay in here? Stay. He's a vampire with bloodlust, and your blood is the first thing he's been able to smell or taste in years. Sure, he stopped earlier, but you were almost dead. You want to lie in bed with him? Have at it." In a fury, I rip the comforter down and fluff the pillow. "A nice place to rest your head."

She rolls out of bed and stomps across the floor and slams the bedroom door behind her.

"Was that necessary?" Emmett says, rolling on his side and propping his head on his hand.

"You're being reckless."

"You care?"

"You know I fucking care, you asshole. You almost killed her, and she almost killed you. You both are walking a line to destroy one another."

"And you don't want that?"

"No."

"You care for her," he says, smiling.

"Fuck no. I care about you and this family. She's nothing to me."

"You keep telling yourself that. You want to fuck her."

"I want to fuck something, but not her."

"You want to fuck me?"

His offer catches me off guard.

When I don't answer immediately, he smiles. "You can if you want. I know it's been a while, but I don't mind. Your cock has to be close to exploding."

"I don't need to fuck you."

"I know you don't *need* to. I'm simply asking if you want to. No strings. You aren't going to the club and as much frustration that's simmering inside of you right now... you're likely to kill someone. I can take it. Plus, it's not like we haven't done it before."

"We've done it in groups."

He shrugs. "No attachments. No strings. Just a quick fuck to help you."

My cock is aching. Throbbing.

He smiles and rolls over on his knees, putting his ass in the air.

"Fuck me," I mumble, as my resolve fades. He's right. If I fuck someone right now, I'll likely kill them. I need someone who can take the full force of me.

"That's your job."

I can't help but chuckle as I slide my boxers off and walk over to stand behind him, fisting my cock in my hand. Just the touch of my hand nearly has me coming. I grab the lube that's sitting on the nightstand and coat my cock and Emmett's ass before pressing my fingers in.

He bucks, but I make quick work stretching him and opening him up as his moans urge me on. A few minutes later, my cock presses at his entrance and I slowly sink in.

A moan escapes my lips as he presses back on my cock, swallowing it in. "Goddamn E."

"Fuck me Jax. I don't want it easy," he growls out. "Let out all your rage and frustration you have with her, because of her, about her. I don't know. But whatever it is, get it out. So when you fuck her, you don't destroy her."

"I'm not fucking her."

"You will."

Eager to shut him up, I slam into him so hard he lurches forward on the bed.

"There he is. Let it out, wolf."

"Shut the fuck up, vampire." I slam into him again as tingles shoot up my spine, and my nails dig into his hips, holding him in place.

A growl unleashes from deep inside of my chest and my wolf is there again.

"It's because of her," he calls over his shoulder. "You can feel your wolf inside of you for the first time in how long? You're scared."

"I said shut up!"

Digging my feet in, I unleash on him. Unleash all the fear and pain. Fear that this is just a tease- a temporary feeling, and the pain. Knowing the kind of deep ache and pain that's going to come when he's gone again. Callum thinks she's the end all be all for our problems, but I think he's only kidding himself. He knows true fae, but this. Her. She's different. She didn't come out when other true faes do. She doesn't have her powers yet, and it's her against the whole damn world.

I'm not getting my hopes up, only to get let down.

EVERLEE - VAMPIRE VOYEUR

MY BODY IS STILL buzzing from what just happened. It was completely unexpected, but so needed. I've never had three men at once, and holy shirtballs... it was everything I could have ever wished or dreamed about. I've read about them, these harems, in my books and they do things to me... make me feel things. But to experience it... I can't wait to tell Lizzy.

Lizzy.

It feels like forever since I've seen her. She probably knows I'm not at the safe house anymore and is freaking out. I'm surprised there aren't fires all around town where she's scorching the earth to find me.

Images of Lizzy huddled over a table with a map and candles and shells, or whatever else she uses, play through my mind like a video. She's probably using one of her fancy locator spells and coming up empty, which could be a good thing or a bad thing. Or... Shit.

What if it's not coming up empty? The guys said this house is protected, but how protected? Samara surely has a witch on her team who can conjure up a locator spell.

They've probably ransacked my apartment to get whatever they need.

Is that why she was here earlier? Because she was testing them?

"Come on in. The water's fine," Knox calls from my bathroom.

He ran up to me after I stormed out of Emmett's room. Jax is infuriating. Like deep down infuriating... like beneath the skin, muscles and bone. At like a molecular level kind of infuriating.

When I walk into the bathroom, Knox is in the shower with his hand outstretched.

"What are you doing?" I ask with a smile on my face.

"I'm going to take a shower with you and help wash the come that's dripping down your leg," he chuckles.

"You don't have to."

"I know I don't, but I want to. I enjoy the water, I enjoy you, and I enjoy your breasts."

"Thank goodness you enjoy me, more than my breasts."

"They're tied. I can't very well say you and breasts at the same time." He tries, coming up with a variety of combinations that sound like brou or yousts.

After a few tries, I pat the air, laughing, and step into the shower with him.

"Is the water too hot? It's hard for me to tell sometimes."

"Water is perfect."

He extends his arms, wrapping them around my back and bringing me in, making sure the water stays out of my face. He plants a kiss on my forehead, then runs his hands down my cheeks and tilts my head up to look at him. "How do you feel?"

"I feel fine. Great."

"Not sore?"

The water beads and runs down his face and is almost mesmerizing to watch. The way it dances on his skin and how his skin nearly glows under it is magical.

"What?" he asks with a reserved smile on his face.

"Nothing."

"Something. You were just staring at me."

"You're just beautiful. Radiant. That's all."

"Well, shucks, you're going to make me blush."

"I doubt that." I push against his hard chest playfully.

"You are all those and more, Everlee. From the moment you walked up on stage, I knew there was something different about you."

"Different? Did you know I was a true fae who was going to blow up your life?"

"Not in so many words." He laughs and grabs my shoulders. "Turn around and let's get you cleaned up so we can try to get a little sleep before the sun rises."

He takes great care in washing my hair and rinsing it, before washing my body with a soap that smells like pumpkin and cinnamon and maybe vanilla? It's seasonally appropriate whatever it is, but still smells fresh and not over the top.

When we get out of the shower, I slip on another pair of underwear and steal Knox's t-shirt. Just as I'm about to climb into bed, I hear a gigantic crash. "What was that?" I jump and run into the hall.

"Nothing," Knox says, reaching for my hand, but I pull out of his grasp. "You need to get back in the room."

Another crash with growls mixed in echo across the house.

"No. Something's wrong." I follow the sound down the hall.

"It's nothing." The edge in Knox's voice is hard to ignore. I can tell he wants me to go back to my bedroom, but I can't.

"Emmett. He's in trouble!" I run to his door and push it open to find Jax buried deep in him. Emmett pulls away, only for Jax to grab him and press into him again. Rough. Commanding.

They both pause and stare at me, eyes wide. I don't move as my mind tries to process what I'm seeing. Is this why Jax wouldn't have sex with me?

Knox is beside me a moment later with his hand on my back.

Jax's eyes lock on mine as he presses into Emmett and my stomach tightens, my eyes widen, my pulse quickens. He shakes his head with a smirk when he catches my reaction. I feel like this is payback for the times he's watched me fuck or orgasm with my eyes locked on him.

His hand slides up Emmett's back as he pushes his chest to the bed as he grinds into him slowly. Gone is the rough and angry Jax, and here in his place... is this one... sex God. His body. His muscles on full display. The way his ass clenches with each thrust into Emmett is intoxicating.

"They sometimes do this when Jax is angry."

"They fuck?"

"Yea. Emmett loves fucking men and women and while Jax usually only fucks females, him and Emmett have a bond. A love that transcends. Plus, Emmett likes it rough sometimes and can take Jax when he gets in these moods."

"What made him like this tonight?"

"Well, little fae. If I had to guess, I'd say you."

"Me?"

"Will you two fucking leave?" Jax growls from the bed.

My eyes narrow to thin slits before I turn and walk back to the room.

"You so want to fuck her," Emmett rags.

"Shut the fuck up and take my cock like a good fucking boy."

I heard them speaking. Excited, I grab Knox's arm. "I heard them."

"Yea." Knox frowns. "When he's in a mood, he's pretty hard not to hear."

"No. I mean, I heard them. Like super hearing or something."

He raises his head in understanding. "Congrats." He pats my butt. "Now, let's get you in bed."

He closes the door behind us and climbs into bed after me, cradling me in his arms. His lips brush against my ear as he whispers, "Next time we can get some rope, because seeing you tied up on stage made me so hard for you."

My stomach clenches as my hand slides over the tops of his and our fingers interlock.

"Good night."

"Rather good morning, love." He kisses the back of my head and I drift off to sleep.

JAX - CUSTOM PIZZAS AND AIR REPAIR KITS

EMMETT KNOWS ME BETTER than anyone. While vampires and werewolves rarely get along, we forged our bond in the depths of despair and anger. We have a common enemy, and it's not each other.

It's Samara.

She tricked us and used our words against us, leaving us mere shells of who we were before and, through that, a brotherhood was formed. We aren't the only four she's done this too, but the others are too stupid to understand what she's taken or don't care.

Some work for her, doing her bidding and recruiting others so she can grant their wishes. We've tried to do research on Djinn to figure out what she gets from granting wishes, but there isn't a lot of literature on it.

It's rumored that Djinn were the first species created after the true fae began to evolve and they would use their magic to grant wishes for the mundanes, sometimes hurting them or others. The true fae told them to stop and not interfere with the humans, but the Djinn didn't listen, so they were banished. The Djinn would return and again, would cast their spells, taking money from the humans. This happened repeatedly until the true fae bound them to items around their house- lamps, bracelets, hairpins. For good measure, they buried the items in caves or at the bottom of the sea.

While hunters were responsible for the Great Fall, the rumor is the Djinn, who'd been found and released from their confinements, sought revenge on the true fae and granted wishes to those hunters. Mundanes would've never been able to defeat the true fae otherwise.

No, it was methodical attacks.

Which is why we need to be careful with Everlee.

If she is a true fae, which I'm still not convinced she is, then Samara will stop at nothing to find her.

BHRING BHRING!

"Someone's at the door!" Knox exclaims, running down the stairs.

He's been with Everlee since she left Emmett's room last night. He looks all happy and bouncy, which is irritating as fuck.

"No shit!"

"Jax," Callum drones, setting his coffee cup down. Emmett uncrosses his legs at the stove and just watches Knox fly by.

He bounces past me and down the hall towards the front door, just as Everlee is walking down the stairs in only a shirt. I immediately hold my hand up to stop her, in case Samara decided to pay us another visit. She stops immediately, tensing, and the shirt floats back and forth, causing the hem which is sitting high on her thigh to expose a hint of her panties. Immediately, I want to slam my fist through something. I hoped fucking Emmett last night would have worked whatever feelings I have about her out, but it didn't. It only made it worse.

I heard her walking down the hall last night before she got to Emmett's room and I hoped when she walked in on us, she'd be hurt or angry. But no. No. She was fucking turned on. It didn't seem to bother her that I stood by the door and watched her be fucked, then fuck her. Had Knox not dragged her away, I'm fairly certain she would have stayed and probably fucking masturbated to us, even though she just got her world rocked. She is the daughter of a succubus, so she will have a heightened sexual appetite, but damn. *And the daughter of an alpha wolf, so she will have fight in her as well,* my subconscious reminds.

The night before we found her, I did a background check on her to see who we were dealing with. Firstborn of an interspecies couple, she had all the makings to be something great, but when she didn't ascend the fae ranks on her birthday, or several years after, she became little more than a mundane. The only thing she had going for her was her brother was a rare phoenix, and her dad was an alpha wolf. She didn't have many friends, and those she had, she pushed away. Except for one. A wild child witch named Lizzy-

"Wow!" Knox exclaims from down the hall, completely enraptured by whatever he's hearing.

Who the fuck is at the door? I grumble to myself.

Walking through the hallway, I stop behind Knox and who other than the wild child witch, although she seems to be selling something. She's tall. Taller than I would have expected, wearing a dark green dress with a brown plaid cap sitting on the side of her head.

"Oh, hi there!" She waves, moving her entire body like a super spunky chipmunk. "I'm Gisebelle Givens. You can call me Gizz."

"Jizz?" I already knew her name wasn't Gisebelle, and admittedly my inappropriate joke was a little immature, but seeing Everlee pop down the stairs this morning without a care in the world irked me.

"Gizz. Or Gisebelle, if it's too hard. I'm going around selling–"

"No thanks. Not interested."

"You don't even know what I'm selling," she huffs.

"It doesn't matter. I'm not interested."

"Jax," Knox pouts. "Listen to her!" His eyes are bright like a child who's just been told they can buy whatever they want in the candy store.

His love and fascination with the humans or land dwellers is... irritating. It makes him more gullible, and it's what got him in trouble with Samara. He lived in the ocean and would watch the people on land and envied their lifestyle, their relationships, the access to both land and sea they had. It was something he longed for, which is what sent him to search out Samara.

When he wished for a life like the mundanes on land, she took his selkie skin, forcing him to stay on land. Without it, he can't shift. Sometimes he disappears for several days at a time and when he comes home, I smell the ocean breeze on him, the salt in his hair.

He hasn't said that he misses the ocean, or his family there, but I know he does. He's hurting even though he won't share it with others, so now I find myself protecting him even when I don't want to.

Which also irks me.

"Fine, I will listen, but I'm still not interested."

Lizzy's face brightens as she inhales a deep breath to walk me through her entire spiel that she just laid out on Knox. "So, before I start again, is there anyone else in the house?" She looks over my shoulder.

I shift, blocking her view, knowing she's looking for Everlee. "No."

Her eyes narrow, and she nibbles on the inside of her jaw before she changes course. "Excellent. So what I'm offering today is a great deal! When this handsome man right here," she points to Knox, "opened the door, I thought to myself,

self, he looks like a man who enjoys custom, fancy pizzas flown in from all over the world."

"And I do!" Knox looks at me bright eyed and bushy tailed and I just roll my eyes.

"Yes! He does!" She points. "I'm offering you a subscription service. Once a month or once a week," she looks over my shoulder again, "to delicious pizzas! You get the ingredients from different locations each week or month, your choice."

"My choice?"

"Yes!" Her eyes light up excitedly. Unfortunately for her, I still don't give two shits and if she was being honest with herself, neither did she because she wasn't selling subscriptions for pizza. She was here looking for Everlee. "So what do you say?" she peers over my shoulder again, and again, I move to block her.

"Still not interested."

She huffs and Knox slumps his shoulders.

"But wait, there's more."

My eyes grow wide in mock excitement. "Tell me! My breath is bated."

"HA!" She pokes me in the chest. "You're funny, in a smartass kind of way. You're waiting with bated breath. Classic."

"Did you just call me a smartass?"

"Did I?" She cocks her hip to the side. We've both clearly read one another and she knows she's not getting anywhere past me.

"So, what are you selling? If I had a chair, I'd be on the edge of it."

"Jax, don't be rude."

"I have..." she looks around quickly, trying to come up with something. "Ah yes! We just got this in..."

"I'm sure it's brand new." Since it didn't exist two seconds ago...

"An air repair kit for your oven. You may find yourself needing one of those when you start cooking all your delicious pizzas."

"An air repair kit?" My brow peaks up, curious about how she's going to sell this. "Is it like a band-aid for the air? Do you just take it and pluck it somewhere?" I ask holding my hands up, simulating repairing the air.

Her eyes narrow again, and she looks over my shoulder.

"Is there something I can help you with? You seem overeager to find something in my house."

"This is your house?"

"Well, ours," Knox chirps and I grind my teeth.

"You're a couple. The. Sweetest!" She clasps her hands and puts them under her chin. "Can I be real with you?"

"No," I quickly answer, but she ignores me and keeps talking.

"I feel like we know each other well enough, to be honest. I'm not selling air repair kits or custom pizza subscriptions."

"No." Knox frowns.

"No," I feign shock and disappointment.

"I'm looking for someone."

"Oh," Knox tenses up.

"My best friend. I think she's in trouble."

"She?" Knox frowns, all the pieces clicking into place.

"Everlee McKinley. I'm a witch and I've been tracking her."

"And you tracked her here?" I press.

"Not exactly."

"So you just picked our house, or are you going to all the houses along this street offering your amazing pizzas?"

"No. I picked your house based on some intel I had."

"Intel?"

"Have you seen her?"

"No."

"Lizzy?" Her voice chimes behind me, and I cringe. "Lizzy!" She's running up to the door, but I block her.

"Ev!" Lizzy claps her hands, then glowers at me, "You haven't seen her? Really?"

"Do you two want to calm the fuck down? You can't announce to the entire world she's here."

"Let her in!" Everlee says, pushing me out of the way.

Lizzy tries to step in, but she's blocked by the invisible protection spells on the house.

"Impressive," Lizzy says, pumping her eyebrows and feeling around the air like a mime.

Knox starts to speak, but I put my hand over his mouth. "You don't know her. How do you know this isn't Samara, pretending to be the best friend, so we let her in?"

"I'm not that slimy Djinn," she retorts, face full of disgust.

At least we have that in common, but I still press. "Seems like something someone would say impersonating her."

Lizzy ignores me and looks at Everlee, then smiles, "You look good, mamacita. Someone has finally fucked you." She lifts her nose in the air. "Recently." She pumps her eyebrows.

"Can you smell sex on her?" Knox asks, amused.

"No, she can't." Everlee laughs, answering for her. "She just has a sixth sense with my sex life. It's creepy as fuck. We call it her sexth sense. Can we please let her in, so we don't have to stand here at the door? Knox?"

"Yes! Lizzy, please come in." Knox waves his arm, allowing her to pass.

"Thank you, Knox." She smiles, then cuts her eyes at me with a 'fuck off sucker' stamped across her head.

And then there were two pains in my ass walking through the house. Well, three, if I include Knox.

As soon as the door closes, they fall into each other's arms, hugging and shrilling. Fucking help me.

Lizzy grabs Everlee by the shoulders and pushes her back. "How are you? I went to the safe house, and you were gone and your phone was there, and I haven't been able to track you. I've been panicked! Why didn't you call?"

"I've been busy," Everlee says, guiding her into the kitchen.

"What? Fucking?"

"Lizzy," she blushes and smacks her on the arm.

"Careful," Knox whispers over my shoulder.

"What?"

"Your face is smiling. I'd hate if you broke something since it hasn't done that... well, ever."

"Shut the fuck up!" I shove his shoulder and he stumbles into the fridge.

"Ass."

Shrugging, I grab a cup and sit down.

EVERLEE - HOUSE OF THE DRAGON

Lizzy's here! I can't believe I'm staring at her beautiful face! Not being able to talk to her over the last several days has nearly killed me. We've gone for days without talking before, but this was different. She didn't know where I was and that's what bothered me most. Her, worried about me.

"So which one was it?" she asks without hesitation as soon as we sit at the island.

"Lizzy."

"I can guess." She looks around at Knox and Jax. "Well, it's definitely not grumpy."

Jax cuts his eyes at her, but doesn't respond.

"Was it you?" she asks pointing at Knox. "Or you?" She points at Callum, then Emmett.

"Going on a witch hunt?" Jax drones, looking completely unamused.

"So original. You would think for as old as you are, you'd have a better joke."

He rolls his eyes, but he doesn't leave. Instead, he picks up a paper and holds it in front of his face, and pretends to read. Maybe he's reading, but I doubt it. Something about his body language and the fact I find it nearly impossible to concentrate when Lizzy's around tells me he's just using it as a prop.

Lizzy grabs my arm, mouth open wide. "You dirty whore."

"What?" I don't know why I ask. Lizzy isn't the kind of person who you need to ask to talk. She just does. She holds nothing back, either. No filter. What you see is what you get.

"All of them? They all have that Everlee glow. Well, except for grump, which is probably why he's a grump. Because he wanted to and didn't."

Emmett's eyes cut at Jax, but he doesn't speak.

When I look at Jax, I find his eyes peering over the edge of the paper at me. Watching me. My stomach flutters and my pussy pulses, so I shift in my seat a little. I can't help but think he's smiling, but I can't tell. Maybe I'm hoping he is, so I have proof he isn't as much of an asshole as he lets on.

"I'm not answering you."

"You just did." She shimmies her shoulders, "Yes, queen!!!"

"Is there something we can help you with? How did you find her?" Jax asks.

"Right. That. So after I went to the safe house and didn't find Ev there, I was worried. Naturally."

Naturally, Jax mindlinks.

I snap my head in his direction and he looks at me with a curious brow.

"I went to her place. Didn't find her there. Ran a tracking spell. Couldn't find her there. So I backtracked, hoping you may have gone back and when I was leaving the safe house the second time, I heard some people talking down the street, so I did what every good witch does and shifted into a cat."

"Good call, since there are tons in the area."

"Right! Oh my Goddess. I've never seen so many."

"Your story?" Jax drones behind the paper.

I knew he wasn't reading it!

"Right. So I'm walking around and see these vampires talking to Samara. The guy was a complete douche. Just seemed like a real prick, ya know?"

"Yea. I know the type," I reply. Jax shifts in his chair, making me smile. Score one for Everlee.

"Anyway, they tell her y'all took her. Well, I didn't know it was y'all at first. I just had a name, so I did some digging around and tracked it back to Allure, where Samara was losing her shit because she thought you had her and were lying. So I devised my excellent pizza plan and headed over."

"You had me convinced. I was ready to sign up," Knox chirps happily.

"You're cute, like in a puppy dog kind of way."

"He's a selkie."

"Ah, makes sense. Golden retrievers of the ocean."

"And what are you?" She looks at Callum. "Power. Dominance. Sex appeal. Wisdom."

Callum shifts uneasily, so I try to divert her attention. "Was it the best idea you coming here? What if Samara is tracking you?"

"Admittedly, probably not the best idea, but I had to get eyes on you. I had to know you were ok. Your parents and brother are freaking out."

"You can't tell them you found me, though. Samara will find out and know I'm staying here."

"What is your plan? You can't just stay here forever."

"I know. I'm still working on it."

"I can help if it would get you out of here faster," Jax chimes.

"Will you just put the paper down and join the conversation? We all know your ass ain't reading it, so you can stop pretending. Casting your googly eyes at Everlee. Damn. You should have just fucked her," Lizzy snipes.

Jax stares at her in utter disbelief, puts his paper down, and walks out of the room without speaking.

"That works too," she calls after him.

"Damn. Broody McBroodyville."

"He isn't too bad."

Lizzy laughs out loud. "You want that wolf dick. That's the only reason you're saying that. I mean, hell, who wouldn't? He's fine as hell. Do you think he howls at the moon when he comes? Asking for a friend." She gives me an overdramatic wink.

I smack her arm, rolling my eyes.

"I like you," Knox says, sitting down beside her.

"I like you, too. I don't want to stay long. I've got shit to do and people to bewitch. I'll be in touch soon. In the meantime, try to figure out a plan. Samara wants you bad, and nothing good can come out of that."

"You should probably watch your back, too. If she knows you two are friends, she'll come after you as a way to get to Everlee," Knox adds.

"Yea. I've been moving around quite a bit and covering my tracks. I have another witch from Helsgard who's been helping me."

"Tony?" I ask, bouncing my shoulders playfully.

"Stop," she blushes.

"Ooh, someone has a crush."

"Go on!" Knox says, clasping his fingers together and resting his chin on them.

Callum clears his throat. I forgot he was still in the room, standing against the wall, with his foot propped up, looking sexy as hell. Emmett must have left when Jax did. Are they together? Why does the idea of that turn me on so much?

Lizzy stands from the bar and reaches over to give me a hug.

"Please stay safe," I say, inhaling her scent- hints of frankincense and rosewood. Her signature smell.

"I love you," she smells me back, then whispers. "Now go get your pussy pummeled."

I catch a soft grin from Callum and Knox and roll my eyes, shaking my head. "They can hear you. They're shifters."

She whispers back, "I know, and you're welcome."

She squeezes me one last time. "I don't want to leave you." She pushes me away, "But I must. I'm determined to learn about the Djinn and the true fae and figure out how we can keep you alive. Well, assuming she wants to kill you after she studies you. I see your future in tiny little jars with labels on them."

"That's morbid as fuck." I smack her arm.

"Yea, probably. But it gives me motivation." She walks over to Knox and holds out her arms. "I like you. You seem sweet and fun. Look after my girl." She gives him a tight hug.

"Oh. Such a good hugger," Knox chimes.

She walks over to Callum and holds her hand out. "You seem like a handshaker, and less like a hugger."

He smiles. "You... are interesting. I'm glad I got to meet you today. You've answered a lot of questions on my mind."

"I have? Like what?"

He smiles coolly.

"I'll take that as a *you're not telling* kind of smile."

"Stay safe."

"I'm going to go out the back if that's ok?"

"Sure," he says, guiding her to the back door, and I follow a step behind him.

She shifts into a black cat a moment later and weaves between my legs before she bounces down the back stairs.

We watch her jump on the fence surrounding the property and prance along like a cat without a care in the world, then close the door.

Callum turns to me and brushes the hair out of my face, staring at me. "She's an odd bird."

"Yes, she is."

"But she seems loyal."

"Very."

"That's good." He pulls me into a hug and I go willingly, wantingly. I know wantingly isn't a word, but it just feels right to say in this moment.

I was scared this morning that things would be weird after last night, but... they aren't. It seems... natural.

Natural to fuck three guys, and want to fuck the fourth?

His hand rubs up and down my back and I nearly melt into his touch.

"Careful," I warn with a sultry tone.

He chuckles and pushes me away. "We have lots of work to do. We need to figure out a weakness with the Djinn, so we can use it against her to protect you. Fortunately, I think most fae don't know enough to care about you."

"Ouch."

"I meant you being a true fae. The Great Fall resulted from Djinn and other dark fae who'd aligned with the Djinn, creating hunters from mundanes in exchange for a variety of things. Land, wealth, power. I don't know if they ever got what they were promised or just killed after the Great Fall. If I had to guess, it would be the latter for most. There aren't a lot of Djinns, and they're spread far and wide and have lived in the shadows for a long time. It wasn't until somewhat recently, I learned they were the ones behind the Great Fall. Something Samara shared as a way to punish and torment me more."

"There aren't a lot?"

"No, they are one of the few fae that can't reproduce. They were created thousands of years ago, soon after the true fae. I imagine there are more in the world, but the true fae banished and bound them to everyday items and then buried them, sunk them, destroyed them. Every thousand years or so, mundanes unearth buried artifacts with a Djinn trapped inside. Fortunately, Djinn are a selfish creature who don't play well with others, so while they live their lives, building their power, they also wage a war amongst themselves, seeking to destroy anyone who could impede their power."

"So can we find another Djinn and use them to kill Samara?"

He laughs. "I don't think that would work out the way you want it to. Djinn hate true fae more than other Djinn."

"Maybe if I can show her I'm not like the true fae who bound them?"

"Doesn't matter. You still have their blood line in you. Soon you will have their power and their memories. It just takes time."

"Is there a way I can speed up my powers?"

"No."

I growl out in frustration. "I feel so alone."

"You aren't alone. We're here."

"But why? Why are you here? What do you get out of it? Why help me? You don't even know me?" I push away from him and stare at him. I'd been so blinded with lust that I never stopped to ask myself these questions before. Why did they want to help me? They have to be getting something out of it.

Callum's eyes fall on my face and a frown crosses his lips.

"Are you using me? Getting me to trust you so you can trade me for your power back?"

"No. Goddess no!"

"Then why?"

He snaps like a twig breaking in the wind. "Aren't these questions you should have asked before you came to our house? Before you slept with us?" His eyes harden. He's mad. "I'm going to the library," he huffs and storms out of the room.

Knox looks between Callum and me.

Well, now, I feel guilty. I just... I feel lost and alone. I don't see a way out of this mess because I know so little about this world. Sure, I've lived in the fae world all of my life and knew they existed, but for the last several years... I've distanced myself. They all represented something I'd never be. Would never have. I stayed away and under the radar until I exposed myself in the most public way possible and now I'm scrambling to catch up. To learn about who I am, when others around me already know.

"I didn't mean... I'm just... lost."

Knox walks over and gives me a hug. "We all are. Callum more than others. He holds himself responsible for the Great Fall, for not protecting the true fae. He rescued Aleida on the night of the Great Fall, but she'd already been injured. She was the last of the true fae and, to help them live on, he had to get her to the Cliffs of Morgai."

Flashes of my dream come back to me in pieces.

"I saw it. In my dream."

"Your shared memories."

"That was Callum? The dragon?"

"Yes. For the last several hundred years, he's dealt with the guilt that he didn't get Aleida buried in time, and then when you walked into the club, it was like a weight had been lifted off his shoulders."

"But why?"

"I don't know if I should be the one telling you all of this."

"I need to know. I need to understand. Right now, I feel like everyone knows everything about my life, my history, who I am, and I'm just wading through the dark waiting for something to get me. I need to understand. Need to take control back."

He nods and takes a deep breath. "The true fae raised him. They found him nearly dead in a cave and rescued him..."

EVERLEE - LET THE WOLF OUT

THE NEXT SEVERAL DAYS go by in a monotonous routine. Breakfast, library, dinner, bed and repeat. We all sense the danger looming over us because of my situation and their lies to Samara.

Callum and I spend most of our day in the library studying and reading up on true fae and Djinn, trying to understand everything about them. Callum has collected thousands of books over the years, and even though we are systematically going through them, there isn't much about the Djinn. They have a few mentions in some books, but it's very surface level. Nothing about the full extent of their powers or what defeats them. If they can be defeated...

If they could've been defeated, then why didn't the true fae do it? I know they were the founders of the light fae and were a benevolent creature. So much so that it cost them their lives in the end, but why not stop them? Self-preservation would have to outweigh their moral code, wouldn't it?

I guess that's a dumb question because it didn't. Even when the hunters were killing them, they didn't defend themselves against the humans.

That's not me though. If someone comes after me, I will strike back.

Does that make me a dark fae?

I've never had to align myself with the light or the dark because I've never had powers. I always considered myself in the middle and would often joke I was the gray fae.

Since Knox told me about Callum, I understand why this is so important to him and what he's getting out of it. Callum is a dragon. A protector. Protector of the weak and the true fae. He's made it his mission to guard me, feeling the guilt of what happened years ago. I'm his chance at redemption for his soul. And a way out from under Samara's thumb. He knows that Djinn and true fae are connected.

The light and the dark.

Yin and the Yang.

We just need to figure out how to crack the code between us.

I apologized to him, and he said he forgave me, but things still seem a little tense around the house. Jax still seems to hate me, Emmett, while nice to me is still fighting urges to kill me, Callum seems... I don't know... confused. And Knox... he brings a smile to my face every time I see him or think about him.

Knox floats in and out throughout the days and tries to help read through the books, but he can't stay focused long enough. He brings us food, and will oftentimes, slip in behind me on the bench at the window and will either rub my shoulders while I read or will simply wrap his arms around me and hold me.

He yearns for connection. Love. And I find it so easy to give it to him. Quite the contrast to Jax, who just seems to carry a darkness around with him. It's a wonder he and Knox get along. I mean, sure, Jax is constantly telling Knox to fuck off, but there's a love under all the words, all the motions, that is bright as day. I know if anyone were to try to harm Knox, Jax would be the first one in line to lay them out. Without hesitation. Without question.

I can't help but wonder what he would do about me if I was in trouble. I'd like to think he'd protect me. That he doesn't really hate me as much as he seems, but I don't know.

Him and Emmett haven't been home much, and when they are, they're downstairs with blood donors. It's been a revolving door, so much so that Knox has even mentioned it. I don't know why they bring them here, seems dangerous letting people into the house, but I'm sure they have protections in place I'm unaware of.

Some of my superpowers have started to come in and get stronger and more consistent. When my super hearing came in, I didn't tell anyone at first, although I don't know why Callum didn't know. I imagine it was confusing at first when I was answering questions or contributing to conversations that were happening in other parts of the house. When I realized what was happening, I quickly got it under control and used it to my advantage, listening to Jax and Emmett talk about me. Did I feel a little guilty for eavesdropping? Yes. But I wanted to know what Jax's problem was with me.

Is with me.

All I gathered was Emmett giving him a hard time about Jax wanting to fuck me, but denying himself the pleasure of my pussy. Which Emmett said was fantastic, so that made me happy. Jax just denied it, but said nothing else.

Mindlinking came in the day after. I'd been getting snippets of it for a while, but it's been inconsistent at best. Now I'm able to control it. Reading through the texts, I've gathered I should also get super speed at some point, and potentially flight. Not all true fae could fly, but some could. That would be pretty fucking cool. I'd always wished for that when I was in school and having to trek fifteen minutes across campus. Often times, I would kill time on my walks, trying to figure out how I could just hover.

Last night after dinner, Knox and I were playing around. He grabbed me from behind and was trying to tackle me to the floor and I accidentally created a little light ball and shot it across the room. Callum told me the fae call them Luxpheras and that it's basically photokinesis. Building and storing energy. He shared that when he was little, he was scared of the starless nights, so Sofrai and Feyra would create these Luxpheras to dance in the air, simulating stars for him. While they used it to calm a child down, he pointed out they are very dangerous. The extent of their power is still unknown, since most true fae didn't document or use the lights for bad.

Hopefully, my super speed will come in soon. Each time something else is unlocked in me, I feel like I'm one step closer to this being over. One more piece of armor in my invisible suit. One more thing in my arsenal I can use to fight against Samara when the time comes, so these guys don't have to.

My fork dangles on my finger as the last bite of lasagna sits on my plate. It's my second helping that I didn't want to want, but needed to have. It's delicious. Absolutely the best thing I've ever put in my mouth. Emmett truly is a master chef and the fact he can't taste the food he prepares and it's still wonderful absolutely blows my mind.

"Want to go on the roof tonight?" Knox asks.

"The roof?" I stab the last piece of lasagna and stare at it.

"Yea, you've been reading and studying a ton. You need a break. We all do."

"What have you been doing?" Jax barks. His eyes catch mine for a second before they dart back to Knox. My heart beats twice and my stomach tightens for a second and I can't understand how he has this hold on me. It has to simply be the fact that we haven't fucked. Like the whole want what you can't have type thing.

"What have you been doing? Does Emmett need you to hold the blood bags for him?"

He shoves his last bite in his mouth, then walks his plate to the sink.

"Wolf got your tongue?"

"Knox," Callum reprimands.

"What?" he defends. "I'm tired of his constant pissy attitude."

Jax locks eyes with me again, then walks out of the room.

What was that? Was he going to say that it's my fault he's in a pissy mood? That if I wasn't here, then everything would be fine?

"Excuse me," I say, pushing away from the table and walk upstairs. I'm tired of the glances and the scowls. I'm tired of his little snide comments to me. I want to know what I've done that is so bad.

"Everlee," Emmett warns, clearly picking up on my frustrations.

"I'm fine," I answer back without turning around.

"*Should we go after her?*" Knox asks Callum from downstairs.

Block it out. Block out their conversation. Focus on Jax and what I'm going to say to him.

When I get to his door, I stand outside of it for a second to calm my breathing, then I knock.

The door cracks open, but no one answers, so I let myself in.

Did he leave it open because he heard me coming or did it just not latch?

Does it matter?

"Hello?" I call out, pushing the door closed behind me.

The light in the bathroom is on with the door open, so I walk towards it. When I get about two steps away, I realize I may walk in on something I don't want to and stop.

Fuck. I didn't really think this through.

Do you ever? My subconscious chimes.

Slowly panicking, my heartbeat races as I look around like a caged animal. Do I cower and leave, or do I stay and face him?

"I can hear you," he says quietly, like he was expecting me.

Pulling in a deep breath, I stomp towards his bathroom door and push it the rest of the way open, nearly choking on air.

He's standing in front of the sink with only a pair of tight black boxers on, which are sitting low on his hips. The muscles in his back flex as he stands upright from slightly bent over, washing his hands. He has a set of tattoos, of stars with different phases of the moon going up his spine. Rather down. From the top of his neck down beneath the elastic of his boxers. My legs twist together and I can't ignore the satisfied smirk on his lips I see in the mirror's reflection.

Frustrated, both emotionally and sexually, I stomp up to him and grab him by the shoulders and spin him around. "What the fuck is your problem?"

He looks down at my hands still pressing on his chest, then back up to me. "You barged into my room, then came into my bathroom."

"One I did not barge in. The door was open. And two, you all but invited me in here."

"I didn't know my acknowledgement of your heady pants was an invitation to come in here and assault me." His words are slow and calculated, cool, but hot as fire.

My eyebrows nearly jump off my face. "Assault? Are you so delicate that me spinning you is assault?"

That did something. His eyes flash with fire and he steps forward, closing the already non-existent space between us, pushing me back against the wall, chest pressed to mine. "I'm not delicate." His hands wrap around my wrist and pin them above my head.

I know I should be scared right now, but fuck, I'm turned on. Fight it. Fight the lady boner. "No, just an ass."

"You haven't seen me be an ass yet."

"Pretty sure I see it every day."

He leans forward so his lips are less than an inch from mine, and he stands there, breathing me in. My lips part and my body shifts as arousal pools in my pants. I stopped wearing panties because I lost three pairs in one night and since then, I stay in a near constant wet state. It's like my pussy has a mind of its own and is hanging around yelling out for cock. Spritzing her sex like a love beacon. Only she's not getting any cock and I'm left dealing with wet panties. I don't like the feeling that I've pissed myself all day.

He smiles, "So easy."

"I'm not." I push against him, but he plants his foot and pushes me back.

"Aren't you? You didn't seem to have a problem fucking most of the men in this house. Pretty sure you'd fuck me right now if I said yes."

"Because I enjoy having sex makes me easy? Do you not enjoy having sex? Does that make you easy? Why is it that women aren't allowed the same indulgences as men without being labeled something derogatory? You're such an ass."

"So you wouldn't have sex with me right now?"

"No!"

Lie!

"No?" His one word comes out silky smooth as he leans in closer, before he moves to the side and kisses my neck, sucking on my skin.

My knees buckle slightly. This is not how I thought this was going to go. Fuck.

"Not even, now."

"No," I pant out, desire and need coursing through me.

He shifts my wrists to one hand and uses his other to slide down the inside of my arm, leaving a trail of goosebumps in its wake and stops just above the hem of my pants.

A whimper escapes.

"Still no?" His words are like silk dancing around me.

My tongue can't move, so I just shake my head.

"Let's see, shall we?"

My stomach is so tight, I'm pretty sure I just grew another two pack on my abs. Because that's how easy it is... just clench really hard so you don't fucking orgasm and boom, you got abs.

His hands start to dip under the hem of my pants and I don't stop him when he pauses. He leans back in, pressing his body against mine as he kisses on the sensitive spot under my ear again. I'm a fucking puddle. A puddle of liquid fervent desire.

His hand slides down and over my clit.

"See. I think you were lying to me," he says, nibbling on my ear. "You are very, very, very, very wet." He shoves a finger inside of me and I arch my back into him, gasping out. "I think you would do anything I asked you to right now, wouldn't you?" he asks, watching me. His eyes are drinking me in as his teeth scrape over his bottom lip. His arm continues to move as he adds another finger inside of me, slowly pushing me closer to my orgasm. "Wouldn't you, little fae?"

My head presses back against the wall as my hands greedily run up his chest and claw at his pecs as my orgasm is right on the edge. My muscles start to clench and my mouth parts to prepare for the moan that is about to escape and then nothing.

Nothing.

He slides his hand out of my pants and looks at me, eyes turning to black.

"Now, you can rightfully call me an ass." He sucks my arousal off his fingers and drops my wrists, pushing away from me.

"Are you kidding me?"

"I don't kid little fae."

Rage pulses through me. "Why!" I shove him backwards, catching him off guard, "Are you–" I shove him again. "Such–" One more time, "An asshole?"

He grabs me by the shoulders and pushes me backward. "Stop pushing me."

"Fuck you!" I yell into his face, straining against the grip he has on my shoulders.

"No thanks," he says coolly.

Before I know what's happening, my body is on fire. We both look down and his eyes grow wide with shock, as do mine. I'm glowing, like a light blue flame is dancing around my body.

All the cockiness has drained from his face and in its place is concern. Good. Let him be concerned.

"You need to stop."

"Are you scared?"

"Everlee! Fucking stop!" He lets go of me and backs away.

"Not such a tough guy now, are you?" I press my hands to his chest and he growls out. Deep and ferocious.

"Everlee," his tone has changed once again. Confusion?

Cracks fill the air. His cracks. He's shifting. His wolf.

A second later, a large black wolf is standing in the bathroom in front of me, head down, body tense.

CALLUM - F UNIT

Fucking Jax. Why does he do this? Why does he try to push everyone away? Knox and Emmett both eye me from across the bar as the pants and moans fill the air. He's fucking with her. We all know it, because the bastard won't let himself feel anything but anger towards her. To him, she is light. Hope. And he won't let himself feel that, or her. He's going to push and push to try to put out her light, but he can't. She is a force to be reckoned with, and he may have met his match with her.

Daughter of a succubus and an alpha wolf. She will take any challenge he throws at her and come out on top. He thinks he can break her, but he hasn't let himself get to know her, to know he's fighting himself.

"*You need to stop.*"

"*Are you scared?*"

"*Everlee! Fucking stop!*"

Knox presses away from the bar. "I feel like we need to get in there. This seems to be escalating quickly."

"*Not such a tough guy now, are you?*"

"Yea, maybe we should," I agree, pushing away and following Knox up the stairs.

A growl echoes through the house and Knox mumbles, "Shit."

"Damn it!"

"*Everlee.*"

Bones cracking filter through the hallways. A second later, the air shifts and my hair stands on end.

"What the fuck?" Knox yells from Jax's bathroom door.

I already know what to expect before Emmett and I skid to a stop behind him.

Emmett's fangs drop as he tenses behind me.

"Ev, you need to get out of there," Knox warns, hands gripped tight on the doorframe. "I wish I was in the pool right now," he mumbles under his breath.

"What happened? I thought he didn't have his wolf," Everlee squeaks out.

"He didn't, but obviously something you did brought it out."

"Me? She shakes her head and flops her hands. "It was the light... the Luxphera. He made me mad and my whole body started glowing. I touched him and that's when he growled and then this."

Jax. Jax. Everlee mindlinks.

Everlee, leave. I don't want to hurt you.

The wolf takes a step forward.

"You're not going to hurt me."

Fucking hell, why can't you ever just listen?

Why can't you? I'm not leaving Jax. I'm not fucking leaving.

My wolf doesn't trust you. You scared him.

Well, tell him I'm sorry. She shakes her head, then holds her hand out in the air towards the wolf, but not touching it. "I'm sorry. I didn't mean to scare you. Your bipedal fae just really pissed me off. He's good at doing that, it seems."

Everlee! Jax barks through mindlink.

Bipedal?

"And it seems I make him mad too, which he honestly deserves."

The wolf growls, taking another step forward, and Emmett tenses behind me.

"Emmett, do you need to leave?" I ask him.

His eyes cut to me, then back to the wolf. Wolf, because in Emmett's eyes, gone is his friend and there is his enemy. They met after Jax's wolf was taken from him, which is probably why they've been able to get along so well.

"I'm fine."

Knox, get her, Jax commands.

"Don't you fucking come near me," she barks back, holding her hand out. "I've got this."

I'm a fucking wolf, Everlee! Jax growls, but it's more of frustration than anger.

"My dad is a fucking alpha wolf. You don't think I've dealt with my fair share of pricks before?"

Her courage is so fucking attractive. And irritating. I just want to scream.

"Listen here, wolf. I'm a friend, not a foe. We're all friends here. You may remember me? I'm sure your fae is always thinking about me. Probably can't get me off his mind."

Not helping, Jax snipes.

"Did she break the spell Samara placed?" Knox asks.

"No. I don't think so. When she's not around, blood has no taste. It's almost like she temporarily blocks the spell or something."

"So if I walk away, then Jax will come back?" Everlee asks thinking it over, her eyes flittering between us and the wolf.

I guess him shifting in the middle of the bathroom wasn't the best idea. He probably feels like a caged animal.

"Let's try that. The wolf, regardless, needs space."

When I glance at Emmett and Knox, they both just look at me and shake their head. They aren't moving without her and neither am I.

"Ok. Ok." Everlee looks at the wolf. "I'm going to leave." She takes a step towards us and Emmett and Knox both shift.

Wait, Jax cries out, and she stops. She heard it in his voice. We all did. *Nevermind. Go.*

"Jax." Her voice is soft and full of pain. She knows he doesn't want her to go because that probably means his wolf goes and he's wanted him back for so long.

Go.

Everlee turns her back and walks out of the door, then runs through the room and down the hall.

"Give him some space," I say, running after her.

By the time I get to her room, the hairs on my arms stand and then fall. He's back. Jax is back.

My knuckles knock softly on the door. "Everlee?" I push the door open and find her laying in bed curled into a ball. "Everlee?"

Her sniffles pull at strings on my heart and I want to wrap her in my arms. Before I know what's happening, I'm climbing into bed and pulling her into my arms. "It's ok."

"It's not ok. I know why he doesn't want me here. It's because I'm like this big tease. He's been feeling his wolf. Hearing him. And tonight, he shifted. He shifted." She rolls over and looks up at me. "He's going to be so mad at me. He won't forgive me. I showed him what he's been longing for and when I'm gone, so is his wolf."

"He's not going to be mad."

She snort chuckles. "Have you met him? He's always mad."

"Well then, this won't be any different." I smile and brush my lips across her forehead.

"I want to talk to him and apologize. Which pisses me off almost as much. He's such an ass. He was teasing me and when I was about to come, he fucking walked away. I was so mad... and now fuck! I just want to hold him. Ugh!" She pounds her fist against my chest.

"Jax is a complicated guy. He's fiercely loyal, but he doesn't let many people in. His problem is that he wants to let you in, but he's scared. You came like a force into our lives and have blown our family apart." I hurry to add, "In a good way. In a very good way. We were all sort of just moving through life before you, and now there is a purpose.

A renewed sense of energy. We always talked about going after Samara. Fighting to break her spell, but we didn't know how to. We've been waiting for you. You are the piece that we didn't know we were missing and I know it sounds crazy because it hasn't been very long, but I felt you when you walked in to the bar. My whole body knew."

"You speak of family... and a question has been on my mind."

I know what she's going to ask. It's the same question we've been asked a hundred times. "Go on."

"You all don't seem to have a problem with someone else laying in my bed or holding me in their arms..."

Chuckling and running my finger down her arm from her shoulder, I answer, "Yes. We don't mind with anyone in this house. We are a family, a unit. We share. But if you went outside of this house...and another man held you, then I think at this point we would all very much care. Even Jax." I gently tap the end of her nose.

We lay in bed for a while, listening to each other breathe. She keeps twisting and turning, but she's not talking. Just gnawing on her lip, or running her fingers up and down my arm.

"Do you want to go see him?"

She turns and looks at me with a shocked face, then nods slowly. "Guilt is tearing me up inside. I didn't mean to make him shift."

"I know. Go see him."

"But... we're-"

I cut her off. "We're fine. Go see him. I will see you tomorrow morning. Maybe we'll work on controlling your Luxphera."

"What if he doesn't want to see me?"

"Then come to my room."

She smiles and rolls out of bed. "I'm going to shower first."

My dick twitches at the thought of joining her, but she doesn't need me right now. She needs Jax and Jax needs her, whether or not he wants to admit it.

When the bathroom door closes, I head towards the library. I need to find the connection the true fae and Djinn have in relation to spells. Between Emmett's ability to taste blood and Jax shifting, there is definitely a connection. Even I've felt an itching on my back where my wings used to be like they're trying to grow back, but only when she's close.

We need to figure out how she can permanently reverse the spell.

EVERLEE - ONE STEP FOWARD, TWO STEPS BACK

AN HOUR LATER, I'M standing in front of Jax's bedroom door. That's how long I take to shower and get the courage to make it down the hall this far. I don't know why I'm so scared. Usually I wouldn't give a fuck about his thoughts or how rude he is to me, but this... when- if he pushes me away will be a whole other level.

Trying to push the anxiety out, I take a few rapid, deep breaths, then knock on the door. Oh Goddess, what if he answers? What am I going to do? Going to say? Shit. I should have had a plan before I came down here.

What if he doesn't answer? That would be the best thing.

Yes. He's not going to answer. I'll just leave.

I start to turn around when the door handle clicks.

Damn it.

He's standing there, chest exposed, with his arm above his head resting on the door frame, wearing only a pair of tight black boxers that sit so freaking low on his hips. Goddamn wet dream.

"I... uh..." I was speechless before, but now I'm speechless and drooling. Not a great combo.

He pushes the door open a little more, inviting me in without speaking.

His room is pitch black, with the hint of the moon shining through his window. I step in and pause just inside the door, not really knowing what I'm doing. What we're doing...

The door clicks, and he brushes past me and walks to the bed.

Stunned, I look around. He hasn't said a word to me, but I *feel* his feelings. Well, at least I think I do. He feels... sad isn't the right word, neither is depressed, almost like he's given up, but not that either... he's just very melancholy, but not that either.

As my eyes adjust, I notice the room has a light blue glow, highlighting the edges of things like they're covered in soft neon lights. Is this my night vision?

He's lying in bed, with his hands clasped together under his head.

This is not what I expected. I need the fight, the condescension, the fire. Not this Jax.

"Are you going to just stand there?" His words roll off his tongue.

"I... uh..."

He pats the bed.

What in the fuck is going on? Am I dreaming again? Who is this man?

"Is that all you can say?" There's a hint of amusement in his voice, causing a wave to pass through my body. It's a hint of him. Just a glimpse.

Heart racing and skin clammy, I walk over and climb into bed. Leaving ample space between us. His sheets feel like satin on my bare legs, slick and cool to the touch. After my shower, I decided to put on one of Knox's shirts. I needed to wear something of his, so his positive energy would flow through to me.

Seriously, what the fuck is going on?

The hairs on my body are standing on end, reaching out towards him, wanting to touch him, but I don't move.

Call me marble, because I'm a breathing statue.

"You're wet."

My legs clench together. My clit is throbbing like it always does around him, but I wasn't even thinking about anything sexual. Granted, just looking at him when he opened the door did it.

"Your hair."

"Oh. Right. Yea. That." I shake my head to clear it, staring at his ceiling.

"What did you think I meant?"

He rolls over to his side and stares at me and goddess, do I want to look, but for the sake of my panties I don't. Right? Right? My resolve is fading. Shit. Don't look. Don't look. Think about your panties. About your pussy.

I roll over, tucking my arm under my head.

Damn it.

His eyes are glowing as they watch me. Residual magic from when he shifted?

"I... uh... Well..."

He chuckles, "At least you've added another word."

Why is he being so... nice? I had prepared myself for a battle, not this.

"Shut up," I snap, shoving his shoulder and he lets me push him over.

The room is silent, and a few minutes pass.

"Look." I prop myself up on my elbow and he slowly turns to look at me. "I'm... sorry. About earlier."

He says nothing and just stares at me like he's waiting for more.

"About the... light thing... and the... wolf thing."

"I know," he whispers.

He knows? No damn you to Helsgard for what you did. No verbal lashing. Just a simple, I know?

He rolls over onto his back. "I'm also sorry... for earlier."

"What?"

"For... you know... teasing you."

"Yea, that was pretty fucked up."

He cuts his eyes at me, and my pulse quickens.

"You have to stop that," he warns, rolling back onto to his side to look at me.

"Stop what?" I pant out.

"That."

"I'm not doing anything."

"You're always doing something," he admits softly and the air changes yet again.

"I don't... I don't mean to."

"I know." He rolls over again and sighs, like he's battling something inside.

"Did Callum say something to you?"

"What?" he spits out.

"You're... being... nice. I was not expecting this."

"I can be nice."

"You just aren't. Ever. To me. I don't know what I did that makes you hate me so much.""Hate you?" His words are laced with surprise. He rolls over and his hand is on my cheek, turning it towards him. "I don't hate you. I just can't be around you."

My face twists with so much confusion it hurts. "That doesn't even make sense."

He sighs and rolls back over like I'm a child who doesn't understand a simple concept, which is frustrating as hell. I'm smart. I pick up on things that others miss. But Jax. He's an enigma locked in a box. He internalizes everything and lashes out.

After a few more minutes of tense, awkward silence, I toss the covers off and move to roll out of bed.

"Where are you going?" he asks, surprised.

"You literally just said you don't want me around. So I'm leaving. Last I checked, laying in your bed is pretty much as close as you can be to someone."

He grabs my wrist and pulls me back into the bed. "You don't listen. I didn't say I don't want you around, just that I can't be around you."

"Different words, but same meaning."

"No." He pulls me with enough force that my ass is sliding across his satin sheets and into his chest. "You... you infuriate me."

"All the more reason for me to go. I'm like gas to your flame. I didn't come in here to fight. I said what I needed to say, so I can go."

"Damn it, Everlee. Just shut up. Stop talking." He presses his forehead to mine, and I can't ignore the tangle our legs have ended up in.

He doesn't need to tell me to shut up, because I can't speak even if I tried. A ball has lodged itself in my throat as my eyes flicker between his and his lips. His eyes are glowing, his mouth is wanting... I hate the way my body reacts to him.

He's breathing slowly, eyes closed like he's fighting the same battle I am.

"You... I don't want things... ever. The more you want things, the more opportunity you have to be disappointed." He shifts his forehead off mine, but rubs our cheeks together as he inhales. "You are here for now until Samara is no longer a problem. Then you're going to leave."

"I... I don't have to."

"You're a true fae. The first in several hundred years. You aren't going to stay here," he says, like my staying is the dumbest idea.

"Don't tell me what I'm going to do or not do."

He laughs and buries his face in my neck, inhaling a deep breath again, causing tingles to shoot over my body.

"Jax," I pant out. I can't deal with being teased again. The strain in his voice, in his movements, makes me think he's not doing this on purpose, but I can't. I think I'll explode if I get that close to an orgasm again without release.

His hand slides up my body and wraps around the back of my neck, while his thumb presses just under my jawline. Frustration is pulsing out of him, through his fingers, as he stares me in the eye. His eyes flicker wildly between mine and down to my lips, like he's trying to convince himself not to kiss me, to take what he wants.

He growls at himself, turning away, like there are two voices in his head. One telling him to take what he wants and the other warning him against temptation.

"I can go," I whisper so softly that even I can barely hear it.

"Fuck it." He turns his head back to me and presses his lips to mine and kisses me. Kisses me hard. Kisses me like it's the only time he will kiss me, so he wants to feel it all. Savor it all. His tongue presses in and I nearly melt. This man and his kiss. A moan sneaks out and dances between us as the heel of my foot digs into his ass, driving our bodies closer together.

Oh my. A ripple of pleasure passes through my body when I feel his hard cock press against my entrance through our clothes.

His hand tangles in my hair and pulls tight, but the pain quickly turns to pleasure. In one swift motion, he rolls us over so I'm straddling him. He pulls my hair backwards, so my lips slip off his and my face is towards the ceiling. He attacks my throat, biting and sucking and licking. My clit is throbbing, needing to feel his cock. His hands make quick work of my shirt, pulling it over my head and he pauses for a moment, drinking me in.

Guys have never looked at me the way he does- these men do. They want me.

Me.

His hands grip the outside of each breast as he squeezes them together and kisses them, while my hands rove over his body, through his hair. I return the favor and pull his hair hard, jerking his face up and press my lips to his neck. His throat vibrates under my lips as he chuckles, then flips us back over and slides his body over mine. He growls out as his chest brushes over my nipples before he slides down, planting kisses over my breasts and down my stomach.

"Jax," I whimper. He slips a finger into the front of my panties and pulls down just low enough for his tongue to brush across my clit one time, before he releases and my panties cover me up again.

My head digs into the bed as want completely consumes me. He slides down my body further, planting kisses on the inside of my knee as I try to wiggle and writhe. His hands stretch up my body and he pulls my panties off and down my legs, before he flicks them to the floor and slides back up.

"Perfection." He lowers his head agonizingly slow between my legs, blowing a warm breath over my pussy and I'm pretty sure a tear is building in my eye. His tongue swipes up my center and over my clit and I nearly come undone. It won't take me very long to have an orgasm because his teasing is driving me wild.

"Jax," I whimper out, latching my hands onto both sides of his head. "I need you."

He sucks on my clit and then snakes his fingers up between us and presses a finger inside of me, then quickly adds a second.

"Oh my goddess," I cry out, my body instinctively riding his fingers and his face at the same time.

His fingers move with expert precision, gliding into me and hitting all the right spots inside of me, bringing me closer and closer to the edge. He lifts my legs and places them over his shoulders, then locks his arms around them as he dives in. Hungry. Something unleashes inside of him as his tongue spears me. Lapping and sucking.

"Jax. Jax!" I cry out, my orgasm hitting me fast and hard. My hips are bucking, rather trying to buck, but his arms have them locked in place while he continues to lick and suck, pushing my orgasm further and further, drinking up my arousal.

"Jax," I pant out. "You need to stop. Can't. Take. Anymore."

But he doesn't listen. He's wild, dropping my legs and then slides up my body, kissing my neck before he takes my lips in a passionate kiss. My nails dig into his back as my body rubs against his, feeling his cock between my legs.

Need consumes me. My hands slide down his body and loop in the waistband of his pants as I start to pull down. The head of his cock pokes out before his hands latch around my wrists.

"Stop."

Gut punch. "Jax," I cry out, head spinning with lust and confusion.

"I can't have sex with you."

"What?" I balk, staring up at him.

"I can't. Once I stick my dick in you... you're mine."

Heat flashes over my skin. "Jax," I try not to whine. "You just... made me come... so hard."

He smiles, "I know." His tongue runs over his lips. "This was me making up for what I did earlier."

"You were hard then, and you're hard as fuck right now. Your cock is going to fall off."

He laughs. "It's not going to fall off."

"Jax." I tug on his boxers, but his hands clamp tighter.

"Everlee," he scolds.

"We don't have to have sex, but at least let me give you release." My hand slides over his hard cock and his hips reflexively buck up into it, seeking friction. "Please. Let me give this to you," I say, pressing the palm of my hand over his cock, before I slide it back up and slip it into his boxers.

Fuck me, he's huge. I mean, I knew he was huge because I saw it when he was fucking Emmett, but goddamn. To feel it under the palm of my hand.

I want it in me.

I need it in me.

Creating more space for my hand to roam, I angle it so the waistline of his boxers slips over his cock, freeing it from its constraints. Saliva pools in my mouth as I start to slide down.

"No."

"We aren't going to fuck."

"I said it can't be inside of you. Your fuckable mouth counts too, little fae."

"Are you kidding me?"

"Do I strike you as the kind of man who would joke?"

I growl out, causing him to laugh. "Fine, but it won't be as enjoyable."

"I think it will be just fine."

"I don't want it to be just fine though," I say through gritted teeth, irritation surging through me.

Gripping his cock tightly in my hand, I slide it up his length.

"You can't be too rough with me, little fae. I'm a werewolf."

"Let's find out, because right now I've never wanted to suck a dick so bad and you're keeping that from me, so I'm pretty fucking pissed."

He laughs. "Lay down and shut up." He rips his boxers off and throws them to the ground and for a second, I'm hopeful that he's going to fuck me, but I've also learned Jax is stubborn and will not bend.

He grabs my wrists and pins them above my head and rolls his hips over mine, so his cock slides between my glistening pussy and over my clit.

"This... this is so fucking close to sex...it's unfair."

"I'm not inside of you."

"Who cares? You fucked Emmett."

"Emmett's different. You're different."

I growl out and wiggle my body, trying to get my wrists free, but he only clamps tighter, pressing his cock up between my pussy, letting it slide back and forth on top of me.

"You're so fucking wet." His head dips down as he clamps onto my neck.

"This isn't fair."

"Then tell me to stop and I will."

"Fuck you!" I chomp out.

"Already told you we won't be fucking."

Anger prickling under my skin and with my body pinned to the bed under his thrusting hips, I do the only thing I can do. I turn my head and bite at his neck. And I don't hold back.

He unleashes a growl so loud and so fierce that I freeze, completely stunned.

"Everlee. Don't fucking do that again," he pants, eyes glowing.

At first, I think it's because he's mad, but then I realize it's because he likes it. Really likes it.

"Do this?" I bite again.

His back arches, sending his hips gyrating into me with such speed and force, I'm fairly certain my precious little nub is going to be bruised tomorrow. And who the fuck calls it a nub, anyway? I hate that I just did, but at this moment in time, that is the only thing that sounds appropriate.

"Everlee," he murmurs against my skin. Teeth pressed, ready to mark, but he pulls away and rests his forehead on the pillow.

Wanting to help with his release and feel his cock, I thread my hand between our bodies and circle my fingers around his length, giving him something to press into. It's so slick, covered in our arousal, that it slides in with ease. He groans in appreciation, so I tighten my grip around him and he loses control, thrusting and pumping, riding my hand and my clit.

"I'm going to come again."

"Come for me, little fae. Come all over my cock."

My legs hook around his and lock on the inside of his knees while I press up into him, riding the length of his cock, moaning his name just as he presses off me and watches himself explode on my chest.

"Oh, goddam." He rolls off me to the side, and we stare at the ceiling.

After my heart has slowed down, and it doesn't sound like I've just ran up a flight of stairs, I grumble, "I would have rather fucked you."

"Me too, but it's not going to happen." He sucks my nipple in his mouth quickly, then kisses it before rolling off the bed. "I'll be right back. I'm going to get a towel for you."

I snarl at him, causing him to laugh as he walks into his bathroom. His ass must have been what artists used for their artwork. So muscular and smooth. The kind of ass you just want to smack and grab and do lots of fun things with. And those two dimples in his lower back...

"You're moaning," he calls from the bathroom.

Embarrassed, I snatch a pillow and hold it over my face while I scream into it.

This is definitely not what I planned. I wanted to apologize and was prepared for a fight. Not two orgasms and him being... vulnerable. Well, his version.

"Hey Ev," he calls and just as I push the pillow off, he throws a towel in my face.

"Ass." I snatch it off my face and rub his come off my chest and then through my legs to soak up as much of my arousal as possible, then throw it back.

While he's putting it back in the bathroom, I roll off the bed to find my underwear that he's tossed somewhere in the room.

"What are you doing?" he asks, walking back in, still completely naked.

"Looking for my underwear. Where did you put them?"

He wraps his arms around me and throws me onto the bed. "You don't need those tonight."

"Who are you right now?"

"Shut up." He crawls in bed behind me and wraps me in his arms.

"You want me to go to sleep with your dick pressed up against me? The same dick you won't use to fuck me?"

"Can you handle that?"

"Can and want are two different things."

"Good night." His arms pull me to him tightly and I'm at a loss for words.

This Jax is a completely different man than I've seen. He's playful, fun, but still stubborn as shit.

JAX - MAN IN CHAINS

<hr>

I'm such an asshole.

The morning sun is filtering through the curtains and Everlee is in my bed. Naked. Chest down, arms spread out like a beautiful starfish.

What the fuck did I do?

Last night shouldn't have happened. I was weak. She- she makes me weak.

She also makes me furious and hot. So fucking hot. I've wanted to sink my cock inside of her since the moment I laid eyes on her, but I can't. She's different. But when she bit me last night, I almost lost all resolve. My wolf responded and was driving me wild.

Damn it!

I shouldn't have... did what we did last night.

I've tasted her and now she's all I want for breakfast, lunch, and dinner. I want to live on my knees in front of her pussy and make her moan my name. But I can't. What happened last night can never happen again.

It was a mistake.

A weak moment. And I'm not weak. I'm unattached. I'm selfish.

FUCK!

Being selfish is what got me into that mess last night. When I turned into my wolf... words can't explain what I felt. He wanted to run, but we couldn't. He didn't understand that it was all temporary. When she left, so did he.

The confusion he felt when she ran out of the bathroom nearly broke me. It only took a minute before I shifted back and my wolf was gone. I laid on the floor as he struggled to get back out, hitting that invisible barrier that has blocked him for so long. But I still felt him inside of me. Pacing. Angry.

When she came knocking on my door, excitement fluttered through me, through him. She looked sad, and I wanted to hold her, while at the same time, my wolf wanted to be near her. To him, she was an opportunity. An opportunity for freedom.

And me, the selfish prick, wanted to continue feeling my wolf, so I talked to her, kept her around. When she tried to leave, I should've let her go, but my wolf cried out, so I stopped her. She likely couldn't hear the guilt in my voice, but I could. And I hated it.

All the emotions. All the pain, and fear, and wanting... it became too much.. When I kissed her, that was all it took. I lost control and I *don't* lose control.

"Do you want to go out with me?" Emmett asks from somewhere in the house. It's still very early, so he's probably in his room.

"Yes. I need out of here." Guilt rips through me as my eyes fall on Everlee again, still asleep.

I don't want to leave her- my wolf doesn't want to leave her, but I have to. He doesn't understand. It's not healthy to stay around her.

Several minutes later, I'm standing in Emmett's room with him sitting in his chair by the window with a smug look on his face. "Told you that you wanted to fuck her."

"Shut the fuck up," I scoff, only causing him to laugh. "And we didn't have sex."

"I know. I listened to every delicious moan and groan. She wanted your cock bad. Why didn't you give it to her?"

"I don't want to talk about it."

He cuts his eyes at me as he walks into the hall. "I want to be back to cook them breakfast. I've been slacking on my duties since she's been here."

"I know. Knox tried to cook breakfast a few days ago and nearly caught the whole damn house on fire."

"He still owes me a new pan. Fucker destroyed it and that's a hard thing to do."

We're in our black Audi, driving away from the house minutes later.

"So you want to talk about last night?" he asks, casting a side glance over his shoulder.

"No."

He sighs, clearly not the answer he wanted to hear. He's always been the 'talk through your feelings' kind of guy. Not me. I'm a 'push them down so far that you grind them into non-existence' kind of guy.

"Fine. How about this? Everlee is supposed to help us break the spell that Samara cast. When she does that... what does that mean for us? Last night when you were in your wolf form... I had a hard time controlling my feelings. It was like millennia of hate was seeping out around us."

"I felt it too." For so long, I'd been focused on getting my wolf back, I haven't stopped to think about what that means. What I could lose. Emmett is my best friend, but vampires and werewolves are archnemesii. Is that even a word? It feels like it should be a word.

"I'm also concerned, because I'm scared I'm going to go back to being a ripper again. While the inability to taste anything has truly sucked, I haven't killed anyone."

"So you don't want her to break the spell?" I wasn't sure how I felt about that. I wanted my wolf back, but at what cost? Could Emmett and I try to remain friends? If he can't control his bloodlust, then I know there's no way.

"I want her too, but... also... I don't. When- if she breaks the spell, then she leaves. I can't explain it, but... I don't want her to leave. I don't know if my feelings are jumbled up because with her around, I've been able to taste blood again, but... I don't know if it's something more."

"I was a dick last night."

"Before or after you teased her and nearly made her come?"

"All the above. I shouldn't have teased her, but..." I growl out. "She gets under my skin. I don't know how or why. And then last night when she came back... I was selfish. I didn't want to lose my wolf and when she's around, so is he."

"That's why you didn't fuck her? Because you were guilty?"

"You sneaky fuck?"

He cuts his eyes at me. "You need to talk about your feelings, brother."

I growl and look out of the window. "It doesn't matter if I talk about them or not. Last night was a mistake and won't happen again. It's for the best."

"Makes sense. Don't get attached and just fight your feelings because nothing can go wrong then. Your feelings will just stop and disappear."

I caught every ounce of sarcasm in his words, but ignore him.

We turn down a small alleyway beside a large building we just purchased several months ago. It used to be a dance club twenty years ago and has sat vacant and empty since. We want to do something with it, but we don't know yet. We've talked about reopening it as a dance club, but we aren't sure.

"She's like a vixen, Jax. She's not going to just disappear quietly or gently into the night. She's got too much spirit and fiery personality."

"She *is* a vixen." A vixen who is worming her way into our lives and making a home there. It hasn't been very long, but the bond... the pull drawing us all together is undeniable.

Like our past lives were intertwined and we've just been waiting.

We enter through the side door into a hall that leads to a two-story room. The painted black walls are chipping with several holes throughout where looters have come in and trashed the place in years past. Torn booths sit haphazardly on the floor, while dangling lights hang overhead. We make our familiar trek upstairs into the office that sits in the back corner and punch the code in to unlock the door. It's the only thing we've done to the place since we bought it.

When the door opens, the iron chains jangle together as the forlorn man backs into the corner to hide.

EVERLEE - BACK DOOR, ONLY DOOR

WHEN I WAKE UP, Jax is gone. I'm not shocked or hurt, maybe I should be, but while last night felt amazing, it also felt temporary. Even in those last moments before we fell asleep, when he pulled me in tight, it almost felt like... he was treasuring the moment while it lasted. I saw a different side of Jax last night. A more vulnerable side. One that I don't think he will ever share again.

My stomach growls. A gentle reminder I need to fill it, so I roll out of bed, gather my clothes and pad down the hall to my room. I don't take the time to actually put clothes on, because at this point, everyone in this house has seen me naked and I've also never been shy about my body.

Twenty minutes later I'm walking down the stairs into the kitchen and find Knox and Callum sitting at the bar nibbling on muffins and drinking coffee and tea. I've learned that Callum likes his coffee, while Knox seems to prefer his morning tea.

Knox looks at me and starts pumping his eyebrows. "Good morning."

A blush tinges my cheeks. "Good morning."

"I'm glad you and Jax made up."

"I'm not sure we did."

"Sounded like it. Although it's kind of shitty he didn't let you play with his cock. What a glorious cock it is."

"Did you listen to the whole thing?"

"Would you be mad if I said yes?"

My stomach tightens and I feel my eyes pulse.

He sees my reaction and smiles. "I knew it, you little kinky fucker."

"Shut up."

"Can't. I have no filter and just say what pops into my mind."

"It's true," Callum says, standing up and planting a kiss on my forehead. "Emmett was supposed to cook breakfast this morning, but got held up with something."

"So, again, I had to fill in."

"You didn't cook again, did you?"

"Stop! That was just one time. And no. I would have, but Callum made me go to the bakery down the street and buy muffins." He opens his arm wide to show the assortment of muffins on the stove.

"I didn't know what you would like, so I got all kinds."

"That you certainly did." There are enough muffins to feed a small army. Lemon zest, chocolate chip, blueberry, raspberry crumble, pumpkin, and several other ones that I'm not sure what they are.

"He may have gone overboard," Callum chuckles.

"That doesn't seem like something he would do," I laugh and Knox just sticks his tongue out playfully.

"Fine! Next time, I'm going to only pick one for you and it will be squid flavored topped with roe."

My stomach churns at the visualization of a squid muffin. "Not cool dude."

Knox is laughing as I grab the double chocolate chunk muffin.

"Excellent choice," Knox coos, holding up the wrapper of his. "You're going to want some milk though."

"What? No squid muffin?" I can't help but smile when Knox is around. He just exudes charm and light and... pure happiness.

"*Everlee*," Lizzy calls.

"What's wrong?" Callum asks, reading my face.

"*I'm outside. Open up the door. My ass is cold.*"

"Lizzy. She's here. Outside," I answer, completely confused. Why is she over here? Did something happen?

"Lizzy? Why?" Callum asks, walking to the front.

"*Back door. Only door.*"

"She's at the back," I chuckle at her dirty little joke. I swear sex is on her mind all the time, or at the very least, inappropriate sexual jokes, usually at my expense.

Knox walks to the back door and standing there looking up at us is a black cat with emerald green eyes.

"Come in," Knox invites, stepping out of the way.

The cat walks in, then shifts into Lizzy, her hair unkempt on top of her head. It's been so long since I've seen it free of ties or braids that I forgot how much hair she actually has.

"Good morning, men! Everlee!" She reaches over to give me a hug, her bare breast rubbing against my shirt.

"Let me get you a blanket," Callum offers, with a modicum of concern.

"That would be great. I'm freezing. Ooh, are those muffins?" she asks, walking over to the stove.

"Help yourself," Knox offers.

Callum hands her a blanket just as she's finding a seat beside me at the bar and Knox is getting her some hot pumpkin and vanilla tea.

"Well, isn't this cozy? I see you're taking care of my girl." Lizzy pumps her eyebrows at me and smirks. "It's about time someone is. Rather somefour."

"Lizzy," I subtly scold.

She looks at me with a dumbfounded look, then rolls her eyes. "Fine."

"What's going on? Why are you here?" Callum asks before I can.

"Geez. Can't a girl come say hi to her BFF? Her sister from another mister?"

"Liz."

"Fine. I see it's business only with you all. I've found something I wanted to share."

"About Samara?"

Lizzy nods, because she's stuffed the rest of the muffin in her mouth, then speaks in garbled words, "Sorry. Starving."

Knox grabs her another and leans across the counter, putting it on her plate.

She nods and holds it up in the air. A wordless thank you before she peels off the wrapper.

"So, what did you find?" I press.

"Tony brought a few books from Helsgard, so we were doing some research last night."

"Last night?" I tease.

"Stop," she blushes, then mouths 'later'. "Anyway, we went through all the books and couldn't find anything aside from the usual Djinn are dark fae who are believed to have wiped out or contributed to the mass execution of true fae. So we took a quick trip to Helsgard."

"You just went to Helsgard?" Knox asks equally parts shocked and impressed.

"Tony arranged it. But that's not what's important. What's important is the book we *did* find. It was old. Super old. We had to use magic to flip the pages, because they encased it in an airtight box to prevent it from further deterioration." She takes another bite of muffin. "You would think with all the advancements of our magic, we'd be able to find a way to protect historical works."

"Or perhaps just rewrite them?" Callum notes, with a hint of sarcasm.

"That would be a lot because the book is huge. And if that weren't the only problem, you don't know what's in the book because all the pages are blank. It only reveals what's on the pages when you ask it a question."

"So there could be a wealth of information in the book. You just don't know until you know?"

"Yes. Very frustrating. Tony and I stayed up all night asking it a variation of questions about the Djinn fae. All we came up with was the rules and then something else."

"Go on," Knox urges, hands clasped under his chin.

"Oh, look who's back," Jax snipes, walking into the kitchen with Emmett following close behind. All the guys pass a silent telling glance between one another like they're checking in, but I don't know for what. Jax's eyes fall on me and a heat races across my skin, before he turns away just as quickly to grab a drink out of the refrigerator.

"What is this nonsense?" Emmett asks walking over to the muffins, picking up one briefly before putting it back down.

"You were out, and we didn't know when you'd be back," Knox defends. Emmett fills a pot with hot water before putting it on the stove and then grabbing a blood bag out of the fridge.

"Looks delicious," Lizzy says monotone before her eyes snap at me. She sometimes has a bad habit of inside thoughts slipping out.

"Better than me eating your friend," Emmett retorts.

"When you say it like that, I don't know if you're being kinky or not," Lizzy claps back.

Emmett stares at her for a second in awe, then chuckles.

"Anyway, as I was saying... there's a small blurb about something called the Mist of Morreux that has been locked away in Pandora's box. It also mentioned another book- the book of Maldor, but it's been lost for a while and I've only heard whispers of the mist, so I don't know how it could help. I wanted to come and see if you all have come across it because there isn't much in the book."

The room shifts and I get a feeling they have, even though no one is jumping to say anything, so I press, "Surely you must have heard about it at some point, Callum?"

He looks at me, studying my face, then takes a breath. Before he can speak, Jax calls his name, nearly shutting him up, but Callum holds his hand out. "Yes. We have heard of the Mist of Morreux. When Samara used our wishes against us so many years ago, we were very upset. We searched high and low for something that could reverse the spell or end her."

There's a strange weight in the air, between all the guys, like they know something they aren't saying and are curious how far Callum's going to go. Emmett's stirring boiling water, trying to pretend like he's not paying attention. Knox is fiddling with the paper wrapper of his muffin and Jax... well, he just looks confused... maybe angry. When I catch him looking at me, he quickly looks away.

Callum continues, "We found the Book of Maldor and in it, it spoke of Morreux. He was a dark wizard hundreds of years ago. After the Great Fall, and without the true fae around to provide guardrails, he sought infinite power. He practiced in the dark arts, gathering artifacts from all over and would leach out their powers. He became very powerful, but at a cost. As the power grew within him, he began to lose control and it started feeding off of him. Some say he grew weaker and his hair fell out and that he turned to skin and bones, then died."

"Some say? You don't believe that?" I ask, sliding forward on the edge of my chair.

Callum studies me for a minute, then shakes his head. "I don't. There were rumors a black mist in the shape of a man walked around. Some mistook it for the dark shadows of another realm, but this was a man, not a shadow."

When I glance around at the guys, I can't help but watch Jax. His body language. He's not happy, but he's also not saying anything.

"How was he stopped? I assume he was stopped because I haven't heard of this Mist of Morreux floating around and killing people."

"He was stopped. But it was very tricky. Weapons and magic did nothing to hurt him. He was -is, very powerful." Callum glances up at Jax and gives him a sorrow-filled glance. Like we are getting closer to a truth, the truth, some truth.

"Helsgard worked with members of both the Seelie and Unseelie courts to come up with a series of strategically planned attacks. They were able to break off pieces of the... mist so they could study it. They quickly learned they had to keep the pieces separated. When it came together with other parts... or pieces- I don't know what you want to call it, it began to move and think."

Eyes snapped wide open in shock. I glance at Lizzy, who is just as enraptured in this story as I am. Jax catches my attention when he shifts, propping his foot against the wall and crossing his arms. I'm dying to know what is going through his head right now. To know how all of this relates to him, because it definitely does. I'm still just missing some key pieces.

"*Are you ok?*" I ask him.

His eyes settle on me, watching me for a moment before he tosses me a wink and nods his head back towards Callum.

"Think?" Lizzy whispers, mostly to herself.

A shiver runs up my spine just visualizing this dark mist moving through the air with thought.

"So what happened? Do they have him all contained together, or are parts of him scattered around? If someone gets enough parts, will it then come back? How do you contain a mist?" I ask rapid fire, thoughts moving a mile a minute.

Callum chuckles and places his hand on mine. "They found a way to contain it. Rather, a poor boy in a village did, by accident."

My brow creases, but I try to hold my tongue.

He smiles, like he's about to go into another story. "Before the mist existed, many, many years ago, there was a beautiful flowering tree called the Urgsam tree. This tree was beautiful. Its trunk was hearty and smooth, with a mixture of light brown and cream swirled through it. It had large green leaves with flowers that hung like pink and yellow bells looking like ballgowns around the tree. At night, the tree would almost glow and sparkle. There weren't many of these trees that existed and some believe the Gods planted them throughout because no one ever saw them grow. They were... breathtaking."

"I've never heard of it."

"Most haven't," he says, frowning and etching his nail into the countertop.

"I don't know what started the rumors, but because of their beauty, people thought they were magical. Believed they held a mystical property. So the humans cut them down. They'd seen the fae and heard rumors of their powers. They believed this tree was the cause." He shakes his head and his face falls. "It was a beautiful tree that held no mystical powers."

"They cut down all the trees?" A ball of pain forms in my chest, thinking about these beautiful trees that were destroyed for no reason.

"It took them a while to realize they had no magic. The magic was simply the beauty of the tree. They abandoned the trees and tried to sell the trunks for scraps, but no one wanted them. So they just littered the ground until they turned to nothing. A poor village boy found a scrap piece of wood and carved a ring box for his mother." He pauses for a second. "Now all of this was happening at the same time Helsgard planned their series of attacks on Morreux. I don't know the specifics, but somehow a piece of Morreux ended up in this boy's ring box for his mother. This boy's ring box was the only thing that was able to contain the mist. Helsgard went out in search of this Urgsam wood, but by this time, most all the wood was gone or had been destroyed. All they could find were little chips."

"So what happened? They obviously found a box," Lizzy asks with her muffin paused halfway to her mouth.

"Helsgard had expanded their search for the Urgsam tree and found it in another realm. They were meeting with a woman named Pan on her island for an unrelated matter. She wouldn't say where she got the box from, only that it was a gift. Helsgard took it against her wishes, but said they would name it after her."

"Pandora's box," Lizzy and I sigh in unison, everything starting to click into place.

"So you have the Book of Maldor?" I ask.

Callum and Jax pass a glance at one another and I don't miss the slight head shake Jax gives Callum.

"We don't have the book anymore."

"Where did it go? We can just go get it."

"I don't know where it is."

"Well, fiddlesticks and biscuits." Lizzy swipes her arm in an awe shucks kind of movement.

"Do we know how the mist can stop Samara?" I ask, grabbing my trash and throwing it away. The skin on the back of my neck prickles, but I fight the urge to look at Jax. I know he's watching me. I can feel it. My skin can feel it.

Lizzy pants loudly and fans herself.

"What's wrong?" I ask, completely confused and concerned.

"You two," she points at Jax and me. "I can't handle the glances and the heat radiating between you two."

"Liz," I scold.

"What? I can't help it. I'm an empath. I can't handle you two being horny around me. Hell, all of you. It makes me feel... things." She shivers her shoulders.

Jax rolls his eyes. "Why is she still here?" "Because she's my best friend and my sister." I defend, then add. "Unfortunately, sometimes."

She grabs her chest, then bats her hand softly at me. "I don't do well in quiet or serious situations. It's like I'm allergic and shit just comes out of my mouth. I have no filter."

"You don't say?"

"Why are you in such a pissy mood?" Knox jumps in.

Jax presses off the wall and steps towards Knox, who falters a bit in his step, but holds his ground.

"Let's get back to business. I can't stay gone long," Lizzy says, attempting to cool the room. While she has an uncanny ability to say the most inappropriate shit all the time, she can also read a room. Usually when she does stupid shit, it's because she's testing her own theories that are percolating in her mind. She's always been the action-reaction kind of thinker. Why waste time thinking through things? Just try and watch, then move on. Efficient, but it's also gotten her into trouble on several occasions.

"Mist? Samara?" I ask, giving our conversation a direction.

Callum continues, "The theory is that Morreux will feed off her darkness, weakening her enough so that we may capture her and bind her and Morreux to a lamp or something else and then bury it where no one can find it."

"Well, that seems to be the only theory we have right now," Lizzy says, pushing away from the bar. "I need to get back. I will do some digging and see if I can find anything about the book or Morreux. Maybe Tony has someone he trusts at Helsgard that will help with either. They are interested in Everlee."

"Do they want to give her some protection?" Jax scoffs. "Or maybe handle Samara for us?"

"They try not to interfere until something has happened."

"What the fuck kind of sense does that make? Wait until Samara kidnaps her or kills her... then they will do something?" Jax yells.

"Look. I didn't say I agree with it, but they can't do anything right now. Their hands are tied, plus Samara is powerful. Only thing equal in power is... her." She points at me.

Being silly, I throw my hands out to the side with jazz hands.

"Whatever!" Jax sneers, then walks upstairs.

"So broody." Lizzy wiggles her fingers and I just cast her a look. She looks back at Callum. "Look, Tony and I want to help. While Helsgard won't step in yet, they sent Tony, and he's reporting back. He's trying to get a few guards here, but they're being difficult. I'm going to keep looking into a few things and if you find out anything, I'm but a mere incantation away. Or a phone call for the more modern folk in the room." She slides a business card across the counter.

"Betty's Bitchin' Rides?" Callum asks, confused.

"No. Flip it over. That was the only paper I had. Although if you ever need a ride, Betty is your girl. A little wild child, but she'll be discreet."

"Thanks," Callum says slowly.

"Anytime! Take care of my girl. In all the ways that matter." She puts her finger through a hole she makes with her other hand.

"Fuck Lizzy. Go!" I slap her arm.

Captain Inappropriate.

She looks at the bowl of gummy bears on the counter and motions to take some. "These aren't sugar free, are they?"

"No," Callum answers, confused.

"Whew! Last time I had some sugar free ones, they lit my ass up. I've never shit so much in my life. It was like a small dragon had crawled up my ass and breathed fire out of it. Brutal. Definitely don't recommend."

Callum looks between Knox and me, then back to Lizzy, completely speechless.

Without missing a beat, she shrugs then continues as if she didn't just have the largest over share of the century, "I shall shed this skin and go forth into that good day!" She drops the blanket at the same time she shifts into a cat and saunters across the room to the back door. Do I see an extra swish in her step? Absolutely. The sass is nearly dripping out of her.

JAX - FEEL THE WOLF

TODAY SUCKS, AND IT'S not even lunchtime yet. The tips of my nails dig into the palms of my fist as I walk up the stairs, walk down the hall, and up the last set of stairs. I need to go for a swim. I need to punch the water. I need to let all of my emotions and stresses out.

This is why you don't allow yourself to get involved with people, or get close to people. They will only hurt you.

Images of Brady sitting chained in the corner of our office etch themselves permanently into my brain. He looked so bad. Worse than I've ever seen him. Nothing more than skin and bones- a fraction of the man he used to be.

His skin is so pale it's almost translucent and wisps of hair lay scattered across his scalp. The iron chains binding him were meant to protect him, meant to slow Morreux from poisoning him, consuming him, piece by piece. Emmett has been feeding him his blood to help prolong his life, to buy us more time so we can figure a way out of this.

He's my brother. Not by blood, but a brotherhood forged in battle and in triumph. He's seen me in my darkest days and at my best.

My clothes fall to the ground and I dive into the pool and sit on the wet pebbled surface, waving my arms back and forth slowly to keep me under water, staring into the blue. I'm not a selkie like Knox, but I can hold my breath for over two minutes. Today, I'm going to push it to three.

Memories of what used-to-be, play on repeat- cutting at me like a thousand razor blades. Brady and I running through fields of battle, fighting for territory and domination, our wolf's paws digging into the surface- dirt and grass flying into the air. The camaraderie, the brotherhood.

Gone.

He's nothing more than a shell. A better man would let death consume his friend. Take away his suffering.

But I'm not a good man.

I'm a selfish man.

A man determined.

And I know Brady could never forgive me if I let him die the easy way. He's a fighter and as long as he is fighting, I will fight for him. With him.

My lungs burn with need, so I push off the floor and breach the top, sucking in a big gulp of air.

"You had a few more seconds before I was coming in there after you," Knox says, sitting on the edge of the pool with his feet dangling in the water. When I don't speak, he continues, "How was he?"

I swim to the edge of the pool and prop my arms on the edge beside him. "Not good. Not good at all. I don't know how much longer he has Knox. He's pale and nothing but skin and bones."

He pats his hand on my shoulder. "I'm sorry Jax. We have Everlee now. Maybe she can help."

"I don't know Knox. Maybe if she was more experienced. She has no control over her powers right now. She's no more use to us than a child."

"That's harsh."

"I don't mean it to be," I sigh, "But it's the truth."

"She's getting stronger every day."

"I just don't know if it will be soon enough. He's dying and I don't know how much more Emmett can give. He's already consuming three times his normal amount for Brady and for Everlee."

"Everlee?"

"He tries to keep himself full, so it minimizes the urges he has. He doesn't want to kill her."

"Well, that's good. I like her Jax. Like really like her."

"You're infatuated. It's something new."

"No. It feels more than that. She feels like a missing piece."

He feels the same thing I feel. No matter how hard I try to fight it or deny it, she just seems to fit. Which is just as frustrating. I know Callum feels the same and if I had to guess Emmett, too.

"Well, we're running out of time."

"Maybe if she saw him, she could help. Maybe use her light ball."

"She has no control over it, Knox. She's a liability. We can't risk it. She'd likely kill him and I could never forgive myself or her."

The hair on my arms stands on end as tingles move across my entire body.

"What the fuck is that?" Knox says and then looks at his feet. "Jax?" His tone is panicked.

Knox's feet are gone and in their place a pair of flippers.

"It's fucking Everlee." A growl rumbles deep in my chest, then bellows out.

I leap out while Knox slides in. His body turning into a seal.

Jax! Knox cries out.

The joy in his voice is almost so much it's heartbreaking. It's temporary, this feeling. When Everlee stops doing whatever she's doing, it will be gone. She doesn't do it on purpose, but it's evil. Not her. Never her. Just the whole damn thing.

Another growl echoes out as my hands and arms turn ridged by my side, clawing, fighting for transition.

Fuck. I need to get inside.

I can't transition again. I can't deal with the feeling of my wolf, only for it to disappear.

"Everlee!" I yell out.

Silence.

Another growl.

Moving with speed, I leap down the set of stairs to the hallway with our bedrooms.

Nothing.

Another pull. The first crack.

Stop wolf! We aren't shifting.

Let me run. I need to run.

No. This is temporary.

How in the fuck am I feeling her? Last time when she left, so did the magic.

She's getting stronger. She's mad.

No shit. On both accounts.

I could almost feel her rage seeping through each pulse.

Needing to hurry, I run down the hall and look all around the kitchen and dining room.

Nothing.

Library.

Maybe she and Callum are fucking again.

Jealousy shoots down my spine.

The speed with which I'm moving doesn't afford me the opportunity to open the doors gently. Instead, they burst open, nearly flying off their hinges.

I'm not prepared for what I find.

Callum is standing in a shredded white button down with his wings spread out wide to the side, staring out of the large bay windows. Scales of blue and gold shimmer in the late morning sun.

"Callum," I choke out, skidding to a stop.

He turns around, his face unreadable.

Judging by his wingspan, I bet he's a massive dragon.

"Where is she?" I spit out.

"Downstairs."

I rush to the wall with the secret entry and nearly rip the book out of the wall and press the button.

"Don't stop her yet." His words are soft, wanting, as his wings fold in around him, hugging him.

My heart aches for him. They don't understand. They should not relish in this moment. They should not want this moment. It's fleeting until we can reverse the spell. They will understand later, even if they hate me now.

Eyes adjusting immediately to the dark, I leap down the center of the spiral staircase and land with a soft thud. I'm standing behind her in less than a minute, hand gripped on her hip and spinning her around.

"You need to stop," I warn, skin itching, wanting the shift.

Her eyes meet mine, and there's pure fire dancing in them.

Shit.

EVERLEE - LUXPHERA

WHAT THE FUCK? NO more use than a child? A liability? His words repeat over and over again in my head. I get it. I'm not the true fae they have known, but damn it. Give a girl some time. I can be.

The hairs on my arms stand on end and a tingle dances on my skin. My hands get hot and there it is. A light ball, the size of a pearl and growing.

Watch it.

Pour my rage into it.

The ball continues to grow until it's the size of a melon. Instinctively, I throw the ball into the darkness and when it hits the far wall, it lights up the room.

Again.

Eager to prove them all wrong and show I have control, I stare at my hands, willing another ball to form.

But nothing.

"Damn it!" I shake my hands, staring at them. "Come on!"

Nothing.

If willing something to happen made it happen, then I would have the largest light ball known to fae. I have to prove to them- to Jax - that I can be useful.

Come on, light ball. Luxphera!
A spark of a light flickers in my hand.
Yes! Yes!
Imagine the ball. Imagine the Luxphera.
Darkness surrounds me as I close my eyes and concentrate on the ball.
My hand tingles and when I open my eyes, there is another ball. I throw it out into the darkness again, illuminating the room.
Again! I command myself.
The ball forms easier this time.
I repeat this over and over again, until I create them on command.
After Lizzy left, I needed some space. I'm pretty sure Lizzy is going to do something stupid because she had that look in her eye. It's the same look she's had since we were kids. She thinks she hides it from me, but I just don't call her out on it, because she'd change and I wouldn't be prepared for her shenanigans. Only this time it isn't chemistry class or Janice's hair color. This is my life, and I'm stuck here because I don't have control over my powers and what's worse is that Jax sees it. And calls it out.
Another light ball shoots into the dark before a hand wraps around my waist and spins me around.
"You need to stop," he warns, eyes glowing gold.
"You need to leave," I retort, trying to shove him off.
"Fucking hell, Everlee. Stop!" he growls, tightening his grip.
"What's the problem? Is it because I'm useless or a liability?"
Am I being childish right now? Absolutely. But fuck it. I'm pissed. Pissed at myself and pissed at him. Frustrated that he's right and I don't have control over these powers. I want to help, but right now I feel like nothing more than a bump on a log, waiting to be scraped off by Samara.
Placing my hands on his chest, I shove him away. Hard.
He slides back several feet.

Whelp, I guess my super strength came in.

His head rotates partially to the side. "Everlee," he warns in a low tone laced with venom.

"Leave. I'm practicing and I'd hate if you got hurt. I'd never be able to forgive myself. Or you." The sarcasm is dripping off every word, playing back his words for him. There's no way he can't pick up on the fact I'm mocking him.

He rushes over to me in the blink of an eye and grabs my wrist, shoving me backwards into his transition cage. "Are you fucking kidding me right now? You're pissed about that?"

"Get off me Jax," I command through set teeth.

"Every word I said is true, and you know it. You *are* a liability. Just because you're a true fae... it doesn't mean shit."

"Get off me," I repeat, pushing against him, but he doesn't budge, this time using his shifter strength to keep him in place.

"Tell me you feel confident using your powers. Tell me!"

My knee travels up with an unforgiving swiftness, knocking his balls into his throat. His hands release as he bends over, holding his stomach.

"What the fuck, Everlee?" he growls out, eyes glowing even more gold. It's his wolf. I can feel it at the edge, waiting to come out.

Pushing myself around him, I take off into the darkness of the room.

While I don't think Jax will hurt me, now I'm not too sure. His wolf is there and I'm pretty sure I just pissed him off.

"Get back here, Everlee!"

"No."

Silence dances around me just before the gust of wind blows my hair in my face.

"Don't run from me, little fae." His words are smooth like silk. Dangerous silk that has a mind of its own and wants to wrap around your throat and strangle you.

My heart is pounding out of my chest, an equal mix of fear and arousal.

His hand wraps around my throat as he pushes me back into the wall. "You should have listened to me." He leans down, running his nose up my cheek into my hairline.

My breath is shallow as moisture pools between my legs. No. This is not allowed.

"Get off me, Jax!" I press against his hard chest, but he doesn't budge.

"Is that what you want, little fae?" His nose touches mine as his lips pause just above mine. Taunting. My body betrays my brain, as my chin tilts up to take his kiss, even though I know I shouldn't.

Instead of kissing me, he smiles. "So easy, little fae. So eager for attention."

"Fuck you!" I spit out through set teeth.

He chuckles low in this chest. "Wouldn't you like to?"

"Wouldn't you? Your boner is poking me in the stomach."

He looks down and, using the brief distraction, I break his hold on my throat, duck under his arm, and push him against the wall before running away.

His shadowy chuckle lingers in the dark behind me, echoing and bouncing off the walls. Captivated by the darkness and the echoes within, I stop and turn around. Did he give up?

That's when I feel it. Every hair on my body stands like iron filings searching for a magnet. My hands instinctively raise, readying to fire Luxphera into the dark.

The growl sounds just as a beast of a wolf leaps from the darkness, claws outstretched and teeth curled over white-hot gums.

Stunned, I fall back onto the floor and push backwards with my hands and feet as the wolf comes to a stop standing right above me.

"This isn't funny, Jax!" I hold my hands up in front of him, a blue glow flowing between my fingers, dancing like smoke on the skin. "I don't want to hurt you."

A second later, the wolf shifts back into Jax, who is crouched over top of me, completely naked. My eyes meet his, then flicker away, uncomfortable with the way his gaze makes me feel.

"Everlee," he pants, as his eyes dart wildly across my face. A mixture of anger and want twisting and fighting.

I shake my head, breaths coming in shallow, short puffs.

He leans down, so slowly that it's almost like he isn't even moving. He's giving me time to stop him. To say no. But I can't. I won't.

Our lips touch, and his tongue explores. I part mine, letting him in. His body lowers just a bit, so his chest brushes against the outside of my clothes and his forearms rest on the floor. Our kiss deepens as he continues to explore, pulling moans out of me one after the other.

One hand reaches up and tightens in his hair, pulling him down to me while the other rakes up his back as I lift my body into his, grinding against his already hard cock. Our bodies continue to rock into one another, seeking friction, seeking release, as our kiss gets more wild and needy.

And then...

Nothing.

He stops and pushes away so fast, I'm pretty sure my mouth and tongue are still moving and kissing the air.

When my brain catches up, I slide into a sitting position and stare at him. "What the fuck, Jax?"

"I told you. I can't."

"No. You can. You're choosing not to. There's a difference!"

Completely stunned, I push myself to standing and brush down my shirt. "You are a coward. You're scared of getting hurt, so you push everyone who cares about you away."

"You care about me?" he scoffs. "You barely know me."

"What the fuck does that have to do with anything? I can care about someone I just met, or someone who I've been around nearly every hour of every day for the last week. Who rescued me from a jackass vamp and who is protecting me now. So, fuck you. Don't make yourself feel better by saying that we haven't known each other long enough. If you didn't care about me, then you wouldn't be pushing me away. You'd have already put your dick in me like you do to other women."

He takes a step forward, then stops. Rage glows in his eyes.

"See. Coward." I nod my head in his direction, then turn to leave.

I don't hear him coming. I only feel his hand on my wrist, grabbing me and turning me around.

"I'm not a coward," he seethes, breathing on my neck. "You want me to fuck you, little fae? Do you want me to press my cock so deep inside of you that you can taste it on your tongue?"

"Not anymore." I try to lie convincingly.

He chuckles, "I know you're lying, little fae. I can smell your arousal, and I'm fairly certain if I slipped my hand into your pants, I'd feel how wet you are for me."

"Try it and I'll break your damn fingers," I spit back.

"Before or after you let me get you off?"

I should move. I should get away. But I can't. I'm glued to this spot, needing to feel him. Wanting to feel him.

He leans in and plants his lips softly on my neck and I lean to the side, giving him more access. He chuckles as he sucks my skin in hard. Pain quickly turns to pleasure as his hand slips under my shirt and around my waist, holding me in place.

"Tell me to stop, little fae."

The words are on the tip of my tongue, but my mouth doesn't move.

"Coward," he whispers before he punishes my mouth with his kiss. My knees buckle as a moan eases itself out of my throat.

My hands run up his chiseled abs, up to his pecs before I grab his shoulders and pull him towards me, pressing my body against him.

"Fuck me, Jax."

He pulls out of the kiss, lips still touching mine, and smiles. "Now you want me to?" He pulls back, drops his hand from under my shirt, and stares at me.

"You fucking asshole."

"Because I had to prove a point?"

"Yes!"

His smile is mirthless. "I'm not fucking you. I've already told you."

"Fine. Then I will just get myself off while you watch."

"Everlee," he growls, and his eyes flash again.

Seeing that fills me with such joy that I feel like I'm about to explode. If he wants to fuck around, then so can I.

I slip out of my shirt and pull down my pants. Lately, I've been opting for no panties or bra, because why? Knowing good and goddamn well I can't stand and have an orgasm without collapsing into a messy goop on the floor, I lay down and spread my legs in front of him.

"Everlee," he hisses.

Ignoring him, my left hand snakes up my body, rubbing over my breast and rubs my nipple between my finger and thumb. For good measure, I throw out a groan and arch my back while my right hand slides down my body and dips between my legs. "Oh, I guess I was wet. Very, very wet," I say, looking at him and blinking slowly.

Because that's always sexy. Nothing sexier than the ye ol' slow blink. But one must practice the blink, which I have done. Too fast and it's not sexy, too slow and it will look like you've ingested toad's tongue poison or something equally bad and are falling asleep.

"You need to stop."

"No." I add another finger in before pulling it out and spreading my arousal on my clit.

"Fucking stop, Everlee."

"Make me."

Our eyes lock and the world stops moving.

"Damn you," he says, and in the blink of an eye, he's on the floor, leg pressed between mine, his mouth over my breast.

Without wasting time, my hand clamps around the base of his cock and I guide it towards my pussy.

"We shouldn't be doing this," he mumbles against my skin. "Tell me to stop. Make me stop," he begs, with the head of his cock pressed at my entrance.

"No." My teeth bite into his neck.

He mumbles a curse, then plows into me with such force that it sends me sliding back onto the floor. He pauses with his cock pressed deep inside of me, letting me stretch around him. "Damn you." His lips press against mine and his kiss is deep and needy. And bruising. Definitely bruising. My lips are going to be so swollen.

He drags his cock out and slams into me again, working through his frustration and desire to fuck me. He moves faster and faster. My body responds with tingles and moans and noises that I didn't know I could make. Wanting to be on top and ride him, I hook my leg around his and time it with his thrust and flip us over.

He looks at me wildly, his eyes still glowing gold. His wolf is there at the surface. I can almost sense him.

His head falls to the side. "You want to ride me, little fae?"

Nibbling on my bottom lip, I nod, before my hands rub over my breast and I move my hips, rocking them back and forth. His head digs into the floor as satisfaction rolls over him in waves and then his hands grip tight on my thighs. Nothing about his moves are light and fluffy. They are all rough and with purpose, with perhaps a bit of anger. Angry that he feels the way he does. Angry that he can't stop himself. Angry that he likes it.

And then that's when I felt it. Our eyes meet, both of us confused, but also wanting.

JAX - KNOT NOW

■ - ■

WHAT THE FUCK IS that?

I know what *it* is, but I don't understand why.

She's ours, my wolf chimes

No the fuck she's not.

You don't see it yet, but you will. She is ours. Theirs. She completes our family.

No.

Yes!

My knot is swollen and thumping at the base of my cock. I want to pull away from her, I want to run. I don't want to knot her, but I can't move. My wolf. He wants to claim her. I want to claim her.

Fuck!

This was not supposed to happen.

She feels it, eyes looking at me curiously, but she's not moving. She's not hiding.

Needing to sink my cock fully inside of her again, I flip us over and pause, staring in her eyes with my cock pressed right at her entrance. She lifts her head slowly to press her lips to mine as her other hand wraps around my length and guides it to her pussy.

As I sink into the kiss, I sink into her. Slowly. But then need consumes me. Lust consumes me. I slam into her, eager to feel her wrapped around my cock, squeezing it, trembling around it. She was close before.

Goddess, she feels like a dream. So tight and perfect.

"Oh, my..." she pants out, but the rest of the words fade away and are replaced by groans. Deep groans. Appreciative groans.

Claim her, my wolf urges.

"Oh, fuck me," she whimpers out and I'm not sure if it's a plea or statement.

I take it as the former, and swiftly and fervently press into her, driving her up the floor with each thrust. I'm not gentle as I rock into her with a want unlike anything I've ever felt. I need to feel her writhing under me, begging, pleading for more.

Mark her.

This is a bad fucking idea.

Mark her! She is ours!

Why did I want my wolf back so badly? He's a demanding little cuss.

Her hands wrap around my neck, lifting her head off the ground and she kisses me, biting my lip, and sucking hard. She's rough and wants it rough. I pull off her lips and suck on her neck, hard enough that everyone will know it was me. As if on its own, my mouth opens, preparing to mark her, but I pull away.

I can't mark her.

Knot her.

A tingle moves down my spine and my body feels on fire at the thought of knotting her. I've been holding back, not pressing all the way in, letting her pussy rub against my knot, but not fully giving it to her.

"More Jax. Give me more!" she pleads.

My lips fall onto hers, to silence her. Her tongue pulses in and out as her hands dig into my back, holding me to her.

Fuck it. I need to feel her wrapped around me. All of me.

I press in slowly. Fully.

She cries out and stops moving as my knot enters her, stretching her.

Oh fuck. She has a hold on me, strangling me.

Stars. I'm seeing fucking stars dancing around my head.

"Are you ok?" I ask, watching her take shallow breaths. "Am I... hurting you?"

Gone was the roughness, and in its absence, was concern. Concern I'm the selfish prick and I've taken too much. I haven't knotted anyone... ever. Never felt the need to. Why her? What was so special about her?

"No... No... I'm... good."

My head drops. "I don't believe you."

"It's just... tight... really tight. So much pressure inside of me."

"I can pull out..." My head falls to the side, because I'm locked inside of her. "Well, I can try, but it will hurt."

"Don't you fucking dare." She squeezes around me and I growl out.

"Oh, little fae. Don't do that again, unless you want me to fill you with my come."

A smile pulls at her lips and she squeezes again, but this time not as hard. She's teasing me.

My hands fall to the floor as I fight the urge to not fucking come inside of her right now. I have rules and rule number one is you don't come before she does. Ever. But goddamn it, she's trying to make me break that rule.

Fuck that.

She will come before me. I will make sure of it. I sit up and she cries out as the pressure moves inside of her. My finger swirls around her clit and her eyes nearly roll into the back of her head.

"Jax," she moans out my name. "I want to..." she pants out in heady breaths. "Top. I want to top you."

Something tugs at my heart and my stomach. Damn her.

She takes control, not waiting for an answer, and pulls me on top of her, then rolls us over. I could have stopped her, because her strength is no match for me, but I don't. I want her to top me. I want her to ride me, so I can watch her perfect breast bounce, and see every eye roll as need and pleasure consume her.

With her legs spread on either side of me, she sinks further onto my shaft and her eyes nearly bulge out of her head as my knot presses into her further.

"Oh, fuck me," she whines, slow with her movements, like she's analyzing the feel of my knot inside of her. Where it feels the best. Where it doesn't.

She takes a minute before she grinds her hips into me. My left hand travels up to grab her breast, as I let her explore my knot, while my other hand finds her clit. It only takes two circles, and she's moaning my name.

"Fuck, Jax." She's rocking faster now, riding my cock as my finger presses against her clit. A second later, she screams out as her head falls back. A soft glow dances around her body and I fucking lose control.

Her pussy has a strangle on my cock and I explode inside of her, raising to sit, wrapping my arms around her back and swallowing her moans. I've never felt something so intense before.

She keeps moving and grinding while her pussy pulses around my cock, and I come inside of her.

"Everlee," I whisper, brushing her hair off her face. "Did I hurt you?"

"Jax," she whimpers. "No. I... liked it. Like it. I want... more."

"More?" I can't help but chuckle.

"You're a vixen, aren't you?"

She shrugs, nibbling on her bottom lip.

"Oh, little fae. Don't do that," I say, rubbing my thumb over her lip, pulling it from her teeth.

We stare at each other without speaking as I slowly rock my hips into her. Watching her micro expressions, the way her lip trembles with each thrust or the way her eyes flutter.

"Jax," she whispers my name as pleasure trickles through her.

"Damn, Everlee." Running my hands down her chest, I hold her hips tight as she rocks into me slowly. "Goddess, I want to fuck you."

Her eyes snap to mine, full of clarity and understanding. "It was you."

"What?" I pause.

"That one time in the library when I was with Callum. You said those same words. Well, thought those words. I heard you."

"Did I?" I ask coyly as I lay back and clasp my hands together, placing them under my head. She smiles at me and continues to rock, so I savor the feel of her hot, wet pussy wrapped tight around me.

"Come for me, little fae."

She rocks faster and faster, as much as she can, with my knot still pressing just inside of her entrance. It's almost too much to take. Her. Her pussy. The sounds she makes.

Twenty minutes and two orgasms later, she is laying on top of me, sweat covering both of us. Through all the groans and wet slaps, we both somehow missed the door opening and closing.

"Told you that you wanted to fuck her," Emmett says from behind us, arms crossed.

"Fuck off," I chuckle and throw the closest thing to me at him.

"Called it," Knox says from beside him.

Everlee lifts her chest off mine and looks at them laughing, then collapses back down.

"Fuck, Jax. What did you do to her?" Callum laughs with a modicum of concern.

"I fucked her properly, since you assholes haven't."

"That's messed up," Knox says, batting the air.

"She's not correcting me."

"Because she's passed out," Callum chimes.

"No." I look down at her and brush the hair out of her face, then listen to her breathing. "Shit. She is. She just fell asleep."

"I'll grab her," Callum offers, walking over. I ignore the look in his eye. The one that looks like he is a proud papa. These men. They are fucked in the head. Who else would be so happy I slept with a woman?

Not *a* woman.

The woman.

The one we can't seem to get off our minds. Who's had a grip on us from the first second Callum felt her walk into the club.

Damn it.

EVERLEE – MORNING AFTER

A BRIGHT LIGHT PIERCES through my eyelids, stirring me from sleep. I'd been tinkering on the edge for a while, and ignored the pitter patter of feet through the room. But when the curtains are thrown wide open and the light slices through the darkness, there's no more hiding.

"Wakey, wakey, eggs and bakey."

Knox.

When I roll over, he's walking around the room in nothing but a satin black maid's apron. Nothing. But.

His perfect ass is exposed as he hustles to the door to grab a tray.

"What is this?"

"How sore are you? Jax was concerned, but too much of a coward to come check on you."

Coward. The word brought back memories from last night. It was tossed around as both a warning and a method of foreplay that resulted in Jax knotting me.

I was knotted.

"I'm *knot* too bad." That's a lie. I'm pretty sore. I think it was round three or four that did me in, but I couldn't get enough of him. I wanted more. Hell, I still want more. I feel like an animal in heat.

He sets the tray on the bedside table. "You have some tea that Callum made. There are lots of herbs and such in it. He said it's an old fae recipe meant to promote healing." He holds his hands by his lips and whispers. "I tried it on the way up here and it tastes like cat piss."

My cheeks hurt from grinning so much. "You've tasted cat piss?"

"It wasn't my proudest moment and a gross misunderstanding. Gross and gross." He opens his arms wide.

"What's that?"

"Emmett offered you some of his blood. Just pumped... or drained... I don't know what you would call it. I added the celery as a garnish. Gives a new meaning to bloody Mary, huh? I call this the bloody Emmett." He sits on the edge of the bed and the skirt rides up his legs and exposes his cock for a second. "My apologies, my lady." He fixes the skirt.

I grab his hand and hold it under mine for a second as he just stares at me with a smile on his face. "You're probably the sweetest person I've ever met."

"You're going to make me blush." He waves the air in front of his face.

"Idiot," Jax says from the door, looking hot as sin. He's wearing a black suit with matching jacket, over a white button down. "For the record, I was coming up to see you with the tray before this little shit stole it and came up here first."

"Lies," Knox says, winking at me.

"How are you?" Jax asks, his face dropping all hints of humor.

"I'm ok."

He cocks his head to the side.

"Fine. A little sore, but that's why I'm going to drink Emmett's blood." My face twists as the words fall out of my mouth. Never in a million years did I ever expect I would say that.

"He's just a greedy fucker who wants to get inside of your head for a bit."

"I'll make it good for him then." I smile and tilt the glass back. It goes down a lot easier than I expected.

"I'm pretty sure he was jacking off while he poured that. Something about the hormones or something makes it taste better," Knox quips.

"Seriously. Just stop talking." Jax snipes.

"What? It's the truth. Ask him."

"No."

"Then you'll never know, so just shut your hole and know your role."

Jax's eye quirks up and he steps into the room, causing Knox to hide behind my back.

"You're using her to shield you from me?"

"No, to hide my erection. Your look just made me hard."

I can't with him. He loves poking Jax and Jax lets him.

"I'm leaving."

"Where are you going?"

"I have to run to Allure. Samara wants to talk about the business."

"You run it with her?"

"Not really. She owns it, and we oversee the business side. She usually stays out of it. More like a figurehead, which is why I'm confused she wants to see me."

"Do you think she knows about me? Do you think it's a trap?"

"I don't know. But I can't *not* go.

"Well, please be careful."

He tosses me a wink, pats on the doorframe twice, then turns to leave.

I don't have a good feeling about this. Something in my gut is tearing me up inside.

"*Please be careful. I don't have a good feeling,*" I mindlink Jax one more time for good measure.

"*I'll be fine.*"

Famous last words.

"Well. What do you want to do today?" Knox asks, bouncing on the bed.

"I need answers." I roll off and realize I'm wearing Callum's shirt and nothing else. "After I shower and get dressed."

"Emmett is cooking you some breakfast downstairs. He said I wasn't allowed to buy anything else."

Scents of sausage waft through the air. "It smells delicious. I'll be down in a minute."

Knox leaps off the bed and scurries to the door. I'm still smiling when I walk into the bathroom with images of his ass hanging out of the apron playing on repeat in my mind.

Twenty minutes later, I'm downstairs. Knox has his head in the fridge, ass still on display. Callum is at the end of the bar reading the paper and Emmett is behind the counter, near the stove, watching me as I walk into the kitchen with a smile on his face.

"I've made a most excellent egg, sausage and cheese quiche with a hashbrown crust." Emmett says, waving his spatula in the air as he walks over to greet me.

"It smells delicious."

"How are you feeling?" he asks, planting a kiss on the crown of my head.

"Good. Better. Thanks."

"I wasn't jacking off... for the record."

Knox pulls his face behind Emmett's shoulder.

"Darn." I wink, causing Emmett to laugh.

He cuts me a slice of quiche and serves it to me on a plate, sliding it over the bar with a cup of coffee.

"You're spoiling me."

"Because I'm treating you the way you should always be treated? Sounds like you haven't been with the best men."

"No. I suppose not."

"Is that N-O-T or K-N-O-T? Too soon?" Knox asks, grabbing a slice of quiche and taking a seat beside me.

My mouth is salivating after I put the first bite in my mouth. It's so good... and flavorful. It's a shame he didn't get to be a world-famous chef. He would have been amazing.

Every bite brings me closer to an empty plate and heightens my nervousness. Ever since last night, after hearing Jax and Knox talk, I know they are keeping someone from me. Which I mean really, it's not like they owe me anything, but still. Based on what they were saying, it doesn't sound like whoever this person is has a lot of time. I want to ask them, but I'm also scared they are going to shut me down and I don't want to deal with that. I feel like we're in a good place right now and I don't want to rock the boat... but I also have to know.

"What's wrong, buttercup?" Knox coos beside me, laying his head on my shoulder.

"What do you mean?"

"Well, you inhaled your breakfast and now you're toying with the last bite."

"Am I?" Didn't realize how observant he was.

I shove the bite in my mouth, each chomp of the teeth giving me more courage.

"So last night I heard some things."

"So did we," Knox laughs, running his fingers up and down my arm.

"I'm serious... Emmett? Where did you and Jax go? Who did you see? What's wrong with him?"

Knox sits up from his seat, Emmett straightens his stance, and then they both look at Callum for direction.

"Callum?" I press.

He folds his newspaper and lays it on the counter and looks at me. "Brady. His name is Brady."

"What's wrong with him?" I can tell by the look on his face he doesn't want to tell me, but I don't know why.

"Let me start with a background."

This can't be good.

"After all of us found each other... after Samara... we were angry and wanted revenge. Wanted to make her pay. Wanted to reverse the spell."

"Makes sense."

"We knew she was too powerful for us, so we needed to find something that would help us make it an even playing field." He pauses for a second, then continues, "We found the Book of Maldor and in it we learned about the Mist of Morreux and Pandora's box. So Jax and his brother. They aren't blood brothers, but they grew up together and were- are- nearly inseparable... anyway, they went out looking for the Mist of Morreux. It led them to the Jungles of Joran. But this wasn't any regular jungle. It has powers and magic laced throughout it. But it also had something bigger. Helsgardian soldiers from the Seelie Court."

"They were protecting the box?"

"Yes. Jax and Brady barely escaped with their lives. They ended up in a small town outside of the Jungle walls and came across a poor beggar man. He spoke of a boy who had a ring box that caught some mist and said it sometimes talked to the boy. The boy's father thought the devil was inside the box and made the boy throw it in the trash, but instead the boy sold it to the beggar man for two quid. The same beggar man they were talking to."

"They traded the Book of Maldor for the ring box of mist, hoping it was, in fact, Morreux. The beggar man said he had never opened it to verify, but he often heard the voice the boy talked about. He was happy to be rid of it. They pushed themselves getting home and were tired. One night while Jax was sleeping, the voice of the mist became too loud and Brady tried to quieten it. No one knows exactly what happened, but the Mist of Morreux was freed from his box and flew into Brady, where he's been ever since. It wasn't a lot, so it took some time for it to get a foothold on him, getting stronger and stronger. When they got back, we all realized what had happened."

"Not before?"

"No. Jax beats himself up that he didn't notice it earlier. But our guess was because it's just a small fraction of the mist, it was weak, so it took some time to grow powerful enough to show symptoms in Brady. We noticed he started getting paler, weaker, more irritable. It was like the mist was literally sucking the life out of him. Brady would beg us in one breath to save him and the next he wished for us to kill him. So we eventually made the hard decision to lock him in iron chains, hoping it would slow the mist down long enough for us to find a solution. Emmett's been feeding him his blood, to help heal him and regain his strength."

"But it's not really helping anymore," Emmett sighs.

"That's what Jax and I were talking about last night. You can possibly help Everlee."

"Me?"

"With your light... I was doing some research." He pauses, waiting for a jab, then realized Jax isn't here, so he continues, "and you, true fae, have all kinds of powers."

"Yea, but I can't really control them."

"We can try to help you. If we can get the mist out of Brady and into Samara, then it will feed on her, killing her."

"Morreux was powerful. Why wouldn't it just strengthen her?" I ask.

Callum chimes in, "We don't know what it will do."

"But we have to try something!" Knox yells, then reigns himself in. "If we lose Brady, we lose Jax."

My heart aches in my chest at Knox's admission. Even though he and Jax give each other a hard time, there is an undeniable, unbreakable love at the foundation of it all. These men... they are worming their way into my heart and... I can't. How would loving four men really work?

Knox continues, "Look, all I'm saying is that we can search through texts and find some way for her to extract the mist out of him... once it's free, it will go into Samara."

"Knox," Emmett starts, with that tone you know won't be reinforcing any kind of idea. "You're saying that we have to get Brady and Samara and Everlee in the same room. Everlee will have to figure out a way to fight off Samara, while at the same time extracting a powerful wizard fae, whatever he is, from Brady, without killing him so that it will fly into Samara?"

"Yes." The look on his face is of an innocent, wide-eyed boy. Not the man in front of me. He wants it to be true and simple and doesn't want to face the reality that it's anything but. He's hopeful, always positive, so why would this be any different? He needs to believe this can work. If he doesn't at least believe that, it will break him. Because he isn't wrong. From what I've seen, if we lose Brady, even though I've never seen him, I fear we'll lose Jax. And I don't want that to happen. I was finally able to chip away a bit of his hard exterior last night. I can't, don't want to, lose him.

JAX - CAUGHT IN A WEB

THE HEAVY WOODEN DOORS feel like thousand-pound weights under the palms of my hand as I push them open. There is no one at the front desk, which is not unusual in the early morning hours, just an odd thing to see. When I push the next set of doors open, the lights are on and the room is large and empty. It's always weird to see this room in the light. In the dark, it's filled with mystery and intrigue and a bit of the forbidden. In the light, it just looks like a bland, open room with a bar on one side and doors around it. It's almost cringy.

"Hey!" a voice shouts to my left.

I jump, not expecting to see anyone here, but find Harlow behind the bar, wiping down glasses. "Hey."

"Are you looking for Samara? She just got in. I'm usually on my own for hours in the morning, and now I have both of you here." She laughs and continues cleaning glasses.

I don't know much about Harlow. Only that she's a harpy and a good worker, though she keeps to herself. Historically, harpies have been treated badly because the Gods used them to do their bidding, but she seems different. Maybe? It's hard to say.

"Yea. She wanted to meet with me about something."

"Sounds ominous. Do you think it's about that girl?"

"What girl?"

"The girl that was here last week. With the light?"

"I don't know."

"Have you seen her?" She hurriedly adds, "I only ask, because I served her at the bar, and felt like we hit it off."

Harlow has barely said two words to me ever and now wants to have an entire conversation with me? Something seems odd. "I... no. I haven't seen her. Can you tell me what she looks like? I know we're all supposed to be finding her, but I never saw a picture. I just heard that she could be dangerous."

Harlow studies me for a second, then laughs awkwardly. "I'm not great at descriptions and it was dark. About this tall," she motions with her hand. "Maybe a bit of fire in her eyes.

I know that look well- the fire. Images of her riding my cock flash through my mind as passion and anger battled for control last night.

Stop.

I need a clear mind when I meet with Samara. She uses words to weave you into a web of deceit until you find yourself stuck in the middle, unable to get out. She'd be better represented as a large blood-sucking spider because that's what she is. Tricking and luring you in under false pretenses until you can't see you're stuck in the middle with her fangs in you, sucking your life away until you're nothing more than a shell of what you were.

The hair on my arm stands on end. Something doesn't feel right here, almost like Harlow is searching for information. How can she not describe her if she served her? Is this Samara pretending to be Harlow? I know she can shift, but why Harlow? "No, I haven't found her."

"Well, when you do, tell her Harlow said hello."

"Ok... I really need to get going. I don't want to keep Samara waiting." I wave and continue walking, the tightness in my gut feeling more and more like a heavily weighted rock. Moving along the demonstration rooms on the right side of the floor, I sludge down the hall and find the set of stairs that lead to the offices. Samara's is at the end of the hall- a black door with golden trim around the door. Not painted gold, but actual gold, much like the rest of the items in her office. All expensive marbles, gold and crystals.

My knuckles knock softly.

Silence.

I knock again, "Samara?"

"Jax," I hear called from behind me.

Samara is walking up to me wearing a long black dress that hugs every curve of her body with her hair hanging down to her waist. Her nails are pointy and painted black, matching the color of her heart if she had one.

She doesn't.

Should have been my first clue not to trust her when I came to her all those years ago, but no. I was selfish and trying to get out of an arranged marriage to a pack alpha's daughter.

"Any news of the fae girl?"

"None."

She lets out a hum, then lays her hand on my arm. "Come with me. I want to show you something."

This can't be good. "I thought we were going to talk about the business."

"We are." The way the last word hangs on her tongue makes the hairs on the back of my neck stand. I can see her spinning her web right around me, but I don't know how to get out of it. Only thing I can do now is buy myself time and not creep further into the center.

She leads me back downstairs to the large circular room with elevators that either take you to Eden or to Infernus. Eden being mostly whites and golds, a place where light fae can explore safely. An Infernus, mostly reds and blacks, where the dark fae come out to play. Where they torture and torment.

With confidence, I know we're going to Infernus. Nothing about Samara says light and happy. No, she was born from the depths of hell. I think the only reason she created Eden was so she could torture the light fae who had allegiance to the true fae. It's a reminder of the power she wields over the fae community. Most have forgotten what she did, or don't seem to care as long as they're safe from her wrath, but those of us who remember... we will get retribution. And now with Everlee, maybe it's a sign the true fae will soon be reborn. Perhaps that's why Samara is so eager to eliminate her or hide her away. Everlee will be a sign of hope for those who haven't forgotten.

We enter the elevator, and she presses the button for Infernus.

It's funny really. You can choose. Heaven or hell. Light or dark. You always have a choice.

"So Jax," Samara's words are smooth like silk. Silk that's been caught on fire. Burns, but does not melt. Just turns black.

"Samara."

"I feel you and your... boyfriends? What do you call them? You are all together, aren't you?"

"We are a family. They are more my brothers."

"Brothers that share and fuck each other?"

Why is she so interested in this?

Before I can answer, she continues, "Wasn't there another? What was his name?"

Where is she going?

"Ah, yes. Brady was his name, I believe. What ever happened to Brady?"

"He died." It wasn't a complete lie. His spirit is gone. It has been for a while. I used to feel him, see it in him. Now. He's a shell of a man barely hanging on. I know I'm being selfish by keeping him alive, but at this point, it's keeping the mist contained. Brady would want to go out fighting. Fighting for the protection of people who don't even know his name. He died many years ago, and who remains now is the warrior shell.

"Died?" she screeches in mock horror, throwing her hand over her mouth. "Oh my. I had no idea."

I don't miss the fact she doesn't offer words of condolences. Would it matter? I wouldn't believe a filthy word out of her mouth.

She glances down at my balled-up fists and I catch myself and release.

"Well, moving on."

Yes. Moving on.

"Can I be honest with you?" she asks, placing her hand on my arm and I try not to flinch or jerk it away.

"Always."

She pushes open the main doors into Infernus and now we're standing in a large room with four large doors that are the gateways into themed play areas. A wooded area, a playhouse, an aquarium, for the water fae, and a fourth I've never been allowed in. No one has. It's Samara's private room.

She walks towards the fourth room and pauses in front of it like she's contemplating something, then shakes her head no and pushes the doors open.

Hesitating, I walk in after her. The room is dark, and it's not until the doors shut and lock behind me that the lights flick on, revealing a large, stark white room. So white that it's creepy as fuck. Large white tiles line the floor, with a large white circle, seven feet or more in diameter, pinned against the wall with white cuffs. It's like a BDSM x-cross but on a wheel. There is a single table in the center of the room with a single white sheet draped across it and behind it is a white shelf with empty jars.

"Are you ok?" she chuckles, watching my face as I look around the room.

I'm getting the feeling this is some sort of room that she performs... dissections of fae and then stores their body parts. Is that what she's planning on doing to Everlee?

"Fine," I say, trying to swallow the bile down.

"I thought you would be. Of all your... brothers, as you call them, I thought you would be the toughest. The others aren't strong enough to handle what needs to be done."

"What exactly needs to be done?"

"Well, finding Everlee, of course, and studying her."

"You plan to... cut her apart piece by piece?"

She laughs an evil laugh. The kind of laugh that slices you deep to the bone. "Of course not. What kind of monster do you think I am?"

The kind of monster that erased the entire species hundreds of years ago. "Well, you just brought me here... so I didn't know."

"No. Silly. I need Everlee. No, this room is for you."

Before the words can fully register in my mind, my vision blurs and darkness consumes me. The last thing I remember is my body hitting the floor.

KNOX - INVITING IN THE DJINN

THE FADING LIGHT FILTERING in through the library window matches my attention span for these books.

Fading.

"Where's Jax? He's been gone all day?"

Callum, Everlee, Emmett, and I have been reading and researching all day, learning as much as we can about true fae, Djinn, Mist of Morreux, and anything else we think could be of use.

Callum told us of a time he saw a fae remove a sickness from a town's person. He said that the fae, with its light, somehow extracted the sickness out. But apparently not all fae can do that, and many that tried, killed the humans. The humans were on death's bed, so it was a long shot if it would work, so they were ok with the risks and it allowed the fae to practice. But there was nothing in the books about that and Everlee would likely kill Brady, so she refused to even try.

Emmett had the idea of trying to extract juice out of an orange, but she just kept exploding the oranges. After twenty-three attempts and a room filled with orange pulp, she gave up and went back to reading. She's been reading one book about Djinn for several hours, but won't say what's so interesting. She just says it's about their history, so she's just learning everything she can.

My stomach rumbles for the hundredth time. A gentle reminder of how hungry I am.

Emmett went downstairs about an hour ago to prepare dinner, and I've called Jax five times now and he hasn't picked up. Something feels off, and I think the others are feeling it too.

"I'm going to go downstairs and check on dinner and Jax."

"He'll be home soon. He's the one who suggested the meal tonight to Emmett before he left. It's his favorite meal, so he won't miss it."

"Unless something is wrong with him."

"Samara can't kill him. Djinn can't do that. One of their rules," Everlee calls from across the room before she puts her head back into her book.

"There's a lot worse things to do to a man than kill him," I mumble as I walk out of the room.

When I get to the kitchen, Emmett is preparing the roast beef, slicing it into strips and placing it in a dish.

"Have you heard from Jax?"

"Yea. He just called. Said he will be here in a minute."

"Asshole. He can't answer my calls, but he can call you?" I walk out of the backdoor to meet him and give him shit when he gets here.

Ten minutes later, I hear the roar of his car pulling into the driveway.

He steps out and looks at me, smiling.

What the fuck? Jax never smiles at me. What did Samara do to him?

"Knox. Missed me that much?" He asks, shutting the door.

"Where have you been?"

"Where do you think I've been?"

"With Samara. Well, that's what you said this morning."

He looks at me but doesn't speak.

"You didn't go see Brady, did you?"

"Brady?" His voice drops and his brow furrows in confusion.

"I know you can't really see *him* anymore, but... maybe talking to him would help."

Jax says nothing, but only shrugs.

"Are you feeling ok? Samara didn't do anything to you did she?"

He laughs. "No. What do you think she could do?" He glances at the door, then back at me.

"What? You can smell it, can't you? Emmett's been cooking all afternoon."

"Yum."

Yum?

He must have had an eventful day, because he is definitely not acting like himself. "Everyone will be glad you're home. I swear it's been torture. I was about to track you down when you showed up."

He chuckles, but doesn't speak as he follows me up the stairs. I hold the door open, but he stands at the top, looking back at the car like he's forgotten something.

"What are you doing? Come on in, we're starving. We can get whatever it is after dinner."

"Right," he smiles and takes a step hesitantly into the house.

"Oh, thank Goddess you're home. Knox has been losing his damn mind with worry."

"Knox. So funny. I'm fine. Just got busy discussing business with Sammie."

Emmett looks at me, then at Jax. "Sammie?"

"Sorry. Samara. I guess I just got used to hearing the name so much today."

Emmett nods one time.

"I'll go get Callum."

"And-"

I cut my eyes at Emmett. "Yes. I'll tell him to hurry. You don't need to tell me twice."

Something about Jax isn't sitting right with me. He seems different, which could be explained, but he's not been a dick to me, so that definitely seems odd. And Sammie. He never calls her Sammie.

Emmett looks at me, studying me for a minute, then nods. "Should I start plating?"

"No. You know how Callum is about his studies. It's always just one more chapter until he's at the end of the book. I will try to get him to hurry, though."

Emmett nods. We can't mindlink because he's not a shifter, and if Jax really is Samara, then I don't know if she picks up the super hearing Jax has. I don't think she would pick up his abilities. Fuck! Why did I invite him in? That would have been the test.

When I push the library door open, Everlee starts to say something, but I rush across the room and clamp my hand on her mouth. She looks at me, pissed and confused, but I shake my head.

Callum stands up, tensing. "*What's wrong?*" he mindlinks both of us.

"*I think we have a problem. Everlee, when I remove my hand, don't speak.*"

She nods, but is still confused.

"Callum, it's time for you to put the books down and come eat dinner. *I think something has happened to Jax.*"

Everlee whirls around, eyes wide and opens her mouth to speak, but I clamp my hand around it. If she could shoot lasers out of her eyes, I'd have a hole straight through my head right now.

"*I think Samara is here, pretending to be Jax. Callum, say you need to finish one more chapter.*"

"*I just need to finish this chapter. How the fuck did Samara get into the house?*"

"*No. Emmett has worked for hours and I'm starving. I may have inadvertently invited him, her, in. He, she, was looking at the car and I said, come on in, it's time to eat. Blah blah*

blah. I didn't know at the time. We can just uninvite him and that will push her, him, out. Goddess, this is confusing."

"You're sure it's not Jax?" Everlee asks, picking at her nails.

I hold her hands. "He smiled at me when he got here."

"Oh."

"Yea. And then just a minute ago he called Samara, Sammie."

"Oh."

"Footsteps! Coming!"

Everlee panics, looking from left to right, then darts across the room and tucks under Callum's desk. There's not enough time to get her down the passageway behind the bookcase.

Callum sits in his seat just as the doors are opening.

"Jax!" Callum calls.

"I thought I would check on you. See if Knox needs back up."

"You are the best, Jax!"

He smiles and shrugs, but doesn't speak.

"Yea, not Jax," Callum agrees.

"Don't uninvite her. See if you can get any information," Everlee chimes.

"Ok. Let's go downstairs. I'm starving."

Jax walks around the room. "Were you reading by the window or at your desk?"

Callum pushes the chair under the desk. So far that Everlee has to be some sort of contortionist to mold around the base.

"That was me," I chime. "I was reading before I went downstairs to find you."

"Reading about..." he picks up the book and looks at it, "History of the Djinn."

"Well, you suggested I read it," I lie.

"I did, didn't I? You rarely ever listen to me."

"You aren't lying." I chuckle and feel sick to my stomach. That's not my book, and Jax would never tell me what to read. Damn it!

"Well, let's eat dinner. If we all keep disappearing, then Emmett will wonder what's happened to us."

Jax drops the book on the window bench and makes his way to the door. All I can see when I look at him is Samara. All I can hear when he speaks is her voice. How the fuck are we supposed to get information about Jax without tipping our hand?

When we walk out of the room, Callum closes the doors. Jax leads us down the stairs with me in the middle. I cast a quick glance over my shoulder and Callum nods.

When we get downstairs, Emmett has the table set with four plates.

Praise Helsgard.

"I was about to send a search party for you all. You all kept disappearing."

"Are you expecting anyone else?" Jax asks.

"No. Should we? You didn't invite Samara over, did you?" I laugh.

"No," he chuckles.

"You were with her all day. What did you do?"

"Nothing much."

"Nothing much? For hours? You had to do something."

"Why are you pressing this?" he asks.

"Sorry. Didn't know if she had any more information on Everlee."

"Isn't that your- I mean, our job?"

"Yes. But we haven't found her. We had the one lead, but she seems to have fallen off the face of the realm," Callum chimes.

"What if-" I slap the table. "What if she has?"

"What?" the entire table asks in near unison.

"What if she's in a different realm?"

"You don't believe that, do you?" Jax asks.

"Well, possibly. She'd have to have someone at Helsgard to help her access the Bifrost," Callum chimes.

Jax nods without speaking. "That would make sense why no one seems able to locate her."

Emmett's eyes meet mine with a what the fuck glance stamped across his head. He seems to have picked up on the problem at the table and is wondering why we aren't fixing it.

"So, did you stay in Samara's office all day, or did you go somewhere else?" I ask. I've never been great at playing the mental minefields like Jax and Callum are.

"You seem to be very interested in my day."

"Well, you said you were going to tell us all about it when you got home, so I'm sure he's just curious. You know how Knox is. Dog with a bone. Or in his case, seal with a ball."

Idiot me, barks like a seal and claps my hands.

I regretted it immediately, but as if we needed any more proof that this wasn't Jax, he didn't say a word. It would have been a perfect opportunity for him to say something along the lines of 'shut the fuck up' or get up and leave in some over the top fashion.

"Well, she took me down to Infernus."

"Oh my God. Did you sleep with her?"

"No! I mean," he brushes his hair behind his ear. Hair that's not there. Force of habit, I suppose. "No."

"So then, what did you do down there? Isn't it only sex rooms?"

"Well, she has the other room. You know."

No, we don't know. Well, not really. "Oh, right."

"Can we please stop asking so many questions," Emmett chimes. "I've prepared this meal and plates are empty," he says, standing up to plate.

"One thing first," Callum says, standing up. "Samara, you are uninvited in our house. Please leave."

He chuckles, then pain contorts his face as the spell that's been put in place makes it uncomfortable for him. "What are you doing?"

"Samara, did you think you could fool us? Where's Jax?"

In a swirl of black smoke, Samara appears and gone is Jax. She has an evil grin spread across her face. "He's alive, if that's what you're asking, seeing as how I can't directly kill anyone."

"Directly?"

"Well, if you hang a bleeding werewolf up to dry, and..." she shrugs, "vampires or something else were to find him. Is that really my fault?" Her evil laugh echo throughout the room as she's being pulled towards the closest door. "Neat party trick. Maybe I should do it on the room Jax is in, so you can see him dying but not get to him. It would serve you right for holding out on me."

"We ar-"

"Oh, please!" she yells, throwing her hand in the air. "I know that little bitch is around here. You can hide her all you want, but are you willing to sacrifice Jax for her? I'm betting no. So just hand her over and you'll get Jax back."

"For the last time, we don't have her. You're welcome to check around the house, but since you're on your way out, it may make it difficult," Callum retorts.

"You may want to turn over every stone then, because you have about two days before he's either drained of blood or someone else finds him. It would be such a waste if he were to die. Such a handsome body. Perhaps I'll make him wish he were dead. What is a girl to do in that case?"

"You don't lay a finger on him," I fire.

"Oh, so possessive." She cackles as she slips out of the house. "I prefer fava beans and a nice wine, for dinner anyway." I follow after and slam the door shut.

By the time I get back to the kitchen, Everlee is already downstairs with a determination set on her face, and a fire in her eyes.

I hold my finger up. "You need to stop and wait."

Her eyes widen like I've slapped her. "You can't be serious. You heard her."

"Yes, but we can't just run in there without a plan. That's what she wants. What she's expecting. If we do that, she has the upper hand."

Everlee is seething and her body is glowing with a light blue mist dancing around her.

"I didn't think true fae were supposed to be violent," I tease, trying to lighten the mood in the slightest.

"Well, being kind and benevolent didn't work out so well for them the last time and seeing as how I'm the first in how many hundreds of years... I would argue retribution and forging my own path are allowed."

We need to get her to calm down and see reason, not fly off the handle and endanger herself. I glance at Emmett, who cocks his head to the side, knowing what needs to be done, but doesn't want to do it. He needs to use mind compulsion on her.

He steps towards her.

EVERLEE – LETTING THE SUCCUBUS OUT

. . . .

As soon as the door clicks locked, I leap down the stairs and stand in the kitchen. She has Jax. She's hurt him. I knew he shouldn't have gone. What the fuck was he thinking? What were any of them thinking? Did they really think she was going to wait idly by?

No.

She's going to force their hand.

Our hand.

Knox walks back and sees me standing there, stopping in his tracks. "You need to stop and wait."

Is he fucking kidding me right now? "You can't be serious. You heard her."

"Yes, but we can't just run in there without a plan. That's what she wants. What she's expecting. If we do that, she has the upper hand."

Rage boils through me as a heat dances across my body and my nails bite into the palms of my hand.

"I didn't think true fae were supposed to be violent," Knox teases, trying to lighten the mood.

"Well, being kind and benevolent didn't work out so well for them the last time and seeing as how I'm the first in how many hundreds of years... I would argue retribution and forging my own path is allowed."

Knox looks from me to Emmett, and I know what's coming. I can read Emmett and he doesn't want to do it. He steps towards me and I set my eyes on him and hold up my hand. "I swear to Helsgard, if you take one step closer to me, I will blast you backwards with my light." I form the ball in my hand, causing him to pause and the others to take a step back. "I'm fine if you want to talk, but do not and I repeat do not, try to compel me. I'll never forgive you."

Emmett holds up his hands and takes a step backward. "Fine. Let's sit down and enjoy this meal that I really spent time making. We will enjoy it and then we will formulate a plan. We will get him back."

"Fine," I huff.

Emmett lets out a puff of air as Callum and Knox take a tentative seat at the table. Emmett holds his arm out, guiding me to a seat before he sits down.

Knox and Callum eye me cautiously, while Emmett is moving with slow moves, like he's ready to catch me if I try to run.

"You can all calm down. I told you. We can talk. I don't want to wait a second, but I know that's what we need to do. So please enjoy your food and stop thinking I'm going to run off."

"You give us your word?" Knox asks. "Because a true fae's word is everything."

"Yes. You have tonight, but I can't and won't promise more than that."

"We can deal with that," Emmett says, sitting down beside me.

"Good, because that's all you're getting." I smile at him.

"When we get Jax back, don't tell him you cooked this meal. You know it's his favorite."

"I've been trying to mindlink him about this meal tonight," Knox chimes.

"What an ass." I jab.

"What? I need to keep him pissed, so he keeps his fight. I don't know what she's done or is doing to him, but he needs to fight. So, I'm giving him something to be pissed about. I'm probably the only one that can do it."

"That is true. You seem to have a knack for getting under his skin."

"It's a hard job, but someone has to do it."

"Is he responding to you?"

"No. I don't know if he's even getting the messages honestly. I don't know how far we can mindlink and I don't know if there are any magical barriers in place between us, blocking the messages."

We finish eating dinner and it's very good. Probably the best meal I've ever had, but I can't fully enjoy it knowing that it's Jax's favorite and he's not here.

Because of me.

We move to the library, and Callum takes out a large roll of paper and swipes the contents off his desk. They clatter to the floor as he unrolls the papers.

"What is this?"

"This is the layout of Allure, Eden, and Infernus."

"You did this?"

"Yes. We continually walk as much of the property as possible to build this out. I wanted to know every square inch of that building in case something ever happened. I knew it was only a matter of time."

He flips to the Infernus drawings. "Why is this blank?" I ask, pointing to an open space on the drawing.

"That is her private room. We can't get in there," Callum says, running his finger over the paper, tracing it.

"Do you think that's where he is?"

"Perhaps. As far as we know, there aren't any extra rooms in Eden or even in Allure's main level." He flips to those pages to look over them, validating his theory before flipping back to Infernus. "The only place it could be, if he was being kept at the club, would be Infernus."

"What if she's moved him?"

Emmett chimes in, "She wants us to find him, so she won't make it hard. She wants you."

"Just because I show up doesn't mean you get Jax back."

Knox adds, "She said it. She said, 'So just hand her over and you'll get Jax back'. I was doing some reading today and a Djinn's word is their contract. She has to give Jax back."

"Yea, but it doesn't say when or in what condition."

Knox puckers his lips. "Well, shit. I read it as immediately. A trade. A person for a person." He rubs his chin, "But she is a Djinn and is notorious for using words against us and to her advantage."

"Then you need to figure out how to word your demand in such a way there's no wiggle room for her to manipulate."

"Everlee, we won't trade you for Jax."

"The hell you aren't. He's your family and I'm a nobody."

Callum rushes me and wraps me in his arms. "Don't say that. I know we haven't been together for very long, but there is a connection with you. A connection that has been forged hundreds of years in the making. You are not a nobody. You are..."

"A somebody?" Knox inserts.

We all look at him.

"Damn it, it was just such a magical moment, and I just got wrapped up. I was trying to help. It sounded so much better in my head, like a suave, 'somebody', but when it came out, it was like huh huck, 'somebody'. I'm sorry. I've ruined your moment." He slaps his forehead.

Overcome with emotion, I hold my arm out towards him, bringing him into a hug. "It wasn't a huh huck moment. It was very sweet."

He buries his face in my neck and I give him a quick kiss on his temple.

"Ok. Fine. We aren't trading me for Jax. So, what are we going to do?"

We spend the next several hours planning, replanning, and planning again. Coming up with phrases and word-smithing the crap out of them to get them down to their most basic meaning so she can't use our words against us.

Tomorrow, Brady will get his revenge. We will use me to trade for Jax, then use Brady to kill Samara. Emmett will feed Brady his blood and then we'll remove his iron chains and hope the Mist of Morreux consumes Brady and in that brief second when Brady dies before he transitions to vampire, the mist will vacate Brady's body and flow into Samara. It's a tight window, but it has to work. It's the only plan that we could come up with where nobody dies, and even this one is not one hundred percent guaranteed.

It's almost midnight when we leave the library and when I tell them I want to take a shower to clean this day off of me, they guide me towards a bedroom I've not seen yet. It has an enormous bed in the middle with various toys hanging on the wall. Before I can say anything, they tell me that's not why we're in here and then guide me to the attached bathroom.

It's the largest bathroom I've ever seen. There's an enormous bathtub in the middle that could easily hold six to nine people and a row of waterfall shower heads along the back wall.

"This is huge."

"That's what she said," Knox teases.

"Do you want a bath or shower?" Callum asks.

Seconds tick by as my mind thinks through each. Why is this such a hard question? After more time than should have passed, I answer, "Shower." Maybe I'll get in less trouble this way.

Emmett takes off his clothes and leaves them on the shelf. He turns on the showers one by one to make a continuous rainfall shower that is at least ten feet long. Knox follows. Removing his clothes, then bouncing across the floor.

"When I said I was going to take a shower, I didn't mean you all had to join me as well."

"Little fae, we aren't leaving your side tonight."

Because they don't trust me not to go after Jax on my own. Fair. I gave them yesterday and since it's past midnight, it's technically tomorrow. I'm sure being with Samara for so long has them naturally dissecting words for loopholes.

His hands gently lift my shirt, then pull down my pants. He places them on the shelf, quickly slips out of his and guides me over.

Yep. This isn't going to work. How can I not want to fuck three deliciously desirable men when they are standing around me, hot and wet?

Callum guides me under the water from behind. He presses his body against my back and gently wraps his hand around my neck and tilts it up so the water washes over my hair and back. Emmett's to my left, squeezing shampoo in my hair, while Knox is rubbing a loofa across my body, slowly. Very slowly.

"Oh," I moan out as Emmett's fingers dig into my scalp and Callum's wrap around my hips and hold me to him.

I'm getting wetter and wetter and it's not from the water gushing over my head.

We shouldn't be doing this. Not when Jax is alone and suffering.

Callum, sensing my hesitation, leans down and whispers in my ear. "You're the daughter of an alpha wolf and a succubus. Take from us to strengthen you. You're going to need it tomorrow."

Surprised by his words, I turn to look at him, our face an inch apart. "What about you all?"

"We'll be fine. We have Emmett to heal us. You get your power from sex. You are a true fae, but your mother's blood runs through you."

"Take from us. Jax needs you tomorrow. All of you. He'll get the warrior of the alpha wolf's daughter, but she needs to be unbreakably strong."

I stare at him for a moment, and hadn't noticed the other's hands had stopped moving as well. Leaning forward, I take his lips in a tender kiss, but it quickly escalates as his tongue presses in. Guilt is chipping away at me, but I have to do this for Jax. I've felt it for a while, the strength I get from fucking, but I didn't want to admit or acknowledge what it was, because I don't have the full powers of the succubus.

Callum steps around while Emmett falls behind me and Knox drops to his knees in front of me. Emmett's hands cup my ass, and before I know what's happening, I feel him there. Like there, there. With his tongue and... oh my... my hands clamp on Knox's head for support at the same time his tongue enters be from the front and Callum clamps around my breast.

My knees are going from weak to strong repeatedly as wave after delicious wave flows through my body as my orgasm builds, getting closer and closer. As I try to clamp and hold it at bay, that's when I feel it.

Oh Goddess.

No.

No.

NO.

My stomach gurgles. You better not fucking fart. Holy fuck. Oh, he just put a finger in. Goddamn it. My eyes snap shut. Praying. Begging. For it to stop. But I can't stop. My orgasm is so close that my body has taken over, rocking into Knox, fucking his face, while Callum inserts two fingers inside of me.

Oh, goddamn.

More pressure is not what I needed.

Oh my Goddess.

Oh my Goddess.

I can feel the gas bubble working its way down, so I try to squeeze and hold it up. Hold it in. I try to tell the guys to move, but I can't get the words to form on my tongue because it won't stop moaning. Another finger in my ass. Ohhh, baby lord of the faedom. With the amount of pressure inside of my body that bitch is going to come out on a high c. Cccccccc, remove a finger then a b. Fucking find a song and get the notes keyed up because they will be able to play it with my ass in about t minus five... four... fuck.... Two... I scramble. Moving faster than I've ever moved before, lifting myself off their fingers and tongues and out of their grasp, I run to the bed. As far away from them as possible. I flop down and they are all stunned and then I feel it burst inside me. A silent psssh in my lower abdomen.

What does that mean? Did the stink corrupt my insides? Would it have been better to come out? Is it like a dutch oven inside waiting to surprise them? Like farting under the covers.

"Everything ok?" Callum and the boys ask in near unison.

"Yes. I just... I wanted your cocks in me and standing... standing... I just... I want all of you." Hopefully that was convincing enough, because telling them I was about to light them up with a gas bomb while playing the fucking monster mash on Emmett's face with my ass was not an option.

Knox and Callum walk over while Emmett cleans himself up. Trying to play off my gasgate situation, I reach for Knox and pull him towards me, pressing my lips to his. His hands swiftly wrap around my back and carry me into the middle of the bed as his body presses on top of me.

"While I want to put my dick in you, I also wasn't done licking your pussy. I want you to drown me with your come."

My eyes pulse as his words set me on fire.

He kisses me on the nose, then slides down my body and plants himself between my legs, his tongue swiping up my middle before he sucks on my clit. His arms lock around my legs as he licks and presses his tongue in, sending tingles up and down my spine and causing my leg muscles to tighten.

"I really need a… cock in me," I whimper through watery eyes.

My orgasm slams into me, causing my body to bolt off the bed and wrap my arms around Knox's head as I hold him to me. Between nearly coming earlier and now, it just hits me in waves. Over and over again.

Knox is moaning as he laps eagerly, which seems to only intensify my orgasm.

"Now I'm going to fuck you, little fae. First your mouth, then your pussy, and last, your ass. I want to claim every hole of yours tonight," he says, pushing me back on the bed and crawling over me.

All I can do is nod, as excitement has robbed me of words. He lines his cock up over my mouth and presses it at my lips. Slowly, I part as he presses in, further and further. I tilt my head back and relax my jaw, taking him as far as I can until he's singing my praises and I'm gagging. He pulls out and I wrap my hand around the base of his cock as he thrusts in, hitting the back of my throat each time. Without warning, he slides down and slams his cock in my pussy, causing me to arch, sliding backwards on the bed. "Oh damn. You feel so good. So tight." He presses in hard and fast until I'm moaning his name. "That's my good girl." He flips us over, so I'm on top of him just as Emmett crawls on the bed. The entire time Callum is watching us, stroking his cock.

Emmett scoots in close and lines his cock up along Knox's and for a moment I panic, thinking that he's going to press in, but as Knox slides out, Emmett shifts me, so I slide onto his cock.

"Seamless."

"Oh," I moan out, eyes watering. Emmett's cock is a touch longer, but not as wide in girth, but the piercings make up for it. It feels... amazing.

He sits me back on his lap, his chest pressed to my back, while his hands come up and grip my breasts as I move up and down on his shaft.

"E," Knox says, sliding out from under me.

When I turn to look at Emmett, his fangs have dropped and his eyes are pulsing. "You good?"

He grunts out, then with speed I've never experienced, he falls back and twists me around on his cock, so we're chest to chest. Pressing my hands on his ribbed abs, I rock and grind on his cock, feeling every bit of his piercings hit spots inside of me I didn't know existed.

"My turn," Knox says, pushing me over. "I've claimed you in two holes and now for the third." He continues the prep that Emmett had started... before my moment.

His fingers move and swirl before he presses in slowly, pausing at the tight ring of muscle, allowing me to adjust to his size. I gasp as my head drops forward and my hands grip the sheets as he continues to push further and further, deeper and deeper. With both of them inside of me, the pressure is almost too much to take, but it feels divine.

My mouth greedily bites and sucks on Emmett as Knox presses in, then drags his cock out slowly.

"More," I beg.

"I'm all the way in, love."

I growl out, then press back onto both of them.

"Oh shit," Knox and Emmett say in unison.

"I love to watch you take their cock," Callum hums.

"Would you like it more if your cock was in my mouth?"

"Would you like it more?"

"I would."

"You're a fucking dream," Knox hums, moving his hand to my clit and swirling it around.

His touch makes me buck a minute, pulling a grunt out of Emmett before I settle back on their cocks. When I reach up to grab Callum's cock, he pushes my hand out of the way. "No little fae, I'm going to fuck your face and watch you take it all."

"I think technically I'm going to watch her take it all," Emmett says from below us.

Callum smirks, "Yes. You're going to watch her suck my cock."

He wraps both palms around the side of my head, fingers digging into my scalp. My eyes are already watering with anticipation.

"Open up, little fae," he murmurs, with his cock pressed at my lips. The promise of his words causes a tingle to shoot through my spine and a heat to flush across my body.

Following his command, I open up, eyes staring directly at him. His thumbs softly sweep over both sides of my head before he pushes in, but I want control. I suck him in hard, shifting my head forward to devour his cock. His muscles tense as his hands grip tightly on my head as a puff of air escapes from between his lips. He drags his cock out as he watches me, wondering if I'm going to take more. With the head of his cock still pressed at my lips, I roll my tongue around the tip, licking off all of his arousal.

"You want my cock, little fae?" he asks, running his hand down his shaft. "Do you want me to unload my come down your throat and all over your face and chest?"

I lean forward to take his cock in, but he backs up, head tilted to the side.

His words are cool, his gaze dark. "Are you trying to dominate me, little fae, while you're on your knees taking our cocks like the good little fae you are? You can't dominate me. I'm a dragon. I don't let anyone dominate me." His hands tighten in my hair, pulling against my scalp. The sting quickly turns to pleasure. He thrust up suddenly, his muscles clenching as his cock pushes in deep, hitting the back of my throat. Tears immediately fill my eyes.

"Swallow me down, little fae. Take all of it." He pulls his cock out and slams it in again, rough and fast, hitting the back of my throat.

Knox and Emmett are moving in timed unison with Callum's claiming thrusts, and as my orgasm creeps up, my body takes over. The heat returns and all the guys groan.

"Callum..." Knox whimpers. "She's glowing."

A heat dances across my body. I can't see it, but I can feel it.

"I can't-" Emmett cries out.

I don't want them to stop, they can't stop. I grab Callum's cock and hold it in my mouth. A frenzy takes over as I bob on his cock, sucking and licking. I can't get enough of them. I need them. I feel... I feel this power being leached from them, feeding into me. I suck faster, grind harder.

Minutes later, Callum is bucking wildly as his orgasm gets closer.

"Fuck, Everlee."

He's mine. They're all mine.

"I'm going to come so hard down your throat," he warns, panting out.

My eyes look up to meet his and I'm rewarded with his glorious tattooed skin, his muscles tightening as he pumps into me, control bouncing between the both of us.

"Oh, fuck!" he screams and a moment later he stops moving and his dragon wings shoot out of his back, stretching wide. A beautiful indigo blue and gold. He roars up at the ceiling as his hands clamp tighter on my head.

"Oh shit," Emmett and Knox say in unison.

He takes over control and fucks my face, hard. Need consuming him. His dragon taking charge.

"You are going to swallow all of me down, little fae." Two pumps and he's exploding down my throat, so hard and so fast I don't even have time to gag.

My hand clamps around his balls, rubbing and massaging, as I suck harder and harder, leaching every bit of his come out that I can. His wings curl around him as he stands over me, hands still tangled in my hair, but without the tight hold.

"Goddess be damned little fae." His eyes are glowing like blue dancing flames as he watches me.

He pulls his cock out of my mouth, and without warning I wrap my hand around his leg and bring him to me and bite the inside of his thigh.

His growl shakes the house and panic tears through me. I don't know why I did that. "Fuck. I'm sorry." I did it with Jax and now Callum.

His fingers tilt up my chin and his cool gaze rakes over my body. He doesn't speak, then drops my head and pulls away.

I look down at Emmett, whose eyes are wide with shock. "You trying to get yourself killed, little fae?"

"I didn't mean..."

"You didn't mean to mark him?"

"I don't know what's going on? I've bitten everyone but Knox."

"Don't worry. I'm not feeling the slightest bit jealous. Not at all. Not even a little bit."

I look over my shoulder at him. "But I want to bite you, too."

His eyes perk up, as do his thrusts. "Little fae, you have to stop glowing blue. You're pulsing out your power over us and if my seal cock pops out in your ass, well, let's just say it won't be something either of us will ever forget."

"I'm not trying to do it."

His hand works on my clit while Emmett's thumb runs along the inside of my wrist. His eyes are hungry, wanting.

My orgasm is building, and it's going to completely rip me apart from the inside. Moans and wet slaps fill the air as we move faster and faster.

"Bite me," I command out.

"What?" Emmett asks, shocked, eyes full of pain.

"Bite me. My wrist. You don't stop and I will use my light to blow off your cock."

"I think I just came," Knox teases from behind.

"Everlee." Emmett's hand clamps around my wrist like he's fighting for control.

"I trust you."

"I don't trust me."

"You've stopped before."

"Oh, fuck!" Knox yells out, exploding inside of me. "Damn. I didn't mean... shit. Just you... your commands... it's just so fucking hot."

I laugh, sitting up on Emmett after Knox pulls out, then reach behind me and wrap my arm around Knox's neck, pulling him in for a kiss. I suck on his bottom lip, then bite. "That's just a little taste, because I plan to mark the fuck out of you."

His eyes roll into the back of his head. "You just made me hard again."

He walks away to clean himself up and now it's just Emmett and me. Callum is still in the room, wings spread wide, watching us. Dominating. Protecting. Artist could have painted his picture in years past with how regal and powerful he looks. It's captivating.

Lust and the need for control flow through me, so I slowly grind my hips on Emmett's cock, taking all of him. "You feel fucking amazing." His eyes are so dark right now, they're almost black. "I want you to fuck me with your vampire speed while you suck my blood."

"Ev," he pants, licking his lips. His inner demons fighting for what he wants to take and the fear of taking too much.

"Emmett." My finger plays with my clit and I can feel my pussy pulsing around his cock, a little teaser, before my body explodes around him. "Remember, I will blow off your cock." I hold my hand up, happy to see the blue flame dancing like smoke.

"Fuck," I could see his resolve fading, so I push myself up on my knees so he can properly fuck me from underneath. He starts slower with each thrust, coming faster and faster. "Everlee," he whimpers.

"Emmett. Fucking suck me." I don't even feel like myself when I say the words. It's like a part that's been hidden inside of me has come out of her shell.

"You are your mother's daughter," Callum notes, still watching.

Emmett breaks and pushes off the bed so he's holding me on his lap with our chests pressed together, while his cock hits so deep inside of me it feels like he's touching my lungs. His tongue licks the base of my neck before his teeth sink in and I fucking explode. The pain and sting of the bite are quickly replaced with this euphoric feeling, and my orgasm slams into me. Suddenly, a wave of intense desire and pleasure swells around me and I can't get enough. "More!" I command, tangling my hands in Emmett's hair, holding his head down and my body onto his and he unleashes. My entire body is singing and pulsing as my orgasm continues to throb, making my entire body tingle. My muscles are tense and my pussy clenches tight around Emmett's cock, feeling every rib of his piercings.

He growls and tosses his head back, blood dripping down his chin, eyes completely feral as he bucks his hips up one more time and unloads inside of me, eyes on fire.

I'm completely entranced, needing more and more. I press him back on the bed, pull off his cock and climb up his body and hold my pussy over his mouth. "Fucking suck."

His eyes meet mine and we're completely lost in one another.

I'm completely lost.

My body feels like an inferno, using their orgasms to fuel my impossible sexual need.

Not taking no for an answer, I rock my pussy over his mouth several times, letting our combined releases mix with the blood on his chin, giving him a taste of both.

"Ev," Callum calls from the head of the bed, with concern laced in his voice.

My head snaps to him, like I'm being possessed by a sex demon, eyes on fire. I don't speak and I'm not sure the sound that would come out.

I turn back to Emmett, grab both sides of his head and continue to fuck his face slowly, letting his tongue rub on my clit. "Stick your tongue inside of my pussy and then bite me. I want to come down your throat at the same time you're drinking my blood."

"Goddamn what did I miss?" Knox says, walking back in.

I ignore the look Callum gives Knox and keep my eyes focused on Emmett, still rocking. I press my pussy down harder as my orgasm is building again. Something about the control I have right now, the pressure on my pussy and the idea that I'm about to come down his throat is like a drug.

"I think her latent succubus traits from her mother are not so latent anymore."

"I need more," I whine out. My body is on fire, needing touch, needing to feel.

Knox jumps on the bed behind me and grabs my breasts and kisses and sucks on the opposite side of my neck that Emmett just bit.

Emmett's tongue swipes up, then presses in. I tangle my hands through his hair and he looks at me one more time and then bites. My head falls to the side as my hand wraps around Knox's neck, holding him to me. The power I have right now is intoxicating.

My eyes slowly find their way to Callum, who is still watching us, and I feel a sadistically sweet smile spread across my lips. Knox moves around and takes a breast in his mouth and bites and sucks on my nipple, sending pleasure straight to my pussy. Another orgasm is there on the edge, so I slide my hand down, eyes still on Callum as I play with my clit. His hand is now firmly wrapped around his hard cock as he pumps.

His wings spread out to the side as he growls out in frustration, and my stomach tightens with excitement. Little puffs of air pulse out of my mouth, tears stream down my face and my orgasm unleashes again. Emmett's hands clasp around my hips and he holds me to his face, sucking and moving his tongue, swallowing all of me down. Knox clamps his teeth around my nipple and I arch backwards, causing a light to shoot out of my mouth before it hits the ceiling and falls like stars around us.

The room freezes.

"What the fuck was that?" Knox cries out, falling back on the bed.

Emmett retracts his fangs and slides me off his face. "Ev?"

"I don't know what that was," I say, completely shocked. "Callum?"

He's always been true fae all-knowing. "I don't know what that was."

"It was like a fae orgasm firework. Like a faegasm firework."

"Knox," Callum scolds.

"I know, I know. Shut the fuck up."

We all stop moving and talking and look at one another. Jax.

He's not here.

For a moment, I forgot about all the problems surrounding me. I forgot about Jax being gone, Samara wanting to kill me. Guilt eats away at me. "Damn it." I roll off the bed and walk towards my room. As the door shuts, I hear Callum tell Knox to leave me and I'm equal parts thankful and sad. The dichotomy of these emotions and feelings tears a hole through me.

Feeling emotional, I climb into the shower and turn the water onto hot. I don't wait for it to warm up, but let the cold pellets act as a punishment. Sure. I can try to reason that part of me, the succubus parts within me, needed to feed to help us become stronger, because I'll need all the strength I can get for when I go up against Samara, but the other part of me knows I was just being selfish.

Twenty minutes later, I climb out of the shower and wipe the steam off the mirror. My skin is red hot and my eyes look tired. They're immediately drawn to the two dots on my lower neck and I gently brush my fingers around them. It's tender to the touch along with other parts of me. I may have gotten a little carried away tonight, but at times, it didn't feel like me. It was like I was a vessel for something else inside of me.

When I walk into the bedroom, the guys are sitting on the bed, and I pause.

Callum holds his hands up. "We don't need to talk. We just want to be near you."

"You're bruising," Emmett says, pointing at my neck. "Here." He bites his wrist and offers it to me. "I won't say anything else. I just don't want you to be sore tomorrow."

I can't help but smile. These men with their concern. I walk over to Emmett and tilt his wrist up to my mouth. His blood works its way through me, taking away the physical pain and soreness etched within the muscles of my body.

We don't speak anymore, as we all climb into bed- Callum and Emmett on either side of me and Knox between my legs, with his head resting on my stomach.

EVERLEE – STOPPING THE DJINN

A THIN LAYER OF sweat moistens my skin, waking me from sleep. I don't know what time it is, but I know it's early in the morning, because the sun is still sleeping and fire stings my eyes. Through the course of the night, Knox has rolled off me and is now laying between Emmett's legs with his arms wrapped around one of them.

These men… they have found a way inside of my life and inside of my heart. There is a connection that is deep and was completely unexpected. It's like… I know them each on a foundational level, but yet I don't know them at all. I care for them, all in different ways. Knox is fun loving and always happy and smiling. He lights up a room without even trying. Emmett is a ripper vampire who drinks blood from bags so he won't harm anyone. He enjoys cooking for others, even though he doesn't eat. Callum is the silent, but effective leader. He rules with passion and an iron fist and commands any room he walks in to. And then there is Jax. The werewolf without a wolf. The fighter, loyal beyond measure and the one in need of love, but guards himself. The one who would sacrifice his life for one or many and who holds the world on his shoulders but refuses to share it with others so they don't have to endure the pain.

These are my men, and I have to protect them.

Trying not to shake the bed, I draw my feet up, then press my heels into the mattress to push me up. Sitting with my back against the headboard, I look at the men sprawled out around me and take a mental picture.

Moving at the speed of a sloth, I tuck my legs under me, then use the headboard to pull myself up, taking most of my weight off the bed. I step across Emmett's head and place my foot on the side table, careful to avoid the lamp and shift my weight. When I'm off the bed, I don't even bother trying to find clothes in my drawers for fear it would wake them up.

Tip-toeing down the hall, I go back to the large bathroom we started in last night and grab my clothes off the shelf and slip them on. I hasten to the kitchen, grab my phone and the card Lizzy gave me off the middle of the counter, and make my way outside.

The sun is peeking over the houses in the east, casting an ominous purplish orange glow on everything. I hurry down the sidewalk and duck into an alleyway out of sight and punch in Betty's number.

"Betty's bitchin' rides. How may I be of service?" she answers the phone in a very chipper voice. Not one that I would expect at just past five in the morning.

"Betty? This is Everlee. I'm the friend that you picked up with Lizzy at the bar."

"Everlee dearest. Quite some trouble you're in."

"Yea. Listen... If you don't want to be involved, then I totally understand..."

"Pshh. I's say, if I's ain't in trouble, then I must be dead!" I can hear her slap her knee through the phone just before she lets out a deafening cackle on the other end. "I'm always lookin' to stir some shit up, but I draw a line at hippogriffs.

Them bitches are meaner than the dickens. I don't trust any animal that has more than one... animal. You know what I mean? Like, which personality am I getting today? The horse? The eagle? Or Dullahans. If I can't look a man, or woman- I don't discriminate- in the eye then," she blows out a breath, "ooh weee. No thank you. Oh! And kappa. I mean seriously... they just give me the heebie-jeebies!"

"Noted. This is neither of those. And really, I just need you to drive me."

"Oh. Yea. I's can do that. You should have just said so."

I pinch my lips together, but don't speak.

"You at that house with those men still?"

"What?" I croak out.

"Ah shit. Forget I said that. You weren't supposed to know I knew. Lizzy told me not to tell you, but I've been watching the house."

"Are you here now?" I peek around the brick corner of the building.

She laughs like I've just told the funniest joke. "Lordy no. I just left about five minutes ago. Give me two shakes of a troll's bat and I'll be there."

She hangs up, and I can't help but stare at my phone like I'm being pranked. Obviously, Lizzy trusts her and if she does, then I should and will.

To her word, she's parked out front of their building a few minutes later. I poke my head out and wave her down to the alley I'm at.

"Well, good day," she says, tipping her invisible hat. "Might I trouble ye for a ride?"

She has to be on some sort of witch's weed or joojoo juice.

"Ye might." What am I doing? It's too early. I shake the nonsense out of my head. "Yes, I need to go to Allure."

"Ay! Revisiting the scene of the crime?"

"I guess you could say that."

"You wouldn't be plannin' on gettin' into trouble there, would you? Lizzy said if there was trouble, then I needed to let her know."

"No trouble." It was a lie. I knew it and I'm fairly certain Betty knew it, but she didn't let on.

We pull up out front of Allure ten minutes later. The sun is higher in the sky, but still casting ominous shadows on the ground. I try to ignore the creepy feelings they're giving me and choose to think positive thoughts.

The large wooden doors stand before me again and dread fills me.

Shit!

Why did I think coming here alone was a good idea? It's like that part in the movie where everyone is yelling at you for making a stupid mistake. That is me. I am that stupid mistake.

Before I can turn to leave, Samara pushes the doors open and stands there in a long, black dress. "I was expecting you much sooner." She smiles, then nods her out. "Didn't know you knew how to drive a motorcycle."

I look behind me and see the motorcycle with Betty's bobble head bouncing in the breeze. "Well, why not learn? You never know when you'll need to drive one."

"Yes. Whatever." She bats her hand flippantly in the air. "Come in. I'll take you to him."

"Is he alive?"

"Does it matter? You're going to come in anyway."

She looks behind me and when I turn, three vampires and a Dullahan step out of the shadows. "Friends of yours? Or fae, you've tricked and manipulated into doing your dirty work?"

"So mouthy. Perhaps we can fix that when I cut your tongue out. Do you know how much true fae tongue goes for in the underground? More than a leg, which is surprising. I guess it's not really all about the size," she jeers. "And speaking of size, Jax." Her eyes grow wide. "Wow. I can see why you'd want him back."

A vampire grabs my arm and shoves me forward, igniting the fury within. My body flushes and I feel the blue flame flowing through to my hands. "Touch me again and I will be the last thing you see before a true fae gives you your true death, fucker."

His hands retreat into the air and he takes two steps back along with the others.

"Oh, stop being pussies. She's a newborn fae. She doesn't even know how to use her powers."

"Do you want to try me?" I clap the air between my hands and a ball forms.

Samara takes a step back into the door.

"Now who's the pussy?"

A smirk curls on her lips, and her back straightens. "Do what you want. Without me, you'll never be able to get to Jax, and he will die. Is that your wish?"

My eyes lock on hers, but I don't dare say a word. Of all the research I've done, you don't speak about a wish unless you're sure you want it cast. She's a vindictive, deceiving bitch who will use any means necessary to win.

She laughs. "I guess reading all those books in Callum's library served you well."

"Guess so."

"Now, enough with all of this posturing. Let's get you inside to your beloved Jax. I'm sure he's *dying* to see you." She watches me for a second, and when I don't move, she continues, "Perhaps it will be easier like this." She tosses her hand in the air and, in a swirl of purple mist, she turns into Jax. "Hey baby."

It takes a minute for my brain to catch up with my eyes. When I see him standing there, a flutter tingles in my stomach, then I remember it's not him. It's her and the rage and hate return. I need to find Jax and figure out how to make a trade that she will agree to. The guys will never be safe as long as I'm around them. Last night, we put together a plan, but it had holes in it. Namely, they were going to be here. She would use me against them, and them against me.

No.

She wants me, so me she'll get.

"Let's go. Let's figure out a trade."

Each step I take feels like more and more weights are being added around my ankles.

CALLUM - CATCHING UP

BUZZ!

BUZZ!

Who is at the door this early in the morning?

I roll over in bed and immediately realize Everlee's gone.

"Shit! Wake up! Ev is gone!"

Within seconds, Knox and Emmett are rolling out of the bed.

BUZZ!

CRASH!

"What the fuck? Are we under attack?" Emmett asks.

Racing through the hall, I come to the back door and standing there is Lizzy and a man behind her. Tall with broad shoulders and light brown skin that causes his green eyes to pop.

"Lizzy. What in the hell is going on?"

"We have a problem." Her gaze travels down my still naked body. "Gah damn and so does Everlee's vagina. Fuck! Are you part dinosaur? Do dinosaur shifters even exist? I mean, I see the books on those smutty social media groups. Fuck Debbie and Dallas, give me Debbie does Dino! Nope! Focus Lizzy!" She scolds herself, biting her fist, then continues. "Fuck. I can't concentrate!" She whips her hand around and the next thing I know, I'm wearing a pair of dino boxers. "Better. Everlee–"

Knox and Emmett come to a rush behind me, boxers on. "What happened?"

"That lucky bitch. Good for her. I've always said she was too much for one man." She swipes her hand across the air like you would when showing a spread of food on the table. "Anyway, Everlee went to Allure."

"How do you know?"

"May I come in?"

"Well, you already blew the door off the back of the house."

She looks at it. "I'm sorry about that, but I knew Everlee was in trouble and I was worried about you all as well. Didn't know if Samara had done something."

"You were worried about us?" Knox sighs.

"Yes. Ev seems to like you all and well, I needed to make sure you were ok and if you were, then get you to come help me get her back before she does something stupid."

"Come in. I'm going to put clothes on."

"Thank the goddess." Tony huffs beside her and puffs out his chest a little. Lizzy asks, "What? Even though we may be something– I'm still not sure yet, and I can appreciate a fine male specimen. Especially if it's one my friend is with. I don't want to bone them, but damn. Pieces of art."

"You're weird."

"Not the first time, or the last time, I will hear that. Now go, hurry! We don't have a lot of time to waste. She offered to make a trade." She looks around at everyone. "Oh, the brute is gone. She's going to make a trade for him?" she snarls, then holds her hands up. "Only kidding, but also not. I don't want her trading for anyone. I want my Everlee back."

"Fuck," I sigh, rubbing my hands against my forehead. I knew she was going to leave. If Samara has taught me any-thing, it's that words matter. And Everlee said she wouldn't go after her yesterday, but that left today wide open, which is why we didn't want to leave her alone last night and also because, well, we simply didn't want to leave her alone. She has a hold on us. And we fear that after all this is done, she will be gone, but I hope not. I don't know what's in store for us, but it needs her in it.

When we come back down a few minutes later, Tony has the door lifted back into place, while Lizzy works her magic to fix the hinges.

"Let's go. We can talk in the car," I command, not wasting anymore time.

Lizzy and Tony follow us out without speaking. I climb in the driver's seat, Emmett takes the front passenger seat, while Knox, Lizzy and Tony climb in the second row.

There's a thick layer of tension and concern in the car as we drive past building after building. We turn down the small alleyway beside the old club we recently purchased.

"Where are we? This isn't Allure."

"This is our plan. The plan Everlee was supposed to be part of before she tried to-" I pound my fist on the steering wheel. "I should have known."

"I'm sure she cares about you all and is trying to protect you. It's such an Everlee thing to do."

Emmett runs inside, while Knox instructs them all to move to the third row. Without hesitations or questions, they move.

When Emmett carries Brady out, the chains are still wrapped around him and he looks frail. No wonder Jax was so upset. It's been several weeks since I've seen him and it looks like it's been years. He's mostly bald and his skin is so pale it's almost translucent.

"What the fuck?" Lizzy mumbles out. "What happened?"

"This is Brady," Emmett says, laying his near lifeless body across the backseat and climbing in with him.

"He's our back-up?"

"He is everything," I correct.

"He can't even walk." As if realization hits her, "You sneaky fucks. You found it."

"Found what?" Tony asks, not keeping up.

I stare at her in the review mirror. Her eyes are wide with shock and something else.

"We didn't find Pandora's Box, but we found the ring box and traded the Book of Maldor for it."

"That's why." She puts all the pieces together. "How are you going to get it from him to Samara?"

"Everlee was going to stun Samara with her light while we unchained him. The Mist would ravage what little life is remaining of Brady, and when he dies, the Mist would need a new source, and it's clearly attracted to power."

"So it would go to Samara." Lizzy nods. "But Everlee is powerful too. What if it goes after her?"

"Everlee is light. Light would destroy the dark. He wouldn't go after her."

"But Brady wasn't a dark fae," Knox chimes with a modicum of concern.

"No, but Brady was the only one around at the time the Mist was out. While Brady may not be a dark fae anymore, he was at one time."

"Won't the Mist of Morreux only make Samara stronger? He is a dark wizard, after all?" Tony chimes.

"That is a possibility, but she already has so much power. We're hoping the Mist will move swiftly, consuming the power, thereby killing her."

"So now you're going to have a mist that has gained the power of a..." he looks at Brady. "I assume werewolf based on some tattoos on his arms, and a Djinn who is how many thousands of years old? He'll be stronger than the Mist that's in Pandora's Box. And assuming you still have the ring box with the Urgsam wood, he will be too big for it. With his power, he will grow in size."

"That's why Ev left. She knew this idea wasn't going to work out. It's why she's going to trade herself. To protect all of you. All of us."

"Fuck!" I slam my hands on the stirring wheel! "Fuck!"

We're at Allure a few minutes later.

"Tony. You're from Helsgard. Do you all have something that can contain it?"

"No. I was on the task force, studying the Urgsam wood, but it's unique and unfortunately, it's all been destroyed. We have found scraps, but nothing of note. We're trying to intertwine magic within the fibers of the wood so we can use smaller pieces, but we've been unsuccessful so far."

I feel like this is unraveling. Samara has Jax and now has Everlee, who will trade herself for Jax, but she doesn't know Samara like we do. Samara will use her words and twist them. The only option is to give Brady a warrior's death and hope we can contain the mist, but Tony is right. He will be bigger after being in Samara. Fuck! How did we miss that? How did I miss that?

I've been studying the mist for hundreds of years. Why? How could I have missed that? I've failed them. I've failed everyone. I've failed Sofrai and Feyra again.

"Everlee! Are you here?"

"Callum?" Everlee answers, her voice is scared, panicked.

"We're here."

"I'm sorry."

"Sorry? Sorry for what?"

Her words sound like a goodbye. Fuck! "Everlee. She needs us!"

"What do we do with Brady?" Emmett asks.

I look between Tony and Lizzy. Tony is shaking his head, while Lizzy is nibbling on her bottom lip, torn. She knows the implications.

"Bring him. Maybe we can somehow trap her with the chains. The iron will take away her powers, slow the progression of the Mist and buy us some time. Buy you some time," I say, looking at Tony.

"Helsgard won't let you keep her. They'll want her."

"All the better."

Tony nods.

We climb out of the car and stand at the front doors.

"Let's go fuck some shit up!" A voice calls from behind us. Standing there is an older woman with pink spiky hair wearing an ACDC shirt with holes in it.

"Who are you?"

"Betty."

"She's a friend," Lizzy chimes. "And a powerful witch."

"Fuck it! Let's go!" Knox chants, pushing the large oak doors open.

EVERLEE - THE DJINNS WISH

NERVES COIL LIKE A knot inside of my stomach with each step we take further into Allure.

The large oak doors shut behind us, and seconds later, I hear the gentle rumble of a motorcycle. They probably aren't paying attention because they aren't expecting a motorcycle to drive itself away. I'm torn with how I feel. Irritated because she's going to tell Lizzy, who is no doubt going to get the guys, which is what I was trying to avoid, or happy for the same reasons, because part of me- ok, a big part of me- is scared shitless.

We talked through the plan last night and I felt good about it until I thought the whole thing through. They're going to have to let Brady die for a shot the mist will go into Samara and not strengthen her, but make her weaker. But even if it does, she gets weaker and Morreux gets stronger. If she dies, his mist is unleashed into the air again and will infect one of us. It will be never ending because the ring box they have will no longer fit the mist after Samara, and chances are not even after Brady. Sure, we can wrap Samara in iron to buy us time, but she's a powerful Djinn. She and Morreux will fight against being bound by iron.

No, the only solution is to avoid all of that and make a deal with the Djinn. Jax in place of me. Brady lives a little longer, and the guys have more time to find a solution for the Urgsam wood.

Tugging my shirt down and straightening my back, I walk behind Samara. Only the Dullahan follows behind us, since the vampires seem to hang by the front door.

"Where is Jax?"

"All in due time, child."

We walk down the corridor that I vaguely remember running down after the Shibari demo. It's silly to think how much has changed in such a short period of time.

A few minutes later, we take an elevator down to a place called Infernus. The colors are red and black and the heat on the floor feels significantly hotter than the main floor. If this is supposed to simulate hell, then she's doing a great job.

My heart thumps faster and faster with every step we take, and a thin layer of sweat covers my body.

"Everlee?"

Jax. His voice sounds weak.

"*Jax? Jax! I'm coming! I'm getting you out.*"

"*Why did you... come, little fae? You should... have stayed away.*"

"*Are you ok?*"

"*Great.*"

Before I can reply, we're walking into a large white room and Jax is chained to a large wheel hanging on the wall, with his head hung to the side and blood dripping down his naked body.

"What have you done to him?" I ask, running over. My hands fly over his body, checking all the cuts. "Get these chains off him! He can't heal!"

"Oh. Can't he?"

"You have me! Let him go."

"Is that your wish?" she asks, all too eagerly.

I stare at her without speaking. Fuck! I spent most of last night lying in bed coming up with the exact phrasing I was going to use for my wish. This was not it!

Turning back to Jax, I lift his chin, and his weary eyes look at me. "You need to just hold on. I'm going to get you out of here!"

Samara laughs behind me. "How do you plan to do that?"

"Clearly you wanted me for a reason, so here I am."

"Here you are, and I didn't have to do anything. Well, not much." She shrugs apathetically.

"Jax. Are you ok?" His eyes meet mine and he gives me a slow wink.

"He's fine. For now."

"What do you want with me? You've been searching for me, so here I am."

She walks over, and I freeze as her hand runs through my hair. Jax jerks the chains behind me as soon as she touches me. "Feisty. Save your energy, werewolf. You'll need it."

Eager to put space between us, I jerk my hair out of her fingers and take a step back, bumping into Jax. "Don't touch me."

She smacks her lips like she's tasted something atrocious and flicks her fingers in the air. "Nasty." She walks back to the table that is standing in the middle of the floor. "You know. I expected more. The fae I killed–" she laughs, "Silly me. I can't kill. One of the few rules I can't break. Anyway, when those true fae were killed so many years ago, it was a little disappointing. Not because they died, obviously, but because they didn't fight back. So good. At least that's what they wanted everyone to think. They were ruthless, vindictive creatures who pretended to be light fae, but deep down, they were darker than the darkest."

"Do you want to explain why?"

"Explain? Explain? No, child. I don't need to *explain* anything to you. You are a nothing. A nobody. You may be a true fae, but you are nothing like them. You are weak. At least they had power, even though they never used it. You're just pathetic!"

Rage envelopes me and before I know what's happening, a light ball is firing out of my hands at her.

She easily deflects it then looks at me wide eyed. "Stupid fae." She fires back a flame, and it hits me square in the chest, sending me sliding backwards on my ass.

Jax growls from the side of the room.

I look at my chest and see the redness fading quickly.

"Neat trick," she laughs. "Vampire blood won't be able to save you."

"You can't kill, remember that pesky rule," I say, standing back up. My shirt is completely ruined, with a large hole in the center and tattered edges flapping around.

"It's not that I can't kill you. I can. Just as a penalty, I get sucked back into my bound object until someone finds it and wishes me out. Why do you think I have my friend here?"

"So, you plan on killing me?"

"Yes. I've rid the world of your kind once already and I will keep doing it over and over again until you all get the point. Seems poetic, doesn't it? You all kept banishing the Djinn away."

"Banish, not kill. There's a difference."

She bats her hand in the air, then holds it up.

Jax lashes out, using what little energy he has to fight against the chains.

"Seems like you upset him." Her words drip with apathy.

"Wait!" I'm losing control of this situation, if I ever had it to begin with. "What if I can offer you something? A wish that gets you what you want and you don't get banished?"

"Why would you do such a stupid thing?" She scoffs.

"Because it would mean that you have to let Jax go and give back the powers you have tricked people out of."

"No!" Jax cries out.

I don't bother looking at him because it would only break my heart. He's done battle countless number of times and risked his life for others. It's time someone does that for him. For them.

"Fine. Let's get this over with then. I don't need the rest of your harem showing up and ruining this."

"I have to be thoughtful in my wish because I know how you are."

"Glad my reputation precedes me."

The fact she is so proud of what a horrible person she is makes me absolutely sick.

"You!" She points at the Dullahan behind me. "Go check and make sure no one is coming. I don't need her here wasting time for an ambush." She looks at me, throwing her hand in the air. "Go on! Make your wish!"

"I need to think about how to word it. I want Jax to be safe. I want all the guys to be safe. I want their powers back for them. I want your spell broken on everyone who's had their powers taken by you."

"Sounds like you want a lot."

"Simply, I just want to undo all the horrible shit you did."

"That! That is what you should wish for, just like that!"

"No." I roll my eyes.

"Darn. I could have had a lot of fun with it." She taps her chin with her pointy fingernail and I just want to punch the smug look right off her face.

"Sorry, not sorry."

She snarls her lips at me. "I'm getting impatient. Perhaps killing you would just be easier after all. There really isn't a downside because..." she pauses, trying to remember the Dullahan's name. "Well, whatever his name is... he will bring me back out with a wish."

"Will he? He didn't seem to be too happy to be your lackey."

"He is plenty pleased with me."

"Out of curiosity, what did you take from him?"

She thinks about it for a minute. "You know I can't remember. It doesn't matter, anyway."

"Well, it may. I know four men who hate you with every fiber of their being and if they were tasked with being the ones to bring you back out, all could rest assuredly that wouldn't happen. Tell me, if you're banished away to your..."

"Nice try. I wasn't born in the last century. You will not find out what my object is. I don't need you using it against me."

"Worth a shot."

"Valiant effort."

I shrug off her sarcastic praise. "Regardless, if you go back to your... whatever it is... doesn't that break your spell?"

She looks at me, but doesn't speak for a moment, then smiles. "No, it doesn't."

Damn. I don't know if she's lying.

"*Everlee! Are you here?*"

"*Callum?*"

"*We're here.*"

Damn it. Panic tears through me. I look at Jax and he's even paler than before and the puddle of blood at his feet is even greater. This has to happen now. If he has Brady, then that's going to set the other plan into motion. The plan that could hurt a lot more people than just me.

No. I have to do it now to save them all. Callum, Jax, Emmett, Knox and Lizzy. She's probably with them because there would be no way they could stop her. Goddess love the stubborn ass!

"*I'm sorry.*"

"*Sorry? Sorry for what?*"

"What? What's going on? Your face. They're here, aren't they? You were stalling." Her words come out in rapid fire as her hands flail by her side. "I wish you would just hurry and make your wish!" Her eyes grow wide with concern and her hand claps over her mouth. "No, no, no, no."

I'm too confused and stunned to speak. She is terrified right now. What did she do or say?

I replay her words in my head over and over, saying them slower each time to dissect what she said, and then it hits me. She asked for a wish.

My heart races. What does this mean? If she wishes for something, then what?

She shoots a red light out of her hand, but I dodge it.

Why is she trying to attack me? Is she trying to kill me now, so that I can't make the wish? Is me making a wish now, a worse punishment for her than death?

The doors burst open at the same time she casts another ball at me, knocking me on the ground. I turn to look at my guys with Lizzy, Tony, Betty, and Brady. My heart swells.Lizzy rears her hands up, but I shoot a light ball at her. Tony steps in the way and conjures up a shield to block it.

"Ev! What the hell?"

"Stop!"

Samara fires another light ball at me, but I roll out of the way.

"She's going to kill you!" Lizzy yells.

Callum, I have an idea. Trust me.

Ev.

Callum! Unlock the chains from Brady. Get Lizzy to help.

Another red ball hits beside me, grazing my leg. I let out a scream, eyes still focused on Lizzy.

Tell Lizzy to stop. It could ruin the plan.

Callum mumbles something to Lizzy, and she cuts her eyes so hard at me, I feel like they're cutting across my skin.

Another red ball comes at me, but Tony's shield he used on me shoots across the space and blocks me.

With the chains off Brady, I turn to look at Samara. As soon as I open my mouth, she starts rapidly firing off red balls at me. Lizzy creates a shield and moves in front of me, blocking me.

"You better know what in the fuck you're doing, princess."

Betty joins her side, screaming some sort of slur of words that make no sense. It almost sounds like a battle cry, but again, superconfused.

"I wish," I say slowly and clearly.

In a panic, Samara twirls into a smoke and floats through the air, and unleashes a flurry of red balls onto me.

"What the fuck is going on?" Lizzy asks, shielding both of us with her magic.

I don't answer her because I don't want it to ruin the wish I've already started. It's exactly what Samara is trying to get me to do. To mess up my wish, but I continue, "That the Mist of Morreux-" Another wave of blasts comes at us.

"Fuck! She's nearly invisible!" Lizzy shouts.

I continue louder, enunciating every word as best I can given the constant rain of hellfire that's coming down on us right now. "That is currently inside of Brady," I point at him, unsure if that helps or hurts the wish, "Be moved into Samara right now."

The red fire balls stop, the smoke settles to the ground, and she stands up, face fallen.

Everyone is quiet as we all stand and wait.

"If this is your wish, then so it must be granted." The words torture her as she says them.

She flicks her hand in the air and waves it at Brady. The mist slowly rises from his limp body and floats in the air above him for a moment, before it floats over to Samara. The mist, as if having a mind of its own, rotates into a long vertical oval and hovers for a moment. A second later, it pulses into her.

EVERLEE – TRAPPING THE DJINN

- -

SAMARA SCREAMS OUT, HEAD tilted towards the sky as her hands shoot down to her sides. After a few seconds, her head rotates back down to look at me, eyes black as the night. She smiles an evil smile and holds her hand up. "Did you think that would work?" Her voice is a combination of her shrill with the low tones of a demonic voice. "I feel... powerful. Wow!"

"We need to get out of here," Lizzy says.

"Add this to the list of things I don't fuck with!" Betty mumbles, holding her hands higher as she retreats closer to the door.

"Fuck!" Emmett yells near Jax, pulling his hands back. "I can't get the chains off without getting burned."

"No, you don't. He's mine. You all are!" she yells as she raises off the ground and hovers in the air.

She fires another light ball, but now they're black. It explodes at Emmett's feet and he goes flying across the room.

"Emmett!" I yell, running after him, but she throws a fireball at my feet, causing me to jump backwards.

My eyes are glued to Emmett, watching to see if he gets up. "Come on. Get up," I urge quietly from across the room.

"Oh, stupid girl, what have you done?"

"You can't make wishes. You made a wish. I granted it."

"You simply made a wish." She laughs, her evil voice echoing through the room. "And now you're all going to die. They deserve it. Entrusting their lives to a foolish true fae. It's a wonder your lot survived as long as they did."

Fear and rage consume me, dominating for dominance. "Go!" I command the room, as I form a light ball in my hand.

"They're no match for me. A mere pebble against a beast."

I fire it off at her, and she dodges it.

Summoning all the strength I have, I let the rage, and fear, and passion for these people fill me. I fire the light balls off in rapid succession, repeatedly. I'm not even trying to hit her, just release enough energy into the room to give the guys back their power, if only temporarily.

"If this is-" I fire off more. "Your wish-" Three more. "Then so it must be granted."

Callum lets out a deafening roar of his dragon, shaking the entire room.

Her eyes grow wide and she falls to the ground. "No! NO!"

Tony runs over to Jax and uses magic to pop the iron cuffs off his wrists and ankles. He falls to the ground and Emmett is over a second later, feeding him his wrist.

"No. This can't be!" Samara shouts, the black smoke around her vanishes, leaving her hunched over on the ground.

Jax lets out a ferocious growl and leaps into the air, shifting into a werewolf, teeth bared, and pulled back over his white-hot gums.

"No. This can't be." She looks around the room.

"Thanks for telling me how to *grant* the wish."

She screams out, pounding her fist into the ground, before she turns into smoke and funnels like a small tornado into the bracelet on her wrist. It clatters to the ground, along with the others she was wearing, and we all just stare at everyone without speaking or moving for a moment.

Jax and Callum both shift back into their human forms and then all eyes turn to Brady. He slowly sits up, some color returning to his cheeks, but he's still very weak.

Emmett is by his side a moment later, feeding him his wrist. Brady coughs at first, trying to suck in air and blood at the same time. He calms himself then grabs Emmett's wrist again, sucking and drinking, to the point Callum and Jax have to step in and pull Emmett away.

"Sorry," Brady whispers.

His face fills out some, but he's not better yet. One hundred years can't be corrected in a few minutes, but at least he looks like there's hope for him.

Tony walks over to the bracelet on the ground and carefully picks it up.

"What do you think you're doing?" Jax barks.

Startled, Tony turns around and looks from him to Callum.

Callum nods, "It's ok. He's going to take it to Helsgard."

"We trust them? Him?"

"Yes. We do," Lizzy chimes.

"I don't know you well enough for your word to mean shit to me." He looks back at Callum, who looks at me.

"Yes."

Callum nods, and Jax rolls his eyes. "Fine." His eyes narrow at me as he walks over, and he wraps me in his arms and buries his nose in my hair. "You shouldn't have come."

"I haven't, yet."

He pulls his head away to look me in the eye, a slight twinkle in his. "You know that's not what I meant."

"I wasn't going to leave you to die." I try to push away from him, but his arms lock tight around me and he brings me in close for a hug, then kisses the crown of my head.

"You didn't leave me," he whispers and the ache is so real it shakes me to my bones.

"I'm not leaving. You're stuck with me. You all are."

"Goddess help us."

Feeling exhausted and relaxed, I press my cheek against his chest, breathing in his scent.

"I can't. Damn. Dick all out. I've already seen Callum's today, and now yours," Lizzy chimes, waving her hand. Suddenly, a pair of boxers with wolves howling at the moon with hearts on them appear around his waist.

He looks down, then from her to me and closes his eyes.

A warmth rushes over me as I watch him and everyone move around. There's a peace in the air. A calmness. I don't know how long it will last, so I appreciate it now.

Lizzy wraps her arms around me from behind. I lean my head against her shoulder and breathe in her signature scent.

"I thought you would have come in here and laid her out." She thrusts her wrists into the air like they shoot webs, making pew pew pew noises.

"I would have, but I knew I wasn't a match for her. She's much older and stronger, so I didn't have a chance. I had to outsmart her. I got lucky when she got so frustrated, she made a wish of her own. It slipped out really and once I figured out what she'd said, I knew I had an opportunity."

"And if you couldn't outsmart her, or wouldn't have gotten lucky?"

"Then I was prepared to sacrifice myself for everyone."

"Well, that's the stupidest fucking thing ever," Lizzy pouts.

"I can agree with Lizzy on this," Jax says, running his hand down my back.

Lizzy clasps her hands together under her chin. "He likes me! He really likes me!"

"I wouldn't go that far," he says deadpan.

Lizzy pats the air playfully in front of him and he simply rolls his eyes and walks over to Brady. "Well, this couldn't have worked out more perfect. You trapped the mist and Samara inside of her bracelet."

"Yea. Now it's simply up to Helsgard to keep her there."

"Well, they've done a good job with Pandora's box, so?"

"Liz?" Tony calls from across the room.

"Liz?" I whisper, nudging her arm. "Only those close to you get to call you Liz."

"Stop." She blushes.

"Oh, we're so not done with this."

She winks at me and flits across the floor to meet Tony. They have their heads together, and I assume it has something to do with taking the bracelet back to Helsgard.

I pull in a deep breath and blow it out slowly, savoring the moment. It's done and over. Samara's gone, the Mist of Morreux is gone, everything can go back to the way it was. I look around the room at my guys helping Emmett and Brady stand. Well, not everything.

I don't know where this leaves the guys and me at. Will they still want me around now all of this is over?

As if sensing my question, Knox runs over and wraps his arm around my neck. "Let's go back to the house. We have some celebrating to do!"

KNOX - BREAKING GLASS

IT'S JUST AFTER NOON when we get back to the house. Tony and Lizzy take off to Helsgard to lock Samara and the Mist away for good, before she can accidentally escape, and Betty just disappeared. Not exactly sure where she came from or where she went, she sort of just floats in and out like the wind. An interesting character.

"I'll cook us up something to eat," Emmett calls, pulling food out of the fridge.

"I'm tired. Do you mind if I find a place to crash?" Brady asks.

"We have the transition cage downstairs," Jax teases.

"Yes! That would be great."

"No. I was only kidding!" Jax says, lightly shrugging his shoulder into his friend.

"I'm not," Brady's face falls. "I still feel like parts of him are inside of me. Like he's somehow etched his way into my bones." He shakes his entire body. "I swear I can still hear his whispers. I'd hate for something to happen to any of you. I'd never be able to forgive myself."

"Don't say that."

"Fine. How about this? The bars of the cage can hold up an old and weak man as I rebuild my strength."

Jax lets out a little laugh and smiles, but when he sees me looking, he stops and rolls his eyes. He must've hurt his face, since it's not used to anything but a scowl.

While Jax and Callum move downstairs to set up Brady, Emmett gets to work on our lunch and soup for Brady. Emmett wants to ease him back into solids since it's been a long time. While Everlee and I cuddle on the couch, I watch him scribble notes on a piece of paper while I absentmindedly rub Ev's hair. I'm fairly certain he's making up an entire meal plan for Brady to help him get his strength back.

Everlee hasn't said much since we've been home, but she's also had a lot to deal with over the last several weeks. I imagine with the weight of Samara off her shoulders, she may not know what to do. Since she is a true fae, we need to reintroduce her properly into society. Both light and dark fae, who lived hundreds of years ago, may have residual feelings towards her, but we will support her every step of the way.

"You know..." she says, voice low and relaxed.

"What?" My hand pauses for a moment, then continues rubbing her scalp.

"I didn't realize it before, but do you think the bracelets she always wore were more like chains imprisoning her to her talisman? I mean, sure, she tried to hide it and make them seem like a choice, by adding more, but she had to wear her prison every day."

I push away and stare at her. "Do you feel bad?"

She shrugs her shoulders. "I mean, she's a vile and horrible person, but I'm just saying... it probably sucked to be her. To be reminded every day that you're a tool being used. It's sad really."

Leaning back on the couch, I pull her in and tuck her head under my chin after giving her a quick kiss on the forehead. "I love how powerful, yet thoughtful, you are."

She looks up at me, her wide eyes droopy, and smiles. She plants a kiss on my neck, then tucks her head back into place. A few minutes pass, and I can feel her weight change as she sinks into me a little more and her breathing becomes deep and slow.

The guys come back up for lunch and see her asleep on me, and I swear they melt into putty just looking at her. This woman. This fierce warrior with a backbone as strong as steel and a heart made of gold has irrevocably changed us.

"You all eat. I'll grab a bite in a little while."

"She can sleep on her own," Jax snaps.

"If you were in my position, would you leave?" I pop my brows up because I already know the answer.

He doesn't respond and blows out a breath before he walks to the dining room table.

When I hear the guys talk about their powers at lunch, I slink out of Everlee's hold and lay her on the couch, covering her with a blanket.

"Now you join us?" Callum teases.

"Shut it. Do you all have your powers back? I've been meaning to ask."

They look around at one another and disappointment paints their faces. "No."

"Really?" I'd been too scared to go into the pool to see if I had my skin back. Perhaps it was silly to think if she disappeared, so did all the darkness she cast. "They aren't just gone. They're somewhere. I bet they're at Allure."

"Do you want to go look?" Emmett asks.

I look over my shoulder at Everlee.

"She's not going anywhere. Callum and I will stay here with her while you two go back to Allure," Jax offers.

Emmett nods and takes his plate to the sink.

"I'll clean those up," Callum nods.

"Ok. If something happens to Brady, I have a bag of my blood in the fridge. Just warm it on low heat in half a pot of water for a few minutes. It should last him until I'm back."

"He'll be ok."

"Let's go," I say, grabbing the keys off the counter.

"Emmett can drive," Jax jabs.

"Oh stop. I don't hit curbs. They literally jump out in front of me!"

"Yea, right."

"You know, I only hit them when you're in the car. I think it's your fault. You make me nervous."

"I'm going downstairs to sit with Brady."

"He was sleeping when I left," Callum says.

"I know. I just want to make sure he doesn't get scared when he wakes up in a new place. It's been a lot."

"Ok. After dishes, I'll sit with Ev."

"Look at us." I clasp my hands together. "One big, happy family!"

"Emmett, take him before I do something I'll regret," Jax warns. The glimmer in his eye tells me he's only kidding, even though he'd never admit it out loud. He's happy.

Emmett and I get to Allure fifteen minutes later.

"This feels weird. Right?" I ask, walking up to the large oak doors we hadn't closed only hours ago.

"Completely. I didn't expect it to feel this way. What are we going to do about the club?"

"Do we tell people she's gone, or do we continue to manage?"

"We need to talk with the guys when we get home. It's a big decision."

"What about tonight?"

"We still have several hours to figure it out."

We push the door open and walk in. The lights are on and there's a clinking of glasses up ahead in the main room.

Harlow is behind the bar cleaning glasses and getting the bar area ready.

"Hey!" she calls at us. "What are you two doing here?"

"Just checking on a few things."

"Have you all seen Samara? I need to ask a question about tonight."

"Can we help?"

"Sure. I always expect to see her here, but you can help too. Madame Dubois is coming in tonight for another demo, but wanted to change the content up a little."

"Sure. Whatever she wants to do is fine."

"Really?"

"Yea. Can you handle telling her when she comes in tonight?"

"Sure. But aren't you all going to be here?"

"We have to take care of some things, so we won't be here, but if you need anything, please call."

"And Samara?"

"She had to take a trip. It was unplanned, but we will find out when she gets back."

It's hard to ignore the brief look of excitement on her face when she hears that Samara's gone. She was like a dark cloud that hung over everything. Suppressing fae and their happiness.

"Ok, well, we need to go check on something in the office. If you need anything, let us know."

She nods and smiles.

When we get into Samara's office, we look around the pristine room. A red velvet couch sits against the right wall with a variety of colored gold and indigo pillows. Against the back wall is a large bookshelf with a few books, and other gold statues and hourglasses, with a large ornamental desk sitting just in front of it. A crystal chandelier hangs in the middle of the room, casting shimmers on the floor and walls and looks like it was ripped out of a palace somewhere. The design of this room is odd. Eclectic.

"It's weird being in here. I can't help but feel she's going to just pop up any second and torture us."

"Hopefully, if that's the case, then Helsgard would send word," Emmett says thoughtfully.

"Yea." I flip through the papers on Samara's desk, looking at contracts and supplies. "You know... I kind of wouldn't mind becoming the owner of this place. I love how it allows people to explore their kinks in a safe environment."

"You just like getting picked for shows, you kinky fucker."

"Maybe that too," I laugh.

"I don't see anything," Emmett says, pulling out the last drawer of her desk. "Throughout the years, we have scoured and mapped out every room in this building, but there's one space that's a mystery."

"Go on."

Emmett steps outside and is back a few minutes later. "It's behind this wall."

"Do you think she has a secret room? It would totally make sense."

We quickly go through and rip everything off the shelves, looking for hidden levers, switches or buttons, but find nothing. "Well, that sucked," I pout.

"Just because we haven't found it yet, doesn't mean we won't. Let's think through Samara and who she is. Get in her mind."

Heaving, I mumble out, "No thank you."

"She had the ability to shapeshift and turn into smoke. So, what looks like that?"

"What if you just use your vampire strength?"

"I don't want to destroy this place if we don't have to."

I was trying not to be impatient, but I don't think he understands. They've all been able to still use their gifts to some extent. But me, the closest I came, was in the pool for only a few minutes. Without my skin, I'm land bound. No ocean, no water. Now I have the chance to get it back, and any second without it is a second too long.

Emmett knocks along the back wall on the right side of the room, so I do the same on the left. I don't know what I'm looking for, but I hope I'll know when I see it- or hear it.

There's a knock on the door and we both freeze, looking at the mess on the floor. Before we can move, the door swings open and Harlow is standing there.

"One more-" She stops and looks at us, then the stuff on the floor.

"We can explain!" I blurt.

"I don't know if I want you to." She turns out of the room, then stops and lets out a sigh. "Fuck."

"What?"

"Look. Something has seemed weird for the last several days. She's been... just more. And then you all today. She never goes away and then this... Tell me. Is she gone?"

Emmett and I look at each other, not sure how to answer.

"Of course she's gone, or else you wouldn't be in here destroying her office. I don't need to know the details, but," she lets out another sigh. "It seems like you're looking for something... important. And... maybe others are looking for it too."

Is she hinting that she knows something?

"And maybe one time someone saw something they definitely shouldn't have, but has been too scared to... see... if what they saw led to... what they're looking for."

"Would anyone care to share what *they* may or may not have seen? Hypothetically, of course. And would it make this person feel safer if they were told that Samara wouldn't be a problem for the foreseeable future?"

Harlow relaxes her shoulders and stares at us for a moment. "Fuck it!" She runs across the room and grabs the large hourglass with black sand off the floor, flips it over and sits it in the middle of the desk. She grabs the golden lion statue off the floor and sits it in the middle of the bookshelf, facing the hourglass.

"What the fuckkkk is this nonsense? Do we have to wait the entire hour?"

"No. Just... give it a second."

A red laser shoots out of the lion's eyes and through the hourglass. As soon as the sand filters low enough, the laser shoots through the glass to the opposite side of the wall. A lock clicks behind us and the entire bookshelf rotates.

"You just happened to stumble across this?"

She shrugs her shoulders as Emmett pulls the large door open. "Oh my..." his words drop off and Harlow and I both hurry to see.

"Oh, shit." In front of us is a room way larger than the blueprints allow for. We step through the door and feel the temperature change significantly. "Did we just walk through some sort of portal?"

"I don't want to know... do I?" Harlow asks.

There are shelves upon shelves of glass jars. Hundreds. Thousands.

"This is it," Harlow whispers, stunned.

"It's like her trophy room. How are we going to find our jar?"

"Do we just break them all? And see what happens? Will they just return to their owners?" Harlow asks, drawing closer to a jar in front of us, watching the silver, sparkly mist float inside.

"Let's try one?" I ask.

She grabs the glass and drops it on the ground, shattering it. The silver mist floats up, then glides out of the room.

"That was anti-climactic."

Hope filling me, I look at Emmett for guidance. I know what I want to do, but I need him to tell me I'm wrong.

"It would take us months to go through these jars," he intones.

I nod, but don't speak.

"Do you want to break them all?" he asks.

"It makes sense, right?" I ask, looking at Harlow.

"I think so." There's a twinkle of hope in her eyes.

We all nod in agreement, then just stand there.

Seconds turn to minutes.

Awkward silence.

I don't do well with awkward silence.

"Fuck it." Seems to be our motto. I swipe my arm across the shelf closest to me and watch the bottles burst on the ground. The silver mists float up, then float out of the room.

"Ok then," Emmett says, stepping forward.

Harlow grabs our shoulders and stops us. "Get behind me. I've got this."

She steps into a forward stance, hands by her waist. "You may want to turn around and cover your ears."

Cautiously, we do as suggested, and a moment later, a sonic scream pierces the air behind us just before thousands of jars burst apart and fall to the ground.

We turn around and see thousands of sparkly silver orbs float into the air and, as if almost commanded, they fly past us out of the room with such force that it knocks us onto our ass. We lie there, completely in awe, as the orbs fly overhead looking like shooting stars in the night sky. I don't know how long it takes- ten minutes, twenty minutes, an hour, before they've all passed. We stand up and look around.

"Maybe all of them at the same time wasn't the best idea." I chuckle and we all burst into full belly laughs.

"Well, do we feel different? Did it work?" Harlow asks.

"I'm scared to find out. If it didn't, then I don't know what else to do," I say, worry tearing a hole through my stomach.

"Should we rock, paper, scissors for it?" Emmett asks.

"I'll do it," Harlow says, stepping up. Her face twists. "A little fair warning. She took my demon, so..."

"Demon. Cool... cool, cool, cool."

She smiles, "I won't hurt you, as long as you don't try to hurt me."

"Yea. Deal. Don't hurt the Harpy."

She smiles and takes a deep breath. "Here goes nothing." She closes her eyes.

We wait, but nothing happens. No. My heartbeat races. "It didn't work."

"I haven't tried it yet. I'm too scared." She giggles nervously.

"Oh, shit. You scared me."

"Here." Before I can do or say anything, Emmett steps forward and bites my neck.

"Ow, fucker!" I push him off.

My blood is coating his lips when he looks up at me. He licks his lips then smiles, "Tastes like candy."

"Seriously?"

"Yea."

"It worked?"

"Yea!"

Without warning, Harlow shifts into her demon form and gone is the beautiful winged woman, and in its place is a horribly ugly creature with dark leather looking skin, pointed ears, eyes too large for its face, and pointed razors for teeth.

I scream out and naturally jump into Emmett's arms.

The harpy's eyes follow me and smiles before shifting back into Harlow.

"What the fuck!" I say, pushing myself off Emmett and standing back up.

"I gave you a warning."

"She's right." Emmett says, like he wasn't scared. If he had a heart, I'm sure it, too, would be pounding out of his chest.

Harlow looks at us, humor dropping from her face. "Thank you. Sincerely. I won't ever forget this. A harpy's word is their bond. You have me in your service, for whatever you need."

"Well, if you want to keep managing the bar, that would be outstanding." Emmett smacks my arm like I was being insensitive.

"What?"

Harlow laughs. "I can do that, but anything else in the future. Let me know." With that, she turns away and walks through the door. Emmett and I follow and don't speak as we walk to the car.

When we pull into the driveway, he looks at me. "Are you nervous?"

"Nervous that when I get in the pool I'm not going to shift? Yea. I'm fucking terrified, man."

He squeezes my shoulder affectionately.

EVERLEE - BITES AND FLIGHTS

KNOX HAS BEEN ON the roof for the last two hours and hasn't come out of the pool. He may never come out. In fact, Emmett, being the guy he is, went to the store and got fresh fish and delivered them on a platter for Knox. I about puked, but Knox was beyond happy and so it was hard not to be happy for him.

Everyone has their powers back, the evil villain is locked away- hopefully for forever, and Brady is getting stronger every second. Everything is wonderful. Great, in fact.

I dry the last dish from dinner and put it back in the cabinet when a pair of hands wrap around my neck with a firm grasp. "Tell me, little fae," Jax whispers in my ear. "What should your punishment be?"

"Punishment for what?"

"Your little stunt earlier."

I push back into him, but his grip tightens, and he pushes me further into the counter, causing the edge to bite at my hips. "You mean when I saved your ass?"

A low chuckle rumbles deep from within his chest. "Did you save me?" His warm breath dances across my skin and travels down my chest. "Look at you. So needy."

"Fuck you," I seethe, between set teeth.

"Wouldn't you like to?"

"Don't you? I can feel your hard cock pressed against my back right now. Is that what you want? To fuck me?"

He growls and presses his body harder into me, so I'm bending over the cabinet. His free hand slides under my shirt, across my back, then dives slowly into my pants, rubbing over my ass before he reaches my clit. "You're fucking drenched. Do you want to fuck me, little fae?"

"No!" I spit out the lie as quickly as I can.

His finger brushes over my clit and a moan escapes as my knees buckle for a second. This man and his hands. Damn him.

"You don't want me to fuck you?" His teeth bite into my neck, and he sucks, causing my body to betray me and ride his finger.

"No," I grind out.

He pulls my pants down so my ass is sticking out. The cold air stings against my hot pussy for only a second before Jax is standing behind me, pants off and cock angled between my legs. "You know the best thing about me having my wolf back?" he asks, slowly inhaling the air by my neck, causing my nipples to harden.

"What?" I ask, closing my eyes, pressing my head against his shoulder, loving the way his cock feels under my pussy.

"I can hear you better..." he nibbles on my ear, "see you better," his hand clamps around my breast, "and eat you better." He presses two fingers inside of me, lifting me onto my toes, before he pulls out and sucks my arousal off his fingers.

Goddess be damned. My eyes roll into the back of my head and I feel my entire body tighten and clench.

"Seems like you want to fuck me though," I grit out.

He chuckles, grabbing my hair near the root and pulls me to standing. His free hand roughly runs over my breast and pinches my nipple between his fingers as I pant out. His lips brush my ear. "Little fae. I want to bury my dick so far inside of your sweet pussy and never take it out." He bites my neck again and sucks hard.

I straight up whimper and lose all control, reaching down to grab the tip of his cock and hold it up while I ride my clit across the top of his shaft.

He groans in satisfaction, then pulls off my neck. "I'm going to mark you tonight. You are mine."

I nearly come at his words.

Something consumes me and I push back with all my strength, so he stumbles backward against the kitchen island, hands pressed on the edges as he watches me. I jump onto him and wrap my arms around his neck and my legs around his waist.

"In my kitchen?" Emmett whines, walking in.

I reach my arm out to him. "You can join... Jax in my pussy."

Emmett's eyes grow wide.

"Now this I want to see," Callum says, walking in and propping himself on the wall.

A second later, there's an undistinguishable noise and crash before Knox appears, jumping down the stairs, completely nude and still dripping wet from the pool. "I heard join and pussy!"

I laugh. "I'm not sure I can get three in there, but you're welcome to take my ass."

"Praise the pixies!" he says, grabbing his erect cock.

"Fuck, do we have to include him?" Jax groans.

"I am all of yours or none of yours and I much rather the former."

"Well, I've already claimed you, so I'm not giving you up."

"I'm so in!" Knox chimes.

"Same," Emmett says.

"Looks like you have your harem, little fae," Callum says, pushing off the wall. "But if you are all ours, then you will take us all. Tonight. We're going to break you, so you'll never look at another man again. Want another man again. We will fill every hole of yours at the same time and then fill you with our come repeatedly. You won't be able to walk, because your legs will be mush. You won't be able to talk because your throat will be raw. When you move, you'll be reminded of us and our cocks. Is that clear, little fae?"

"Callum, please stop talking. You aren't scaring her, only turning her on more. Her pussy is so wet she's running down my stomach and cock and my wolf is going fucking crazy to mark her."

"Let's go upstairs."

My legs tighten around Jax and I use my muscles to prop myself up so I can sink onto his cock. "While I'm on your cock." I kiss the tip of his nose.

"Fuck me," he mumbles under his breath with a gleam in his eye.

"I plan to."

"I'm sure you do, little fae. You may have a little succubus in you, but you're about to feel what it's like to have all of us in you, too."

He starts walking and the way his cock moves inside of me sends me reeling. I don't want to think about orgasms, because that will make me come. Although, I imagine tonight will make up for the last six months...

Emmett is laying on the bed when we get in the room, while Callum is getting undressed and Knox is grabbing lube. He looks at Jax. "I've got bottom, because I want you to fuck both of us."

My poor bookstore. I'll be calling out tomorrow and the next day because I already know I won't be able to walk. I eagerly climb off of Jax and slide down his body as I move to Emmett.

"Come to me. Come on me. Just come, little fae." He winks at me.

Wanting to feel his piercings rub along the inside of my hyper sensitive walls, I waste no time climbing on top of him. His hands grip my waist as I slide down.

"You feel like home," he murmurs, and that causes my heart to pulse.

My eyes catch on his as I rock. A second later, his fangs descend and his eyes pulse. "Same rules apply. You don't stop, and I'll blow your cock off."

He winks at me.

He loses control and fucks me with his vampire speed, and my orgasm crashes into me.

"Un-fucking-fair. I walk away for two seconds to get some lube, and she's already had an orgasm."

"Don't worry Knox. She's going to have a lot more tonight," Callum says.

Jax walks over to the bed, after Knox puts some lube in his hand and presses his fingers in and stretches me. Two dicks at one time? What was I thinking?

"Are you ready for me?" Jax asks, pressing his cock at my entrance but waiting.

"Yes."

Emmett shifts his cock out some while Jax slowly presses in. There's so much pressure, but when he pulls out Emmett inches out a little more. He presses in again, this time going a little further, and holds it. He's taking short, shallow breaths, then pulls out. He presses in again, Emmett going with him and lets out a moan.

"Goddamn, you're so tight with us in you." Jax pulls out and then presses in again, picking up speed until he's fucking us. "Fuck, E. Your piercings."

Knox hops on the bed and, with the lube on his finger, works my ass, prepping it for him.

"Ohhh!" I scream out when Knox puts a finger in.

Everyone stops. "Are you ok?" Emmett asks.

Trying to catch my breath, I mumble out, "Good. Sooo good."

Jax leans over and starts planting kisses on my spine, causing my ass to shoot out. Jax moves again while Knox continues to work me open.

Several minutes later, he's at my entrance and everyone freezes. "Are you ready?"

"Mmhmm."

"Words," Callum commands.

"Yes."

Knox eases in slowly, pausing at the tight ring of muscle, then drags his cock out. He presses in again, this time going further, and we all let out a collective sigh.

After another minute of him pressing in, pausing, and applying more lube, we all move slowly.

"You look like a queen taking their cocks," Callum says, running his hand up his hard shaft.

"Your turn."

He smiles and steps onto the bed, lining his cock up to my lips. He doesn't ask if I'm ready. He doesn't wait. He just grabs onto the side of my head and claims my mouth, sending his cock to the back of my throat. He's moving in perfect rhythm with the other guys and I'm being fucked from all sides with me in the middle. The central piece. These are my men.

My body is humming, buzzing, then suddenly my orgasm slams into me. The wave peaks and I cry out as I clench around all of their cocks, sending them into a frenzy of grunts and thrusts, pushing their own orgasms along. My hand reaches up and wraps around Callum's cock and I lose control, sucking him in hard and fast. Tears stream down my face as he hits the back of my throat repeatedly.

"That's right, little fae. Be a good girl and gag on my cock." His dragon wings shoot out from his back and his eyes turn a bright blue as a growl rumbles out of his chest.

Needing more, I press back on the guys, seating myself fully on their cocks.

"Oh, fuck," someone cries out. Between the moans and wet slaps, it's hard to make out the voice.

Jax unleashes a growl and a second later his hands are moving the hair off my neck and he clamps down, biting me.

Marking me.

A shot of electricity moves through my body, lighting it on fire as I cry out. The pain is quickly replaced with a pleasure that I've never experienced before. A flush sweeps across my body from my head to my toes as my body sings.

"Man, she's glowing again..." Knox cries cautiously.

"Ev?" Emmett asks.

"Good. All good."

Knox cries out as his orgasm unleashes inside of me. He begs me to stop, but I don't, pressing back and fucking them all.

Unable to stand anymore, he pulls out. "Ev," he pants, bending over with his hands on his knees.

Before I can respond, Jax and Callum both growl out at the same time as they both unload inside of me. Eagerly, I swallow Callum down and reach up to grab his balls, massaging every ounce out of them. "You suck cock like a fucking goddess."

"And she tastes like one too," Emmett says, sitting us up once Jax and Callum pull away. "Let me taste." He tilts my chin up and presses his lips to mine, pushing his tongue in and licking up the remaining part of Callum. I rock and grind, riding his cock while we kiss.

"Suck me," I command, just as Knox walks back in from cleaning himself up.

"She's so demanding," Knox teases.

I brush my hair off my neck and tilt my head towards Jax's bite mark. Emmett runs his tongue from my collarbone up to my neck, then bites.

Jax and I both sigh out at the same time. It's like he can feel what I feel. It's heaven. Pure bliss. It's like every fiber, every cell in my body, is singing in pure joy. His speed picks up as he comes inside of me before he stills, unlatching from my neck. It felt so good. I'm not sure I would have known if he was killing me.

When we stop moving, I slide off him and roll onto the bed. Callum climbs over the top of me and starts planting kisses on my breasts. "Oh, little fae. We're just getting started." His wings shoot out to the side as he presses his cock deep inside of me. "Have you ever fucked while flying?"

My eyes grow wide with a mixture of excitement and fear.

"Cal, you haven't had them in so long," Jax warns.

Callum wraps his arms around my back and starts flapping his wings. He flaps them slow and steady and in seconds we're levitating off the bed. I look on either side of me, because obviously if you are off the bed on your right side, there's still a chance you aren't on your left, *she says sarcastically.*

My hands move to wrap around him, but they'd hit his wings, so I do this sort of weird arm dance looking move, then stop.

He smiles, "Wrap them around my neck. I won't let you fall."

I wrap them around his neck and he kisses me slowly as he continues to thrust his cock inside of me.

IN. THE. FREAKING. AIR.

"Let your body relax. Trust me." He looks at me, his blue and golden eyes sparkling.

"Ok." I let go and my legs, arms, and head fall towards the ground, while his thrusts pick up speed.

He flaps his wings and we go a little higher and I feel my entire body clench and he lets out a moan. "Can't do that, babe. I will come right now and there's so much more I want to show you first."

True to their word, they claimed every hole multiple times, and I had twenty-three orgasms before I fell asleep. I don't know what the future holds exactly, but for the first time in a long time I'm so excited.

Epilogue

"Pass the potatoes"! Lizzy cries, reaching out her hand.

"No," Jax snaps back.

"Ev," Lizzy whines. "Tell your boy I don't want to lay the witch's elbow on him," she says, rubbing her elbow.

"You don't scare me."

"Jax. Please?" I ask, sticking out my bottom lip and rubbing his leg.

He looks at me, but doesn't move, so I inch my hand up higher. He still doesn't move, but a sly smile crosses his lips. I move my hand to the bottom of his shorts. A moment later, I see another hand on his leg sliding up and nearly explode in laughter. Knox has his shoulder shrugged and touching his cheek as he bats his eyelashes quickly at Jax.

Jax looks at him and his eyes darken and a ferocious growl escapes.

"Fine." He holds up his hands. "You weren't complaining last night, though."

"Knox."

He sticks out his tongue at me just as Jax hands Lizzy the potatoes.She grabs them, then scoops out a spoon for her and Tony. They've been together since they came back from Helsgard. They were there for two weeks, having to explain all the events that led up to them locating the Mist of Morreux and trapping a Djinn with it. Callum, Jax, Emmett, Knox, Brady, and I had to go up for three days of questioning. It was scary, because even though we did them a huge favor, they were not thrilled with the way we handled it. Apparently, we didn't know what we were doing and put ourselves and many others in danger.

We think Tony worked some backroom deals to get them to take it easy on us since our hearts were in the right place and at the end of the day, Helsgard got what they wanted. Tony said they needed to make a show of force for everyone watching, so they put us on a one-year probation. We can't get in trouble during that year or else we'll end up in a Helsgard prison.

No. Thank. You.

Brady is mostly back to normal, although at times he still has moments of weakness. We've remodeled the basement and made it his permanent home. Out of the cage, of course. There's an access door from outside so he can come and go as he pleases, but for the most part he stays around the house. He's so thankful, he's become the driver for the house. I think it allows him some freedom, but also keeps the guys close by in case something happens. He would include me in all that too, but I don't feel like I did much to help him throughout the course of the Mist.

Knox has taken over Allure and now manages it. I help when I'm not running the bookshop. He's a brilliant manager there, even though Jax had his doubts at first. I've learned that Knox is one of those personalities that is always joking, but when something matters, he digs in and digs in hard.

Jax and Callum remodel the club they had Brady in and name it Vixen after me. After little fae, it's their next favorite name to call me. It's opening in another three or four months. Lizzy has already been coming up with themed events they can do there to get business. As you can imagine, Jax has been super thrilled. At least that's what he pretends. I'm pretty sure he actually likes several of her ideas, even if he won't admit it.

And last, my dearest Emmett. He followed his dream of owning a restaurant. He's calling it the Good Life. It's very simple, but elegant. He's digging into his French roots and recipes and going to make it truly exquisite. We're here today to sample several of the dishes he's thinking about offering there. He's not sure if he wants to do small plates so tables can mix and match or if he wants to make it standard size. Whatever he decides, it's going to be great.

Ok, I guess this is the last piece. Me. I'm great. Living my absolute best life. My parents are going to visit in a month. They know about the guys and have been on several video chats with them. Of course, my mother couldn't be happier for me. Four men. Can you imagine? My brother is also happy for me. He's trying to convince my parents to accept his choice of joining a mundane's firehouse for a job. He wants to give back to the humans and thinks that a fire station is the best place, since fires can't hurt him. I'm happy for him. I'm happy for everyone.

I'm just happy in general.

BLOOPERS

EVERLEE – WHEN KNOX IS GIVING A LESSON IN THE MIDDLE OF A GROUP FUCK

Knox's finger is playing around my ass as something wet and slippery slides over it. "You're so tight. Just relax. If you want me to stop you, just say the word, or think it."

Think it? "I can do that?"

"Mindlink? Yes. Just practice, pushing your thoughts out and receiving thoughts."

Jax chimes in, "Dumbass, you think that teaching her how to mindlink while she's being fucked by the three of you is the best time?"

"Maybe she learns best this way?"

"Shut the fuck up."

"What? She's going to be choking on Callum's cock. How else can she tell me to stop?"

I chuckle, which sends me into slight convulsions, feeling Emmett's cock tighten inside of me when I do that. "I'll try to mindlink and if not, I'll figure out a way to let you know." A low moan dances out of my mouth as Emmett continues to push my orgasm closer and closer.

What's Coming Next?

There are at least 3 more books (plus 1 or 2 of Beckett and Will). I was going to do a quick check in at the end of this book for our fave fivesome, but then I kept writing so now it will be a Thanksgiving book.

About the Author

Hi friends! Follow me below for all the updates, behind the scenes and bonus content!

You can always email me at authorsnmoor [at] gmail.com or message me below. I do rely more on facebook, Insta and TT for most of my communication.

Website
Etsy Shop AuthorSNMoor
Tiktok@authorsnmoor
Instagramsn_moor
FacebookSN Moor Author — Author SN Moor Fan Group
GoodreadsS.N. Moor
Amazon

www.ingramcontent.com/pod-product-compliance
Lightning Source LLC
Chambersburg PA
CBHW031002190726
48285CB00004BB/1439